Peter Hume Brown

George Buchanan, Humanist and Reformer

A Biography

Peter Hume Brown

George Buchanan, Humanist and Reformer
A Biography

ISBN/EAN: 9783337029173

Printed in Europe, USA, Canada, Australia, Japan

Cover: Foto ©Raphael Reischuk / pixelio.de

More available books at **www.hansebooks.com**

George Buchanan

HUMANIST AND REFORMER

A Biography

By P. HUME BROWN

EDINBURGH: DAVID DOUGLAS

1890

PREFACE.

THE foundation of all the biographies of Buchanan is a short Latin sketch written two years before his death—in all probability by himself, at the suggestion of his friends. On this sketch we have two commentaries, one by Sir Robert Sibbald (1707), the other by Ruddiman, both of which add a few details to its somewhat meagre outline. The only considerable biography of Buchanan is that of Dr. David Irving, the second and last edition of which appeared in 1817. The excellent account of Buchanan in the *Dictionary of National Biography*, by Mr. Æneas Mackay, is also deserving of special mention. During the seventeenth and eighteenth centuries Buchanan was the subject of interminable controversies; but the main sources of our information regarding him are those which have just been named.

The idea of writing a new biography of Buchanan was seriously entertained both by Sir

William Hamilton and Mr. James Hannay; but there is now a special reason for the work they contemplated. Of the seventy-six years of Buchanan's life, more than thirty were spent abroad ; and this period of his career has hitherto been all but an entire blank. Recent histories, however, of the very institutions with which, during those years, Buchanan was mainly connected, bring vividly before us the world in which he moved, as well as the aims and interests of men of his type during the sixteenth century. Read in the light of this fresh knowledge, his writings acquire an entirely new interest and significance as the expression of his character and genius.

As this biography is meant to make Buchanan known to those who are never likely to read his two Latin folios, translations have in almost every case been given of the various passages quoted. It will be seen that these translations have been made on two distinct principles. Where only the exact sense of the passage had to be considered, a closely literal rendering has been given ; where the tone and spirit were essential to its appreciation, the precept of Cowley has been followed, and the attempt made to reproduce something of " the way and manner " of the original.

The accompanying portrait of Buchanan is that which appears in Boissard's *Icones* (1597). This portrait is the one approved by David Laing, who commissioned Mr. D. W. Stevenson to follow it in executing the bronze bust in Greyfriars Churchyard. The Buchanan bust in the Wallace Monument, at Stirling, by the same artist, is also after this portrait.

By the kind permission of the Senatus of the University of St. Andrews a reproduction is given (in the vignette) of a sketch of St. Leonard's College, over which Buchanan presided for some time as Principal. The original sketch, in the possession of the University, was made by John Oliphant in 1767, and represents the building as it then stood. From its ruinous condition it had ceased to be used as a college twenty years before.

The edition of Buchanan's works to which reference is made throughout is that of Ruddiman, in two folios (Edin. 1715). In that edition there is a full bibliography of Buchanan. Editions of his works that have appeared since 1715 are specified as the works themselves come up for notice.

I would here take the opportunity of specially thanking Dr. Dickson of the Register House for his great kindness on the frequent occasions I have had to consult him. In my search for traces of Buchanan I also owe much to the courtesy of M. Tamizey de Larroque, correspondent of the Institute, of M. Chatelain, librarian at the Sorbonne, and of Professor Hagen, of the University of Berne. To Professor Masson I am indebted for several valuable suggestions made by him after a careful perusal of my manuscript; and I have to thank Mr. R. C. Christie, author of *Etienne Dolet, a Biography*, for information which, from his special knowledge of the sixteenth century, he alone, perhaps, could have supplied. My specific obligations to certain other gentlemen I have acknowledged in the proper place.

P. HUME BROWN.

April 1890.

CONTENTS.

CHAPTER I.

PARENTAGE AND EARLY EDUCATION.

1506-1520.

CHAPTER II.

REVIVAL OF LETTERS AND RELIGIOUS REFORM IN PARIS— BUCHANAN'S FIRST STUDIES THERE.

1520-1522.

CHAPTER III.

MILITARY EXPEDITION—STUDIES AT ST. ANDREWS.

1522-1526.

CHAPTER IV.

PARIS—THE SCOTS COLLEGE AND SAINTE-BARBE.

1526-1535.

CHAPTER V.

REGENT IN SAINTE-BARBE AND PROCURATOR OF THE GERMAN NATION.

CHAPTER VI.

SCOTLAND—QUARREL WITH THE FRANCISCANS.

1535-1539.

CHAPTER VII.

BORDEAUX.

1539-1542.

CHAPTER VIII.

BORDEAUX—OCCASIONAL POEMS AND TRAGEDIES.

CHAPTER IX.

PARIS—PORTUGAL.

1542-1552.

CHAPTER X.

EROTIC VERSES AND PARAPHRASE OF THE PSALMS.

CHAPTER XI.

FRANCE—ENGAGEMENT WITH THE MARÉCHAL DE BRISSAC.

1552-1561.

CHAPTER XII.

THE *DE SPHAERA* AND OTHER POEMS.

CHAPTER XIII.

SCOTLAND—RELATIONS WITH THE COURT.

1561-1567.

CHAPTER XIV.

THE *DETECTIO* AND VERNACULAR WRITINGS.

CHAPTER XV.

SERVICES TO EDUCATION IN SCOTLAND.

CHAPTER XVI.

TUTOR TO KING JAMES—PUBLIC LIFE.

CHAPTER XVII.

POLITICAL OPINIONS—THE *DE JURE REGNI APUD SCOTOS.*

CHAPTER XVIII.

HIS HISTORY OF SCOTLAND.

CHAPTER XIX.

CORRESPONDENCE.

CHAPTER XX.

LAST DAYS—CONCLUSION.

GEORGE BUCHANAN

THE LIFE OF GEORGE BUCHANAN.

CHAPTER I.

PARENTAGE AND EARLY EDUCATION.

1506-1520.

For continental scholars and men of letters during the latter half of the sixteenth century the most distinguished person then living in the British Islands was the Scottish humanist and reformer, George Buchanan. The testimonies of Buchanan's contemporaries place this fact beyond question. Buchanan owed this eminence to his mastery of Latin, then the international language of Europe; in the composition of Latin prose and verse, Buchanan had, indeed, hardly a second in Britain, so that he easily stands as the representative British humanist of his own day. The terms in which the humanists of the sixteenth century speak of each other must always be taken with large modification; of their friends their laudations are apt to be as meaningless as their denunciations of their enemies. Yet, when all allowance has been made for uncritical superlatives, the testimonies of Buchanan's most eminent

A

contemporaries leave us in no doubt as to his immense reputation. What the great printer, Henri Estienne, said of him, and Camden approvingly repeats, was generally received as true — that Buchanan "was easily the first poet of his age". So long as Latin continued to be the language of literature, Buchanan's fame on the Continent remained unimpaired; for Grotius in the next century he was *Scotiae illud numen*; and Milton's antagonist Saumaise spoke of him as "the greatest man of his age". Even into the eighteenth century, as we shall see, Buchanan still retained on the Continent a certain vitality as a man of letters. In the present century he has been but the shadow of a name; yet it is curious proof of his once brilliant reputation, that, as by a kind of echo, he is even now rarely mentioned on the Continent except as "the celebrated Buchanan."

In England, Buchanan remained a living force in literature for much the same period as on the Continent. In the sixteenth century, Roger Ascham and Sir Philip Sidney acknowledge his supremacy in the world of letters; and in the seventeenth, Milton and Cowley speak of him with the highest respect. For Dryden, Buchanan as a writer of history was "comparable to any of the moderns, and excelled by few of the ancients." Buchanan was still well known in England to the close of the eighteenth century. Warton, for example, speaks of him as "a popular modern classic," and Boswell has recorded a characteristic tribute which Dr. Johnson paid to him. "Ah! Dr. Johnson," said a certain Scotsman, "what would you have said had Buchanan been an Englishman?" "Why, sir, I should not have said, had he been an Englishman, what I will say of him as a Scotchman, that he was the only man of genius whom his country ever produced." And on another occasion Johnson declared that "Buchanan not only had great knowledge of the Latin, but was a great poetical genius". It is significant, however, that Porson confessed that he had not even heard of such a person as Buchanan.

By Scotsmen, Buchanan has always been regarded as one of the great characters in their national history. "There are not, perhaps," says Mr. Hill Burton, "above three or four names holding so proud a place in the homage of his countrymen as Buchanan's." His countrymen are proud of him as their most distinguished scholar, and as one of the very limited number of British writers who, with Hume, Adam Smith, and Scott, have achieved a European reputation. His association with Mary Queen of Scots has assured him an undying memory so long as her tragic fortunes remain a theme of interest. In his capacity as tutor to James VI. he has a place in the traditions of his country which he could not have gained by all his skill in the imitation of classical Latin. In spite of his foreign training and classical affinities, his countrymen have always recognised in him the typical Scotsman, as strongly and distinctively marked as Knox or Carlyle himself. It was Buchanan, indeed, who supplied that famous phrase—*praefervidum ingenium Scotorum*—which has been accepted as the happiest characterisation of the national temper of his countrymen.[1] But the most signal tribute to the great per-

---

[1] It should be said that Buchanan did not actually use this phrase. It seems to have been suggested by the following sentence in his

sonality of Buchanan is the amazing transformation
which, in common with Virgil and Rabelais, he has
undergone in the minds of the people.   Buchanan,
the fastidious scholar of the Renaissance, the translator of the Psalms of David, the author of a serious
History which fills a thick folio volume, has been
transformed into the court fool of his royal pupil,
and his name associated with an obscene jest-book,
of whose indecencies he is as innocent as Virgil of
the black arts that popular imagination ascribed to
him.   Yet in spite of the enduring place he holds
in the memory of his countrymen it cannot be said
that he is a living force in their minds.   By the very
conditions which made his European reputation he
has forfeited his portion in the present intellectual
life of his country.   It is not only that the two folio
volumes which make up his works are written in a
dead language.   The themes on which he expended
his best powers are largely inspired by circumstances which, from their very nature, could have
no abiding interest for the mass of his countrymen.
The object of the present biography is to show what
it was in Buchanan that won him the admiration of
his contemporaries, and what share may be fairly
assigned to him in the general development of the
national life of Scotland.

GEORGE BUCHANAN was born on the lands of
Moss, or Mid-Leowen, near Killearn, in Stirlingshire,
about the beginning of February 1506.   The exact
spot of his birth was a few yards from the river
Blane, and about two miles to the south-east of

History: "ne Scotorum praefervida ingenia in errorem inemendabilem
universam rem praecipitarent".—*Hist.* p. 321 (D).   As usually quoted,
praefervidum almost invariably appears as *perfervidum*.

the village. Part of the house in which he was born, consisting of a thatched roof resting on oaken spars, existed till as late as 1812, when a modern residence was built almost on the site of the ancient one. From the oaken spars of the original cottage a table and chair were made, which are now in possession of the present owners of the modern house.[1] These are the only relics of Buchanan now to be found in his native district. There is a tradition in the neighbourhood that Buchanan was born, not in the house above mentioned, but in a *shieling* among the hills behind it. As his birth took place in February, however, the season of the year renders this improbable.[2]

In the cursory account he has given of his own life, Buchanan, with the proverbial weakness of Scotsmen, does not forget to mention that the family to which he belonged, though in narrow circumstances, was yet of honourable descent. Like other clans, the Buchanans had their legendary ancestor. In the case of the clan Buchanan, this ancestor was Anselan Buey (Fair) Okyan, son of Okyan, provincial king of the southern part of Ulster. By reason of the share he had taken in a general massacre of the Danes, Anselan was forced to flee to Scotland in 1016, during the reign of

---

[1] *New Statistical Account of Scotland.*

[2] There can be no doubt whatever that Buchanan's birthplace was the house immediately on the banks of the Blane. "During the lifetime of the late proprietor, who died in 1808, in the ninety-fourth year of his age," says Irving, "the farm-house in which Buchanan was born was twice rebuilt: but on each occasion its original dimensions and characteristics were studiously preserved; and an oak beam, together with an inner wall, has even retained its ancient position. The present building, which may be considered as a correct model of Buchanan's paternal residence, is a lowly cottage thatched with straw; but this cottage is still visited with a kind of religious veneration."—*Memoirs of Buchanan*, p. 2 (Edin. 1817).

Malcolm II., landing on the north coast of Argyll, near the Lennox. For his distinguished services against the Danes in their attacks on Scotland, Malcolm rewarded him with the grant of several lands, those of Pitwhonidy and Strathyre being specially mentioned. By marriage with one of the Dennistouns, a noted family of the Lennox, Anselan also gained a small part of the estate of Buchanan, though the greater part of that estate was granted to him by Malcolm.[1]

The first historic Buchanan was Anselan, chamberlain to Malduin, Earl of Lennox, the seventh in descent from Anselan Buey. This Anselan obtained from the Earl of Lennox a charter of Clareinch (Clarines), an island in Lochlomond, in 1225.[2] The name of this island was adopted by the family as their slogan or war-cry. The son of this Anselan, Gilbert, was the first to assume the territorial name of Buchanan.[3] Two of his descendants, previous to the most illustrious of all the Buchanans, have a claim to be specially mentioned. Sir Alexander Buchanan, who accompanied the Earl of Buchan to France during the regency of Albany, has the credit, on fairly good grounds, of having slain the Duke of Clarence at Baugé with his own hands, and of having carried off the Duke's coronet.[4] Another descendant, Maurice Buchanan, who acted as treasurer to the Princess Margaret, wife of the Dauphin (afterwards Louis XI.), has on the highest authority been accredited with the authorship of

---

[1] Buchanan of Auchmar, *Essay upon the Family and Surname of Buchanan.*   [2] *Ibid.*   [3] *Ibid.*

[4] This story is told in the Book of Pluscarden. For a commentary on the story, see Introduction to vol. x. of the *Historians of Scotland*, by F. J. H. Skene.

the Book of Pluscarden.[1] It will be seen, therefore, that Buchanan could justly claim for himself that, on his father's side, he came of an honourable stock.

It is, however, to the Buchanans of Drumikill, a younger branch of the family, that Buchanan belongs. As Buchanan's family and clan connections had a very direct bearing on his life and opinions, it is necessary that these should be clearly understood. The first of the family of Drumikill was Thomas Buchanan, the grandson of Sir Walter Buchanan and Isobel, daughter of Murdach, Duke of Albany, and Isobel, heiress of Lennox.[2] To Thomas, first of Drumikill, succeeded Robert, the grandfather of George Buchanan. Thomas Buchanan, the father of George, was son and apparent heir to this Robert.[3] On his father's side, therefore, we see Buchanan's connection with the family and clan of Lennox — a fact that claims to be specially noted in speaking of a time when, as Mr. Froude has said, "social duty in Scotland was overridden by the more sacred obligation of affinity or private bond". It cannot, of course, be maintained that his connection with the house of Lennox determined Buchanan's choice of the side he came to take in the great political and religious questions

[1] Skene, *Proceedings of Society of Antiquaries*, vol. ix. p. 447.
[2] Buchanan of Auchmar, *Essay*.
[3] In biographies of Buchanan it is usually stated that his father was the second son of Thomas Buchanan of Drumikill. But the statement in the text is proved by a deed, dated 5th August 1531, now in the possession of Mr. H. D. Erskine of Cardross. I have to thank Mr. Guthrie Smith of Mugdock Castle for drawing my attention to this deed. In Buchanan of Auchmar's day it would appear that certain persons inclined to the statement made in the text. Auchmar himself, however, did not accept it, and he has been followed by subsequent biographers of Buchanan.

of his time, and that his detestation of the Hamiltons was prompted by mere clan rivalries. Yet, in spite of his humanistic training and long sojourn abroad, Buchanan never forgot that he was a Scotsman in the first place, and in the second a Lennox-man, the hereditary foe of the Hamiltons. How strong such ties still remained throughout a century when new principles thrown into society affected the deepest springs of men's actions is curiously shown in the case of one who even in greater degree than Buchanan might be supposed to have been superior to feelings of this nature: Knox himself, all absorbed as he was in his great mission, declared to Bothwell that he could not forget that three of his ancestors had served the Bothwell family.

It admits of conclusive proof that on his father's side Buchanan was of Celtic descent. *Anselan*, the name of the legendary founder of the Buchanans, is simply the Gaelic *Auslan*; and Macauslan was actually the name of the lairds of Buchanan.[1] The Macauslans and the Macmillans were branches of the same clan, and of the Macmillans an authentic pedigree exists which places their Celtic descent beyond question.[2] Not only was Buchanan, on his father's side, a Celt by birth; in all probability Gaelic was his mother tongue. Till his fourteenth year he must have lived mainly at Killearn and Cardross, Menteith, and in both of these districts the prevailing language must have

[1] *Proceedings of Society of Antiquaries*, vol. ix. part ii. p. 449.
[2] Skene, *Celtic Scotland*, vol. iii. p. 489. The *Okyan*, which Buchanan of Auchmar gives as the patronymic of Anselan Buey, appears in the Macmillan pedigree as *Cainn*. I am indebted for guidance on these points to the kindness of Mr. Skene.

been Gaelic.[1]   The introductory chapters of his
History of Scotland also prove that he was perfectly
familiar with that language.[2]   That he had the
feelings and prepossessions of a Celt, his writings,
prose and poetry, abundantly prove.   When he
celebrates, as he frequently does, the valour and
glories of the Scots, it is the Celts of whom he is
thinking ; and when he speaks in his History of the
English immigrations in the reigns of Malcolm and
David, it is with no feeling of the benefits they
actually brought to the country.

On his mother's side, Buchanan came of an
equally honourable stock.   Her name was Agnes
Heriot, of the Heriots of Trabroun, a family of considerable importance in the county of Haddington.
The lands of Trabroun, near Lauder in Berwick-
shire, consisting of about 400 acres, were originally
granted to John Heriot for military service by
Archibald, Earl of Douglas—the charter being confirmed by James I. of Scotland in the nineteenth
year of his reign.[3]   In this charter the Earl desig-
nates John Heriot as "squire and heir to his con-
federate, James Heriot of Niddry-Marshall".[4]   It
is perhaps worth noting that George Heriot, the
founder of the magnificent hospital in Edinburgh,

---

[1] The following story told of Buchanan has all the marks of truth,
as he certainly knew Gaelic, and the humour of the story is thoroughly
characteristic.   A woman whom he met in France gave out that she was
devil-ridden, and could speak all languages.   Buchanan tried her with
Gaelic ; but, finding her ignorant of that language, protested that the
devil was at least ignorant of Gaelic.—Man, *Censure of Ruddiman*,
p. 329.

[2] I am assured of this by Mr. Skene.

[3] Steven, *History of George Heriot's Hospital*, where a pedigree of
the Heriots of Trabroun is given in the Appendix to the second edition
(Edin. 1859).

[4] "Dilecto armigero suo Johanni de Heriot, filio ac heredi dilecti con-
federati sui Jacobi de Heriot de Nidri-Marshall."

was a scion of the same family of the Heriots of
Trabroun.[1] As George Heriot was nineteen years
of age when Buchanan died, he may have had
direct personal intercourse with his famous relative.
The Heriots of Trabroun, it should also be added,
were of Teutonic descent, so that in Buchanan we
have that fortunate blending of races which Lord
Brougham found so happily realised in himself.

Besides George, Thomas Buchanan and Agnes
Heriot had other four sons and three daughters, all
of whom reached maturity. Of the other members
of the family, Patrick is the only one with whom we
shall casually meet in Buchanan's biography. Like
George, Patrick also chose learning as his pursuit,
and gained some distinction as a scholar. He died
before his more famous brother, who has commemorated him in his autobiography and in the following
fine epigram :—

> Si mihi privato fas indulgere dolori,
>   Ereptum, frater, te mihi jure fleam :
> Nostra bonis raros cui protulit artibus aetas,
>   Et nivea morum simplicitate pares.
> At si gratandum laetis est rebus amici,
>   Gratulor immensis quod potiare bonis.
> Omnia quippe piae vitae et sinceriter actae,
>   Praemia securus non peritura tenes.[2]

The family was always poor, the lands of Moss
being neither extensive nor productive, and Thomas
Buchanan seems to have suffered, while still a young
man, from the same disease which at an equally early
age afflicted his son George. His father, Robert of
Drumikill, could afford him little assistance, as his
own affairs were equally unsatisfactory. On the
death of her husband, while her family was still

---

[1] Steven, *History of George Heriot's Hospital.*   [2] *Epig.* ii. 23.

young (George was probably only seven), Agnes
Heriot found herself reduced to the greatest straits.
It was indeed, her son tells us, only her excellent
qualities that enabled her to rear her numerous
family in the face of the difficulties with which she
had to contend.[1]   Poverty was to be Buchanan's
own constant companion to the very close of his
life, so that this early acquaintance with strenuous
self-denial was perhaps the best discipline he could
have known.   At the same time, this life-long
prospect of actual want, though it never drew from
Buchanan the pitiful complaints and cringing appeals
of Erasmus, doubtless helped to sour a temper not
naturally very uniform or accommodating.

A deed dated 21st July 1513 still exists, in which
a lease of certain lands near Cardross, Menteith,
is granted to Agnes Heriot and her sons, Thomas
Buchanan the younger, Patrick, Alexander, and
George.[2]   When he was about seven years of age,
therefore, Buchanan must have left Killearn for Cardross in the district of Menteith, and the tradition of
that neighbourhood is that he actually passed his boyhood there.   We have no certain record as to where
Buchanan received the elements of his education.
He himself says only that he was educated in the
"schools of his native country".   The tradition in
the neighbourhood of Killearn is that he attended
school in that village; and a writer of somewhat
dubious authority states that he attended the school
of Dumbarton.[3]   In the records of Dumbarton no trace

---

[1] The family motto of the Heriots of Trabroun is *Fortem posce
animum*.

[2] This deed was found in Cardross Castle.   The lease was renewed
in August 1531.   In the renewed lease Buchanan is styled Mr. George.
By that date he was Master of Arts.

[3] Mackenzie, *Lives of Scots Writers*, vol. iii. p. 156.

of Buchanan as a pupil can be found; yet in the
account he gives in his History of the capture of
Dumbarton Castle by Captain Crawford in 1571 he
describes that fortress with a minuteness of detail
which suggests the familiarity of boyhood. The
schools at Killearn and Dumbarton, it may be said,
were both of some repute. It is as probable as not,
therefore, that Dumbarton and Killearn were the
"schools of his native country" to which he himself
refers. At Dumbarton especially we may be certain
that Buchanan would have ample opportunity of
preparing himself to take his place in the schools of
Paris. There is indeed excellent reason for believing that, with the exception of the Netherlands,
no country in Europe was better provided than
Scotland with schools for what was then primary
and secondary education. Of the Low Countries it
has been remarked that "whereas in other countries
universities preceded grammar schools, in the
Netherlands universities were a development of the
grammar school".[1] What is here said of the Netherlands applies in large measure to Scotland. It was
the pursuit of higher education that took so many
Scottish students to the continental universities;
and it was the perception of this fact that led to
the foundation of St. Andrews, and afterwards of
Glasgow and Aberdeen. We have documentary
evidence "that grammar schools existed in connection with most of the cathedrals, abbeys,
collegiate churches, principal burghs, and even in
towns which have since sunk into obscurity".[2] In

[1] Mark Pattison, *Essays*, i. p. 243 (Clarendon Press, 1889).
[2] Grant, *Burgh Schools of Scotland*, p. 72 (Collins, Glasgow, 1876).
The introductory chapter on the Burgh Schools of Scotland previous to
the Reformation is based on written records of unquestionable authority.

Scotland, in fact, centuries before the Reformation, education was placed within the reach of all classes.[1] In these schools Latin was the chief subject taught; but, curiously enough, Greek also seems to have had a place in certain of them. The Latin taught in Scotland in Buchanan's day must have been far indeed from the classical standard which he himself ultimately attained; and as for Greek, Buchanan did not receive instruction in that language even in the schools of Paris, but had afterwards to acquire it by his own unaided efforts.

By his fourteenth year Buchanan had given evidence of such distinct talent that his mother's brother, James Heriot (whose name Buchanan is careful to mention in the meagre sketch of his life [2]) determined to send him to the University of Paris, then the dream of all the studious youth of Scotland. Glasgow University had been founded in 1450, but it had disappointed the hopes of its founders, and was now in a helpless state of inefficiency.[3] It is certain that had Buchanan received his university training in Glasgow, and not in Paris, his career would have been widely different from what it actually was. At Glasgow he could neither have acquired that command of classical Latin which was the basis of his reputation, nor would he have been brought into contact, at the most susceptible period

---

[1] Grant, *Burgh Schools of Scotland*, p. 72. Mr. Grant's researches conclusively prove that the educational advantages of the country made perfectly reasonable the famous Act of Parliament of 1496, enjoining all barons and freeholders that were of substance to send their sons to school till they acquired "perfyt Latin".

[2] This James Heriot seems to have been "Justiciar" of Lothian. See pedigree of the Trabroun family above referred to.

[3] Cosmo Innes, *Sketches of Early Scotch History* ("The University"). Edin. 1861.

of his life, with the great intellectual and religious movements which affected him so powerfully.

Thus early, therefore, began that wandering life which, whether of necessity or choice, was to be Buchanan's fortune, till his final return to his native country when past his fiftieth year. Save perhaps for one short visit, he does not seem to have again returned to his native district. Except for early associations, indeed, the country where his home lay could have had but little attraction for him. To modern eyes the Blane valley is a delightful vestibule to the glories of Highland scenery, and "the varied realms of fair Menteith" are the admiration of every year's tourists. But Buchanan had the feelings of his age and of the classical tradition in the matter of scenery. We have abundant evidence from his writings that the forests and hills of his native districts were the last sights in the world on which he could look with pleasure. It is the smiling plains of France, with their broad, calm rivers, that he thinks of when he wishes to descant on the beauties of nature.[1] His native district, however, has always shown itself proud of his great reputation, and his monument, a towering obelisk, erected in 1788 on the ridge on which the village of Killearn stands, is a conspicuous object in the neighbourhood. This obelisk, it is said, was fashioned after the model of that which commemorates the battle of the Boyne.[2] There is undoubtedly a curious fitness in this conjunction of the names of William III. and Buchanan.

[1] Cf. for example his *Adventus in Galliam*, Fratres Fraterrimi, xxviii.

[2] *New Statistical Account of Scotland.*

CHAPTER II.

REVIVAL OF LETTERS AND RELIGIOUS REFORM IN PARIS—BUCHANAN'S FIRST STUDIES THERE.

1520-1522.

BUCHANAN was more or less directly connected with Paris and its University for the next twelve years— a period, it may be safely affirmed, among the most important not only in the history of the University but of France itself.[1] When Buchanan arrived in Paris in 1520, its University no longer held that place in the mind of Europe which it had held throughout the Middle Ages. There is, indeed, good ground for supposing that even by the middle of the fourteenth century the Paris schools had lost something of their prestige as the intellectual centre of Europe. "The zeal of that illustrious school," wrote Richard of Bury, during the invasion of France by Edward III., "has become lukewarm, nay, even frozen, whose rays once illumined every corner of the earth."[2] Even before that period the most influential thinkers were no longer Frenchmen, and the most important books in theology were no longer

---

[1] On this occasion, Buchanan remained two years in Paris. On his second visit, made some three years later, he remained ten. Later in life he made other sojourns there, two of them of several years' duration.

[2] Quoted by Mr. Mullinger, *The University of Cambridge from the Earliest Times to the Royal Injunctions of 1535*, p. 214.

produced in the University of Paris.[1] Nevertheless,
so long as scholasticism continued to satisfy the
intellectual needs of Europe, Paris remained the
great school to which men were drawn as by natural
attraction. And north of the Alps, to the close
of the fifteenth century, the hold of scholasticism
on men's minds was hardly less powerful than ever
it had been. But during that century a new world
of spiritual and intellectual interests had been
opened up by the scholars of Italy. The literatures
of Greece and Rome had revealed to these scholars
conditions of thought and feeling which made impossible for them the barren subtleties of the
scholastic theology. As their discovery was in
reality an immense emancipation for the human
spirit, it was merely a question of time how soon the
best minds of Europe should be universally drawn
to their side. As it happened, the University of
Paris was the last great centre of studies to open its
doors to the new gospel. Scholasticism was indeed
so bound up with all the interests of the University,
that to break with it would have implied a transformation of its very mode of being. The expeditions of the French kings, Charles VIII. and Louis XII.,
had brought France and Italy into too close relations not to have imported into Paris something
of the new ideals of the Italian humanists ; but
there was no ready disposition on the part of the
authorities of the University to give any important
place to those new studies and new methods which
ran counter to the traditions of their own schools.
In 1498 Erasmus sought and found in Oxford the

---

[1] Kaufmann, *Geschichte der deutschen Universitäten* (1888), Introductory Section.

instruction in Greek which he had sought in vain in Paris. During the latter part of the fifteenth and the beginning of the sixteenth century, teachers of Greek were always to be found in Paris, but the instruction they gave was of the most elementary kind, and they themselves held no assured position in the University. Not, indeed, till 1530 did Greek receive a recognised place in the schools of Paris. In that year Francis I., mainly inspired by the greatest Greek scholar of his day in France, Guillaume Budé, founded the Collége Royal[1] for the teaching of Greek, Latin, and Hebrew. But this foundation was made in the teeth of the most vehement opposition on the part of the University.[2] Even the study of the Latin classics, as they had come to be known through the labours of the Italians, found little favour in Paris; and till nearly the middle of the sixteenth century, the records of the University continued to be written mainly in the Latin of the Middle Ages. Of this Latin style we have a perfect example in the History of Scotland by our own John Major, who, as late as 1530, was one of the foremost figures in the University of Paris.

Such was the general attitude towards the new studies on the part of the University when Buchanan arrived there in 1520. In certain quarters, indeed, strong dissatisfaction was felt at the existing state of things, and within due limits strenuous efforts were really being made to rationalise the traditional subjects of study. In this connection,

---

[1] Afterwards the *Collége de France.*
[2] According to the theologians of Paris, Greek was simply "the language of heretics".

the work of Lefèvre d'Étaples is specially noteworthy.   Lefèvre had studied in Italy, and made
himself acquainted with the results attained by its
scholars.   He did not, however, become a humanist
of the Italian type, preferring purity of form to
sound knowledge.[1]   Philosophy was at first his
main subject of study, and with the lights he had
received in Italy he made it his first great work to
present Aristotle in a rational form to the scholars
of Paris.[2]   This work he accomplished before 1517,
but, as we shall see, Buchanan had not the good
fortune to profit by it.   Even more important was
the work which Lefèvre accomplished in theology.
By his liberal and intelligent handling of the text
of Scripture, he did more than any other French-
man, except Calvin himself, to induce a critical
attitude   towards   the   traditions   of   the   Church.
Lefèvre's philosophical and theological labours were
alike an abomination to the University, and in 1525,
during the captivity of Francis I. after the battle
of Pavia, it succeeded in driving him from the
country.[3]   Buchanan has paid his own tribute to
the work and character of Lefèvre, and there can
be little doubt that he owed a direct debt to this
forerunner of Calvin.[4]

There is no one else in the opening years of the
sixteenth century at Paris to be named with Lefèvre
for general openness of mind and actual achievement.
But that he had a considerable following is conclu-

---

[1] Graf, *La Vie et les Écrits de Jacques Lefèvre d'Étaples* (Strasbourg,
1842), p. 7.   [2] *Ibid.* p. 9.   [3] *Ibid.* p. 119.
[4] Buchanan thus celebrates Lefèvre's services to letters :—

    Qui studiis primus lucem intulit omnibus, artes
      Edoctum cunctas haec tegit urna Fabrum.
    Heu ! tenebrae tantum potuere extinguere lumen,
      Si non in tenebris lux tamen ista micet.—*Epig.* ii. 11.

sively proved by the ready acceptance given to the doctrines of Luther, which, about the date of Buchanan's arrival, had begun to find their way into France. It should be said, also, that certain of the colleges were much more disposed than others to welcome the new lights. The Colleges of Montaigu and Ste. Barbe (with which we shall afterwards see Buchanan associated) may be taken as representing the extreme tendencies of the University. The administration of the Collége Montaigu under Jean Standonck shows what ideals were still possible in Paris, even into the opening years of the sixteenth century. Erasmus, who was a member of this college at the close of the fifteenth century,[1] has given a vivid description of its domestic arrangements and its scheme of studies. Of the latter, it is sufficient to say that their unprofitable absurdity more than anything else made Erasmus throughout his life the inveterate foe of the schoolmen. On the other hand, Ste. Barbe was under more rational management, and at least from about 1525 onwards freely adopted the reforms of the humanists.[2]

But besides the question of the new studies, another matter then engaged the University, of still greater importance, and provocative of still fiercer conflict of opinion. The doctrines of Luther had met with acceptance in unexpected quarters. In 1519, a year before Buchanan's arrival in Paris, Luther's dispute with Eck had been referred to the University for decision. Its judgment, withheld for two

---

[1] As also the Scotsmen Boece and Major. Rabelais has directed his keenest wit against the wretched treatment of the students in this college.
[2] J. Quicherat, *Histoire de Sainte-Barbe* (Paris, 1860), vol. i. p. 150.

years, was an unqualified censure of Luther's
position. As in Buchanan, to the end of his life, the
humanist and the religious reformer remained mixed
in varying proportions, it is important that we
should understand the religious position in Paris
during this period of his connection with the University. It was in the conflicts of the old and the new
studies, and of the old and the new religions, during
these years in Paris, that Buchanan acquired the
bent which he retained till his final return to
Scotland about 1560.

From the first introduction of Luther's opinions
into Paris, it was noted that the men with whom
they found most favour were the zealous advocates
of reform in the University studies.[1] In the
interests of the new learning this was unfortunate,
as scholar and heretic gradually came to be
synonymous terms, and the new studies to be denounced as ferociously as novel tenets in theology.
In the colleges, where the traditions of scholasticism
had come to be regarded with scanty respect, secret
sympathisers with Luther were found in considerable
numbers between 1520 and 1530. In Ste. Barbe,
where Buchanan afterwards acted as regent, all
shades of orthodoxy and heterodoxy were to be
found, Lutheranism very prominently among the
rest.[2] On all these novelties the University
authorities looked with horror and alarm. In
their opposition to reform both in studies and in
religion, there was doubtless much honest zeal,
especially on the part of the theological faculty.

[1] "Le Luthéranisme, né en Allemagne, s'insinuoit en France ; et il
faut avouer que les gens de lettres se portoient volontiers de ce côté."
—Crevier, *Histoire de l'Université de Paris*, vol. v. p. 169.

[2] Quicherat, *Sainte-Barbe*, vol. i. chap. xxi.

Yet the theologians could hardly conceal from themselves the fact that these reforms virtually meant the reconstruction of the entire University—a reconstruction in which their ancient prestige would be gone. The powers of the theological faculty were directed and concentrated by the famous College of the Sorbonne in its opposition to reform. By the nature of its constitution, and by its dogged adhesion to every tittle of the scholastic theology, this College had gained such ascendency in the councils of the University that it came practically to represent the entire theological faculty.[1] Directed by the doctors of the Sorbonne, the opposition of the University to reform in religion was not less formidable than that of Rome itself. Its immense authority was due partly to its fame as the infallible oracle of theological science; but, above all, to the fact that its decisions in every case received the faithful support of the Parliament of Paris.

Next to Rome itself, the theological faculty of Paris had been the main support on which the highest teaching of the Middle Ages had rested. It claimed for itself the right—denied to the Pope himself—of sovereign decree on the truth or falsity of all religious doctrine.[2] Its doctors clearly saw, therefore, that should the reforms in studies and religion take effect, their whole doctrinal system would be discredited, and they themselves dethroned from their pre-eminent place as the advisers of popes and princes, and the teachers of the highest forms of truth. It was this consciousness

---

[1] Thurot, *De l'Organisation de l'Enseignement dans l'Université de Paris au Moyen-Age*, p. 130. The Collége de Navarre was wealthier than the Sorbonne, but it never attained its fame and authority.

[2] *Ibid.* p. 160.

of their very existence being at stake which throughout the whole century inspired their ceaseless war
with every form of what they deemed heresy. ·

During the period of which we are speaking, the
battle between the two parties was practically
fought and decided. The party of reform undoubtedly numbered in its ranks the best spirits
of the University; but in spite of its zeal and
the distinction of its representatives, its existence
would have been a brief one but for the good
wishes and sometimes the efficient services of
Francis I. In this matter, as in all others, Francis
showed his inability to lay down for himself a
settled plan of action and abide by it ; yet it must
be admitted that as far as he could have any motive
at heart besides his own self-gratification, he sin-
cerely sympathised with the new spirit of his time.
Even though eventually he so bitterly disappointed
the hopes of the French religious reformers, they
still acknowledged that the country owed him a
debt for his genuine interest in the cause of true
learning. It may be regarded as conclusive evidence of Francis's undoubted claims to gratitude in
this instance, that Beza in his *Icones* heads his French
worthies with the portrait of that monarch, and
while apologising to his fellow-religionists for its
intrusion, frankly states the debt of learning to a
king "whose vices seemed almost virtues in the
light of the depravity of later times".[1] But during
the captivity of Francis, after the battle of Pavia,
the Sorbonne and the Parliament laid a heavy hand

---

[1] The same acknowledgment to Francis is made in the *Histoire
Ecclésiastique des Églises reformées au Royaume de France*, published at
Geneva in 1580, p. 3.

on the professors of the new religion, burning some, and driving others into exile. In 1529 the theologians gained a great triumph in the burning of Louis de Berquin—"the most learned of the nobles"—the most daring champion of reform in learning and religion, who had hitherto been supported in his defiance of the old order by Francis himself. It soon appeared that the death of Berquin meant the triumph of traditional theology in France, and the precarious existence of the new learning for nearly the remainder of the century. The ill-conditioned zeal of the Lutherans themselves in Paris and elsewhere in great measure lost them the chance of gaining the country. The stupid affair of the *Placards* in 1534, when unseemly remarks on the old religion were inscribed in the most public places of the city, seemed to give Francis the excuse he wanted for throwing in his lot once for all with the party with which he thought he saw that his real interests lay. From this date it may be said that the battle of religious reform in France was lost. In the years immediately following 1520 it had certainly seemed as if the new opinions approved by the most enlightened minds in the University, and favoured by the King, and especially by his famous sister, Margaret of Navarre, had as fair prospect of victory in France as elsewhere. Many reasons have been given for this abortive reformation in France; but the impression we gain from the writings of the time scarcely leaves us in any doubt as to the true one. The relations of France to Rome had all along been so intimate that to break them at any time during the sixteenth century would have implied the dis-

ruption of the French nation. And the University
of Paris, by its immitigable antagonism to all
reform in religion, was undoubtedly one of the
main factors in finally thwarting the forces that
made for such reform. All through the century
the new opinions continued to gain support among
the best educated classes in the provinces; but,
opposed by the Crown and the University, the
French reformers could not but fail to make their
cause the cause of the nation.

It was almost at the beginning of the twofold
struggle above described that Buchanan first found
himself in France, and as he himself came to have
his own share in that struggle, and as the bent of
his life was mainly taken during these very years,
it was necessary that some account should be given
of the great questions at issue.

For several centuries before Buchanan's day the
University of Paris had been to Scottish students
far more than of late years the German Universities
have been to their descendants. Especially since
the foundation of the Scots College in 1325 there
had been a continuous stream of Scots to that city.
An interesting document lately published enables
us to form some idea of the numbers of Scottish
students who might have been found in Paris at
any time during the fifteenth century. This is the
annual account of the German "Nation" of the
Paris University for the year 1494.[1]   In this

---

[1] This account is given in Jourdain's *Excursions Historiques et
Politiques à travers le Moyen Age* (Paris, 1888). It is perhaps worth
mentioning that the name of John Major appears in the list of Masters
of Arts. The entry of his name is as follows : "Iohannes Maior, dyo-
cesis S. Andree. Bursa valet 4 sol." The fee paid by Major is that of
most of the graduates, viz., 1 lib.

account we have the list of the students who in that year paid the fees for the degrees of Bachelor and Master of Arts. Out of the number of eighty-six, twenty-one are Scots.[1] As probably the large majority of students took the degree of Bachelor,[2] and at least three years' study was required of the candidate, we may form some notion of the total number of Scots then attending the University. It would also appear that students were relieved from the above fees on a satisfactory plea of poverty, and such a plea, we may suppose, was likely to be as frequently urged by Scottish students as by their neighbours. At an earlier period than the date of the above account the numbers of Scottish students must have been even larger, since by 1494 the Universities of St. Andrews and Glasgow had both been founded. Altogether, these facts conclusively show to what a large extent Scotland must have been indebted to France for the training of her most useful citizens.[3]

It is probable that the bulk of the Scots students who found their way to Paris belonged to the upper and middle classes. Through the influence of some patron, the Scots College was, of course, open to poor students; but that College

[1] The German Nation included English, Irish, Germans, Poles, and generally all students from the northern countries of Europe.

[2] Thurot, p. 40 (note).

[3] On the Continent there seems to have been a very distinct impression of the Scottish character and intellect. Major (*De Gestis Scotorum*, lib. i. cap. vii.) reports that in his day it was a common French proverb, "Il est fier comme ung Escossois." And Erasmus, in a curious passage in his *Praise of Folly*, in which he enumerates the characteristics of the various European nations, says that "the Scots plumed themselves on their high birth and kindred with the royal family, and also on their skill in dialectic subtleties." At a later day Galileo seems to have had a similar impression regarding the type of the Scottish intellect (MS. in Advocates' Library, Edin., referred to by Tytler, *History of Scotland*, vol. i. p. 288 (ed. 1873).

could provide only for a small number of the Scots who year after year sought the University. The average number of bursars in each of the fifty colleges that had been founded in Paris was only nineteen,[1] and in all likelihood the number provided for at the Scots College would be rather under than above this average. The account of the German Nation above referred to throws some light on the comparative wealth of the students. The fees charged on the attainment of the degrees of bachelor and licentiate were in proportion to the *bursa* or weekly expenses of the student; and an examination of the account shows that the Scots were at least as well-to-do as their fellows. At the same time, it is to be remembered that mendicancy largely prevailed among the younger scholars, and was regarded as no disgrace.[2] By this means, therefore, poor Scots lads, once in Paris, might eke out a living till they had taken the degree privileging them to "regent" or teach in the schools of the University. Buchanan's own case, as we shall see, shows through what hardship and difficulty many a Scots student must have fought his way to learning.

Even the difficulties of the journey from Scotland to Paris were such as might have daunted less hardy students. In reading the Latinists of the sixteenth century we must always make allowance for a certain licence of statement; yet we must suppose that in a sentence of John Vaus, the Aberdeen grammarian, there is at least some element of truth. Vaus paid a visit to Paris in 1522 for the purpose of publishing a grammatical work, and he

---

[1] Thurot, p. 126.   [2] *Ibid.* p. 39.

speaks of his journey as being attended "with the greatest risks by land and sea, and dangers from unscrupulous pirates".[1] In England, lads proceeding to Cambridge from the remoter districts went in a body under a "fetcher".[2] It is possible that some such arrangement may have existed in Scotland in connection with France. Dumbarton,the nearest sea-port to Buchanan's home, had an active trade with France, and small detachments of young Scotsmen may have been convoyed from that port for the opening of the Paris schools in October.

It must have been a remarkable experience for a boy of fourteen, like Buchanan, to be transported from some provincial Scottish town into the extraordinary world that composed the University of Paris. It seems impossible to determine the exact number of students and teachers who made up its society at any given period. When the whole community assembled on great occasions, however, its numbers seemed those of a considerable town. Of the life of the students something will have to be said in another place ; but a few sentences from a writer studiously moderate in all his statements will give some notion of the society into which Buchanan was now thrown :—" Such a world, we may imagine, was not easy to discipline. Not only, like the students of all ages and countries, did they frequent *cabarets* and questionable haunts, and mercilessly fleece every freshman (whom they styled a *béjaune*), but they even committed crimes which in our own day conduct to the convict-prison.

---

[1] "Per maxima terrarum et maris discrimina piratarumque qui injustissimi sunt latrocinia." Cf. Cosmo Innes, *Sketches of Early Scotch History*, p. 272 note. Edin. 1861.
[2] Mullinger, *History of Cambridge University*, p. 346.

They associated themselves with vagabonds and
criminals, swaggered the streets at night in arms,
snapped their fingers at the law, assassinated, broke
into citizens' houses.   The *fêtes* celebrated by the
Nations in honour of their patrons, instead of being
an occasion of edification, were only a provocation
to drunkenness and debauch.   The students scoured
the streets of Paris in arms, disturbed the peace-
able citizens by their shouts, maltreated every in-
offensive passer-by.   In 1276 they even played dice
on the altars of the churches."[1]   As the result of
endless conflicts with the civil authorities of the
city, the students were by Buchanan's day under
somewhat severer restraint; but the records of the
University show that even then there were still
frequent occasions when all discipline was thrown
to the winds.

It is to be remembered that the University
of Paris, as it had grown up through the Middle
Ages, was in many respects something very different from what we conceive as a University.   The
University of Paris did at once the work of an
elementary school, a secondary school, and a university.   Before a student could enter the Faculty
of Arts, he must have learned reading, writing, and
the elements of Latin grammar,[2] and these subjects
he could acquire at the schools of the University.
It was usual for students to enter the Arts Faculty
before the age of fifteen, but, as in the case of
the Scottish Universities, men of all ages sat on the
same benches with mere boys.   The first degree to
be taken was that of Bachelor, for which a two
years' course of logic was required, the candidate

[1] Thurot, p. 40.   [2] *Ibid.* p. 37.

not being under fourteen years of age.[1] Both the
term of study and the subjects prescribed varied at
different periods. Buchanan, as we shall see, completed three years' study before he was made Bachelor, and other subjects besides logic made a large
part of his curriculum. For the degree, or rather
title, of Bachelor, the student received simply a
certificate, and not a diploma—Bachelorship not
conferring the privilege of teaching in connection
with the University. By the age of twenty-one
he might take the degree of Master of Arts, and
thus become a licentiate, with full privilege to teach
in any university of Europe. For the licentiates,
also, the subjects prescribed for examination varied
greatly at different periods; but till after Buchanan's day these subjects were mainly logic, moral
and natural philosophy, mathematics and astronomy.
Having finished his course in Arts, the student
might then enter one of the higher faculties, as
they were called, of law, medicine, and theology.[2]
While pursuing his studies in any of these subjects
he might earn a subsistence by regenting in the
Arts Faculty. If he chose theology as his profession, he could not attain to all the privileges of that
Faculty till he took the degree of Doctor at the
age of thirty-five.

There were various ways in which the scholars
of Paris in Buchanan's day could prosecute their
studies. They might be presented to one of the

---

[1] Strictly speaking, "bachelorship did not imply admission to a
degree, but simply the termination of the state of pupildom".—Mullinger,
p. 352. Scholars and bachelors were called *dominus*; the licentiates,
magister.—Thurot, p. 60 (note).
[2] Licence in Arts was compulsory for the higher degrees in law,
theology, and medicine.

fifty colleges that now made so important a part of
the University. In certain of these colleges the
students both boarded and received instruction as
bursars. They might board at *pensionnats* (*paedagogia*) attached to the colleges, attending the colleges themselves for instruction.[1] Again, living in
private lodgings, they might attend the classes of
some particular college, or the public classes connected with the Nation to which they belonged.
Buchanan has not told us in which of these various
ways he began his studies in Paris; but the fact
that he does not specify any college, and that on
the death of his uncle want of means forced him to
return to Scotland, would lead us to believe that he
was not a bursar. It is probable, therefore, that,
living in private lodgings, he may have attended the
public classes of the German Nation. The students
who lived in this fashion were known as *martinets*,
and, as we should expect, they formed the most
unruly element in the schools. So much trouble,
indeed, did these *martinets* occasion, that in 1463
the Faculty of Arts decided that they would grant
no certificate to a student who did not reside in a
college, a *paedagogium*, the house of some relative,
or that of some well-known member of the University.[2] This decision, however, remained a dead
letter, as till the end of the sixteenth century numbers of students took up their abode wherever they

---

[1] *Paedagogia*, that is, boarding-houses for students, with some members of the University at their head. They were usually attached to
some college. It is possible that Buchanan may have been a boarder
in one of these, seeing he was not a bursar, and had to pay for his own
maintenance. The suggestion in the text, however, we think more
probable.

[2] Thurot, p. 97.

could find quarters.[1]   The German Nation was well
equipped with schools, both for the elementary and
for more advanced instruction of its members.   It
possessed eight schools in the Rue du Fouarre, consisting of two houses, known respectively as the
Magnae Scolae and *Scolae Septem Artium.*   The
Nation also owned another house in the Rue Ga-
lande, at the sign of the *Pomme Rouge,* with land
adjoining the Seine ; another in the Rue du Clos-
Bruneau, having for sign *A l'Image de Notre-Dame.*[2]
    As the two years that Buchanan now spent in
Paris were afterwards placed to his credit at St.
Andrews, he must at once have enrolled himself as
a student of the Arts Faculty.   This implies, as
has already been said, that he had mastered at least
the elements of Latin grammar when he arrived
there.   The studies of these two years he has
described for us in a single sentence.   " Partly of
his own choice," he says, " and partly of compulsion,
the writing of Latin verse, then the one subject
prescribed for boys, made the chief part of his
literary studies." [3]   That two years of the course
required for Bachelorship should thus have been
mainly devoted to Latin would seem to imply that
important modifications had been made on the subjects of study.   The traditional regulation was that
the whole three years should be almost exclusively
devoted to logic—knowledge of Latin grammar
and other elementary subjects being presupposed.

---

[1] Pasquier, *Recherches,* etc., I. ix. ch. xvii. (quoted by Jourdain,
Excursions Historiques et Philosophiques, p. 262 note).
[2] It should be said that by the end of the fifteenth century the
schools in the Rue du Fouarre were closed. After that date, instruction
was mainly given in the colleges and *paedagogia.*—Thurot, p. 98.
[3] *Vita Sua.* See Appendix A.

This statement of Buchanan, however, is borne out
by the fact that in 1452 the Faculty of Arts passed
a law in which it specially insisted on knowledge of
the rules of versification on the part of candidates
for the bachelor's certificate.[1] It would be a
mistake to suppose that this instruction in Latin
necessarily implied a more intelligent conception
of the value of literary studies. Verse-making
in Latin had for centuries been practised in the
cloister schools ; and Erasmus has told us in sufficiently emphatic terms how stale and unprofitable
the exercise could be made. " Heavens ! " he
exclaims, " what an age was that when the dis-
tichs of John Garland were explained to us boys
with laboured and prolix commentaries, and the
largest part of our time was wasted in dictating
and repeating the most foolish verses." [2]

It was undoubtedly in large measure this early
training in Latin verse that lost Buchanan to the
vernacular literature of his native country. His
own fine natural instinct for purity of form, and
this assiduous practice in his youth, soon gained him
a reputation in an exercise in which all his contemporaries strove to excel.[3] As far as contemporary
fame was concerned, it was, of course, an immense
advantage that he should write in Latin. At the
same time, it lost him that place in the hearts of
his countrymen which his genius and intensely
Scottish type of character must certainly have

---

[1] Thurot, p. 84. It is worth noting that Latin versification was
taught by Italians in Paris. The Paris doctors looked with disdain on
an exercise which they considered worthy only of a schoolmaster.

[2] Erasmus, *Opera*, i. 514 f. (edit. Le Clerc).

[3] On this subject cf. Pattison's *Essays*, vol. i. pp. 98, 210 (Clarendon
Press, 1889).

assured him. In extent of mental horizon, as probably in natural poetic gifts, he was superior to his countrymen Dunbar, Lyndsay, and Douglas; but as it has happened, all these three have now a vitality which can never again in the nature of things be his. If, coming at the time he did, he had made choice of his native speech as the vehicle of poetic expression, he would have had behind him what was wanting to all the Latin poets of the sixteenth century, a national impulse and the inspiration that comes of it. Thus inspired by such an impulse, Buchanan might have inaugurated a new tradition in Scottish poetry, and done much to save his country from the intellectual sterility of the century and a half that followed his death.

At the end of two years the death of his uncle forced him to return to Scotland. Want of means and serious illness, he tells us, were the occasion of his return.[1] From his repeated illnesses, which appear in each case to have completely prostrated him, it would seem that Buchanan was naturally of a weak constitution, though doubtless hard fare and excessive study in youth sowed the seeds of the various ailments that afterwards afflicted him.

---

[1] Buchanan's own words are very strong : "Gravi morbo correptus ac undique inopia circumventus."

C

CHAPTER III.

ON his return to Scotland Buchanan had to devote
almost a year to the recovery of his health. Where
he spent this time we have no means of ascertaining.
Probably, however, it was with his mother at Cardross, Menteith, where, as we have seen, the lease
of certain lands had been granted to her and her
sons. By the autumn of 1523 his health was so
far recruited that he was able to take his share in
a great expedition against England organised by
the Regent Albany.[1] This was the only occasion,
so far as we know, in which Buchanan actually bore
arms, yet it is clear that he had in him something
of the stuff of which soldiers are made. In his old
age he recalls that he joined the expedition with the
desire of becoming acquainted with the art of war ;
and in his History, written also in advanced years
and broken health, he invariably speaks of battle
as one who had known great soldiers, and who had
himself felt something of the glow of battle. The
words in which he dedicates his *Jephthes* to the

[1] *Vita Sua.*

34

Maréchal de Brissac, with whom he afterwards came to live on terms of intimacy, are also a curious comment on this side of his character. He says in effect that a great soldier must of necessity have all the gifts that make a great writer, and maintains that it is a popular delusion to suppose that there is any inherent antagonism between war and letters.[1]

It will be remembered that on the death of James IV. at Flodden, his widow, the sister of Henry VIII., had been appointed Regent during the minority of her son. By her marriage with the Earl of Angus, however, she had forfeited the confidence of the Scottish Estates ; and in 1515 the Regency had been transferred to the Duke of Albany, High Admiral of France, son of the brother of James III. By the appointment of Albany, the influence of France in the affairs of Scotland became such as to excite the fear and jealousy of Henry. By force and diplomacy alike, therefore, Henry did his utmost to gain the ascendency in the government of Scotland ; and by way of retaliation, Albany had in the autumn of 1522 made an ineffectual invasion of England.

Of the expedition in which Buchanan was engaged he has himself given an account in the fourteenth book of his History of Scotland. In 1523, during the absence of the Regent in France, the troops of Henry VIII. made one of the merciless English invasions of Scotland. On the news of this invasion Albany had hastened to return to Scotland, making sure he would now have the support

---

[1] " Neque enim inter rei militaris et literarum studium ea est, quam plerique falso putant, discordia."

of the Scots to a man against England. A great muster of troops was held on the Boroughmuir, near Edinburgh, and the Regent marched to the Border with the intention of avenging the disaster of Flodden and the late unprovoked invasion. As the expedition is both interesting in itself, and is a sufficiently picturesque incident in the career of a scholar, its history may be told in Buchanan's own words. The account he gives of Wark Castle is, according to Tytler, "valuable, as, with little variation, it presents an accurate picture of the Scoto-Norman castles of the period".[1]

"When the French auxiliaries, whom the Regent had brought with him, were again fit for service, he levied an army of Scots, and with his united forces proceeded to the Border towards the end of October, with the intention of invading England. He had marched as far south as Melrose, and had led the greater part of his army across a wooden bridge which there spans the Tweed,[2] when the Scots, alleging the same reasons as on the occasion of the expedition to the Solway, refused to pass the Border. Recrossing the river, he marched a short distance down the left bank, and taking up his position directly opposite Wark Castle, proceeded to carry it by storm. A body of cavalry despatched across the river prevented relief from that quarter, and the adjoining country was laid waste with fire and sword. The castle consists

[1] Tytler, *History of Scotland*, vol. ii. chap. vii.
[2] Professor Brewer (*Reign of Henry VIII.*, vol. i. p. 557) corrects Buchanan for saying that Albany threw a bridge across the Tweed. But Buchanan makes no such assertion. He distinctly states that the bridge already existed.

of a tower of unusual strength surrounded by a
double wall. Between the two walls there is a
court of considerable extent, where in times of
war the country-people of the neighbourhood take
refuge with their property. The inner wall encloses
a much smaller area, and is rendered still more formidable by a moat and the turrets that surmount it.
The outer court was at once carried by the French
auxiliaries ; but the English garrison, setting fire to
the straw in the barns, deprived them of their temporary advantage. During the next two days a
constant cannonade was kept up against the inner
wall, and a breach being at length effected, the
French made a second gallant attempt to bear all
before them. The keep itself, however, was still
unharmed, and the garrison poured a steady fire on
their assailants. After the loss of a few of their
companions, the French were again forced to retire
to the main body, and recrossed the river. The
Regent now saw that with the Scots in their present
state of mind an invasion of England was out of
the question. Moreover, he had certain information that a large English force (if we may believe
the English historians themselves), consisting of
40,000 fully equipped soldiers, besides a garrison
of 6000 left at Berwick, was on the march against
him. Accordingly, on the 11th November, he removed his camp to Eccles, some six miles distant.
Thence, in the third watch, he made a night's
march to Lauder, in an unexpected snowstorm,
which told heavily on man and beast. The English
suffered equally from the inclemency of the weather,
and were forced to retire and disband their forces."

As the result of this freak, Buchanan was bed-ridden during the rest of the winter.

Buchanan had still at least a year's study to complete before he could gain his bachelor's certificate. It is to be remembered that the medieval universities, looking to the Pope as their general head, made one great society, existing on the same conditions, and sharing common privileges. Studies at one university were recognised by all the rest, and degrees conferred by one conveyed equal rights in the others. The multiplication of universities during the fifteenth century had necessitated a certain modification of this state of things. Thus, in Paris it was made a condition of licence that a student must either have "determined" at Paris, or at some university which counted at least twelve regents.[1] It was not likely, however, that studies at a university of such immense repute as Paris should not be recognised by any of the universities of Scotland. In the spring of 1525, therefore, Buchanan proceeded to St. Andrews to complete his first stage in the curriculum of Arts. He was specially sent there, he tells us, to sit at the feet of John Major.[2] Logic was the part of his course to which he had now to devote himself; and, as it happened, there was no logician in Europe who had a greater name than Major.

In his own generation John Major was hardly less famous than was Buchanan himself in the generation that followed. It was Major's misfortune that he came at the close of an era, and that he never divined the true direction where the best interests of the future lay. Born near North Berwick in

---

[1] Thurot, p. 52.   [2] *Vita Sua.*

1470,[1] he had in the course of a life wholly devoted
to study made himself a storehouse of all the learning of the Middle Ages. He had studied at Oxford,
and also at Cambridge, where he tells us that " on
feast-days he lay awake many a night to listen to the
melody of the bells ".[2] In Paris he completed his
course in Arts at the Collége Ste. Barbe, taking his
final degree in 1494.[3] As his aim was to become
doctor in theology, he entered the Collége Montaigu, which, under the administration of one of
the most remarkable men of his time in Paris, Jean
Standonck, had become one of the first schools in
that faculty. The Collége Montaigu, we have seen,
was the stronghold of scholastic studies, and for his
adoption into this college Major was indebted to the
one man in Paris who beyond all others was noted
for the sheer ferocity of his hatred of the new learning and the new religion—Noel Beda, afterwards
Syndic of the University.[4] It marks at once Major's
type of mind and the character of his thinking that
he speaks of the Collége Montaigu, which Erasmus
held up to the ridicule of Europe, as "his true
nursing-mother, ever to be named by him with
veneration ".[5] Having taken his doctor's degree
in 1505, he continued to teach the scholastic logic

---

[1] There is some uncertainty as to the exact date of Major's birth.
As he took the doctor's degree in theology in 1505, and as he could not
do this before the age of thirty-five, this gives us 1470 as the date of his
birth. This degree conferred important privileges, so that it is unlikely
he would defer taking it. Buchanan speaks of Major in 1525 as being
in extrema senectute. But in the sixteenth century, as we have said
elsewhere (Appendix A), a man at fifty was considered aged.

[2] Major, *De Gestis Scotorum*, lib. iii. cap. i.

[3] As has been already said, Major's name occurs in the list of licentiates given in the account of the German Nation referred to above.

[4] Major, *In secundum Sententiarum Commentarius.*

[5] Major, *In primum Sententiarum Commentarius.*

and theology till about 1518.[1] As a teacher he
speedily took his place among the first of his
day in Paris. His scholars spoke of him in terms
which, with every reservation, prove him to
have been a man both of unusual power of mind
and commanding personal character. One of his
pupils,[2] himself a leading figure in the scholastic
world of Paris, speaks of him in the following
manner so characteristic of the period : " The true
Gorgonian horse is Pegasus, and Pegasus is that
incomparable master in arts and philosophy, whom
I am unable to praise according to his merits, my
master John Major, who, by the aid of his own
wings, flies higher than the wings of the wind
could carry him, till he surpasses all other spirits in
sublimity."[3] Besides teaching, Major wrote volu-
minously on all the subjects which still had an
interest for the upholders of the old order. It was
during these years in Paris also that he wrote the
only book which of all his productions retained any
value or interest almost from the date of his own
death. This was his combined History of Scotland
and England, written by 1518, and published in
Paris in 1521. This History is written in the extraordinary Latin with the perverse logical forms
of the schoolmen, yet to the modern student it has
an interest far beyond the insipid elegance of many
of the humanists who came to sneer at its author.
Under all its strange limitations of thought and

---

[1] In 1498 the temporary exile of Standonck disorganised the
Collége Montaigu. Major, therefore, while still remaining a member
of that College, gave his lessons in the Collége Navarre. Launoy, *Regii
Navarrae Gymnasii Historia*, lib. iii. cap. xix.
[2] Robert Cenalis.
[3] Quoted by Quicherat, vol. i. p. 97.

uncouthness of movement, Major's History reveals an individuality of character, a clearness and force of intelligence, that fully explain to us the extraordinary impression he made on his own time. In 1518 we find him professing in the University of Glasgow, where he remained probably till 1523, when he removed to St. Andrews to act as teacher of logic and philosophy.

In 1525, Buchanan, with his brother Patrick, matriculated at the University of St. Andrews,[1] and was enrolled as a member of what was then known as the Paedagogium, where Major was acting as one of the regents in Arts. This Institution had been the nucleus of the University of St. Andrews.[2] Till 1430, twenty years after its foundation, the University was still unprovided with any college or paedagogium, such as by the thirteenth and fourteenth centuries had revolutionised the University of Paris. During those years schools were opened simply where convenient premises could be obtained—the result being, as in the case of Paris itself, increasing confusion and inefficiency.[3] In 1430 Wardlaw, Bishop of St. Andrews, granted to the Faculty of Arts a separate tenement where its studies might be conducted.[4] From the terms of the grant it is difficult to understand whether this Paedogogium was founded on the model of those

---

[1] Buchanan is among those who paid sixpence at matriculation. Some paid eightpence, and others are marked *pauper*. By this last designation is meant those who were unable to pay the usual fee.

[2] The name *Paedagogium*, however, does not seem to have been applied till after Bishop Wardlaw's grant. See Maitland Anderson, *The University of St. Andrews, a Historical Sketch*, p. 7.

[3] Principal Lee, *Lectures on the History of the Church of Scotland*, vol. i. p. 16 note.

[4] Lyon, *History of St. Andrews*, Appendix, p. 229.

in Paris, or consisted simply of class-rooms set apart
for the different regents.[1] The Paedagogium does
not seem to have prospered, as in 1512 it is described as "nearly ruined through the defect of its
constitution and the want of learned men".[2] In
that year Archbishop Stewart, the natural son of
James IV., engaged himself to endow the Paedagogium
and erect it into a college ; but his death at Flodden
the following year prevented his carrying his purpose
into effect.[3] About the date when Buchanan came
to St. Andrews the number of all the supposts[4] of
the University averaged from 150 to 200, and in the
year of his own matriculation the number of fresh
students was 76. The fame of Major had doubtless
drawn students to St. Andrews, who, like Buchanan
himself, might have gone more.conveniently elsewhere. But though Buchanan then saw St.
Andrews at its best, and with the lustre of a famous
teacher in its schools, it must have seemed a poor
enough place after the magnificent endowments of
Paris. All that John Major in his notice of the
Scottish Universities has to say of St. Andrews, the
most famous of the three, is contained in a single
sentence, written, however, before he himself had
come there. He speaks of it as a university
"towards which no one has as yet dealt with any
liberality, except James Kennedy, who founded one
small but rich and handsome college".[5]

[1] From the extent of the buildings the *paedagogium* probably consisted only of class-rooms. It is to be noted, however, that such an
institution did not correspond to the *paedagogium* of Paris.—Thurot,
p. 95 ; Jourdain, *Excursions Historique*, etc., p. 262. I have to thank
Professor Seth for his kind assistance on various points connected with
St. Andrews.

[2] Lyon, *Appendix*, p. 254.   [3] *Ibid.*

[4] The supposts were all those in any way connected with the university.   [5] Major, *De Gestis Scotorum*, lib. i. cap. vi.

The teaching of Major was little to the mind of Buchanan. More than half a century afterwards he spoke of his old master as " teaching the art of sophistry rather than dialectics ".[1] When Buchanan wrote thus, at the very close of his life, it was doubtless with a vivid consciousness of years of bitter conflict with the system which Major had incarnated for him in his youth. At the same time, we can have no doubt that Buchanan found such teaching as Major's as unprofitable as Erasmus had found it at the Collége Montaigu. Buchanan's own countryman, Florence Wilson, a humanist like himself, speaks in the same tones of disgust at his early training in the dialectics of the schoolmen.[2] Even when his reputation was at its height, Major was already the mark for the wit of the men of the new order. Melanchthon had selected him as a special object of his attack in his reply to the censure of the Sorbonne on the opinions of Luther. " I have seen John Major's Commentaries on Peter Lombard," he says. " He is now, I am told, the prince of the Paris divines. Good heavens ! What wagon-loads of trifling ! What pages he fills with disputes whether there can be any horsemanship without a horse, whether the sea was salt when God made it. If he is a specimen of the Parisian, no wonder they have so little stomach for Luther." A few years later Major was pilloried for all time by one greater than Melanchthon—Rabelais himself. Among the books in the wonderful library at

---

[1] *Vita Sua.*

[2] " Primi aetatis gradus mihi consumpti sunt in illorum captiunculis discendis ; cujus utinam temporis bona pars utriusque linguae studiis impensa fuisset."—*De Animi Tranquillitate*, p. 250 (edit. Edin. 1751). It is uncertain where Florence Wilson received his university training.

St. Victor's in Paris, Pantagruel found one entitled *The Art of making Puddings,* by John Major.[1]

It has been suggested that Knox (who was a student under Major at Glasgow) and Buchanan owed at least their liberal opinions in politics to Major. It is certainly true that Major held precisely the same views as his two pupils regarding the claims of the people and the rights of kings. But, as we shall have occasion to point out in dealing with Buchanan's own political opinions, these views must have come to Knox and Buchanan from other sources than Major. Major himself, as we shall see, was even in the liberality of his political opinions still only the representative of the best schoolmen.[2]

Of late years it has been conclusively shown that what we know as scholasticism was in its own time and place a perfectly rational system, yielding free and healthy exercise to the best minds of the Middle Ages. If the world outgrew it, and it degenerated of itself into sheer futility, it only followed the course of all great movements that at different periods have absorbed the minds and consciousness of men. Humanism itself was not a century old before its childish absurdities wrought something like disgust in men of saner minds. As Erasmus denounced the trifling of the later schoolmen, so he held up to equal ridicule the Neo-Pagan developments of humanism and the superstitious worship

---

[1] Livre ii. chap. vii. The point of Rabelais' jest is not quite evident. Urquhart's characteristic note is hardly satisfactory.

[2] Crevier speaks of Major as "a doctor famous for his attachment to the principles of the University with regard to the power of the Pope". —*Histoire de l'Université de Paris,* vol. v. p. 82. Major was with certain of the most eminent schoolmen in these opinions also.

paid to Cicero by the stylists of Italy. In the pedantries of modern German erudition we have the same evidence of an exhausted movement as we find in scholasticism at the close of the fifteenth century.[1] The attitude of the modern man of science towards classical studies has its exact parallel in the attitude of the humanist of the Renaissance towards the intellectual interests of the schoolmen.

Although the humanists were wrong in confounding the later follies of scholasticism with the true intellectual movement of the Middle Ages, they had ample reason for their contempt of what passed for logic and philosophy in the later years of the fifteenth century and the opening of the sixteenth. It was in the name of right reason that they ridiculed the barbarous terminology, the triviality of the matter taught, and the interminable hairsplittings in its discussion. At the same time, it is worthy of note that the humanists were not all agreed as to the true attitude that should be taken up towards the studies of the past age. Many of them maintained that to break completely the continuity of public instruction would be fatal to the best interests of learning and religion.[2] There is certainly excellent ground for maintaining that the scholars of the sixteenth century would have approached classical literature in a more intelligent spirit had they possessed something more of the equipment of the best schoolmen.

[1] Mr. Hill Burton relates that Professor Pillans was indignant to find that Porson had never read the Latin poetry of Buchanan. Porson was persuaded to look at it, but flung the book from him in disgust on discovering a false quantity.—*Scot Abroad*, vol. ii. Major thus had his revenge for Buchanan's slighting mention of himself.

[2] Schmidt, *La Vie et les Travaux de Jean Sturm*, p. 294.

In October 1525 Buchanan graduated as Bachelor
of Arts.   This was the same year as that in which
he had matriculated, so that his studies in Paris
must have been recognised by the Faculty of St
Andrews.   His name appears in the second class of
graduates.   As logic was the main subject of examination, we may regard this as another proof of his
distaste for the prelections of Major.   The word
pauper stands opposite his name, as it does against
the names of the majority of his fellow-graduates.
The meaning of this term is not what his biographers
have hitherto assigned to it—an exhibitioner.   All
that it implies is that Buchanan, on a satisfactory
plea of poverty, was excused the payment of the
customary fee on "determining" for his Bachelor's
certificate ; and, as we have seen, this was a common
practice in the University of Paris.

CHAPTER IV.

In 1525 John Major returned to Paris, and the next summer Buchanan followed him.[1] As he had now definitely made choice of the life of a scholar, his course for the next few years was clearly marked out for him. He had first to take the higher degree in Arts, qualifying him to " regent " or teach in connection with the University; and having thus assured a means of livelihood, he could proceed with his studies in any of the three higher faculties. Such, at least, was almost universally the career of students who looked with an eye of prudence to some comfortable settlement as they approached middle life. Maxims of prudence, however, never weighed much with Buchanan at any period of his life; and though when he left Scotland on this second occasion he had doubtless every intention of following the beaten track, he had not been long in Paris before it was brought home to him that such a course had for him become impossible.

His first two years in Paris were passed mainly in the Scots College. It is matter for the keenest regret that at the French Revolution all the documents of this College were either dispersed or destroyed. The College was founded in 1326 by

[1] *Vita Sua.*

the then Bishop of Moray, who bought up the lands of Grisy, a village near Paris, for its endowment. It would appear that it was originally intended only for the benefit of students from his own diocese.[1] Soon, however, it was thrown open to the whole of Scotland, and it was at this College and that of Montaigu that Scotsmen were chiefly to be found during the fourteenth and fifteenth centuries. It has been inferred from an expression in Buchanan's Autobiography that he owed to Major[2] his admission to the Scots College, and on this somewhat doubtful ground he has been accused of ingratitude for his contemptuous reference to his ancient master. A nomination was, of course, required to the bursaries in a college, and it may be that Buchanan owed this service to Major. We have seen, however, that Buchanan was no very distinguished member of Major's class at St. Andrews; and if Buchanan the youth in any degree resembled Buchanan the man, we may feel certain that he made little attempt to conceal his scorn for the teaching of the old schoolman. It could hardly have been as a favourite pupil, therefore, that Buchanan deserved such a kindness at the hands of Major. Moreover, if Buchanan followed Major to Paris, it was not till the summer after the October in which he graduated at St. Andrews. In view of all this, therefore, the charge of ingratitude against Buchanan may as well be abandoned till we have clear proof of his actual obligation.

[1] Mackenzie, *Lives of Scottish Writers.* Mackenzie states that he had his information regarding the College direct from the University of Paris.

[2] Buchanan's words are : " hunc [that is, Major] in Galliam aestate proxima sequutus."

These first two years in Paris, he tells us, were passed in "hard struggle with untoward fortune".[1] As a bursar he received his board and education free. The Scots College being one of the smaller Paris colleges, its bursars would have to attend classes elsewhere—probably in Buchanan's day in one of the larger colleges, where *externes* or day-scholars were received. But while he was in this manner, as it would seem, completely provided for, all that we know of these Paris colleges makes clear to us that Buchanan's experience during these two years was but the common experience of his fellow-bursars. The food and accommodation, even of the best-endowed colleges, were of the most wretched description; in the case of the poorer colleges the fare was not only unwholesome but scanty. The lodging was that of the worst slums in our large cities. However generous may have been the original endowments of a college, in most cases poverty sooner or later overtook it. The deterioration in the value of money seriously affected the weekly allowance of the poor bursar.[2] The income due from the property that formed the endowment of a college was seldom regularly or fully forthcoming. Moreover, as the bursars and the head of the college were merely temporary residents, they had little interest in looking to its permanent efficiency.[3] The result of all this was that, especially in the case of the minor colleges, the life of the bursar was in simple truth exactly such as Buchanan describes his own to have been.

[1] "Biennium fere cum iniquitate fortunæ colluctatus."
[2] A sum of money (that fixed by his foundation) was given every week to the bursar to meet his expenses.
[3] Thurot, p. 129.

D

In March 1528 (at the earliest date possible,
therefore), Buchanan graduated master of arts, and
thus became qualified to act as regent. The next
year we find him on the teaching-staff of one of the
most flourishing colleges in Paris—that of Ste.
Barbe.[1] As Buchanan acted as regent in this college for the next three years, and as, according to
its latest historian, he exerted an influence on its
teaching which affected the entire university, a
brief account of its history and internal arrangement cannot be considered irrelevant.[2]

Two brothers, Geoffroi and Jean Lenormant, of
the Collége de Navarre, were in their own day
among the most famous professors in the schools of
Paris. Their fame attracted to Navarre a large
number of outsiders, for whom they had to provide
accommodation in five or six adjoining houses.
The bursars of the college, however, of whom a considerable number were priests and men in mature
age, at length protested against the disturbance of
their privacy by such numbers of unruly scholars
coming and going at all hours. They carried their
point, and the two brothers left the college. Confident in their popularity, the elder, Geoffroi, took a
bold step, and with no funds for the endowments
usual in such cases, he started the College of Sainte-
Barbe in 1460. The college received its name
from Saint Barbara, who was regarded as a kind of

---

[1] Chalmers (*Life of Ruddiman*, p. 313, note) gives two entries relative to Buchanan from the registers of the Scots College, which were
communicated to him before the French Revolution. The one entry
states that Buchanan was incorporated as Bachelor of Arts in that
college in October 1527 ; the other that he graduated Master of Arts in
March 1528. It is possible that Buchanan remained in the Scots
College till his appointment as regent in Ste. Barbe.

[2] For what follows regarding Ste. Barbe, I am indebted to Quicherat's
Histoire de Sainte-Barbe (Paris, 1860).

Christian Minerva in the Middle Ages. The name may also have been partly suggested by the logical term *barbara*—a play of fancy, singularly characteristic of the later times of the schoolmen.[1] From the very outset, the College had a run of good fortune. A succession of distinguished teachers drew to it a greater crowd than was to be found in any other college except Montaigu, which, under Jean Standonck, about the beginning of the sixteenth century proved for a time its formidable rival. At the beginning of the reign of Francis I. (1515), it was said of Ste. Barbe that the Parliament was made up of its pupils, that the faculties of theology and medicine were mostly recruited from its ranks, and that so many heroes issued from its bosom that it might be fitly compared to the wooden horse of Troy.

Shortly before Buchanan entered Ste. Barbe, it had passed an important turning-point in its history. From the date of its foundation, students from Spain had made an important contingent of its scholars; but in 1526, some three years before Buchanan became regent, the College was peopled by a colony of Portuguese. During the reigns of John II., Emmanuel, and John III., Portugal had made extensive foreign acquisitions, and, as a daughter of the Church, she was bound to do what she could to extend the true faith wherever she planted her flag. Large numbers of missionaries were therefore required, and for the most part these were sent to Paris, still the best school of sound Catholic theology, for their training. At this time one of the most distinguished men about the uni-

[1] Cf. the *Bokardo* Tower at Oxford.

versity was Jacques de Gouvéa,[1] a Portuguese, the
first of this name of a number of scholars, who
played a pre-eminent part in the development of
the new studies. King Emmanuel was desirous
of securing this distinguished Portuguese for the
service of his own country. But Gouvéa had a
more notable scheme in his head for the honour
and interest of Portugal. This was no less than
the purchase of Ste. Barbe for the Portuguese king,
and the settlement in that college of all the Portuguese who studied in Paris. The proprietor of
Ste. Barbe, however, a certain Robert Dugast, of
whom we shall hear again, would not listen to the
proposal of purchase, and Gouvéa had to content
himself with renting the College in the name of the
King of Portugal. The Portuguese possession was
completed by the establishment of fifty bursaries
for the benefit of Gouvéa's countrymen.

But although Ste. Barbe thus became so distinctively a Portuguese college, it must not be
thought that Portuguese formed even a large proportion of its scholars. To make this clear, some
account of the organisation of the medieval College
of Paris is necessary. It is to be remembered that
the university was already old before colleges grew
up in any number. Not, indeed, till the fourteenth
century did they become so numerous as to be a
distinctive feature of its life. We have no certain
knowledge of the numbers of students who at different periods attended the University of Paris ;
but how great they must have been we may gather
from the fact that in 1546, when Paris no longer

---

[1] I give the French form of his name, as that by which he is best
known.

held its ancient place among the schools of Europe, a Venetian ambassador reckoned that the attendance must have been from sixteen to twenty thousand.[1] It was soon found that colleges met the wants of students and teachers alike, that they made discipline more possible, and that they added vastly to the comforts of university life. The number of colleges, accordingly, grew rapidly, and by the end of the fourteenth century there were no fewer than forty. All these colleges were not, of course, equally equipped. In many of them the students simply boarded, going elsewhere for instruction. In others only a part of the course requisite for degrees in arts was supplied. A few only, known as *grands colléges*, or *colléges de plein exercice*, gave instruction in grammar, rhetoric, and philosophy ; and of these Ste. Barbe was one. In describing Ste. Barbe, therefore, we are describing the fully developed type of the mediæval College of Paris.

In most of the colleges (though, as we have seen, not in the case of Ste. Barbe), a band of bursars formed the nucleus. In addition to these bursars there were other students (*convicteurs* or *portionistes*), boarding with the principal, who received from their parents a stipulated sum for their board and education. The regents, also, had the privilege of receiving boarders (*caméristes*) in rooms adjoining their own, and specially provided for the purpose. In this relation the regents were known as *précepteurs particuliers* or *pédagogues*. But the bulk of the students in the *grands colléges* consisted

[1] Jourdain, *Excursions Historiques, etc.*, p. 261. The statement is vague enough ; but it at least suggests how great the number of students must really have been. Luther states that the number of students at Paris was about 20,000. Alfred Franklin, *La Sorbonne*, p. 125.

of students who frequented them only to receive instruction. These students (*martinets*) had no relations with the principal, and made their arrangements solely with the regents whose classes they might wish to attend. It was these *martinets*, a somewhat irresponsible body, who made the most unruly element in the student life of Paris. A curious section of these *martinets* were the *galoches*, so called from the galoshes which they wore in winter. These *galoches*, who have still their representatives in the Paris of to-day, were men advanced in life who sat through the classes from year to year with no other intention than that of passing an idle hour. Still another class of students—a peculiar feature of medieval scholastic life—invariably made part of the membership of a college. These were the servitors, mostly young men of the humblest rank, who did the menial work of the house, receiving in return the privilege of attending whatever classes they wished.

This large body of students was graduated, in the case of Ste. Barbe, into fourteen classes, each class being under the direction of its own regent. The regents themselves were mostly young men between twenty and thirty years of age, on the way to become licentiates in the higher faculties. Their engagement was only from year to year, and in return for their services the principal guaranteed them food and lodging in the college. Regents of philosophy had a claim to benefices in the Church after five years' teaching; but this privilege was not granted to regents of grammar and rhetoric till 1534.[1] From their pupils all the regents received

---

[1] Crevier, v. 286.

certain fees agreed upon, which were paid twice in the year. As the natural result of this arrangement, the regents were on much more friendly terms with their pupils than with the principal. In cases of insubordination they were as often as not the aiders and abettors of their pupils. How the various elements in these colleges held together under a chief whose powers were so inadequate may well excite our wonder. It is to be remembered, however, that the privileges even of undergraduates were so great that few cared to go to such extremes in their defiance of authority as to run the risk of losing them. Large numbers of persons, indeed, actually enrolled themselves as students for the sole purpose of obtaining these privileges; and in litigation it was always a point with the parties to have a student's interests involved in the case.

Of the hard fare, the coarseness, and even squalor of the life in these colleges we have ample testimony from many sources. Erasmus, Rabelais, and Montaigne have alike spoken in the strongest terms of the wretched conditions under which boys were reared and educated. In the school-room the master alone was seated.[1] The pupils lay on straw littered on the floor, and as their dress consisted of a gown descending to their feet, we may imagine what appearance they must have presented in the matter of personal cleanliness, and we can also understand the necessity of one of the rules of the College that

[1] "About 1366 and about 1452," says Thurot, " benches for scholars began to come into use ; but the cardinals Ste.-Cécile and d'Estouteville put down this luxury as likely to have evil results, and insisted that the scholars should be made to sit on the ground as formerly, so that they might have no temptation to undue presumption."—P. 69.

"no student was to carry his hand to his bonnet in time of meals." The spirit of the time showed itself further in the brutal corporal punishments inflicted on the most trivial occasion. According to Montaigne—and his words are of universal application at the time of which we are speaking—schools were the veritable prisons of captive youth, and when you approached one of them you heard nothing but "cris d'enfants suppliciez et de maistres enyvrez en leur cholère".[1]

In one of his earliest poems, which has not merely a biographical interest, but is a document of recognised value in connection with the history of the university, Buchanan has himself given us a vivid picture of the routine of a day's duties in the college.[2] It was written at the close of his connection with Ste. Barbe, and at a moment apparently when he thought a brighter future was before him. The poem is entitled "Of the wretched Condition of the Teachers of Humane Letters in Paris". It is, therefore, the record of Buchanan's daily duties for the space of three years. After some introductory lines in which he bitterly contrasts the unprofitable drudgery of the scholar and teacher with all other pursuits, he tells how the unhappy regent has sat far into the night over mouldy manuscripts, and has at length, exhausted in mind and body, thrown himself on his bed to snatch a few hours' sleep. "No sooner," he proceeds, "has he stretched his limbs than the watchman announces that it is already the fourth hour. The din of the shrill alarm chases away his dreams, and reminds him that his rest is at an end. Hardly are things again

---

[1] *Essais*, livre i. chap. xxv.   [2] *Eleg.* i.

quiet, when five o'clock sounds, and the porter rings his bell, calling the scholars to their tasks. Then in all the majesty of cap and gown forth issues the master, the terror of his charge, in his right hand the scourge, in his left perchance the works of the great Virgil. He seats himself, and shouts his orders for silence till he is red in the face. And now he brings forth the harvest of his toil. He smooths away difficulties, he corrects, he expunges, he changes the text, he brings to light the spoils he has won by ceaseless study. Meanwhile, his scholars are some of them sound asleep, others thinking of everything but their Virgil. One is absent, but has bribed his neighbour to answer to his name at roll-call. Another has lost his stockings, another cannot keep his eye off a large hole in his shoe. One shams illness, another is writing letters to his parents. Hence the rod is never idle, sobs never cease, cheeks are never dry. Then the duties of religion make their call on us, then lessons once more, and once more the rod. Hardly an hour is spared for our meal. No sooner is it over than lessons again, and then a hasty supper. Supper past, we continue our labours into the night, as if the day's tasks, forsooth, had not been sufficient. Why should I speak of our thousand humiliations? Here, for example, come the swarms of loafers (*errones*)[1] from the city, till the street echoes with the noise of their pattens. In they scramble to listen as intelligently as so many asses. They grumble that no placards announcing the course of lessons have been stuck on the street corners;

---

[1] These were the *galoches* above mentioned.

they are indignant that the *doctrinal* of Alexander [1]
is scornfully ignored by the master, and off they
run to Montaigu, or some other school more to their
taste.   Parents also grumble that the days pass by,
that their sons learn nothing, and meanwhile the
fees must be paid."

Under such conditions it may seem wonderful
that teachers and pupils should have had any
vitality left for mischief or enjoyment.   That they
had leisure and spirit for both, the annals of the
University amply prove ; and the picture of this old
student life can hardly be complete without some
illustration of this other aspect which is certainly
to the full as characteristic as the other.   As a
specimen of its holidaying after Buchanan's own
account of its drudgeries we take the following from
one of the historians of the University :—" The feast
of Lendit," [2] says he, " was a day of feasting and
rejoicing for scholars and regents.   This was the
period when their honorarium was paid by the
scholars, who having put their present in a purse or
in a lemon (*citron*) carried it in pomp to the sounds
of pipe and tabour.   The same day a grand caval-
cade was formed to accompany the rector to St.
Denis.   The supposts of the University, masters
and pupils in great number, assembled and ranged
themselves round their chief in the Place de Sainte
Geneviève, and thence all on horseback, marching
two abreast, with ensigns flying and tabours beat-
ing, they traversed the entire length of the town
until they arrived all in the same order at St. Denis,

---

[1] A grammarian of the Middle Ages, for whom Buchanan, with the
rest of the humanists, had a supreme contempt.   Cf. p. 64.
[2] A fair held at St. Denis during June and July.

the term of their journey. The excesses and scandals which this ceremony occasioned led to the desire on the part of most well-disposed people that this custom should be abolished. But," adds he, "it is not easy to suppress customs which favour licence."[1]

As one proof among a thousand of the readiness for all manner of mischief on the part of the regents and their scholars, we need go no further than the page from which the foregoing extract is taken. The passage also forcibly illustrates what has been said above regarding the good understanding between regents and students. "In 1539,"[2] the same writer continues, "the reform desired was as far off as ever. The old licence was still maintained in full vigour, and there arose out of it certain disorders in the College of Ste. Barbe. In spite of the prohibition set forth by Parliament at the request of the University, the regents of this College wished to celebrate Lendit in the manner they had always seen it celebrated; and finding opposition in the principal, Jacques de Gouvéa, they forced the barriers, sallied forth at the head of their scholars with weapons and tabours, and returned in the same manner. Gouvéa appealed to Parliament against them, and obtained a judgment interdicting them from their functions." In the end the University recommended him to make peace with his refractory subordinates.

[1] Crevier, vol. v. p. 347.
[2] That is, some six or seven years after Buchanan had left Ste. Barbe.

CHAPTER V.

IN passing from the Scots College to Ste. Barbe,
Buchanan had moved to one of the most liberal colleges in Paris.[1] Under its principal, Jacques de
Gouvéa, the most radical reforms had been introduced
in the teaching of Latin and philosophy. The old
text-books in both these subjects had been abandoned, and many of the regents were men with all
the new ideals in studies and religion. Gouvéa himself was a devout Catholic; but he seems to have
allowed a large licence of creed among his subordinates. Several of these made their own mark on the
age, though they call for no special mention in the
biography of Buchanan. The names of two students
of Ste. Barbe, however, between 1520 and 1530, can
hardly be passed by without notice. These were
John Calvin and Ignatius Loyola, whom a curious
fate conducted to the same College at an interval
of a few years between these dates.

The Collége de la Marche has been usually named
as Calvin's first college in Paris ; but there is good
reason to believe that Ste. Barbe must claim the

[1] Quicherat, vol. i. p. 152.

honour.[1] If Calvin was actually a student there, it
must have been in 1523, several years before
Buchanan became regent in the College. But Calvin
was again in Paris in 1533, and at this period there is
every probability that he and Buchanan may have
met. In that year those who favoured the doctrines
of Luther were especially energetic in Paris, and Calvin was already recognised as one of the leading spirits
among them. He was also a visitor at Ste. Barbe,
and was on intimate terms with Antoine de Gouvéa
(the nephew of the Principal), whom he had
succeeded in imbuing with his own heresies. Calvin's connection with Buchanan's college is further
marked by the well-known incident of his early life—
the affair of Nicolas Kopp. Kopp was one of the
regents of philosophy in Ste. Barbe, and mainly
through Calvin had been led to take the side of the
religious reformers. The year in which he took this
step, Kopp was appointed rector of the University,
and in this capacity he had to preach a sermon
before its assembled members. Kopp followed the
usual custom, and preached a sermon expressly
written for him by Calvin, which set the entire university by the ears. The result was that Calvin
and his convert had to flee for their lives. By 1533
Buchanan had left Ste. Barbe, but he was still in
Paris, and he himself expressly tells us that at this
period " he fell among the Lutheran sectaries ".[2] It
is hardly possible, therefore, that he should not
have been familiar with the small circle of zealous
Lutherans,[3] in which Calvin was so prominent a

[1] Quicherat, vol. i. p. 207.
[2] *Vita Sua.*
[3] It is to be remembered that the religious reformers in France were
known as Lutherans till past 1540.

figure.   It should be said, however, that in his lines
written long afterwards on the death of Calvin, he
gives no hint that they had ever held personal intercourse.

In the beginning of 1528 Ignatius Loyola had
come to Paris, driving before him his faithful ass
laden with his books.   He had first begun his studies
at the Collége Montaigu ; but in 1529 he had taken
up his residence in Ste. Barbe.   His residence in
this College is connected with an incident which is
at once illustrative of his own spirit, and of the
manners of the time.   Loyola had come to Paris for
the purpose of study ; but he could not resist the
temptation to make converts to his great mission.
Among these converts was a Spaniard named
Amador, a promising student in philosophy in Ste.
Barbe.   This Amador Loyola had transformed from
a diligent student into a visionary as wild as himself, to the immense indignation of the university,
and especially of his own countrymen.   About the
same time Loyola craved permission to attend Ste.
Barbe as a student of philosophy.   He was admitted
on the express condition that he should make no
attempt on the consciences of his fellows.   Loyola
kept his word as far as Amador was concerned, but
he could not resist the temptation to communicate
his visions to others.   The regent thrice warned
him of what would be the result, and at length
made his complaint to the principal.   Gouvéa was
furious, and gave orders that next day Loyola should
be subjected to the most disgraceful punishment the
College could inflict.   This running of the gauntlet,
known as *la salle*,[1] was administered in the following

---

[1] Quicherat, vol. i. p. 193.

manner. After dinner, when all the scholars were present, the masters, each with his ferule in his hand, ranged themselves in a double row. The delinquent, stripped to the waist, was then made to pass between them, receiving a blow across the shoulders from each. This was the ignominious punishment to which Loyola, then in his fortieth year, as a member of the College, was bound to submit. The tidings of what was in store for him reached his ears, and in a private interview he contrived to turn away Gouvéa's wrath. The next day after dinner, when pupils and masters doubtless looked forward with much satisfaction to the expected performance, Gouvéa arose and announced the culprit's pardon, and from that day Loyola became an inmate of Ste. Barbe. As this was in 1529, the year of Buchanan's entrance into Ste. Barbe, he must have been one of the regents disappointed by Gouvéa's announcement. It is certainly odd to think that Buchanan, afterwards the co-churchman of Knox, should so nearly have missed the privilege of laying his ferule on the bare shoulders of the founder of the Society of Jesus.

While there was this liberty of opinion in Ste. Barbe, the advocates of reform in religion and education were very far from having it all their own way either in the university or even in Ste. Barbe itself. Although we are now in the year 1529, it was still only in a very few colleges that the new methods in literature and philosophy had as yet found a place. In 1530, after a delay of fourteen years, mainly due to the University itself, the Collége Royal was founded for the teaching of Latin, Greek, and Hebrew. But to the end of the century the university maintained the same attitude of hostility

and indifference, and not till the year 1600 did it by
formal decree assign a place to Greek in its curriculum of study.[1] As the case of Descartes (born
1596) also shows, the medieval Aristotle held its
place in the schools of France till past the opening
of the seventeenth century.   This obstinate antagonism to all the new lights was mainly on the
part of the faculties of theology and law.   The numbers and influence of the members of these faculties
put the fortunes of the University in their hands,
and their vested interests in the old order made
impossible for them the acceptance of the new.

Ste. Barbe, we have seen, was one of the most
advanced colleges in the University ; but in Ste.
Barbe itself, all the regents were not of the same
mind, and even the scholars offered formidable opposition to any departure from the beaten track.
In the poem lately quoted, it is enumerated among
Buchanan's grievances that the *galoches* made complaint that the grammar of Alexandre de Villedieu
was not used in the teaching of Latin.   On the
subject of Latin grammars, indeed, the battle between the old and the new world was brought to
direct issue, and it was fought with a zeal and determination on both sides that had in it something of
the character of a religious war.   *The Rudiments of*
the Latin Language, by Alexander of Villa-dei,
had been published in 1240, and up till 1514 it had
been the text-book in all the mediæval universities.
It is a curious commentary on human nature that
men were still found far into the sixteenth century
who seriously maintained that the eternal welfare
of youth would be at stake if any other book were

[1] Crevier, vol. vii. pp. 64, 65.

substituted for Alexander. This Grammar, drawn up by a Franciscan monk of the thirteenth century, is written in Latin verses, of which each word is meant to suggest or recall some rule of syntax. As originally composed, it was a lamentable enough presentation of its subject; but in course of time it had become so overloaded with notes, that, in Buchanan's day, it was simply a barbarous puzzle. This subject of Latin grammars continued throughout the whole century to be a source of trouble and endless discussion among the humanists. As the new learning continued to make way in the various countries, numerous grammars appeared, with the result of introducing considerable confusion into the study of the language. In Scotland, long afterwards, we shall find, in connection with Buchanan's own history, that the multitude of Latin Grammars was made a matter of serious discussion in relation to educational reform.

The historian of Ste. Barbe affirms that to Buchanan, along with two other scholars, belongs the honour of introducing into that College "genuine instruction in the classical languages".[1] We have no detailed information regarding Buchanan's methods and degree of success in the conduct of his class during his three years in Ste. Barbe; but it may be regarded as perfectly satisfactory proof of his energy in the cause of the new learning, that in 1533 he published a Latin translation of Linacre's Grammar. The very fact that he undertook such a task proves not only his zeal in the cause of education, but also that he had the courage to make himself an object of dislike to the authorities of the

[1] Quicherat, vol. i. p. 152.

University. It was published in Paris by Robert
Estienne, and ran through seven editions before the
end of the century. The book was dedicated to his
pupil, the young Earl of Cassillis, in a preface which
has the double interest of clearly setting before us
Buchanan's own point of view, as well as the
attitude of the obscurantists to the more rational
methods he so strenuously advocated. The translation was not published till after he had left Ste.
Barbe, but we may safely conjecture that Linacre's
Grammar had been the basis of his teaching there.
After highly commending the singular clearness,
method, and accuracy of Linacre's work, he thus
proceeds : "But I am perfectly aware that in translating this book many will think that I have given
myself quite unnecessary trouble. We have already
too many of such books, these persons will say ;
and moreover, they add, can anything be said worth
saying which is not to be found in authors who have
long enjoyed the approval of the schools ? As for
the novelties, which make a large part of this book,
such as the remarks on the declension of nouns, of
relatives, and certain moods and tenses of verbs,
they think them mere useless trifling. Such
criticism can come only of sheer ignorance or the
blindest prejudice, that will listen only to its own
suggestions, and gravely maintains that departure
from tradition in such matters is to be regarded as
a proof not so much of foolish self-confidence as of
actual impiety. From these persons, so wise in
their own conceit, I appeal to all men of real
learning and sincere love of letters, confident that
to all such Linacre will generally commend himself."

But it was not only in his capacity of regent

that Buchanan made himself felt in university circles. Buchanan had an eager and lifelong interest in education ; but, as will abundantly appear as we proceed, he was in the first place, and distinctively, a man of letters, with the very strong desire and determination to make his voice heard in whatever society he might find himself. It was at this period that he began the habit of launching those epigrams, which make such a considerable portion of his work, at men and things that met his disapproval. We have already sought to indicate the general state of opinion in the University at this particular epoch ; but the influences to which Buchanan was now subjected will be still better understood by considering the men whose sayings and doings were, during these years, the talk of all its schools. As representing almost all the various tendencies in religion and literature, the names of Lefèvre d'Étaples, Briçonnet, Bishop of Meaux and Conservator of the Apostolical Privileges of the University, Guillaume Budé, and Noel Beda, Syndic of the University, were on the lips of every one interested in the future of French religion and scholarship.

The name of d'Étaples, and the great work he accomplished in rationalising University studies, have already been noted. He had been forced to leave Paris in 1525 ; but his example was still the inspiration of those who aimed at reform in learning and religion. Briçonnet was one of those unhappy persons whom fate mocks with a mission beyond their powers. His high birth had given him his prominent position in the University, and, by sentiment rather than from reasoned conviction, he had identified himself with humanism and reform. In

his bishopric of Meaux, in the neighbourhood of
Paris, he had introduced the religious reforms
advocated by d'Étaples, and had surrounded himself with a band of zealous supporters. But Briçonnet was not of the stuff of which revolutionaries
are made. Brought face to face with the Parliament
and the Sorbonne, he consented to abandon the
cause he had undertaken.[1] It must certainly count
for something in the different fortunes of religious
reform in France and Germany, that in the one
case its first champion was Briçonnet, in the second,
Luther. Briçonnet's submission had also taken
place in 1525, during the captivity of Francis, but
this victory of the Sorbonne had only the effect of
quickening the zeal of the more energetic advocates
of reform. Among these was Louis de Berquin,
who, according to Ranke, combined in happier proportions than any other man then living the best
elements in the teaching of Luther and Erasmus.
At every point Berquin was opposed to the theological faculty, and his rash courage and high
accomplishments made him its most formidable
single adversary. From 1523 till 1529 the battle
went on between them, and Berquin, supported by
Francis, and especially by Francis's sister, the
famous Margaret of Navarre, had for a time seemed
even to have the advantage. Twice Francis rescued
him from the Parliament and the theologians; but at
length he passed the limits of Francis's power or
desire to help him, and in 1529 he was burned at
the stake. The name of Budé carried with it
greater weight than that of any French scholar of
his day, and by his solid contribution to our know-

---

[1] Graf, *Jacques Lefèvre d'Étaples*, p. 120.

ledge of classical antiquity, he is in the line of Casaubon and the younger Scaliger rather than that of the Italian stylists and their French imitators of his own century. All Budé's influence went to favour the new studies, and it was in great measure his work that in 1530 the Collége Royal was founded by Francis. Budé's position on the question of religion was that of most of his fellow-humanists. He ostensibly adhered to the traditions of the Church, but the real interest of his life was in the tradition of Greece and Rome.[1] Noél Beda, the last of the group above named, was the veritable incarnation of the scholastic theology, at a time when the life had gone out of it. "In one Beda," says Erasmus, "there are three thousand monks." He pursued every form of what he deemed heresy with such inveteracy of hate, that, in the opinion of his own party, he injured the very cause he had at heart. It was by his efforts more than by those of any one else that Briçonnet had been brought to submission and Berquin burned. At last, in his indefatigable zeal, he persuaded the theological faculty to condemn a book written by the King's own sister. This passed the endurance of Francis, and the University was compelled to pass sentence of exile on its redoubtable champion. It was with this Beda that men like Buchanan had to reckon, when, by pen or tongue, they passed the limits of what he deemed the traditions of the Church in human and divine things.

---

[1] Rebitté, *Guillaume Budé, Restaurateur des Études grecques en France*, p. 201. Buchanan has the following lines on Budé :—

Gallia quod Graeca est, quod Graecia barbara non est,
Utraque Budaeo debet utrumque suo.—*Epig.* ii. 7.

In the conflict of opinion represented by the
names just mentioned it is interesting to note the
different courses taken by the three most eminent
literary Scotsmen then in France—John Major,
Florence Wilson, and Buchanan himself. Major,
we have seen, had returned to Paris in 1525, and he
was now teaching in the Collége Montaigu with a
reputation second to that of no doctor in Paris.[1]
His modes of thought have already been indicated,
and it is sufficient to say that at this moment
he was regarded as "the veritable chief of the
scholastic philosophy".[2] His former pupil and he,
therefore, were in opposite camps, and this at a time
when the strife between them was at its bitterest.
In all probability, it is to this period we must refer
Buchanan's famous epigram on his old master, for
which he has been blamed even by his own friends
and admirers. Sarcasm could hardly go further than
in this epigram ; yet, read without reference to the
circumstances in which it was written, and to the
licence of abuse which the Latinists of Buchanan's day
permitted themselves, it will lead to an utterly false
impression of Buchanan's character. From what
has been said, it must be clear that, in directing his
satire against Major, Buchanan was in reality doing
battle against the system which Major incarnated,
and which Buchanan, and those who thought with
him, were zealously bent on bringing to the ground.
But the truth is, that the standard of fair satire in
Buchanan's day was so different from our own, that
we should be utterly astray in inferring from this
epigram any real badness of heart in the writer. It

---

[1] It is not quite certain when Major returned to Scotland. It must,
however, have been about 1530.   [2] Quicherat, i. 97.

must be added that Major himself had tempted the attack. In a spirit of somewhat affected humility he had spoken of himself as *Joannes solo cognomine Major* ("*Major* by name and not by nature "). Buchanan's epigram is the merciless comment on these words :—

> Cum scateat nugis solo cognomine Major,
> Nec sit in immenso pagina sana libro :
> Non mirum, titulis quod se veracibus ornat :
> Nec semper mendax fingere Creta solet.

> "' Major by name,' thou sayst, 'and not by nature !'
> The greatest liars sometimes speak the truth :
> And in thy endless stream of idle chatter,
> What wonder if thou once hast spoken sooth !"

It is to be regretted that our knowledge of Florence Wilson[1] is so scanty, as from all we know of him he is among the most interesting of the numberless literary "Scots Abroad". A few years Buchanan's senior, he had received his education partly in Aberdeen and partly in Paris, and had early been caught by the new ideals of the century. He had acted as tutor to the nephew of Cardinal Wolsey, was on familiar terms with Bishop Fisher, and was afterwards attached to the train of Jean du Bellay, Bishop of Paris. In accompanying du Bellay to Rome he made the acquaintance of Cardinal Sadoleto in a manner which throws a curious light on that enthusiastic community of feeling between men of all ranks who were devotees of the new learning. It is Sadoleto himself who relates the incident in one of his letters.[2] One evening he had

---

[1] We have no authority for the name *Florence Wilson*. The name always appears as *Florentius Volusenus*.

[2] It should be said that Wilson had fallen sick at Avignon, on his way to Rome with du Bellay. It may here be added that Buchanan probably met Wilson in Paris in 1531. We know that Wilson was there in that year.—*Bannatyne Miscellany*, vol. i. p. 325.

sat down as usual to his books, when his servant
announced that a stranger, by his gown evidently a
scholar, desired to see him. He was annoyed at
being disturbed, but he ordered the visitor to be
admitted. The Cardinal is at once arrested by the
stranger's address, and by the refinement and
choiceness of his Latinity. Questions then follow. Whence did he come, where had he been
educated, what was his past history? All is
answered satisfactorily, and meanwhile Sadoleto
is every moment becoming more and more charmed
by the modesty and evident accomplishments of
his visitor. The stranger's name, he learns, is
Volusenus, and he has come from Avignon to Carpentras, partly to see Sadoleto himself, of whose
fame he had heard so much, and partly to offer
himself for the post of Principal in the new school
of Carpentras, in which Sadoleto had taken such
interest. The Cardinal is delighted at the prospect
of having such a man in his neighbourhood. He
talks over the authorities, and Wilson is unanimously appointed to the post. Here Wilson remained probably till 1544.[1] Two years later, while
on his way home to Scotland, he died at Vienne in
Dauphiné. Buchanan commemorates Wilson in
the following lines :—

> Hic musis, Volusene, jaces carissime, ripam
>   Ad Rhodani, terra quam procul a patria !
> Hoc meruit virtus tua, tellus quae foret altrix
>   Virtutum, ut cineres conderet illa tuos.

---

[1] In 1544 Sadoleto wrote to Claude Baduel, Principal of the Gymnasium of Nismes, offering him the Principalship of his school at Carpentras. This would seem to show that Wilson had held that post, and
was not a simple regent.—Gaufrès, *Claude Baduel et la Réforme des
Études au xvi⁰ siècle* (Paris, 1880), p. 129.

"Here by Rhone's banks (from thy own fields how far !),
Beloved of all the Muses, dost thou sleep :
Yet doth the land that did thy virtues rear,
Meetly, O Florence, thy dear ashes keep."

Wilson has left us a few Latin poems, and a
somewhat lengthy tract, entitled *De Animi Tranquillitate*, in the manner of the philosophical
treatises of Cicero. His poems have little merit as
poetry,[1] and his treatise has nothing of Buchanan's
force of thought and impetuous rush of feeling.
But every page confirms the impression we receive
from Sadoleto's letter—the impression of dignity,
refinement, and moral elevation. In his Latin style
he is a greater purist than Buchanan, and he has
disparaging remarks on the Latinity of Erasmus.[2]
But the interest of Wilson's treatise lies mainly in
the fact that it curiously illustrates the struggle
in his mind between the good Catholic and the
humanist, caring everything for the choiceness of his
style and the genuine flavour of antiquity. After
he has devoted nearly three-fourths of his book to
maxims drawn from the Greeks and Romans, he
suddenly becomes conscious that all this has more
of the Pagan in it than the Christian, and straight-
way proceeds to unsay all he has been saying,
and ends in a strain of the soundest orthodoxy.
Wilson was a humanist, then, but a humanist
who, while keenly conscious of the shortcomings
of the Church, was still satisfied to remain within
its pale.[3] In his case, as in the case of Buchanan,
we cannot but regret that by his humanistic culture

[1] Wilson himself tells us that he had not the advantage of being
trained to verse-making in his youth like Buchanan.—*De Animi Tranquillitate*, p. 165 (edit. Edin. 1751).
[2] *De Animi Tranquillitate*, p. 250.
[3] "Nobis Ecclesiae auctoritas semper plurimi est facienda."—*Ibid.*
p. 251.

his character and talent were lost to his native literature.   He would have been one more of that type
which in Scotland has not had too many representatives—a type which Henryson in the fifteenth
and Leighton in the seventeenth century so finely
illustrate.

In Buchanan's case we have for this period no
such definite expression of opinion as in the case of
Major and Wilson.   He tells us, indeed, that at
this time " he fell among the Lutheran sectaries " ;[1]
but this certainly cannot imply that he now definitely embraced the opinions of Luther, or that he
formally broke with Catholicism.   Equally from the
general tenor of his life, and from the various poems
he was continually throwing off, we are forced to
the conclusion that not at least till near his final
return to Scotland about 1560 did he throw in his
lot with the religious reformers.   At this time there
were many Lutherans in Paris, and there were few
of the Colleges without some members who in
greater or less degree favoured their doctrines.
But as far as Buchanan is concerned it will abundantly appear as we proceed that any seeming in-
clination to side with Luther against the Pope must
be traced to his detestation of the dogged obscurantism of the Sorbonne, and the general ignorance
and degradation of the clergy.   In short, till 1560
Buchanan's attitude towards the Church was that
of Colet, Erasmus, and Thomas More.[2]   It is difficult
to determine the exact periods when the poems
that make up the collection entitled *Fratres Frater*-

---

[1] " In flammam Lutheranae sectae, jam late se spargentem, incidit."
—*Vita Sua.*

[2] And we may add Budé himself, who speaks as strongly as Erasmus and Buchanan against the ignorance and degradation of the clergy.
—Rebitté, *Vie de Budé*, p. 237.

rimi were written, but in none of them, even in those where the satire is bitterest, is there anything to indicate that he had broken with the central doctrines of the Church.

The futility of the instruction that still predominated in the Paris schools, the ignorance and profligacy of those who made the loudest professions of orthodoxy—these were the subjects that now filled Buchanan's mind and exercised his wit. His epigram on Major shows us his contempt for the effete scholasticism ; the following shows his regard for its champions. It is directed against one Gonellus, a Dominican and member of the Sorbonne : " Gonellus, who has a paunch like a balloon, one day heard the old remark that truth lies hid in wine. ' What !' exclaims he, ' have I wasted all my precious years in these tedious and silly wranglings of the Schools ? Good-bye, my grim Sorbonne ; not with you, as I now learn too late, does truth abide. But hail ! goodly taverns, the true and only homes of wisdom.' And from that hour our good Gonellus does nothing but sound the depths of wine-jars. He drinks by night, and he drinks by day. At length, having drained his purse in draining casks, he thus sums up the result of his researches : 'I know nothing, and I possess nothing,' and solacing himself with this pretty jest, he boasts that he is as wise as Socrates." [1] We may conceive how the august Sorbonne must have regarded Buchanan when jests like this went the round of the colleges.

[1] If we may believe Rabelais, the doctors of the Sorbonne must have had a reputation as *bons vivants*. We have seen how he assigns to Major a book entitled *The Art of making Puddings*. To Beda himself he ascribes a work in the same library of St. Victor—*De Optimitate Triparum*.

Buchanan had not been long in Ste. Barbe before
an honour was conferred on him which proves that
he was among the most prominent of the younger
men then frequenting the University.   On the 3d of
June 1529 he was elected Procurator of the German
Nation—an honour which would have befallen him
a month earlier had the Germans who made part of
the Nation not voted against the English and Scots.[1]

The arrangement of Nations, with their Pro-
curators, arose naturally out of the metropolitan
character of the mediæval universities.   From the
twelfth century students had flocked to Paris from
every country of Europe ; and those who came from
the same country and spoke the same language
naturally drew together, and formed a body as
distinct as the conditions of university life would
permit.   In course of time it was seen that this
natural arrangement formed a suitable basis for
regular organisation, and accordingly so early as
1245, in a Bull of Innocent IV., the four Nations of
France, Normandy, Picardy, and England are distinctly recognised.   These four nations and the
superior Faculties of theology, law, and medicine,
made up what were known as the seven " com-
panies " of the universities ; and it was the pro-
curators of the Nations and the deans of the
Faculties, who, with the rector as president, con-
stituted the university tribunal.   The English
Nation was composed of three tribes—Germany,
Scandinavia, and the British Islands, and for its
patron saints it had Charlemagne and St. Edmund.[2]

---

[1] Archives of the University of Paris, Register 16, fol. 169 and 170.
See Appendix B.
[2] This is the King Edmund commemorated in the name St. Edmunds-
bury.   See Major, De Gestis Scotorum, lib. iii. cap. i.

Of its schools we have already spoken. During the Hundred Years' War between England and France, the name "English Nation" became an offence in French ears, and in 1378 the Emperor Charles IV., then on a visit to Paris, expressed the wish that the name should be changed. It was not, however, till 1436 that the designation "German Nation" displaced the other in the University Registers.[1] At the time that Buchanan became its procurator the German Nation in Paris was no longer so important a body as it had formerly been. Some years later the schism of England from Rome, and the religious dissensions in Germany, largely reduced its members; and it is a fact of curious interest, as showing what rending of the peoples had ensued from the general breach with Rome, that in 1541 there was but one member of the German Nation in Paris.[2]

The office of procurator could be held only for one month, but in the event of his giving satisfaction to the Nation, the same person was frequently re-elected several times in succession. Buchanan's predecessor in office, Robert Wauchope, also a Scotsman, who had a remarkable career in his day, was re-elected nine times in succession,[3] Buchanan himself four times.[4] The duties of the office consisted in looking after the money affairs of the Nation, in presiding at its meetings, and in reporting their decisions to the general council of the University. In the register of the German Nation Buchanan has left a memorial of his term of office which at once gives us

---

[1] Jourdain, *Excursions Historiques et Philosophiques*, p. 366.
[2] Crevier, vol. v. p. 367.
[3] Chalmers, *Life of Ruddiman*, p. 313. Chalmers's authority is the Register of the Scots College.
[4] Archives of the University of Paris. See Appendix B.

a curious glimpse into the scholastic life of Paris,
and reveals his own sarcastic habit.

Robert Dugast, who has already been mentioned as the proprietor of Ste. Barbe, was at this
time one of the most remarkable among the principals of the colleges of Paris.   He seems to have
been a man of unusual ability and force of character, and open, moreover, to all the new lights
of the time ; but he was greedy and overbearing
to absurdity.   From his uncle he had inherited
the Collége Coqueret and the Collége de Reims,
and by unscrupulous dealing he had made himself owner of Ste. Barbe.[1] As the result of all
this, he was detested by every member of the
University, and complaints were being constantly
lodged against him.   It is one of these complaints
that Buchanan signalises in the following entry :—

"Pierre Tillier, regent of the Collége Coqueret,
has presented a request to the Faculty of Arts, in
the name of a certain colleague unjustly imprisoned
by the criminal lieutenant, and also in the name of
a certain pedagogue detained in the official prison
at the instance of the principal of the above-named
College, a man detestable by his harshness and
avarice—their crime being that they ate a penny
loaf belonging to the said principal.   The German
Nation, on this point in accordance with the whole
Faculty, has charged Master Martin Dolet to demand
the liberation of the prisoners ; and as regards the
said principal, it declares him fallen from all University privileges, as having violated the statutes
which forbid any member of the University to be
cited before any court whatever before the rector

[1] Quicherat, vol. i. chap. xxix.

has been made acquainted with the affair.   Further, the entire Faculty has declared the said principal guilty of insubordination, and has charged the censors of the Nation to visit the Collége Coqueret, and to use their authority to re-establish order." [1]

In other entries relating to this Dugast, Buchanan similarly enlivens his formal official record.   Thus, another regent is mentioned as " desiring to recover by legal process certain articles of furniture which he declares to be detained by that rapacious harpy Master Robert Dugast, whom the same regent cited before the Faculty.   But the above-named principal, with his usual obstinacy, failed to appear."   From all we know of this Dugast he seems to have fully deserved the worst that Buchanan has said of him.

The year following his procuratorship, 1530, a new University honour was conferred on Buchanan. In one of the elections of the rector during that year, it fell to the Scottish section to choose the elector who should represent the German Nation, and on the motion of their countryman, Robert Wauchope, they unanimously fixed on " that able man, so learned in Latin and Greek, Master George Buchanan." [2]   The next dignity would have been the rectorship itself; but Buchanan had identified himself far too prominently with the new movements in the University, and cast his witticisms about much too freely, to make it possible that the four Nations should choose him as their head.

Buchanan probably resigned his post in Ste. Barbe somewhere in 1531 ; and the concluding lines

[1] See Appendix B.
[2] Archives of the University, Reg. 16, fol. 184.   The reference to Buchanan's acquaintance with Greek is noteworthy.   In Greek, as will afterwards be seen, he appears to have been self-taught.

of the elegy in which he gives the account already
quoted of his duties as regent, seem to commemorate
this step : [1]—

> Ite, igitur, Musae steriles, aliumque ministrum
> Quaerite : nos alio sors animusque vocat.

We may readily believe that Buchanan, with his
fastidious temper and his poet's sensibility, must
have found in the highest degree uncongenial that
dismal routine he has so vividly described.   We
may fairly conjecture, indeed, that under the
happiest circumstances the profession of regent or
tutor, which he was thenceforth to follow, could
never have been grateful to him.   It is almost as
easy to think of Heine or Swift or Burns yoked to
this profession, and finding it their true function, as
Buchanan.   His health was never robust, and by
his mental constitution he had the irritability of the
poet and man of letters.   We must therefore set it to
his credit that, with his late experience behind him,
he chose the mode of life he did, when by a little
compromise he might have found in the Church some
comfortable benefice that would have enabled him
to cultivate his muse in peace.   That the temptation came to him we have some reason to believe.
But he was too deeply moved by the new ideals of
the time in religion, in literature, in politics, to
make the compromise without injury to his best
self.   Accordingly, as we believe, he made what for
a man of his type is the highest sacrifice he can possibly make.   He sacrificed the life that would have
yielded him the best opportunity of cultivating his
special talent.

[1] He acted as regent in Ste. Barbe for three years.—*Vita Sua.*

The engagement on which Buchanan entered on leaving Ste. Barbe was one of a kind becoming every day more common with his .fellow-humanists—that of tutor or companion to the member of some distinguished house.   For those out of sympathy with the Church, and with no predilection for medicine or law, this was perhaps the most comfortable position in which they could find themselves.[1]   Its one great drawback was that, in most cases, such an engagement could only be temporary.   The wandering propensities of the scholars of the Renaissance have often been noticed.   Yet in many cases it must have been as much from necessity as choice that they so frequently changed their abode.   None of them made more frequent migrations than Buchanan himself, and in his case there seems always to have been sufficient reason for each new flight— now the expiry of an engagement, now sickness, now personal risk on account of opinions.

Buchanan's pupil was the Earl of Cassillis, to whom, as we have seen, he dedicated his translation of Linacre's Grammar in 1533.   The young Earl's father, the second Earl of Cassillis, had been assassinated in 1527, and his son, then a boy of twelve, had been placed under the guardianship of his uncle, William Kennedy, Abbot of Crossraguel.[2] Buchanan's pupil, Knox tells us, was one of those children of the nobility made to sign the death-warrant of Patrick Hamilton in 1528.[3]   In 1530 Abbot William obtained a royal licence to pass to

---

[1] The only other occupation for scholars in Buchanan's position was that of assistant to one of the great printers of the time.

[2] Charters of the Abbey of Crossraguel, xxxvii.

[3] Knox, *History of the Reformation in Scotland* (Laing's edition), vol. i. p. 16.

F

Rome by way of France ;[1] and it is probable that his nephew accompanied him on this journey, as Buchanan seems to have been acquainted with him before he became his tutor.[2] It was probably in 1532 that the engagement actually began, and it lasted for the next five years.

Cassillis' long residence in Paris for the sake of his education may be taken as one proof, amongst many, that the Scottish nobility had in some degree realised that the period of feudalism was past, and that other accomplishments were now required of a baron than those which satisfied old Bell-the-Cat. Cassillis came to be one of the prominent Scottish nobles in the protracted regency that followed the death of James v., and we may believe that his five years' intercourse with a man like Buchanan must have placed him at some advantage with his brother barons, both in Scotland and England. In 1558 Cassillis was chosen as one of the Commissioners to represent Scotland at the marriage of Mary with the Dauphin, and on his way home he and other three of his fellow-commissioners died suddenly at Dieppe, under strong suspicion of having been poisoned by the Guises. Buchanan has celebrated his pupil in the following lines :—

> Hic situs est heros humili Gilbertus in urna
>   Kennedus, antiquae nobilitatis honos :
> Musarum Martisque decus, pacisque minister,
>   Et columen patriae consiliumque suae.
>
> Occidit insidiis fallaci exceptus ab hoste,
>   Bis tria post vitae lustra peracta suae.
> Parce, hospes, lacrymis, et inanem comprime luctum,
>   Non misere quisquam, qui bene vixit, obit.[3]

---

[1] Charters of the Abbey of Crossraguel, xxxvii.   [2] *Vita Sua.*
[3] *Epig.* ii. 9. As Cassillis was a little over forty at the time of his

A passage in his History, in which he represents Cassillis as playing the part of another Regulus, deserves to be quoted, not only for its interest in the present connection, but also as a curious specimen of what has found its way into history in the guise of the soberest truth. It should be said that Cassillis had been taken prisoner by the English at Solway Moss, and allowed to return to Scotland, though for very different reasons from those assigned by Buchanan. In the following paragraph we have an account of the debate that arose after an interview between the Regent Arran and the English Ambassador, who, on behalf of his master, had demanded a new set of hostages :—

"The new hostages were refused ; but a question of no less importance arose. What of those nobles (such as Cassillis) who had been made prisoners at Solway Moss, and who had been liberated only after they had left hostages behind them, and given a solemn pledge that, in the event of the favourable overtures on the part of Henry not being accepted by the Scots, they would of their own accord return to England ? The Cardinal's [Beaton's] faction, and the clergy generally, plied the nobles with arguments and precedents to prove that, where the interests of one's country are at stake, goods, kinsfolk, children, everything that one holds dear, must be lost sight of. The decree of the Council of Constance was adduced, which distinctly laid it down that no faith is to be kept

death, Ruddiman thought that the above epigram must apply to the father, who also died by violence. But the line

"Musarum Martisque decus, pacisque minister"

seems naturally to apply to Buchanan's pupil. The misstatement of his age need not be regarded too seriously.

with heretics.   The majority of the nobles, whom
this question concerned, readily accepted these excuses for their treachery.   One only of their number was found, who could neither be won by bribes
nor be constrained by threats to break his pledged
word.   This was Gilbert Kennedy, Earl of Cassillis.
He had left two brothers in England as hostages ;
and now he declared that nothing would induce
him to save his own life at the expense of theirs.
Accordingly, in the teeth of the strongest opposition, he at once proceeded to London.   King
Henry lavished his praises on the young Earl's
steadfast good faith ; and that men might understand that he knew how to honour virtue, he sent
him home laden with gifts, and accompanied by
both his brothers." [1]

It was in all good faith that Buchanan wrote
the foregoing paragraph, and it may be that in the
ordinary dealings of life his pupil was quite up to
the moral standard of his class and of his age.   We
now know, however, what Buchanan could not
have known, that Cassillis was in reality the paid
agent of Henry VIII., and that his magnanimity on
this occasion was purely mythical. [2]   At the same
time, it is but fair to add that a large number of
the Scottish nobles were in the same case as Cassillis, and that their policy finds some justification
in the danger they professed to see from the French
ascendency in Scotland.

---

[1] *Hist. Rer. Scot.* lib. xv.
[2] Cassillis is condemned by a letter of his own found in the State
Paper Office.—Tytler, *History of Scotland*, vol. iii. p. 32 (edit. 1873).

CHAPTER VI.

THE following entries in the Treasurer's Accounts fix approximately the date of Buchanan's return to Scotland, and at the same time give us an interesting glimpse of his close connection with the Court :

"Item, the xvj Februar [1535-6] be the Kingis gracis precept and speciale command to Maister George Balquhannan and Andro Myln, servandis to Lord James, xi elnis pareis blak to be thame twa gounis," etc., and various other "leverays", viz., "hoiss, bonnettis, hugtonis,[1] and doublettis".

" Item [the xxj day of August 1537], to Maister George Buchquhannan, at the Kingis command . . . xx lib."

In July 1538, upon occasion of "the Quenis [Magdalene's] saull mess and dirige, quham God assolze", Maister George Balquhanan received "a goun of Paryse black, lyned with blak satyne", etc. ; also £20 at the King's command.

As, on his return to Scotland, he spent some time in the country with the Earl of Cassillis before his engagement with the Lord James,[2] Buchanan

---

[1] Cassocks (Fr. *hocqueton*).
[2] *Vita Sua*, and Dedication to *Franciscanus*.

must have left Paris in 1535 ; and this date exactly
corresponds with his statement that his second
sojourn abroad lasted ten years.[1] It was during
his stay in the country with Cassillis at this time
that Buchanan wrote a poem which was to have the
most important influence on his subsequent fortunes. This was the poem entitled *Somnium*, in
which he gave mortal offence to the great Order of
the Franciscans, who thenceforward, first in Scotland, and afterwards in England, France, Portugal,
and Italy, pursued him with every weapon at their
disposal.[2]

In a lively figure Scott has very well described
the position of the Church of Rome at this period.
"That ancient system," he says, "which so well
accommodated its doctrines to the wants and wishes
of a barbarous age, had since the art of printing,
and the gradual diffusion of knowledge, lain floating
like some huge leviathan, into which ten thousand
reforming fishers were darting their weapons."[3]
Partly owing to its existing shortcomings, and
partly also, it should be said, to its own good offices
in the past, the old religion in Scotland was even
less able than elsewhere to meet the storm that
now came upon it. By its endeavours in preceding centuries, as we have seen, education was
perhaps more widely spread in Scotland than in any
other country of Europe. From an Act of Parliament passed in 1525, and renewed in 1535, prohibiting the importation of Lutheran books, we
gather that from the very first there was an intelligent and widespread interest in the great religious

[1] *Vita Sua.*
[2] Dedication to *Franciscanus.*   [3] *The Monastery,* ch. xxxi.

movement, as yet associated only with the name of Luther. On the other hand, we have it from friends and foes alike that the bulk of the clergy themselves were dead to that general awakening of men's minds which betokened nothing less than the beginning of a new era. By the time they came to see what many of the laity and a few of their own order had seen long before, it was too late to meet the new conditions.[1]

But not only had the clergy fallen below the educated intelligence of the laity, they had also fallen below its moral standard.[2]   At the very time they should have given least room for criticism, they presented the broadest mark. This moral disintegration was in the first place due to the fact that the ideas on which the Church rested were in the last need of quickening or renewal. The intellectual interest in its doctrines was insufficient to give life to that complicated machinery of the Papal system, which renders it so powerful in periods of religious fervour, but in times of apathy makes it but a cumbrous toy. This intellectual torpor brought with it moral deterioration ; and in that age moral deterioration meant surrender to the coarsest forms of sensual indulgence. If a Loyola was not forthcoming to quicken the Church from within, a Knox must renew it from without.

The decay of the Roman Church in Scotland was organic ; but the process was hastened by circumstances which at healthier periods would have

---

[1] Buchanan himself tells us that many of the monks believed that Luther was the author of the New Testament.—*Rer. Scot. Hist.* lib. xv. p. 292. The testimony of Boece and Major regarding the ignorance of the clergy is in the same direction.

[2] The poems of Sir David Lyndsay, for example, leave us distinctly with this impression.

promoted its vitality. By the battle of Flodden, a
generation of nobles, who had formed the natural
equipoise to the higher clergy, had perished ; and
to the Church thus fell an undue place in the management of affairs.[1]   The long minority of James v.
increased this advantage ; and when James himself
came to the throne, his own policy was to exalt the
bishops at the expense of the nobles.   Arrogance
and luxurious living followed this increase of power
and wealth ; and the lower clergy soon learned the
manners of their superiors.   Hatred and contempt
of its representatives, therefore, worked with the desire for reform to move the foundations of the Church.
A large number of the nobles detested the higher
clergy, and the people were growing out of sympathy
with the lower.   Moreover, the schism of England
from Rome came to be the formidable precedent
which presented itself as the ultimate solution of
the general discontent.   The influence of England
in hastening the Reformation in Scotland is one of
those facts in history which cannot be measured by
any accumulation of details.   Its example was a
great fact that touched men's minds at a thousand
points, and influenced them unconsciously to themselves.

It was further the misfortune of the Romish clergy
that their ways of living and thinking presented
precisely the subjects which the humanists, and,
indeed, the generally quickened intelligence of the
laity, needed for the exercise of their new weapons.
We certainly do no injustice to men like Erasmus
and Buchanan in thinking that their sarcasms at

---

[1] This is Buchanan's own remark, and its justice is evident.—*Rer.
Scot. Hist.* lib. xiii. p. 255.

the expense of the monks were often as much mere
play of wit as the expression of righteous indignation. With the humanists especially, who sought
to make a reputation as poets, the contrast between
the lives and the profession of the clergy was an
inexhaustible subject. For poetry of the highest
type, these Latin poets of the Renaissance had no
great themes on which their genius could work.
By the very condition of their training, and the
mental attitude they cultivated, they cut themselves off from real contact with their native soil.
Their attitude towards the past and present of their
respective countries was too critical to permit of
their producing works of national interest and
national importance. All this certainly applies with
less force to Buchanan than to the contemporary
humanists of France and Italy. That intensity of
national feeling, which has always pre-eminently
distinguished Scotsmen, kept him close to the heart
of his country in spite of his artificial training.
Yet it is the fact that with the exception of a few
patriotic lines, he wrote no poem which is essentially
homebred in its inspiration. His themes were the
conventional ones of all the Latinists ; and in the
three poems now about to be considered he comes
before us rather as the humanist exercising his wit
and his Latinity than as the social and religious
reformer. In another production, which belongs to
a somewhat later period, we shall see that Buchanan
rose to a higher mood in his denunciation of what
he considered the abuses of the time in Church and
State.

The poem entitled *Somnium*, which was to be
the beginning of so many of his troubles, is identical

in motive with a poem of Dunbar known as *How Dunbar was desyrit to be ane Fryer.*[1] Both poets begin by describing how St. Francis, the founder of the Franciscan Order, appeared to them in a dream, and besought them to don his habit. The reply of both is to the same effect. They can be honester men as they are, for vice and knavery are all they can see in the Church. If St. Francis could promise them a bishopric, however, they would gladly listen to his proposals.

> " Of full few freiris that has bene sanctis I reid ;
> Quhairfor ga bring to me ane bischopis weid,
> Gife evin thou wold my soul guid into hevin."

Or, as Buchanan renders it :—

> Pervia sed raris sunt coeli regna cucullis :
> Vix Monachis illic creditur esse locus.

> .   .   .   .   .

> Multus honoratis fulgebit Episcopus aris ;
> Rara cucullato sternitur ara gregi.

We know from this poem of Dunbar that in his youth he actually was a Franciscan friar, though he afterwards renounced the habit. Buchanan in all probability never ceased to be a layman. At the same time, it is noteworthy that both this poem and *Franciscanus*, the most elaborate of all his satires against the friars, open with the question as to the advisability of entering the Church. It is quite possible, therefore, that at this particular period Buchanan may have had serious thoughts of taking such a step. It is to be remembered that about 1537 there was as yet in Scotland no real breach with the Church, though many were calling aloud its abuses. Knox appears to have been in priest's orders till about 1540, and Buchanan himself has told us that there were still men in the Church

---

[1] Buchanan's poem is, indeed, virtually a translation of Dunbar's.

worthy of all respect. Moreover, he could not but be aware that outside the Church his prospects in life must be but dark and uncertain. As he had no predilection for law or medicine, the haphazard career of regent or family tutor was the only one left open to him. He was not a considerable enough person to be promoted to important State employment, and besides, as has been said, the clergy had it much their own way in all departments of the government. Altogether, therefore, it is by no means unlikely that the opening lines of these two poems may record a real struggle in Buchanan's mind.[1]

On the expiry of his engagement with Cassillis, Buchanan had thoughts of once more returning to France. Just at this moment, however, an offer was made to him by James v. to act as tutor to one of his natural sons.[2] This son, Lord James Stewart, is not to be confounded with another natural son of James who bore the same name, and who was afterwards known as the Regent Moray.[3] As the King was now but twenty-four, Buchanan's pupil must have been a mere child. He died in 1558, leaving no record in the history of his country. The significance of this engagement for Buchanan was that it brought him into close connection with the

---

[1] Some lines in *Franciscanus* have been supposed to suggest that Buchanan was at one time a friar ; but the context of the passage does not justify such a conclusion :—

> . . . puerum olim
> Me quoque pene suis gens haec in retia mendax
> Traxerat illecebris, nisi opem mihi forte tulisset
> Coelitus oblata Eubuli sapientia cani.

[2] *Vita Sua.*

[3] The mother of Buchanan's pupil was Elizabeth Shaw, of the family of Sauchie.—Man, *Censure of Ruddiman*, p. 349. The dedication of *Franciscanus* proves that the Regent Moray was not Buchanan's pupil.

Court, and led the King to prompt him to further satires against the Franciscans.

In a letter addressed to Pope Clement VII. in 1531, James speaks highly of the virtues of the Franciscans, yet this can hardly induce us to question Buchanan's statement that it was at the instance of the King he wrote against them.[1] A set epistle from a boy-king to a pope may be taken for what it is worth ; and the fact remains that James fully enjoyed the roundest jest at the expense of the clergy. Buchanan said hard things of the Church, but certainly no harder than Sir David Lyndsay in his *Satire of the Three Estates*, the first performance of which James honoured with his presence.[2] According to Buchanan, James fancied that at this time he had particular reason to have a grudge against the Franciscans, as he suspected them of being concerned in certain plots now afoot against him among the nobility. From the date at which the poem was written, the plot referred to was probably that of the Master of Forbes, who in June 1536 was accused of an attempt to shoot the King at Aberdeen, and in July 1538 was beheaded on this charge. Nothing is accurately known of this affair of Forbes, and there is no reason to believe that the Franciscans were in any way his accomplices.[3]

As Buchanan had already been made to feel the foolhardiness of offending so powerful a body as the Franciscans, it was with some reluctance that he

---

[1] The letter of James to the Pope is quoted by Canon Bellesheim in his *History of the Catholic Church in Scotland* (ii. 139 n.), from Theiner, *Monumenta*, p. 597.

[2] Laing, *Life of Lyndsay* (prefixed to his edition of Lyndsay's Works).

[3] Tytler, *History of Scotland*, vol. ii. chap. ix. (Edin. 1873).

obeyed the King's command to attack them anew.[1]
It occurred to him that by giving his verses an
ambiguous turn he might satisfy the King without
further irritating the Franciscans. Such is the
account of the origin of the two short poems,
each entitled *Palinodia*, which with little variation Buchanan gives in his autobiography and in
the dedication of his *Franciscanus*. If at their first
appearance these poems were exactly such as we
now have them, Buchanan must indeed have had a
supreme contempt equally for the intelligence of the
King and that of the friars. Both poems are, in
truth, far more savage satires than the *Somnium*
itself. The fact, however, that two poems of the
same title stand in the collection of his works,
suggests that, as in the case of *Franciscanus*, alterations and additions may have been made on the
poems as originally written. As they now stand, it
is certainly hard to see how Buchanan could have
imagined that the Franciscans would not resent this
second lampoon tenfold more keenly than the first.

In the first of these two satires Buchanan
imagines himself borne into the heavens and set
down in a vast hall thronged by monks of the
Franciscan order. A sarcastic description of their
general appearance follows. But the crowd is met
to sit in judgment on himself, and he is at once
dragged to the tribunal, where the judge dis-
charges a ludicrous tirade against him for daring
to breathe a word against the Order of St. Francis.
" Away with the knave!" he at last exclaims; "strip
him bare, and let his skin pay the penalty of his
tongue." The brothers need no second bidding.

[1] *Vita Sua.*

" They tear the clothes from my back. They take
turn about at the task. I receive a cut for every
saint in the calendar, nor even when the whole cata-
logue of the saints is called are the brothers weary.
My back is one sore. So, if stories be true, must St.
Jerome have looked when he was flogged for reading Cicero. As soon as I was allowed to speak,
'Profane not, my father, profane not, brothers,' I
exclaimed, 'profane not your holy hands in my
blood. So may your seraphic Order flourish under
ever more glorious auspices. So may the ignorant
and the stupid join your tribe in flocks ; and may
never an old woman be wanting for you to gull.
May the mob never discover your lies, nor see
through your impostures.'" And so on till he
becomes untranslatable. Of its companion piece
it is sufficient to say that it is, if possible, more
merciless in its satire.

We can hardly wonder that the Franciscans were
more greatly wroth than ever on the appearance of
this second pasquinade ; but we must needs wonder
to be told that it was not lively enough to satisfy
James.[1] He demanded of Buchanan another satire,
" which should not only prick the skin, but probe
the vitals ". Annoyed at having satisfied neither
party, Buchanan determined that on this occasion
he would strike out from the shoulder. The result
was his *Franciscanus*, the most carefully elaborated
of all his poems. The poem was only begun at this
time, and it was not till his final return to Scotland,
after 1560, that he again took it up and dedicated it
in its final form to the Regent Moray. In the
additions he afterwards made to it he drew largely

[1] *Via Sua*, and Dedication to *Franciscanus*.

from his intervening experience on the Continent. Doubtless, also, he added touches to what he had already written, as in every respect his poem is the production of maturity.

The poem opens with a statement of the various reasons which should induce men of serious mind to enter the Church. " What a safe haven is to the storm-tost ship, the Church should be to the soul vexed by its own failures to attain true virtue." The remainder of the poem (which consists of nearly a thousand lines) is the reply to any one who may think that by donning the Franciscan habit he is likely to save his soul. The reply is put into the mouth of one who has himself been a Franciscan, and can therefore speak of what he knows. Who, in the first place, he asks, are those who become Franciscans ? Those ruined in purse, law-breakers, the ignorant, the diseased in mind and body, the used-up gambler and voluptuary. Formerly, men when driven to straits committed suicide ; now they turn Franciscans. But it may be asked, How do such creatures impose on the world as they do ? The answer is easy : All have to serve an apprenticeship to knavery. The novice must first learn to fashion his bearing and speech to his new profession. Having acquired these elements, he is put into the hands of some aged friar, who instructs him in all the methods of befooling the people and indulging his own vices with impunity. And here the poet presents the imaginary address of such a counsellor to his raw brother. Much of this speech cannot be described except in the most general terms, but its outlines may be given. The art of arts, he says, is how to make dexterous use of the confessional so as to make

you master of your penitent. Rich matrons are the
most profitable victims. The country is the best
field of operations, for there the people are less keen-
witted than in towns. It is needful that the Franciscan should be eloquent; but to acquire eloquence
the schools are the last place in the world to frequent.
The rules of successful oratory can easily be given.
Cultivate a face of brass; eschew learning; a few
Latin words dexterously applied will supply all that
is wanted; flavour your sermons with frequent hints
of the horrors that await the sinner. Avoid, as you
would the deadliest poison, the writings of St. Paul.
Well had it been for the Church had that apostle
died in his childhood, or that at least he had never
been converted. The golden age of the Franciscans
is gone. People can no more be tricked as of old.
And the poem concludes with a comical story of a
brother who failed in an attempt to impose on
certain stupid Scottish peasants.

This satire is certainly a brilliant performance,
careful in construction, ingenious in detail, abounding
in happy sallies. At the same time, it is not satire
of the type that rises into poetry by the disinter-
estedness of its inspiration, and the very intensity
of its denunciation of evil. There is nothing in
Buchanan here of the prophet's or reformer's fulness of soul, or their burning consciousness of a
divine cause. On its own level, however, it can
hardly be surpassed in its dexterous play of ironical
invective, and in its skill in the selection of points.
Lyndsay wrote as bitterly of the monks, but the
satire of Buchanan is the far more perfect weapon,
and wielded with far higher skill and far keener
purpose to wound.

Two questions suggest themselves in connection with these satires of Buchanan : how far are we to consider them legitimate ; and how are we to regard what to the modern reader is the repulsive coarseness of many of their passages ? If satire be a legitimate weapon at all, it can never have stronger justification than in the purpose for which Buchanan now used it. A society which nominally existed for the noblest of all ends, yet by its position, its prestige, its example, polluting all the sources of the national life—this surely is a legitimate object of satire, and specially so when more effective weapons are out of the question. That such was indeed the real condition of the Church is not questioned by serious historians of any shade of opinion.[1] At the same time we may make too much of these admissions, and draw somewhat erroneous conclusions as to the real condition of Scotland at this period. In the sixteenth century, in Scotland as elsewhere, there took place a great moral and intellectual awakening, and the national mind was violently turned to self-examination and self-criticism. If at any period of its history a people's mind takes this turn, it will never be at loss for the materials of a damning indictment against itself. In such a case it is apt to exaggerate its own shortcomings, and shut its eyes to the saving elements in its own constitution. This was what happened to Scotland at this particular epoch. The nation saw its own deformities, and fortunately for its own highest interests would insist in thinking of nothing else. That the forces on the side of religion and virtue came to prevail is conclu-

---

[1] See Canon Bellesheim's *History of the Catholic Church of Scotland*, vol. ii. chap. vi. (Hunter Blair's translation).

sive proof that there was somewhere stored up the
moral energy which should ultimately reconstruct
society on a new basis.   In the Church itself there
were undoubtedly many persons who preserved its
nobler traditions, and who would gladly have set
about the work of reformation from within.   But,
as has already been said, these persons were neither
numerous enough nor influential enough to make
such a reform possible.   Of the better side of the
dying Church Buchanan himself gives us a pleasant
glimpse in an interesting poem written at the same
period as the three satires just mentioned.[1]   This
poem has a double interest, as marking Buchanan's
own religious sentiments, and as presenting us with
an "interior" in Scottish ecclesiastical society of
that day such as the historians have not led us to
expect.   The Archbishop whose entertainment the
poet commemorates is Gavin Dunbar, who had once
been tutor to the King, had become Archbishop of
Glasgow in 1524, and Chancellor of the kingdom in
1528.   In his History, written long after this poem,
and when he had become a member of the Reformed
Church, Buchanan has still a kindly word to say of
Dunbar, making mention of him as "a good and
learned man, though in the opinion of certain people
somewhat deficient in political prudence".   It should
also be noted, as further bearing on Buchanan's religious opinions at this time, that this same Archbishop solemnly protested in 1543 against the proposal to permit the Bible to be read in the Scots or
English tongue.   The poem is entitled *Coena Gavini
Archiepiscopi Glascuensis.*   "Having sat as a guest
with Gavin, I envy not the gods their nectar and

[1] *Epig.* i. 43.

ambrosia. A feast where was no vain display, but a table chastely and generously furnished, seasoned with talk, now serious, now bright with Attic wit! The guests were equal in number to the Muses, worthy of themselves in doctrine, genius, sympathy, and noble feeling (*fides*). As Apollo led the choir of the Muses, so our host shone above all by his eloquent speech. The talk was of the glory of Him who wields the thunder, how He took on Him the burden of our condition, how the Divine nature clothed with man's frail flesh received no stain of sin, how God descended in the form of a servant, yet His mortal covering stripped Him not of His own Divine nature. Each guest is in doubt whether the school has found its way to the palace, or the palace to the school."

With reference to the coarseness of these satires of Buchanan, as well as many other of his poems besides, the saying of the Abbé Galiani must be regarded as the last word : " One century may judge another century ; but only his own century may judge the individual." When we speak of the coarseness of the writers of a past age it should at once be made plain whether we speak of a coarseness relative to our own or the writer's day. Judged by a modern standard, much of Buchanan's work is objectionable in a high degree. On the other hand, if we compare him even with the most reputable writers of his own century, we find him neither better nor worse than his neighbours. In Scotland we have the flagrant instances of William Dunbar and Sir David Lyndsay, who speak in the vernacular with a licence that fairly leaves Buchanan behind ; and the " meary bourds " with which Knox

enlivens his History of the Reformation in Scotland
may be regarded as marking the limits of the strictest
decorum which the age prescribed for itself. If we
go abroad, we have but to finger the pages of the
Contes et Nouvelles of Margaret of Navarre, the type
of a pious soul and a refined intelligence, to be convinced that a freedom of speech was then permitted
which by no means implied native coarseness in the
writer. In Buchanan's case, moreover, we must
take into account that he wrote in the language of
the learned; and as we shall see with reference to
another side of his work, this must count for more
than is generally supposed in the final estimate we
form of him.

It has always been matter for wonder that Lyndsay escaped the consequences of his unmeasured
invective against the Church, when many persons
less formidable and less distinguished were called to
account. Buchanan, at all events, was soon made
to feel that not even the countenance of the King
would be his defence against the wrath of those he
had offended. The year 1539 was one of vigorous
action against heretics. " In the beginning of that
year," he tells us in his History, " many suspected of
Lutheranism were seized; towards the end of February five were burned; nine recanted; many were
exiled. Among the last was George Buchanan,
who, while his guards were asleep, escaped from the
window of his sleeping apartment."[1] As it had
come to his ears that Cardinal Beaton had offered
a bribe to the King to put him in his hands, it
was evident that Scotland had become too hot
for him.[2]

---

[1] *Rer. Scot. Hist.* lib. xiv. p. 277.   [2] *Vita Sua.*

On escaping from his prison Buchanan made for England. But his adventures were not yet over, as we gather from the letter of Randolph, in which he suggests that his biography should be written while he is still alive to supply the facts.[1] Among other things, Randolph says that he will have to tell " how the Grey Friars prevailed against him, that he was fayne to leave his contrey, how he escapid with great hazard of his lyfe at Godes hand the thievis on the Border, the plague in the north of England, what relieve he found heere at a famous knightis handes, Sir John Rainsforde, the onlie man that mayntaynid him against the furie of the Papists ". Besides what is here stated, we know nothing further of Buchanan's sojourn in England at this time than what is implied in three short poems, two of them apparently written now, the third at some subsequent period. The last is an epitaph on Sir John Rainsford, with whom he found refuge.[2] The terms in which he speaks of Rainsford bear out the words of Randolph. " His house," Buchanan says, " was an altar of refuge to the wretched, an ark of safety to the good." The second poem is addressed to Thomas Cromwell, then near the term of his career. From this poem we must conclude that at no period of his life were Buchanan's fortunes at a lower ebb. Addressing Cromwell as a " haven for the unfortunate and the restorer of primitive piety ", he speaks of himself as " a wanderer, an exile, needy, tossed about by land and sea through every trial which life can bring to man ". And he prays the great man to accept the humble gift he lays at his feet. This gift was a collection of poems, which he speaks of as " sheaves from the poor harvest of a

---

[1] *See* Appendix A.   [2] *Epig.* ii. 24.

barren wit".[1]   As is well known, this was the
universal manner in which poor scholars made their
approaches to the great.   It speaks well for the
native independence of Buchanan's character that
such productions make but a small proportion of his
work, though more even than most of the scholars
of his day he must have known the pressure of
immediate need.

The lines Buchanan addressed to Henry VIII. at
the same period even more strongly confirm the impression of his needy condition.[2]   In the sketch of
his own life Buchanan sarcastically speaks of Henry
as " burning Protestant and Catholic alike, on the
same day, and in the same fire, and as more intent
on safeguarding his prerogative than advancing pure
religion ".   But in these lines he addresses Henry
as if he were an Alfred or St. Louis.   " His virtues,"
he concludes, " place him in the ranks of the gods,
and far above the proudest aspirations of mortals."
This was, of course, but the current coin of courtly
compliment, and has its perfect parallel in the flatteries addressed by Spenser to Elizabeth.   The
University of Paris, having often to address great
personages of questionable character, justified its ill-
deserved eulogies on the ground that though ill-
deserved, they placed before the person addressed
the pattern of what he ought to be.   And no better
apology, perhaps, could be offered for the custom.

Meanwhile, from Henry's indiscriminate dealings
with persons of all shades of religious opinion, it
was in daily risk that Buchanan remained in England.   Once more, therefore, and when he was now
in his thirty-third year, he had to fare forth and
begin the world anew.

CHAPTER VII.

On leaving England, Buchanan once more made
for Paris. It would seem that he regarded France
much as Heine regarded it three centuries later.
" How is it," exclaims Heine, " that France lays
such a spell on every foreigner who may happen to
pass a few years on its soil?"[1] In the sixteenth
century Buchanan bears similar testimony to the
attraction that France and its people exerted on all
cultivated minds. Certain of his panegyrics, indeed, are hardly borne out by his own experiences
in that country. Thus he speaks of her as " the
kind nurse of all true learning", " the common
fatherland of all nations", " the sincere worshipper
of the Deity".[2] The justice of these laudations
may be questioned; yet in speaking thus Buchanan
undoubtedly gives expression to the general feeling
of scholars towards France during the first half of
the sixteenth century. The labours of the best
humanists, as we have seen, were even during this
period thwarted by many opposing forces; yet with
Francis as her king, France was on the whole the
happiest soil for the disinterested pursuit of the best
thought then known. Buchanan's attachment to

[1] *Lutetia*, Letter xliii. [2] *Adventus in Galliam.*

France seems to have been cordially returned.   The
French were still at this period more kindly disposed
to the Scots than to other foreigners; and Buchanan,
by his long residence in their country, and by his
ready acknowledgment of its superiority, had still
further claim on their goodwill.   " Buchanan," says
de Thou,[1] " was born by the banks of the Blane, in
the country of the Lennox, in Scotland ; but he was
of us by adoption."

But on the present occasion Buchanan was not
long to enjoy the society of Paris.   On his arrival
he found his arch-enemy, Cardinal Beaton, engaged
in an embassy there.[2]   As things now went at the
Court and at the University, it would have been an
easy matter for Beaton to have placed Buchanan in
the hands of those who would have effectively
silenced his gibes at cardinals and monks.   Since
Buchanan had left Paris in 1535, Francis had finally
identified himself with the old party in religion
against the Lutheran sectaries.   An active persecution was being carried on in the capital and the
provinces; and no one was safe who gave the
slightest suspicion of a leaning to the new doctrine.
Paris, therefore, was no place for Buchanan at such
a time.   It was fortunate, therefore, that just at
this moment a post was offered to him which for the
next three years provided him with a resting-place
of comparative security.[3]

In 1533 there had been opened at Bordeaux a
great school, which Montaigne, himself one of its

---

[1] Thuanus, *Hist. sui Temporis*, vol. iv. p. 99.
[2] *Vita Sua.* Pinkerton (*History of Scotland*, vol. ii. p. 352) throws
doubt on Buchanan's statement here.   But we now know that Beaton
was in Paris in 1539.—State Papers, Hen. VIII. v. 154, 156.
[3] *Ibid.*

scholars, speaks of as "very flourishing for that time, and the best in France".[1] Planned on the model of the best colleges of Paris, but especially that of Navarre,[2] and supported by the most eminent public men of the time, this school, known as the Collége de Guyenne, had already attracted many of the best scholars in France. The institution had at present the further good fortune of having at its head a man whom Montaigne, the most capable of judges, calls "the greatest principal of France".[3] This was André de Gouvéa, another member of that Portuguese family who played such a distinguished part in the development of education during this period. André was the nephew of that Jacques de Gouvéa, whom we have seen as principal of Ste. Barbe while Buchanan was regent there. During the principalship of his uncle, André had acted as one of his regents, and must then have known Buchanan as his colleague, and as one of the most distinguished of the younger men in connection with the University. About the time of Buchanan's arrival in Paris, Gouvéa had two vacancies in his College, and one of these he offered to his ancient colleague. Buchanan at once closed with the offer, and for the next three years we find him settled in Bordeaux. The other vacancy was filled by Élie Vinet, afterwards himself principal of the College, and with whom to the close of his life Buchanan was united in the closest bonds of friendship.

In the history of what we now call secondary education, the Collége de Guyenne, with the School of

[1] Montaigne, *Essais*, Liv. i. chap. xxv.
[2] Massebieau, *Revue Pédagogique*, 1888.
[3] Montaigne, *Essais*, Liv. i. chap. xxv.

Sturm at Strasbourg, and that of Calvin at Geneva, supplies us with the most interesting and important details for the sixteenth century. Of the college of Guyenne we have the most detailed history from its foundation. From that history, lately written by M. Gaullieur,[1] we may gather how, at an epoch in education in many respects resembling our own, the enlightened men of that time sought to meet the new conditions and new aims of life that had come to them with the revival of letters. It is, of course, beside our present task to give a detailed account of the arrangements and scope of the new College of Bordeaux. In the case of such men as Sturm and Gouvéa, the institutions which they made and fostered form the most essential part of their biographies. But Buchanan, it is to be remembered, never had any part in the construction and direction of the school of Guyenne, and to the end he remained only one of the subordinates of the institution. Still, as for three years he held this post, and as these three years were perhaps among the happiest of his chequered life, some account of his new surroundings seems in a certain degree necessary.

A similar problem to that which confronts ourselves confronted men in the opening of the sixteenth century. The immense progress of science during late years, and the transformation it has wrought in the conditions of modern life, have forced us to reconsider our entire scheme of education. The traditions of humanism that come to us from the sixteenth century appear to be doomed, and the ideal of education that now seems to win most

---

[1] Ernest Gaullieur, *Histoire du Collége de Guyenne* (Paris, 1874).

favour is hard-and-fast apprenticeship to practical life. There is a curious touch of irony in the fact that to-day, as in the sixteenth century, the Sorbonne has become in France the by-word for obscurantism in education. Its reproach to-day is its dogged adherence to these very classical studies it originally did its best to obstruct. The transformation which science has wrought for us in the present century, humanism wrought in the sixteenth. The old scholastic training was outgrown, and in the best minds the belief was universal that in an acquaintance with the writings of Greece and Rome was to be found the best possible intellectual discipline for youth and manhood alike. Then, as now, there were extremists in educational matters. As we have now certain modern men of science who see in the study of Latin and Greek the merest dissipation of energy, so, at the time of which we are speaking, there were many who thought that the only possible line of progress for modern Europe was in the universal adoption of Latin as the vehicle at once of speech and literature. These persons had no promptings to seek for anything that was good in the old studies they sought to displace. Yet in this neglect they undoubtedly missed much that would have rendered more fruitful their study of antiquity. As it happened, the broad instincts of the modern nations led them in far other directions than the humanists confidently anticipated, and it may be that their modern representatives similarly miss the deepest instincts of their time.

The arrangements of the new school in Bordeaux give us a measure of the change that had taken place in educated Europe since the opening

of the century. The school was virtually called
into existence for the teaching of Latin, as that
language had come to be known through the labours
of the humanists. In the ten successive classes
into which the scholars were divided,[1] Latin was the
one subject of instruction through all the school
hours, through all the years of attendance. In five
higher classes, to which outsiders were admitted,
philosophy, Greek, and mathematics were taught.
The arrangements for the last two subjects, however, were so inadequate that only the merest elements could be acquired by the most diligent
scholars.[2] A lecture on the Epistles of St. Paul, on
the first Sunday of every month, completed the list
of subjects taught at this great school, planned
according to all the lights of the time.[3] Bordeaux,
it will be remembered, had been for centuries a
great mart for commerce, and was therefore full of
all the activities of a manifold life ; yet in this
curriculum of its new College not the slightest
provision is made for the practical training of its
future citizens.

From what has been said, it will be seen that
the College in some degree discharged the functions
of an elementary school, a secondary school, and a
university. In the tenth class, pupils were taught
to read and write, and they gradually proceeded
through the Latin course till they were sufficiently
advanced to begin the study of philosophy. In the
subordinate place given to philosophy, as in the
excessive importance attached to Latin, we see all

---

[1] Two more classes were formed by a subdivision of the sixth and
seventh. This change was made before Gouvéa's day.—Gaullieur, p. 104.
[2] Gaullieur, p. 104.   [3] *Ibid.* p. 158.

the new tendencies of humanism. Whereas in the
Paris colleges three years were allotted to philosophy, at Guyenne two were now thought enough.[1]
The methods of instruction in this subject, also,
were entirely different from those followed in the
schools of Paris. Logic and ethics were taught, as
Melanchthon had shown the way, by introducing the
scholars to practical illustrations of these sciences in
the ancient writers—not, as had for centuries been
the case, by books of " sentences " and trifling exercises. In all the classes and in all the different
subjects dictation and learning by heart were practised to what we should now consider an utterly
undue extent. The custom of disputation, which
made so large a part of mediæval instruction, received a strictly subordinate place in the school of
Gouvéa. Only on Saturdays was the practice put
in force, when six scholars of one class sat in judgment on the written compositions of six scholars of
the class below.[2]

The discipline and internal arrangements at
Bordeaux mark a distinct advance on the colleges of
Paris. The pupils did not lie on the floor, but
were seated on benches, arranged, in the case of the
junior classes, in the form of an amphitheatre.
From the list of rules for the conduct of the
scholars, posted in the great hall of the College, a
few may be given as throwing a curious light on
the time. The scholars must be religious and filled
with the fear of God ; they must not think or
speak ill of the Catholic religion ; they must not
read or have in their possession books condemned
by the Fathers of the Church (we shall see that

[1] Quichernt, vol. i. p. 232.   [2] *Ibid.* vol. i. p. 234.

there was some need for this prohibition); they must take in good part their reproofs and punishments, and not use threats or insolent words to their regents; they must speak no language but Latin amongst themselves.[1] Of the extent of the College buildings some idea may be gained from the fact that there were fifteen class-rooms, twenty-six rooms for the accommodation of the regents, domestics, and fifty-six boarders. For the junior pupils there was a distinct building.

We have seen that in the case of the colleges of Paris one of the chief difficulties in the way of discipline was the unsatisfactory relation between principal and regents. As things were arranged in these colleges, the regents as often took sides with the scholars as with the principal. Gouvéa proved his genius as an administrator by putting himself on a rational footing with his subordinates. He made a point of treating them as his equals, showed no favour to one more than to another, gave each the right of inspection and correction throughout the College, and took all of them into council in the work of administration. By such prudent conduct Gouvéa attracted the most distinguished teachers to Bordeaux, and made his institution the most celebrated of its kind in France.[2]

Which of the ten classes was committed to Buchanan is not known; but his duties must have consisted simply in teaching the portion of Latin grammar, and in reading the particular Latin author, assigned to his class. The class-teaching ceased at five in the afternoon; but each regent had his own set of *internes* or boarders, whose studies

---

[1] Gaullieur, p. 106.   [2] Quicherat, vol. i. p. 238.

he superintended in the evening, and from whom he received fees in addition to his public salary. Among his boarders, Buchanan had at one time no less famous a pupil than Montaigne. The subject of Montaigne and his tutors has been a standing puzzle to biographers. In the famous essay in which he gives an account of his early education, he names as his *précepteurs domestiques* four of the leading scholars in France—Nicolas Grouchy, Guillaume Guérente, Marc-Antoine Muret, and Buchanan. That he should have had all these scholars in succession as tutors resident in his father's house seemed a circumstance demanding some explanation. A late writer would cut this knot in a fashion somewhat disrespectful to Montaigne. " The critics," he says, " still dispute what this [*précepteurs domestiques*] means. A foreigner may be permitted the conjecture that the form of speech called *gasconnade* has been employed by Montaigne."[1] The same phrase has misled successive biographers to suppose that Buchanan at some period actually resided with Montaigne in the country in the capacity of private tutor. It will be seen that the college arrangement above mentioned explains the difficulty in the simplest manner. We know that all the four scholars named by Montaigne actually taught at the Collége de Guyenne. When Montaigne, therefore, speaks of all four having been his *précepteurs domestiques*, or, as he expresses himself elsewhere in the same essay, *précepteurs de chambre*, all that he meant to say was that he was an *interne* or boarder with each of them in succession, and had private instruction from them in addition to

---

[1] Mark Pattison, *Essays*, vol. i. p. 126 (Clarendon Press, 1889).

his lessons in the regular classes. The sentence in Montaigne's essay above referred to is our sole source of information regarding his connection with Buchanan. There is consequently no ground whatever for the commonly received statement that Buchanan lived at the country-house of his pupil.[1]

In the same well-known essay, Montaigne has given us some interesting notes on his experiences at the Collége de Guyenne. After speaking of the excessive care his father had taken with his home education he proceeds : " My good father being in extreme dread of failure in that which he had so much at heart, allowed himself to be won over to common opinion, which, after the manner of cranes, ever follows those who go before, and ranged himself on the side of custom, having no longer with him those he had brought from Italy for my early education ; and sent me, when I was about six years of age, to the Collége de Guienne, very flourishing for that time, and the best in France ; and there no trouble was enough for him in the choosing of my private tutors, and in all other things relating to my comfort, in which he made several stipulations against the rules of colleges : though, all the same, it still remained a college." In another part of the same essay he speaks of "Georges Buchanan, ce grand poëte escossois". It will be remembered that by his father's novel plan of education Montaigne had been taught from infancy to speak Latin as his mother tongue. When he went to the College, therefore, he astonished all his teachers by his fluency in that language ; and he specially mentions

[1] Irving noted this, but of course could not give the true explanation.—*Memoirs of Buchanan*, p. 38 (note).

that all his private tutors, and Buchanan among the
rest, had repeatedly told him that they were afraid
to accost him in Latin. As this mastery of the
Latin language was in fact what all the humanists
were aiming at, Montaigne's facility would seem
greatly to have impressed Buchanan. " Buchanan,"
he says, " whom I met afterwards in the train of
the Mareschal de Brissac, told me that he had the
intention of writing on the subject of the education
of children, and that he took mine as a pattern ; for
at that time he had charge of the Comte de Brissac,
whom we have seen since so valorous and brave."
As we shall see, Buchanan did afterwards write a
work designed for the instruction of de Brissac ; but
neither this nor any other of his productions corresponds to this description of Montaigne. Except at
these two periods, we have no reason to believe that
Buchanan and Montaigne had any intercourse. It
is perhaps worth mentioning, however, that long
afterwards, in a letter of Killigrew to Cecil in 1572,
it is stated that a translation of Buchanan's famous
Detectio was sent to " one Montaigne of Mont-
pellier ", supposed then to be writing *The Universal
History of the Time.* Probably Montaigne is here
confused with de Thou.[1]

Another notable person with whom Buchanan
held some intercourse during his stay in Bordeaux
was the omniscient swashbuckler, Julius Cæsar
Scaliger. That scholar had for some years been
settled at Agen, some sixty or seventy miles from
Bordeaux, in the capacity of physician to the
bishop of the place. Here, in the autumn holidays

---

[1] Froude, *History of England*, vol. x. p. 41 n. Montaigne quotes
Franciscanus in his *Essais*, Liv. iii. chap. x. He seems also to have read
Buchanan's History of Scotland. Cf. *Essais*, Liv. iii. chap. vii.

of the schools, he was wont to receive annual visits from the regents of the Collége de Guyenne.[1] None of these learned visitors seems to have been more acceptable to him than Buchanan, and if we may judge from the complimentary verses interchanged by them, the esteem seems to have been mutual. In a few happily turned lines, Buchanan speaks of a visit paid by him to Agen. The roads were all but impassable, and it was wintry weather at its worst; but amid all the discomforts of the journey one hope cheers him—he will enjoy Scaliger's converse at its end. Unfortunately, Julius is absent, and even after five days he does not appear. Buchanan has to return without a sight of his friend; and this disappointment, he concludes, far outweighs all the toil of his journey.[2] Scaliger replied to Buchanan in two copies of verses by no means so happily turned. What is noteworthy in Scaliger's lines to Buchanan is the consciousness they express, in their strained and clumsy manner, of Buchanan's unrivalled skill and genius in Latin poetry. Even in his own day, Scaliger's taste and discernment in such matters were not held of much value, yet the tone of these verses cannot but be regarded as a striking testimony to the impression made on Scaliger by Buchanan's character and talent. As is well known, Scaliger, with all his prodigious attainments, was the most vainglorious of men. His life was a ceaseless wrangle with his contemporaries, and in his attacks on Erasmus he outdid even his own century in the downright brutality of his abuse. With such

---

[1] Jos. Scaliger, *De Vetustate et Splendore Gentis Scaligerae.*
[2] *Epig.* i. 49.

a man we should hardly have expected Buchanan, whose own temper was none of the sweetest, to have put himself on cordial terms. Scaliger's admiration of Buchanan was shared to the full by his greater son. The highest eulogy that has been pronounced on Buchanan's poetry is that of Joseph Scaliger. "In Latin poetry," he says, "Buchanan leaves all Europe behind."[1] And in his elegy written on Buchanan he has spoken of him in a manner that reminds us of Landor :—

> Namque ad supremum perducta Poetica culmen
> In te stat, nec quo progrediatur habet.
> Imperii fuerat Romani Scotia limes :
> Romani eloquii Scotia finis erit.

---

[1] *Prima Scaligerana* (Cologne 1695), p. 37: "Buchananus unus est in tota Europa omnes post se relinquens in Latina poesi."

CHAPTER VIII.

BUCHANAN'S position in the school at Bordeaux was that of a subordinate, and to the end he never attained to the highest honours of his profession on the Continent. In all probability such a position was the last in the world he would have desired. Neither by his temper nor his genius was he fitted for the work of a Sturm or a Gouvéa. A certain irresponsibility, a certain amount of leisure for his own pursuits, perfect freedom from all practical cares—such seems to have been the ideal he had always before him ; and this is but to say that he was the scholar and man of letters in the first place, and in the second place a teacher.

But although by his official position he was only a subordinate, it is evident that he was a marked man among his fellows. His literary gift was recognised from the first as unrivalled. In the case of a great institution like the Collége de Guyenne, occasions were continually arising when it had to address great personages either in its own interest or in the discharge of its necessary

functions.   On such occasions, if we may judge from
the specimens in his collected works, Buchanan was
frequently called upon to exercise his talent.   Thus
he had not long been in Bordeaux when there
came to the city the most distinguished guest it
had ever had the privilege to entertain.   This was
no less a personage than the Emperor Charles v.,
on his famous journey through France, by the
romantic permission of its king, to suppress the
insurrection of the burghers of Ghent.   Bordeaux
with all its institutions did its best to show all
honour to its august visitor ; and on the part of the
College a Latin poem by Buchanan was presented
to the Emperor.[1]   This poem has all the character
of a set performance, and is interesting simply as a
proof that when his colleagues wished to give col-
lective expression to their desires, they naturally
looked to Buchanan as their exponent.   On another
occasion, when the finances of the College were not
quite satisfactory, it occurred to Gouvéa that a
poetical address to the Chancellor of the Kingdom,
known as a generous patron of letters, might bring
some advantage to him.   Buchanan was again
appealed to ; and a historian of Bordeaux thus
tells us of the manner in which he responded :
" Buchanan," he says, " performed his task with
elegance, but above all with *netteté*.   Quite convinced of his own merit and that of his friends, he
made use of no idle flatteries, but simply put the
question to the Chancellor if they might count on
his support, adding with dignity that the Muses
of Aquitaine, thus abandoned, could easily retreat

---

[1] *Silvae*, i. " Ad Carolum v. Imperatorem, Burdegalae hospitio publico
susceptum, nomine Scholae Burdegalensis, anno MD.XXXIX."

elsewhere, certain as they were to find an asylum wherever they might betake themselves." [1]

Besides these performances executed to order, Buchanan, as was his habit till his most advanced years, threw off many shorter pieces at this time, which doubtless passed from hand to hand among the congenial spirits of the city. Only two of these pieces call for particular notice as making an essential part of his biography. The brothers of St. Antony at Bordeaux enjoyed the curious privilege of having two pigs sent into the town free of toll. [2] The brothers, it would appear, somewhat strained their privilege, and their convent came to be literally peopled with pigs. The magistrates having learned that the pious community made a regular trade in these animals, had more than once endeavoured to put a stop to the traffic. This was an occasion and a theme after Buchanan's own heart, and he accordingly launched the following epigram: "When alive, Antony, you are said to have been a feeder of swine; now, when dead, you feed monks. Both, in truth, have the same brains and the same stomach, the same delight in filth and gluttony. In everything they are alike, save one; but therein lies a grievous blunder. Acorns should be the food of your monks as well as of your swine." [3]

The other poem is one which not only, like the above, reveals the spirit and temper of Buchanan— it is a poem which better than volumes of history reveals to us the attitude begotten in the men of Buchanan's day by the progress of humanism. [4]

[1] Dezeimeris, *De la Renaissance des Lettres à Bordeaux.*
[2] Gaullieur, p. 142.   [3] *Fratres Fraterrimi*, xxii.
[4] *Eleg.* iii. "Ad Briandum Vallium, Senatorem Burdegal., pro Lena apologia."

The poem has been a puzzle to Buchanan's biographers, who have wished to make of him an
ardent reformer from the beginning. From its
nature it cannot be analysed here ; but its title
is sufficient to indicate its purport. It is, of
course, a mere *jeu d'esprit* ; but it is a *jeu d'esprit*
which puts beyond question how much more, at
this period of his life at least, Buchanan was the
humanist than the reformer. The point of view of
the poem is one which essentially implies the ironic
and not the theological view of life ; and it would
argue complete unacquaintance with the spirit of
his age to draw from such a poem any injurious
conclusions as to Buchanan's own manner of life.
All that we are justified in inferring from such
effusions of the humanists is that they claimed for
themselves a licence of thought and speech over the
whole of human experience which men of another type
deem it wiser to renounce. It throws still further
light on this strange time when we learn that the
person to whom Buchanan addresses this remarkable poem, Briand de Vallée, was a councillor of the
Parliament of Bordeaux, that it was he who founded
the monthly lecture on the Epistles of St. Paul, and
that Rabelais, who counted him one of his best
friends, could speak of him as the " tant bon, tant
vertueux, tant docte, et équitable président Briand
de Vallée ".[1]

Buchanan found further scope for his literary
faculty in a practice which Gouvéa seems to have
established in his school. It was expected of the
regents (possibly only of those who had charge
of the advanced classes) that they should each

[1] Rabelais, Liv. iv. chap. xxxvii.

write a Latin play every year for representation
by the boys.[1] This practice was encouraged for
two reasons. It gave the pupils that facility in
Latin which was the grand aim of the entire
curriculum of the school. Secondly—and this
is the reason given by Buchanan himself—these
Latin plays, being imitations of classical models,
served to wean the taste of the scholars from the
absurdities of the mediæval mysteries, in which, as
he tells us, the French above all nations then took
especial delight.[2] It was to be expected that the
humanists, who had come to know from antiquity
what the drama might be made, should regard with
disgust these monstrous exhibitions, which in many
cases appealed to the basest passions of the mob.
That there was real ground for this feeling on their
part is proved by the fact that in 1547 the Parliament of Paris was constrained to suppress, by reason
of the excess of their buffoonery, " all mysteries of
the Passion, or other sacred mysteries ".[3] Moreover,
the very language in which the actors in these
mysteries spoke must have been hateful to ears
which found offence in every vernacular. The
Italian scholars had long been in the habit of
writing plays in imitation of the ancients; and in
Germany, towards the end of the fifteenth century,
Reuchlin had produced Latin plays which were
represented by the students of Heidelberg. In
England, also, somewhat later, Nicolas Udall
wrote Latin plays to be acted by his boys at
Eton during the long winter nights.[4]

[1] *Epist.* xxvii.   [2] *Vita Sua.*
[3] Hallam, *Lit. of the Middle Ages*, vol. i. p. 430.
[4] *Ibid.* p. 433.

In his performance of this task Buchanan wrote
in all four plays during his stay in Bordeaux. Two
of these plays were merely translations of the *Medea*
and *Alcestis* of Euripides, a poet for whom Buchanan
seems to have shared all the admiration of Milton.
In the case of the *Medea*, he says (and the fact is
interesting as bearing on the knowledge of Greek
possessed by scholars of Buchanan's standing) that
he did not write it with a view to publication, but
that in setting himself to learn Greek without a
master, he might in the process of translation weigh
more carefully the meaning of each word.[1] Of his
two original dramas, *Jephthes* and *Baptistes*, the
former, as he himself justly thought, is undoubtedly
much the more striking dramatic performance. The
story of Jephthah and his daughter is clearly one
which presents all the materials for tragedy of the
highest order ; and Buchanan, shackled though he
is by conventional forms and a dead language, has
certainly risen to the greatness of his theme.   His
conception of Jephthah and his daughter Iphis is
indeed quite Miltonic in intensity and elevation.
But here, again, we can but express regret that
there should have been lost to Buchanan's native
literature a talent which even under such untoward
conditions could achieve so much.

But if his *Jephthes* be the greater drama, *Baptistes* is much the more interesting in its bearing
on the poet's character and opinions. Of all his
writings up to this date, this drama is the one
which most clearly indicates Buchanan's leanings
in politics and religion.   It is always hazardous to
draw dogmatic conclusions from so impersonal a

[1] *Epist.* xxvii.

production as a drama. In the case of the *Baptistes*, however, the choice of subject is so significant, its bearing on the questions of Buchanan's own day is so obtrusive, that we seem justified in inferring that its leading sentiments express the strong leanings of the writer. Strictly speaking, indeed, the piece is hardly a drama at all, but simply a series of dialogues which naturally end with the death of the Baptist. There is no attempt at a plot, and there is not a single dramatic incident. Its interest for those for whom it was written must have lain simply in the sentiments of the dialogues, and the persons with whom these sentiments might be identified. If the piece was actually represented, the spectators could have had little difficulty in finding modern representatives for all its leading personages. John the Baptist himself, who is for laying the axe to the very root of Jewish tradition, is the unmistakable prototype of any fiery reformer (Berquin, for example), who in Buchanan's own day would be content with nothing less than a return to the ante-papal Church of the first centuries. Malchus, the high priest, who is the intolerant upholder of tradition in all its length and breadth, who insists on finding in every novel religious doctrine an attack on the State no less than on the Church, and who has no mercy in his dealings with what he deems heresy, undoubtedly stood in Buchanan's mind for his own relentless pursuer, Cardinal Beaton. The people of Bordeaux, however, would see in Malchus a personage nearer home, their own Archbishop, Charles de Grammont, as keen a hunter of heresy as Beaton, and who, as we shall presently see, had his eyes on Buchanan

himself.[1]   Herod, with his temporising policy towards the Baptist, could hardly but suggest
Francis I.'s past attitude towards the religious
difficulties of the day ; and Herod's final surrender
of John might with no excess of ingenuity have
found its modern application in Francis's surrender
of Berquin.   To those whose sympathy went with
reform in religion, Herodias the queen, with her
overweening notions of the royal prerogative and
her detestation of all religious novelties, must have
seemed the true prototype of Louise of Savoy, the
Queen-mother, who since the beginning of the
religious troubles had stood by Beda and the Sorbonne in their most intolerant action.

It seems hardly possible that such a play could
have been represented at Bordeaux at this period.
Gouvéa himself, it is to be remembered, was an
orthodox Catholic, and held several benefices in the
Church.   It is not likely, therefore, that he would
permit his scholars to make acquaintance with a
production which so plainly inculcated the most
revolutionary opinions in matters of State and
Religion.   Moreover, in Bordeaux for some years
past, a genuine alarm had arisen at the spread of
heresy in its midst.   So early as 1525 persecution
on account of religion had begun in the town ; and
in 1534 the principal and regents had been sum-
moned before the Parliament to render account of
the fact that books of a heretical tendency had been
found within the walls of the College.[2]   About the
very time *Baptistes* may have been written (1541),
the first burning for heresy in Bordeaux took place.
If we remember also that the eyes of the Archbishop

---

[1] Gaullieur, p. 163.   [2] *Ibid.* p. 153.

were continually on the school, it is difficult to believe that the play was actually put on the stage by Gouvéa. That certain of Buchanan's dramas were represented we have the conclusive testimony of Montaigne, who expressly tells us "that he played the chief parts in the Latin tragedies of Buchanan, Guérente, and Muret, which were represented in the College of Guienne with dignity".[1]

The *Baptistes* is, in truth, but the poetical draft of his famous tract *De Jure Regni apud Scotos*, whose publication long afterwards made him known to Europe as a political revolutionary. In 1576 Buchanan dedicated this drama to King James in a characteristic letter. "This little book," he tells his Majesty, "must seem to have a peculiar interest for yourself, inasmuch as it sets before you in the clearest manner what torments and miseries tyrants endure, even when they appear to be most prosperous. And this lesson I deem not merely beneficial, but absolutely necessary for you, so that you may early begin to detest what it must be always your duty to avoid. Moreover, I wish my book to be a standing witness with posterity that not with your teachers[2] but yourself rested the fault, if impelled by evil counsellors or your own undue desire of power, you should ever depart from the lessons you have received."

Long afterwards, in the critical year 1642, a translation of the *Baptistes* was published under the suggestive title, " Tyrannical Government Anatomised : being the Life and Death of John the

---

[1] Montaigne, *Essais*, Liv. i. ch. xxv.
[2] At the time the dedication was written Buchanan was acting as tutor to James.

Baptist." By one of his editors this translation was assigned to no less a person than Milton. We know that Milton read and admired Buchanan, but this translation is not his.[1] Yet the whole drift of the drama is such as would meet Milton's most ardent approval. To the religious and political situation of 1642 it had an even more piquant application than to the circumstances of the time at which it was written. No Puritan reader could fail to see Charles I. in Herod, Laud in Malchus, and Henrietta Maria in Herodias.

During his three years' sojourn in Bordeaux Buchanan had never been without uneasiness from the action of Cardinal Beaton and the Franciscans. Beaton, indeed, had even gone so far as to write a letter to the Archbishop of Bordeaux, urging him to have Buchanan arrested as a heretic. Fortunately the letter had passed into the hands of certain of Buchanan's most attached friends, who put him on his guard. The death of James V. in 1542 gave Beaton other matters to think of than the heresies of Buchanan, and a plague that devastated Aquitaine diverted the thoughts of his persecutors in Bordeaux. At the end of 1542, or the beginning of 1543, Buchanan left that city, though for what reason has not been clearly ascertained.[2]

---

[1] Professor Masson assures me of this.

[2] There is nothing in the records of the Collége de Guyenne to indicate when or why Buchanan left Bordeaux. Buchanan's mention of the plague does not help us, since such plagues were then of common occurrence. We must therefore fall back on his own statement that he spent three years in Bordeaux. As we can fix the date of his arrival in that city, we infer that he must have left it either at the end of 1542 or the beginning of 1543. It has been shown above that there is absolutely no ground for supposing that on his departure from Bordeaux Buchanan went to reside with Montaigne in the country.

CHAPTER IX.

In 1542, or possibly 1543, therefore, Buchanan left Bordeaux, and from this date till his journey to Portugal in 1547, we all but lose sight of him. In his own account of his life he ignores these years altogether. The true inference from his silence seems to be that during this period he held no permanent appointment. The blank, however, is partly made up to us by a poem belonging to this time, which is noteworthy as being the most minutely personal of all his productions, and which clearly reveals to us what it was in Buchanan that gained for him the affectionate reverence of his friends. This poem bears the date 1544, and from certain of its references we gather that when he wrote it Buchanan was once more back in Paris. As it happens, this exactly tallies with two other testimonies [1] to the effect that along with two other scholars of the first order, Turnèbe and Muret, he taught at this date in the Collége du Cardinal Lemoine. [2]

[1] Moreri states that Buchanan, Turnèbe, and Muret taught in the Collége du Cardinal Lemoine at the same time. If they did so, it could only have been about 1546. Nicole Bourbon assured Ménage of the same circumstance (*Anti-Baillet*, tom. i. p. 328). But M. Dejob (*Appendice* A to his *Vie de Muret*) is disposed to think that Muret, at least, could not have been in Paris at that date.

[2] Jourdain, *Excursions Historiques*, chap. xii.

Unfortunately the records of this College are so defective that no satisfactory account of it is possible as in the case of Ste. Barbe. Founded in 1302 by Cardinal Jean Lemoine, with provision for only three students of arts and four of theology, by the sixteenth century it had taken rank with the first of the Colleges of Paris. It had been founded mainly to favour the study of theology, but from the beginning special provision had been made for the Arts course, and in time it had come to be a *collége de plein exercice.* By the sixteenth century it was one of the schools in Paris that opened their doors most readily to the new studies. In 1528 it took what even at that date was the revolutionary step of instituting a course of Greek ; and it is perhaps worth noting that Bonchamp, the regent who taught it, had as one of his pupils Jacques Amyot, so interesting in the history of literature as the translator of Plutarch. This liberal spirit in the Collége du Cardinal Lemoine explains how Buchanan, now so well known for his zeal for the new studies, found a place there. In the large majority of the Paris colleges he would certainly have been the last man to be admitted within their walls.

The elegy above mentioned is entitled, " Ad Ptolemaeum Luxium Tastaeum et Jacobum Tevium, cum articulari morbo laboraret." Both of these scholars had been among Buchanan's most intimate friends at Bordeaux ; and to the former he has addressed a special poem, which proves that the very closest relation existed between them.[1] The second, de Teyve, had been one of Buchanan's colleagues at

[1] *Silvae,* ii.

Bordeaux, and he afterwards made one of that remarkable band of scholars who accompanied André
de Gouvéa to Portugal.   As the title indicates, the
poem was written in illness—illness so severe, indeed,
that he seems to have had grave doubts as to his
ultimate recovery.   One half of the poem is taken
up with the account of his " case " ; and if we may
draw definite conclusions from its poetical exaggera-
tions, he must have been suffering from a singular
complexity of ailments—gout, dropsy, asthma, and
racking cough.   After he has given this vivid picture of the state to which he is reduced, he turns to
his friends, and addresses them in words which put
us in closer touch with the man Buchanan than almost
any other piece of writing he has left us.   They are
emphatically the words of one to whom friendship is
a necessity, and who had that unbounded confidence
in the affection of his friends which begets enthusiasm.   " Such," he proceeds, " are the dire images
of death and death-bringing want that visit me.
Nor by my side have I my Tastaeus and Tevius,
whose pleasant converse would make the long day
short.   Neither is my sick heart refreshed by the
learning and eloquence of my other friends of the
Gascon school.   Yet amid all my ills tried friends
have not wholly deserted me.   Often Groscollius
expounds to me the virtues of his herbs, and helps
to cheer me by his kind counsel.   Often the skill
and experience of Carolus Stephanus[1] brings relief
to my suffering.   Turnebus, that pride of the Muses,
suffers not a day to pass without the offices of friendship.   And though other blessings fail me, the pious
care of my comrade Gelida supplies the place of

[1] One of the notable family of the Estiennes.

father and fatherland alike. While it is day, my
lot is thus made light. With the coming of night
an army of cares raise their sighs around me, and a
thousand shapes haunt my dreams. In the silence
of the darkness your forms come before me, and
make the night-watches short with beguiling words.
Yet, though vain and all too brief is this delight, 'tis
sweet even thus to know the presence of those we
love. Perchance, also, in the dreams of the night,
I may, ghost-like, stand by your couch, and in words
mingled with sighs bewail the hardness of my untoward lot. And ye, dreams, sweetest pledges of
the night, let not grief for me touch my absent
friends; alone let me bear the burden of my fate.
But if inexorable doom shall move me hence before
my day, late may the tale reach the ears of my
Tastaeus and Tevius. And ye, of one mind and one
soul, cease from tears, and grieve me not with
your lament when I am gone."

Buchanan was now on the verge of his fortieth
year, yet he was still as far as ever from a settled position in life. With his advancing years and uncertain
health, homeless and an exile, he must needs have
had gloomy hours at the thought of his probable
future. As far as is known, he never seems to have
thought of marriage. It is to be remembered, however, that till the middle of the sixteenth century,
marriage was discountenanced among the members
of the lay faculties of law, medicine, and arts. It
was not till 1598, indeed, that doctors of law in the
University of Paris were permitted to marry, the
privilege being granted on the ground that so few
Churchmen then thought of studying law.[1] Only

---

[1] Crevier, *Histoire de l'Université de Paris*, vol. vii. p. 84.

I

in 1576 were Masters of Arts who were married
allowed to teach in the University.[1] What shows
also that a strong prejudice against marriage existed
in the Faculty itself is that it actually passed a
decree in 1588 excluding married men from the
right of voting in their Nations.[2] This objection
to the marriage of public teachers does not appear
to have been so strong in the provinces.[3]

As we gather from a poem written afterwards
in Portugal, Buchanan must have left Paris not
later than 1545.[4] How or where he spent the next
three years has not been discovered.[5] When next
we hear of him it is again in connection with the
great principal, André de Gouvéa, who in response
to an invitation, or rather command, of John III.,
in 1547 set out for Portugal to take the temporary
superintendence of a new college in connection
with the lately founded University of Coimbra.
John, it appears, had very greatly at heart the
success of the new institution. It is said of him
that he was acquainted with every detail in the
working of the various colleges of the University,
and that he knew all the students by name. Coimbra had been the original seat of the University,
but in 1377 it had been tranferred to Lisbon. John
had restored it to its original seat with the inten-

---

[1] Crevier, vi. 331.   [2] *Ibid.* vi. 400.

[3] "Uxorem ducere, extra Lutetiam, in omnibus omnium civitatum
scholis probatissimum est."—*Gelidae Epistolae* xv., quoted by Gaullieur,
p. 191.

[4] *Silvae*, iii. In this poem, entitled "Desiderium Lutetiae", he
states that he has not seen Paris for seven years. As this poem bears
evidence that it was written in Portugal, and Buchanan left that country
in 1552, we are led to the conclusion in the text.

[5] In his History (p. 11) Buchanan casually mentions that he was in
Toulouse in 1544. With the kind assistance of several French scholars
I have made many attempts to come upon traces of Buchanan during
this period, but with no success.

tion that, started in a new career, it should make
an era in the history of his kingdom. With such a
scheme in his mind, he could not but think of the
Portuguese Gouvéa, whose capacity as an administrator had made the success of the Collége de
Guyenne. So early as 1543, indeed, John had been
in communication with him regarding the new
College, and before his present journey Gouvéa had
already made two visits to Portugal in connection
with the same object.

The next five years of Buchanan's life were
spent in Portugal ; and from the fact that out of the
five pages that make his autobiography two are
devoted to the story of these years, it would seem
that he regarded them as the most remarkable in
his life. He had certainly excellent reason for
thinking so. The whole character of this enterprise of Gouvéa, so completely in the spirit of
humanism ; the signal miscarriage of its main object,
the distinction of the scholars engaged in it, the
ill-fortune of most of them ; above all, Buchanan's
own unhappy experiences—all this must have
made him look back on those years as the most
memorable passage in his history.

When Gouvéa proposed to Buchanan to make
one of the band of scholars about to proceed to
Coimbra under his direction, he readily assented.
France, he tells us, was fast becoming an impossible
place for men of peaceful inclinations. All Europe
was either already ablaze with war, or at least
would soon be so. Moreover, it was not as if he
were going forth alone into a strange land. There
would be those with him, de Teyve and Élie Vinet
in the number, who had for years been his very

closest friends. Altogether, the prospects of the
expedition seemed so alluring that Buchanan
thought himself justified[1] in persuading his brother,
Patrick, to make one of the company. It was
towards the end of March 1547—almost, therefore,
on the very day of the death of Francis I.—that
Gouvéa and his band of scholars sailed from Bordeaux for Coimbra.[2]

The institution founded by Gouvéa and his staff
was named the College of Arts. The idea of the
King was to put this College on a level with the
Collége de Guyenne, and the best colleges of Paris,
and so render it unnecessary for the Portuguese
youth to leave the kingdom for higher education.
With Gouvéa as principal, supported by the brilliant scholars he had brought with him, John made
sure that everything must turn out to his wish.
And so at the outset it seemed. Under Gouvéa's
management the new institution was launched
with the happiest auspices; but before the year
was out Gouvéa died, and his death, as it proved,
sealed the fate of the College.

The new College, with its foreign colony of
humanists, had been especially hateful to the
Jesuits, who had by this period secured a firm footing in Portugal. Simon Rodriguès, the celebrated
associate of Loyola, had gained the most absolute
ascendency over the mind of King John; and, on
the death of Gouvéa, all his arts were directed
towards the acquisition of the College for his company.[3] The usual weapons were brought into play.
Secretly and publicly charges of heresy were ad-

---

[1] *Vita Sua.*   [2] Gaullieur, p. 206.
[3] Quicherat, vol. i. p. 241.

duced against Gouvéa's companions. First, three were thrown into the prisons of the Inquisition, and only after long confinement were brought to trial. The trial was a mere pretence, the accusers not even being named; and they were again sent to their dungeons.[1] With such weapons at their disposal, the Jesuits had not long to wait the attainment of their end. One morning the Provincial of their Order presented himself at the gate of the College of Arts with a signed order. The order came from the King, and it bore that thenceforward the College was under the absolute control of the Society of Jesus.[2]

It seems to have gone harder with Buchanan than with the rest of his colleagues. But as his own account of his adventures is the only one we possess, it is best that we should here listen to his own words : " It was on Buchanan, as a foreigner, with very few friends either to take pleasure in his safety, to grieve at his misfortune, or avenge his wrongs, that they heaped the greatest insults and injuries. His poem against the Franciscans was made a charge against him ; yet before he left France he had stipulated with the King of Portugal that this offence should be overlooked. Moreover, his accusers were really unacquainted with the nature of that satire, as the one copy of it had been given to the King of Scots, at whose instance it had been written. He was accused of having eaten flesh in Lent, which, in fact, every one in Spain does; and it was urged against him that he had made certain injurious reflections regarding the monks, in which, indeed, none but a monk could have found

---

[1] Quicherat, vol. i. p. 241.   [2] *Ibid.*

offence. But what gave rise to the bitterest feelings against him was that in a certain confidential
conversation with some young Portuguese, when
the subject of the Eucharist came up for discussion,
he had affirmed that Augustine was far more with
the heretics than the Church in his teaching on that
subject. Jean Talpin, a native of Normandy, and
Joannes Ferrerius,[1] a native of Liguria, gave evidence, as he learned long afterwards, that they had
it on the most trustworthy authority that at heart
Buchanan was no good Catholic. But to be brief :—
After the inquisitors for a year and a half had worn
out his and their own patience, lest they should be
supposed to have persecuted to no purpose one not
altogether unknown to fame, they shut him up for
some months in a monastery, in order that he might
be more accurately instructed by the monks, who
proved, indeed, neither unkindly nor ill-disposed,
though they were utterly ignorant of religious truth.
It was mainly at this time that he translated his
Psalms into various measures. At length, being
restored to liberty, he asked permission of the
King to return to France. The King, however,
requested him to remain, and supplied him with
means sufficient for his daily wants. But sick of
delays and uncertain hopes, he embarked at Lisbon
in a Cretan ship, and sailed for England." [2]

---

[1] This is the Ferrerius known in Scottish literature as connected
with the Monastery of Kinloss. Cf. Stuart, *Records of the Monastery of
Kinloss.*

[2] *Vita Sua.*

CHAPTER X.

BUCHANAN's Latin version of the Psalms, we have seen, was produced mainly during his sojourn in Portugal; and it throws a curious light, both on the man and his time, when we learn that to the same period belong the most objectionable of his erotic verses—those, namely, addressed to Leonora.[1] When we remember, also, that Buchanan had turned his fortieth year when he wrote these verses, we see how entirely factitious was the world in which these humanists lived, how their whole life was a straining after modes of thought, of feeling, of expression, which the Christian tradition they sought to ignore had for ever made impossible. This writing of erotic poetry made, in fact, an essential part of the discipline of the scholars of the Renaissance. If a scholar made any pretensions to be a poet, and there were few of them who did not make the pretension, he must have given proof of a happy turn in speak-

---

[1] This can easily be paralleled. Marc-Antoine Muret, whom we have seen as possibly the colleague of Buchanan at the Collége du Cardinal Lemoine, was one of the most brilliant humanists of his time. In 1552 he delivered in Paris a *Discourse on the Excellence of Theology.* In the same year he published his *Juvenilia* (dedicated to a Councillor of the Parliament of Paris), in which he permits himself the greatest licence of expression; and the next year his *Commentaire sur les Amours de Ronsard.*—Dejob, *Marc-Antoine Muret,* p. 21.

ing the language of Catullus or Tibullus, or others
of the amatory poets of antiquity. The Italian
poets of the preceding century had led the way
in this exercise, and had done to death every
word and phrase in the vocabulary of this species of
poetry. It is needless to say that, in the matter of
absurdity and obscenity, they had fairly outdone
their masters. As Italy had been the inspirer of
the new learning, the example of her scholars could
not but be followed by their imitators beyond the
Alps. The fashion of writing these erotic verses,
therefore, became all but universal in every country
where Latin verse was cultivated—in Scotland,
notably, among the rest.

The remarkable thing, however, is that the
licence of expression in these productions by no
means implies laxity of life in their writers. Beza,
who was certainly one of the rankest offenders of his
century in this matter, solemnly assures us that
though his Muse was loose his life was chaste.
Doubtless there were exceptions, as in the case of
Muret, whose life was an exceedingly practical commentary on the grossness of his verse.[1] But for the
most part the cultivation of this species of poetry
was simply a discipline, an avenue to distinction,
which the humanists, the most hungry for fame of
all the generations of men of letters, could not afford
to neglect. As the subject, however, is one which
is not only of importance towards a true estimate of
Buchanan, but one which touches the deepest life of
the time, it is as well that we should understand

---

[1] M. Dejob, Muret's latest biographer, is of opinion that the charges
of unnatural crime brought against Muret are but too well founded.
—*Marc-Antoine Muret*, p. 55.

how this erotic verse was regarded by the humanists themselves.

In publishing his *Juvenilia*[1] at Paris in 1548, Beza, then in his twenty-ninth year, accompanies them with a dedication to Melchior Wolmar, a man of severe and simple virtue. Wolmar was, in truth, the last man to whom Beza would have submitted for approval what he knew himself to be unseemly. "Although many grave and learned men," he begins in his Preface, "have taken objections to such poems as make up this volume, for my own part I could never help spending some time in composing them, whether from natural predilection, or from a conviction that this manner of cultivating one's style is neither frivolous nor useless. This conviction was deepened by the weight of your judgment, which alone would be enough to make me adopt any opinion. Moreover, from the letter you sent me from Tübingen, I understand that these same verses of mine had the most cordial approval of yourself and Camerarius. Accordingly, I have long had the wish to see them collected in one volume, convinced as I am that no sensible person could find fault with what is given to the world with your approval and on your persuasion." Afterwards, indeed, when Beza had identified himself with Geneva, he had qualms of conscience on account of his youthful effervescence. But at that period he had ceased to be the humanist, and had become the theologian pure and simple. What the dedication proves is,

---

[1] As is well known, the verses to Candida in this collection have their own place in the religious controversies in which Beza afterwards came to be engaged. It should be said that about the time these verses were published, Beza delivered lectures on the Epistle to the Romans and the Epistles of Peter.

that to scholars like Wolmar and Camerarius, the friend and follower of Luther and Melanchthon, the most licentious forms of verse were simply ingenious exercises in Latinity, which afforded rival humanists the opportunity of proving their skill.

There is, indeed, no product of humanism that more clearly brings before us the complete breach it had made with all the traditions of the Middle Ages than these endless lines to Phyllis, Amaryllis, Leonora, Pancharis, Candida, and the rest. The humanists had broken with the scholastic philosophy, and in large degree also with the doctrines of the Church. These verses show that they had also broken with the *sentiment* of the Middle Ages, as expressed in the best troubadours, in Dante, and in Petrarch. That attitude towards woman (so distinct from the attitude of antiquity) which resulted from the combined influence of Christianity and chivalry, and which finds expression in the Provençal poets, is not understood by the erotic poets of the Renaissance. Of the spiritualised passion of Dante, or the "almost unearthly sentiment" of Petrarch, they have no approach to a suggestion. Their love-verses are as purely sensual in their inspiration as those of Ovid or Catullus. Yet, as has already been said, it is hardly accurate to speak of inspiration in connection with them. Their erotic verses are rightly regarded simply as more or less ingenious attempts to reproduce the feeling of an age divided from their own by a new civilisation. It was left for Goethe, the Pagan born out of due time, in his Roman elegies, to reproduce in a modern tongue the unconscious naturalism of classical antiquity.

With one or two exceptions, the love-verses of
Buchanan consist of two sets, those addressed to
Leonora, and those addressed to Neaera. In a certain sense each of the sets constitutes a series. In
those to Leonora he seems to have taken Horace's
ode (iv.13) to Lyce as his model, and tortures his in-
vention through some twenty poems for every term
of abuse. Two of these poems might seem to indicate
that Leonora was a real person, whom Buchanan knew
in Coimbra;[1] but the entire series has so essentially
the character of a mere theme, that it is difficult to
avoid the conclusion, supported as it is by other
evidence, that she is a mere creation of the poet's
fancy. The verses addressed to Neaera are of a
more pleasing description, and everywhere display
Buchanan's talent for piquant turns of thought and
felicitous expression. Like the verses to Leonora,
they are all in one strain ; only in Neaera's case her
beauty and charm is the theme. One, at least, of
these poems, deserves to be quoted as having found
a place in most subsequent collections of epigrams :—

> Illa mihi semper praesenti dura Neaera,
>   Me, quoties absum, semper abesse dolet.
> Non desiderio nostri, non moeret amore,
>   Sed se non nostro posse dolore frui.

> "When I am by her side, Neaera's cold,
>   And, strange ! she weeps when I am gone :
> Think not for love of me these tears she sheds ;
>   At missing mine she sheds her own."

Like Beza, Buchanan came also in his old age
to regret the indiscretions of his Muse. Writing to
a friend in 1566, he says "that he does not know
whether to be chagrined or ashamed at the trifling
character of the greater part of his poems" ; and in

---

[1] *Iambon Liber*, ii. ; *Miscell.* vii.

another letter, dated 1579, he says that "but for the importunities of friends, he would have consigned to eternal oblivion elegies, sylvae, and epigrams alike". But the most interesting reference to his erotic verse is found in a poem addressed to Walter Haddon, one of the Masters of the Court of Requests to Queen Elizabeth, who, after Buchanan himself, holds the second place among the British Latinists of his age.[1] These lines, moreover, deserve to be quoted, as they seem to place beyond a doubt that Leonora and Neaera were mere names on which he exercised his fancy. Haddon, it appears, had called on his friend for a poem, such as he had once known so well how to turn. But Buchanan, now on the verge of his sixtieth year, thus replies: "In vain you challenge an old man to the sallies of his youth. Even in the years when such trifling is more seemly, rarely did the Muse visit me, born as I was in mountainous Britain, in a rude age, among a rude people. Now when declining age has left me a few white hairs, when I have all but told the tale of threescore years, and all my spirits droop, Phœbus turns me a deaf ear, and the Muses hearken not to my call. *It yields me no joy now to sing how the golden hair of Phyllis is dearer to me than the locks of Bacchus, or to indite stinging iambics on Neaera's heartless want of faith.*"[2]

A poem which also belongs to this period of Buchanan's life was once thought to be of the erotic class; but there can be no doubt that the Amaryllis

[1] Hallam, *Lit. of the Middle Ages*, vol. i. p. 501.

[2] Nec Phyllidis me nunc juvat flavam comam
      Praeferre Bacchi crinibus,
  Nec in Neaerae perfidam superbiam
      Saevos iambos stringere.—*Liber Iambon,* i.

to whom it is addressed is simply an allegorical name for Paris.[1] Read in this light, it is interesting as showing how large a place Paris filled in the thoughts of Buchanan. When he wrote it, he was still in Portugal, and had already, he tells us, been seven years exiled from the banks of the Seine, and it is his fervent prayer that his return may not be long delayed.

Another favourite exercise of the humanists, besides that of writing erotic poetry, was the metrical translation of the Psalms into Latin. This exercise commended itself to them for a double reason. It gave them scope for a display of their Latinity, and it placed them on good terms with the Church, and perhaps with their own conscience. The double benefit to be derived from these translations—the instruction in polite letters, and the building up of religious faith—was strongly emphasised by the great German reformers.[2] One of the best known of these versions is that of Eobanus Hessus; and to this version there were originally prefixed commendatory epistles to the author from Luther, Melanchthon, and Justus Jonas. All three equally insist on the happy combination of secular and religious instruction to be gained from such a rendering of the Psalms. Speaking of poetry as the efficient handmaid of religion, Luther has the following characteristic sentence : " I confess to be

[1] Warton thought that the Amaryllis, to whom Milton alludes in Lycidas, was the Amaryllis of Buchanan ; but, as is stated above, there can be no doubt that Buchanan's Amaryllis is merely an allegorical name for Paris. Nevertheless, Warton may have been right in his conjecture.

[2] Knox, in his History, thus speaks of Buchanan's paraphrase of the Psalms : "That singular work of David's Psalms, in Latin metre and poesie, besides many others, can witness the rare grace of God given to that man."

one of those whom poetry moves more deeply,
delights more intensely, and clings to more tena-
ciously, than any prose, be it the prose of Cicero or
Demosthenes himself." [1]   "I give it to you as my
fixed conviction," says Melanchthon also, "that your
edition of the Psalms is of real service, at once in
building up the piety, and in forming the judgments
of the young, and of service, moreover, in rousing
generous natures to the study of poetry." [2]

Of the motives which prompted the humanists
to their innumerable versions of the Psalms, we have
also an interesting statement by one of the most
brilliant of the Italian scholars of the sixteenth
century — Marcantonio Flaminio.   Flaminio is in
the first rank of modern Latin poets, and he shared
to the full the enthusiasm for classical antiquity that
distinguished all the Italian scholars.   But he was also
—what few of these scholars were—a man of virtue
and simple tastes, who ardently desired a return to
purer ideals on the part of the Church. [3]   Such being
his character, his account of the motives that prompted
him to his version of the Psalms has a peculiar
interest.   The lines in which he states these motives
are contained in an address to the reader with
which he closes his book on the Psalms. [4]   In the
main, it will be seen that he regards the subject in
the same light as Luther and Melanchthon—only, as

[1] "Nam ego me unum ex illis esse fateor, quos poemata fortius movent,
vehementius delectant, tenaciusque in eis haereant quam soluta oratio,
sit sane vel ipse Cicero aut Demosthenes."
[2] "Quare et ad pietatem et ad formanda judicia studiosae juventutis,
deinde etiam ad incitandas generosas naturas ad studium poetices,
prodesse hanc psalmorum editionem statuo."
[3] Mr. J. A. Symonds has given an interesting account of Flaminio
in his *Renaissance in Italy*.
[4] "M. Antonii Flaminii in Librum Psalmorum brevis explanatio."—
Venice, 1545.

was to be expected, the humanist in Flaminio prevails over the reformer. "By divine aid, Christian reader," he says, "I have so tempered these strains that, as thou readest, it may wellnigh be as thou didst read the most sacred bard himself. For though word has not been rendered by word, and I have deemed it no sin to add much ; yet have I a good and sure hope that nothing has been added which David himself would disapprove, nothing which does not make clear what is obscure, and, after the manner of light, add some grace to the beauty of the poem ; even as rich-hued roses and violets, garlanding her golden locks, add grace to some beautiful maiden." [1]

In further illustration of the attitude of the humanists towards these versions of the Psalms, we have a singularly interesting passage in the dedicatory letter with which Henri Estienne accompanied his edition of Buchanan's paraphrase. The letter is addressed to Buchanan himself; and in the passage quoted it will be seen that Flaminio and his version are made the subjects of criticism. "If any one should object," says Estienne, "that the Scriptures do not admit of this adornment of verse, I shall tell him what four years ago I told an Italian in Rome. The conversation had turned on Flaminio's version of the Psalms, and I praised the pains he had taken with his task.' 'The whole thing was a wretched mistake,' he replied (he spoke in Italian, but I give you the sense). 'From the time when Flaminio gave himself to the Scriptures, the old grace and neatness of his verse has deserted him. Since he wasted his genius on these subjects, the

---

[1]   . . . . virgini pulcherrimae
Quale decus addunt arte purpureae rosae,
Violaeque flavis crinibus circumdatae.

exquisite taste that formerly distinguished him has
got corrupted. When he now tries his hand at
some secular theme, you no longer recognise the
hand of Flaminio.'[1] 'If, in the translation of Scripture,' I replied, 'you mean that there should be no
false ornament, I am quite of your opinion; for
nothing could be further removed from the spirit of
the sacred writings. But if I understand you to
mean that not even ornaments that combine dignity
and simplicity are to be allowed, then we are as
far asunder as the poles in our way of thinking.
To my mind, this is the very style the Scriptures
demand. I hold, therefore, that Flaminio's mistake
lay in this—that before he attempted the Psalms,
he crippled and enfeebled his powers in the composition of loose and trifling love-ditties. When he
sought to rise into a higher atmosphere, and to
deal with serious themes, he was unequal to the attempt.'" These quotations seem necessary to explain
the spirit in which Buchanan must have conceived
and executed what is by far the most famous of
all his productions. The quotations are interesting,
moreover, as throwing a curious light on the attitude of the humanists to the Christian tradition.

In Buchanan's paraphrase the roses and violets
of which Flaminio speaks are certainly more pro-
fusely strewn than in the versions of most other
scholars. Buchanan, in fact, has not merely done
the Psalms into Latin verse; he has sought to give
to them the form and texture of Horatian odes.

---

[1] "Imo," inquit ille, "(verbis quidem Italicis, sed in hunc sensum), O
factum male: ex quo enim istis sacris se addixit, multum illius carmini
de solita elegantia et lepore decessit. Nam quum omne μυροθήκιον
respuant illa, nescio quomodo ita descivit ab illis quibus antea uti
solebat ornamentis," etc.

Where it was necessary to mark the continuity and development of the thought, he never scrupled to supply what he judged to be the missing links. The result is that in Buchanan's version a Psalm of David ceases to be what it frequently is—a series of disjointed utterances making no organic whole, and becomes a coherent poem with a beginning and an end.   His ideal of translation was that of Cowley in rendering his two odes of Pindar : "not so much to let the reader know what the author spoke, but what was his way and manner of speaking".[1]   As we must think with our better lights regarding Pindar and the writers of the Psalms, both Cowley and Buchanan in their respective renderings were the width of heaven from " the way and manner " of their originals.

But whatever we may think of the merit of Buchanan's version, it was undoubtedly the work that did most for his immediate and posthumous reputation.   It was in the title-page of their two editions of Buchanan's Psalms that Henri and Robert Estienne assigned him the distinction of being *poetarum nostri saeculi facile princeps.*   In the dedicatory letter above quoted, Henri puts the version of Buchanan in comparison with those of Eobanus Hessus, Flaminius, Salmonius Macrinus, and Rapicius, all among the best Latin versifiers of their day, and finds that of Buchanan superior to them all.   This dictum of Estienne was long indorsed by the scholars of the Continent.   " Henri Estienne," says Maittaire, " was the first who placed Buchanan at the head of all the poets of his day, and all France, Italy, and Germany have since subscribed

---

[1] Cowley : Preface to *Pindarique Odes.*

to the same opinion, and conferred that title upon
him."[1]   The tributes to the merits of Buchanan's
paraphrase form, in truth, an interesting commentary on the literary ambition of the Latinists of the
sixteenth and seventeenth centuries. "Virgil,"
says Guy Patin, "never made better verses than
Buchanan, and fifteen centuries were needed to
produce another poet like Virgil."[2]   The saying of
the Père Bourbon, also, as reported by Ménage, has
often been quoted—that he would rather be the
author of Buchanan's Psalms than Archbishop of
Paris. Cowley is more critical, yet he admits
Buchanan's superiority to all rivals. Speaking of
the various translations of the Psalms, he says :
"Bucanan himself (though much the best of all
these translators, and indeed a great person) comes
in my opinion no less short of David than his
country of Judæa." Even in Buchanan's lifetime
his Psalms were introduced into the schools of
Germany ; and so early as 1585 an edition set to
music was published.[3] In Scotland they made a
regular part of Latin reading in schools till a comparatively recent period ; and, according to Mr.
Hill Burton, "their use as text-books gave a
vitality to the teaching of Latin in Scotland it
could not easily achieve elsewhere."[4]

Buchanan's most formidable rival in this his
most famous work has been his own countryman,

[1] Quoted by Hallam, *Literature of the Middle Ages*, vol. ii. p. 147.
[2] Guy Patin, *Lettre* 151.
[3] Irving, *Memoirs of Buchanan*, p. 118.
[4] *Scot Abroad*, vol. ii. p. 33. In a note to the next page, Mr. Hill
Burton states that "it was a fine intellectual treat to find the late Dr.
Melvin of Aberdeen exercising his first form on Buchanan's Psalms".
Professor Masson informs me that they were read on Saturdays in the
fourth and fifth classes.

Arthur Johnston. Round the respective merits of each quite a lively controversy arose during the sixteenth century, and certain of Buchanan's most fervent admirers were even wroth that Johnston should have had the audacity to enter the lists against his great countryman. Nevertheless, a few scholars, both British and foreign, have been of opinion that in elegance of diction, as well as in fidelity to the original, Johnston has the advantage.[1] Johnston himself, however, frankly admitted Buchanan's superiority, and there can be little doubt that he judged aright. Johnston has confined himself almost exclusively to elegiac metre, and he evidently made a point of keeping more closely to his original than Buchanan. But in real poetic feeling and easy mastery of language Buchanan leaves Johnston far behind. For the modern English reader it is doubtless hard to feel either interest or pleasure in any of these attempts to make King David speak the language of Horace and Virgil. Accustomed as he is from childhood to the noble simplicities of the English version, he is apt to find but little satisfaction in the most successful even of Buchanan's renderings. Yet few who know Buchanan's version of the 137th Psalm will refuse to admit that with all its classical suggestions, and in spite of its wide departure from the true spirit of Hebrew poetry, it possesses an inde-

---

[1] Hallam passes the following adverse criticism on Buchanan's paraphrase: "It is difficult, perhaps, to find one of Buchanan's Psalms, except the 137th, with which he has taken particular pains, that can be called truly elegant or classical Latin poetry."—*Lit. of the Mid. Ages*, vol. ii. p. 147. "So different are the humours of critics!" as Hallam himself remarks in a note on this very passage. Hallam's criticism here, as in so many other cases, is that of the scholar rather than the sympathetic reader.

pendent charm of its own that lays criticism asleep. The following renderings of the 23d Psalm by Buchanan and Johnston respectively will give an idea of their different styles of translation. A literal English translation of the same Psalm will bring before the reader the striking contrast between what has been called the "lightning-like effect"[1] of the original and what once passed for faithful translation :—

Jehovah is my shepherd ; I shall not want. In pastures of young grass he maketh me lie down ; by the waters of resting-places doth he gently lead me.

He refreshes my soul ; he leads me in right tracks for his name's sake.

Yea, though I walk through the valley of deadly shade, I will fear no evil, for thou art with me ; thy club and thy staff, they comfort me.

Thou furnishest a table before me in the presence of my foes ; thou hast anointed my head with oil, my cup runs over.

Surely good fortune and loving-kindness shall follow me all the days of my life, and I shall dwell in the house of Jehovah for length of days.

The following is the version of Buchanan :—

Quid frustra rabidi me petitis Canes ?
Livor, propositum cur premis improbum ?
Sicut pastor ovem, me Dominus regit ;
     Nil deerit penitus mihi.
Per campi viridis mitia pabula,
Quae veris teneri pingit amoenitas,
Nunc pascor placide ; nunc saturum latus
     Fessus molliter explico.
Purae rivus aquae leniter astrepens
Membris restituit robora languidis,
Et blando recreat fomite spiritus
     Solis sub face torrida.
Saltus quum peteret mens vaga devios
Errorum teneras illecebras sequens,

---

[1] The expression is Dr. Cheyne's ; and the translation is that given by him in the Parchment Library. Buchanan's paraphrase was, of course, made from the Vulgate. We have no evidence that he was acquainted with Hebrew.

Retraxit miserans denuo me bonus
 Pastor justitiae in viam.
Nec si per trepidas luctifica manu
Intentet tenebras mors mihi vulnera
Formidem duce te pergere ; me pedo
 Securum facies tuo.
Tu mensas epulis accumulas, merum
Tu plenis pateris sufficis, et caput
Unguento exhilaras : conficit aemulos,
 Dum spectant, dolor anxius.
Me numquam bonitas destituat tua,
Profususque bonis perpetuo favor ;
Et non sollicitae longa domi tuae
 Vitae tempora transigam.

We now give Johnston's rendering :—

Blandus ut upilio, me pascit Conditor orbis :
 Ne mihi quid desit, providus ille cavet.
Dat satur ut recubem pratorum in gramine molli :
 Ducit et ad rivos lene sonantis aquae.
Cor recreat, rectique viam mihi monstrat et aequi :
 Illius ut laudes laetus in astra feram.
Non ego degeneri quaterer formidine, leti
 Ante oculos quamvis vallis opaca foret :
Tu, Deus ! es praesto, baculo vestigia firmans
 Ne titubem : vires restituisque meas.
Hoste palam tu das plenis accumbere mensis ;
 Et mihi regales porrigis ipse dapes :
Tu caput irroras succo felicis olivae ;
 Sufficis et larga pocula plena manu.
Me tua defendet bonitas, dum lumine vescar ;
 Per salebras gressus diriget illa meos.
Inque tuis adytis, rerum Pater alme ! morabor ;
 Hic, ubi perpetuo gaudia laetus agam.

CHAPTER XI.

BUCHANAN, we have seen, left Portugal for England
in 1552. His sojourn in England at this time must
have been even shorter than on the occasion of his
former visit. Some inducement, it appears, was held
out to him to make his stay longer; but the state
of the country was such that it was no home for
peaceful students like himself.[1] As it must have
been towards the end of 1552 that he arrived in
England, his description of the state of the country
must refer to the strifes of Somerset and North-
umberland, and the subsequent intrigues of the latter
to secure the accession of his son to the throne as
the husband of Lady Jane Grey.

As the time had not yet come when Scotland
could be a place for men of his tastes, there was
but one other country open to him—France. But
if France had become an almost impossible abode
for the scholar when he left it in 1547, things had

---

[1] " Nec hic tamen substitit, quamquam honestis conditionibus invitaretur. Erant enim illic omnia adhuc turbida sub rege adolescente,
proceribus discordibus, et populi adhuc animis tumescentibus ab recenti
motu civili."—*Vita Sua.*

hardly improved in that country during his absence. Henry II., who had succeeded his father on the throne, was no patron of letters like Francis; and in the matter of religion he had the unwavering conviction that, save where his own interests were concerned, it was the highest crime in a ruler to give any quarter to heretics. The persons who had most influence with him, Diane de Poitiers, Constable Montmorency, and the Guises, all in strict subservience to their own interests, drove him to that policy which before the end of the century was wellnigh to wreck France as a nation. They drove him to the continuance of the fatal wars with Charles V. and his successor Philip, which, as far as Henry was concerned, were to end in one of the most ignominious arrangements France ever entered into—the Peace of Câteau-Cambresis in 1559, the year of Henry's own death.[1] From Buchanan's arrival in France till the date of that treaty the nation was engaged in continuous war either in Italy or on the banks of the Rhine. In Italy, the conduct of the Maréchal de Brissac, with whom we shall presently see Buchanan in honourable relations, won a certain success for France; and the capture of Calais from the English, and the brilliant defence of the lately acquired town of Metz, helped to blind the country to the disastrous results of the policy of the Government. To this mistaken foreign policy was joined the even more infatuated home policy of merciless persecution for religious opinion. As his war with the Emperor forced Henry into an alliance with the Protestants of Germany, he sought to redeem his

---

[1] H. Martin, *Histoire de France*, vol. viii. chap. xlix.

character as an orthodox son of the Church by all
the more remorseless persecution of heretics at
home. Almost at the beginning of his reign, a
chamber, known as *la chambre ardente*, was established in the Parliament for special dealing with all
suspected of heresy.[1] The persecution became so
close and merciless that crowds of Frenchmen were
driven to seek an asylum in Geneva.[2]

Such being the state of affairs in France during
this period, it is certainly noteworthy that Buchanan
should have found himself at his ease in that country,
and that he should not rather have sought in Geneva
a more congenial place of abode. As we shall see,
however, Buchanan was on perfectly good terms
with the Government, lived in intimate relations
with a French marshal known as the foe of all
heretics, and was ready with his congratulatory
odes whenever the occasion demanded them. The
true inference from all this seems to be that
Buchanan's interests as the scholar of the Renaissance were stronger than his interests as the reformer of the corruptions of the Church. But, in
all probability, at no time of his life, not even after
his final adoption of the creed of the Scottish
Reformers, would he have exchanged Paris, in spite
of the Sorbonne, for Geneva and its reign of the
saints.

In one of the very happiest of his shorter poems,
Buchanan has given expression to the pleasure he
felt on finding himself once more on the soil of
France. "Farewell," he exclaims, "a long fare-
well, ye barren wastes and niggard soil of Portugal.
But hail ! happy France, kind nurse of all the arts

---

[1] H. Martin, *Histoire de France*, vol. viii. chap. xlix.   [2] *Ibid.*

of life, with thy wholesome skies, thy generous
tilth, thy vine-shaded hills, thy groves alive with
cattle, thy richly-watered valleys, thy plains gay
with flowers, thy rivers whose far sweep bears
down many a sail to the deep, thy pools, thy
streams, thy lakes, thy seas with their plenteous
stores ; in many a harbour receiving the world as
thy guest, bounteous in thy turn to share thy
blessings ; happy France ! with thy sweet country
homes, thy ramparted walls, thy stately castles,
and thy sons adorned with all the graces of life,
modest, courteous, pleasant of speech. . . . France !
if while I live I love and cherish thee not as one
cherishes and loves the land of his birth, then may
I return to the barren wastes and niggard soil of
Portugal." [1]

At the moment of Buchanan's arrival in France
the country was rejoicing at the repulse of the
Emperor Charles in his attempt to recover the
important town of Metz. As was the invariable
custom on such occasions, every scholar came forward
with his Latin ode in celebration of the triumph of
the French arms, whereby de l'Hôpital said in *his*
ode " warlike Germany had at length yielded to
France her old superiority in battle". As an admirer
of France, Buchanan was pressed by his friends to
add his voice to the rest. He did not quite relish
the task, as it seemed to put him in competi-
tion with certain of his most intimate friends. He
felt an especial delicacy, he tells us, in seeming to
put himself in rivalry with Mellin de Saint-Gelais,
the most popular of the Court poets of the period.[2]
This casual mention of Saint-Gelais as one of his

---

[1] *Adventus in Galliam.*   [2] *Vita Sua.*

intimates is of much more importance to us in an attempt to understand Buchanan than the poem he made to order on the successful defence of Metz.

On the death of Clément Marot, Saint-Gelais held for a brief season, till the appearance of Ronsard, the first place among the vernacular poets of France. He has the distinction of having imported the sonnet into French literature, and he had a certain "witty delicacy" which won for him his brilliant though strictly ephemeral reputation. He was an ecclesiastic and the son of an ecclesiastic ; and he held the post of almoner at the Court of Henry II., so that Buchanan may have experienced substantial proofs of his favour.[1]   But what is to be noted in Saint-Gelais in connection with Buchanan, is thus stated by a great French critic. "Saint-Gelais," he says, "seems to have neglected no contrasts which poetry could offer to his profession, and he often made his ecclesiastical knowledge serve him for sufficiently profane allusions."[2]   His well-known jest at the expense of the doctors who were disputing about the nature of his case as he lay on his deathbed—*Messieurs, je vais vous lever de peine* —may be taken as illustrating the same strain in his character. With a personage of the type of Saint-Gelais it is utterly impossible that Knox or Calvin could at any period of their lives have had a single sentiment in common. Yet Buchanan admired Saint-Gelais' verses, and was bound to him by some tie, whether of sympathy or obligation. It is precisely in this friendly relation with

[1] *Nouvelle Biographie Générale.*
[2] Sainte-Beuve, *Tableau de la Poésie Française au xviᵉ Siècle.*

men like Saint-Gelais, taken together with his contempt for the ignorance of the monks and the obscurantism of the theologians of the Sorbonne, that we
see in Buchanan at this period the humanist pure
and simple.[1]

After his arrival in France in the beginning of
1553, Buchanan appears to have made his home in
Paris for the next two years; and at some time during
this period, as we gather from a letter addressed to
him after his final return to Scotland, he must have
filled the post of regent in the Collége Boncourt.
Of the details of his life during these years we
know nothing ; but we gather from his dedications
to his translations of the *Medea* and *Alcestis* of
Euripides, that his stay in France was not without
risk, and that, like other scholars during this reign, he
was in some danger of finding his way to the Place
Maubert.   He had friends in high places, however,
as these dedications prove—for they are addressed
to no less distinguished persons than Margaret the
King's sister, and one of the princes of the house of
Luxembourg, both of whom, he tells us, had given
him tokens of their favour, and had shielded him
from the attacks of his enemies.

But the closest and most honourable relation
that Buchanan had with great persons in France
was that with Charles du Cossé, Comte de Brissac,
one of the marshals of France.   At this time de
Brissac was in command of the French forces in
Italy ; but Buchanan must at some previous period
have had proofs of his respect and good-will.   In

---

[1] Buchanan has the following epigram on Saint-Gelais :—

Mellinum patrio sale carmina tingere jussit,
Parceret ut famae Musa, Catulle, tuae.

1553, on de Brissac's capture of Vercelli, Buchanan
had written a congratulatory ode, manifestly inspired by genuine admiration for his character and
exploits.   In the following year he dedicated to
him his tragedy *Jephthes*, and accompanied it with a
preface which does honour both to the soldier and
to the poet.   It is in this preface, as has already
been mentioned, that Buchanan puts forward his
argument that there is no necessary antagonism
between war and letters.   Formerly, he says, the
great captain and the great writer were frequently
conjoined.   If this is no longer the case, the poet
and the soldier, at all events, can never dispense
with the function of each other.   The soldier
provides the poet with the material of his song,
and thereby the soldier attains what is his paramount desire—immortal fame.   The happy union
of distinction in war and love of letters is seen in
no one more conspicuously than in de Brissac.   In
all his campaigns he never fails to surround himself
with men eminent for their learning.   Of his love
for learning he has given the most conclusive proof
in the jealous care he has taken in the education of his son.   And Buchanan concludes with an
expression of gratitude for de Brissac's past favours
to him.   "Before you had even seen me," he says,
"and when I was unknown to you except by repute
as a scholar, you overwhelmed me with such proofs
of your goodwill and generosity, that if I have
produced aught of any real value, if any result is
likely to come of my labours, to you must certainly
belong all the credit."

    That de Brissac deserved all that Buchanan said
of him we have the most conclusive testimony from

many sources. There must have been in him, indeed,
a strain of magnanimity which reminds us of the
best types in Plutarch's gallery of heroes. Henry II.
had made him Governor-General of Piedmont, by
way, it is said, of ridding himself of a formidable
rival in his amours with Diane de Poitiers. In
Piedmont, de Brissac's conduct was such as to place
him among the first soldiers of France during the
sixteenth century, and with Admiral Coligny he
shares the distinction of humanising the preva-
lent modes of warfare, and of raising the character of French military discipline. An interesting example is given of the manner in which he
enforced discipline among his subordinates. Since
the Emperor Charles and Francis had interchanged
cartels of defiance on the refusal of the latter to
observe the terms of the treaty of Madrid, duelling
had become more and more the fashion among the
gentlemen of France. In de Brissac's camp the
practice was strictly forbidden; but when the
parties would not be turned from their purpose
they were allowed to proceed on one condition :
they must conduct their meeting on a narrow
bridge spanning a stream, in such fashion that the
combatant who fell must be drowned in the water
below.[1] De Brissac permitted no plunder in an
enemy's country, and when a town fell into his
hands, his treatment of the inhabitants was such
as marked him out from all the commanders of the
period. Of his high-minded patriotism he gave a
striking example, when at a certain critical juncture
he sacrificed his daughter's dowry, and borrowed
money on his own personal fortune to meet the

[1] H. Martin, *Histoire de France*, vol. viii. chap. xlix.

claims of his soldiers.[1]   There was therefore more
than mere courtly compliment in the title of the
fine ode which Buchanan addressed to de Brissac—
De Amore Cossaei et Aretes.

It was in 1555 that de Brissac chose Buchanan
to be tutor to his son, Timoleon du Cossé, then a
boy of twelve. As Buchanan had the young du
Cossé in charge for the next five years, his high
opinion of de Brissac must have been cordially
reciprocated, and it must certainly be regarded as a
high tribute at once to the character and attainments of Buchanan, that a personage of the rank
and stamp of the Maréchal de Brissac should have
chosen him from the crowd of French scholars to
this responsible post. Buchanan had every reason
to be proud of his pupil. "The Comte de Brissac,"
says Brantôme, "was one of the most perfect and
accomplished noblemen I have ever seen in our
Court. I have hardly ever seen one of them who
has not been guilty of some folly in his youth, but
de Brissac was never guilty of any." In another
place Brantôme has the following remark on a
characteristic of du Cossé, which may be set down
to Buchanan's credit as his teacher : "Quant aux
vertus de l'ame de ce Comte, il estoit sçavant, et
lisoit tousjours peu et peu."[2] Yet from the separate
portraits Brantôme has given us of the father and
the son, it is evident that the father had the larger
mind and nobler nature. Nevertheless, a career
as brilliant as that of his father's seemed opening
before the son, when he was killed by a musket-
ball at the age of twenty-six. Buchanan's most

[1] *Nouvelle Biographie Générale.*
[2] Brantôme, *Vie des Hommes Illustres.*

ambitious poem, and that on which he meant his fame should rest more than any other—the *De Sphaera*—is the memorial of his relation with his pupil; for to him the poem is specially addressed.

During the five years of his engagement with de Brissac, Buchanan was constantly coming and going between Italy and France.[1] Of his friendly relations with the Marshal himself H. Estienne tells the following story. "The Comte de Brissac," he says, " was in the habit of admitting George Buchanan, the tutor of his son, to his councils of war. He was led to do this from the following incident. On a certain occasion Buchanan had come down from his bedroom to the dining-room to give some order to a domestic. As it happened, de Brissac with his staff was deliberating in an adjoining hall on matters of the gravest importance. Buchanan, overhearing what was said, muttered some words of disapproval. De Brissac noticing a smile on the face of one of his officers, and the reason being given, Buchanan was called in and asked for his opinion. This he did with such sagacity that all present agreed that his suggestion should be adopted. As it happened, the result confirmed the wisdom of Buchanan's counsel."[2]

The beginning of his poem on the Sphere, and a few short occasional pieces, make up the list of Buchanan's productions during these years. His thoughts, in fact, had now begun to take a new direction, and his humanistic studies gave place to a keen personal interest in the great religious questions of the time. Till his last arrival in France,

[1] *Vita Sua.*
[2] Quoted by Ruddiman in his commentary on Buchanan's auto-biography.

in 1553, there can be little doubt that he still considered himself a member of the Church of Rome. Certain expressions in the poem already quoted, *Adventus in Galliam*, put this beyond question. He there speaks of France as

> . . . cultrix numinis
> Sincera, *ritum in exterum non degener,*

which can refer only to the religious innovations of Germany and Switzerland. In his poem on the capture of Calais in 1558, he speaks of the Pope as *Pater Romanus* in a tone utterly incompatible with Lutheran or Calvinistic leanings. But during his last years in France, he for the first time began to make a serious study of the questions at issue between Rome and the Protestant reformers. His own words are so remarkable that they deserve to be quoted. These five years, he says, he mainly devoted to the study of the Bible in order that he might be able to form definite opinions for himself on the controversies which were then exercising the majority of men. These controversies, he proceeds, were now on the point of being settled at home, since the Scots had got rid of the tyranny of the Guises. Returning thither, he gave in his adhesion to the Scottish Church.[1] Till the very eve, therefore, of his final return to Scotland, and when he was already in his fifty-fifth year, we are bound to regard Buchanan as emphatically the product of the Renaissance, not of the Reformation.

It was probably some time in 1561, after an

---

[1] "Quod tempus maxima ex parte dedit sacrarum literarum studio, ut de controversiis, quae tum majorem hominum partem exercebant, exactius dijudicare posset; quae tum domi conquiescere coeperant, Scotis a tyrannide Guisiana liberatis. Eo reversus nomen ecclesiae Scotorum dedit."—*Vita Sua.*

exile of twenty-two years, that Buchanan returned
to his native country ; and there, with the exception of one flying visit to Paris, and a short sojourn
in England, he thenceforth remained for the rest of
his life.

CHAPTER XII.

By his poem entitled *De Sphaera* Buchanan doubtless thought that he would lay the foundations of his fame deep enough to defy all the vicissitudes of time. He wrote it in Latin, thus securing, as he fancied, an unfailing succession of educated readers; and he chose a theme which, as he confidently anticipated, linked his literary fortunes to the very course of Nature itself. But if he had known it, even when he wrote, modern Europe had rejected Latin as the vehicle of its deepest thoughts and feelings; and what he deemed the eternal system of the universe had been exploded some twenty years before he began to sing it.

In thus choosing the system of things as the subject of his most important poem, Buchanan was only impelled by the necessities of the movement of which he was so brilliant a representative. That movement being essentially imitative and not creative, themes of truly human interest were debarred to him and his fellows. Consequently, when they aimed at the higher triumphs of their art they were almost inevitably driven to subjects of a didactic character. How sorely they were pressed for subjects may be gathered from the titles of some of the

best-known poems of Italian writers of Latin verse.
Thus, we have Vida's poem on the Game of Chess
and his epic on Silk-worms, and the unsavoury
theme of Fracastorius' famous poem. But if a
didactic subject was to be chosen, there could be
few, as Hallam remarks, "which could afford better
opportunities for ornamental digression" than the
system of the heavens.[1]

With the exception of one or two shorter pieces,
indeed, Buchanan has produced no better poetry
than is to be found in many passages of the
Sphere. The poem was written in the full maturity of his powers, and with the full consciousness that he was making his greatest stroke for
fame. And in spite of the exploded hypothesis on
which the poem is based, and of all the obsolete
and grotesque notions with which it abounds, we
everywhere feel the presence of a mind and soul in
living and intimate contact with its subject. It is
perfectly evident that Buchanan wrote the poem in
the conviction that he was not only immortalising
his own genius, but that he was doing the world a
real service in expounding the true theory of the
universe. As we shall see, he was perfectly aware
of the new theory of Copernicus. To show the
folly of that theory, and to denounce the popular
astrology as leading men to unworthy views both
of themselves and the Creator—these undoubtedly
were two motives that had their influence in his
choice of a subject. It is, in truth, this ardent
feeling of an ethical purpose on the part of the poet
that even still gives to his work a certain vitality.

Buchanan's poem is in large measure only a

---

[1] Hallam, *Lit. of the Middle Ages*, vol. ii. p. 146.

poetical paraphrase of the famous text-book of
Joannes de Sacrobosco on the Sphere.[1] Sacrobosco's
book was originally published in the thirteenth century, and since the date of its publication it had
been the text-book of astronomy in all the great
schools of Europe. For brevity and clearness, indeed, it could hardly be surpassed as an exposition
of the Ptolemaic conception of the heavens. In
Buchanan's day it was as popular as ever. His
colleague at Bordeaux and intimate friend, Élie
Vinet, published a new edition of it, in 1540,
with a preface, in which he states that Sacrobosco's
treatise was still unrivalled as an introduction to
the study of astronomy. But the remarkable thing
is that this book, with slight modification, remained
in use till past the middle of the seventeenth century.
In 1656, the Government of Holland gave special
orders that Sacrobosco should have a place in the
schools of that country, at the same time suggest-
ing that such alterations should be made in it as
time had made necessary. As edited by Burgersdicius the mediæval Latin phraseology was altered,
and certain additions were made; but the main
doctrine that the earth is the immovable centre of
the universe is still as confidently asserted as if
Copernicus had never lived.

It was, therefore, no perverse obscurantism in
Buchanan that between 1550 and 1560 he began
this poem with the purpose of expounding and em-
bellishing the Ptolemaic theory, though the epoch-
making treatise of Copernicus, published in 1543,

---

[1] If Joannes de Sacrobosco—that is, John Holybush or Holywood—
were indeed, as some have supposed, a native of Scotland, he must certainly be regarded as the most famous of all the "Scots Abroad".

had shown that that theory could be replaced by one far more simple and satisfactory. It must be remembered that there were more reasons than one why the Copernican theory was so slow to win general acceptance. In the first place—and this was doubtless the strongest reason of all—the entire Christian revelation was supposed to be bound up with the doctrine that the earth was the centre of the universe. More than a century after the death of Copernicus, Pascal did not dare to affirm the contrary ; and it has been noted as a proof of the courage and good sense of la Fontaine that he spoke of the sun thus :—

L'ignorant le croit plat ; j'épaissis sa rondeur,
Je le rends immobile, et la terre chemine.[1]

It is to be remembered, also, that the Ptolemaic theory actually did explain all the phenomena then known, so that to Buchanan and his contemporaries Copernicus passed for a revolutionary of the most unreasonable type. It is not to be wondered at, therefore, that during the sixteenth century the new theory found but four supporters in the whole of Europe.[2] There was still another reason why humanists like Buchanan should regard the new teaching with contempt. Pythagoras, before Copernicus, had taught that it was the earth that moved and not the heavens. But Greek and Roman antiquity alike had rejected the teaching of Pythagoras ; and to question the right reason of Greece

---

[1] The case of Galileo is too well known to require mention ; and, besides, he died in 1642. Milton, it will be remembered, adopts the Ptolemaic system, though quite aware of the claims of that of Copernicus. Addison's hymn, beginning "The spacious firmament on high," written in the beginning of the eighteenth century, is also expressed in the language of the old cosmogony.

[2] Hallam, *Lit. of the Mid. Ages*, vol. ii. p. 227. Hallam names Wright and Gilbert as the only two Englishmen who accepted the Copernican theory during the sixteenth century.

and Rome was a flight of audacity far beyond the scholars of Buchanan's day.

Buchanan's poem consists of five books, the last two being incomplete; and from internal evidence we gather that they were all probably begun during his engagement with de Brissac.[1] That he had the intention of completing the poem appears from two of his letters written long after his return to Scotland. Writing to Tycho Brahé in 1576, he says that for the last two years he has been so prostrate with all manner of ailments that he had been forced to desist not only from higher tasks, but from completing his poem on the Sphere.[2] To another correspondent, also, he writes as late as 1579 : " My astronomical poem I have not so much cast aside, as been forced sorely against my will to give it up."[3] That till within three years of his death, when old age and protracted illness might be supposed to have quenched all his literary ambitions, Buchanan still thought of adding the finishing touches to his poem, is signal proof that he considered the *De Sphaera* the most important effort of his genius. As but few readers are likely to make acquaintance with this the lengthiest of all Buchanan's poems, it may be worth while to note a few of the more curious points in his exposition of the system of the universe.

As has been said, Buchanan closely follows the arrangement of Sacrobosco's treatise. The first book is occupied mainly with an exposition of the nature and arrangement of the four elements, and of the rotundity of the earth. Each of the elements, he says,

---

[1] At least he directly addresses his pupil in the unfinished books.

[2] *Epist.* xv.

[3] *Epist.* xxvii. " Astronomica non tam abjeci, quam extorqueri invitus tuli."

has by its nature a peculiar region of its own, which it finds by virtue of its relative density. Lowest, as being heaviest, is earth ; then water, air, fire, all disposed in spheres, forming successive layers after the manner of the coats of an onion. That the earth is anywhere above water is due to the special providence of God.[1] All the elements naturally tend to the centre; hence the earth, as the heaviest of the elements, is necessarily round, and necessarily forms the centre of the universe. In proving the rotundity of the earth, Buchanan makes use of the same arguments and illustrations as Sacrobosco; but he is able to add one more cogent than all the rest, which was not accessible to the thirteenth century. The earth had been circumnavigated since Sacrobosco's day. Buchanan seems rather to have regretted this fact, for the reason that he saw but one motive in all the maritime enterprise of his century. Avarice, he thinks, was at the bottom of it all; and here he has one of his eloquent digressions which relieve the monotony of the poem. Where enlightened reason failed, the vilest of human motives has succeeded :—

> Quod ratio longis nisa est extundere seclis,
> Illa oculis hominum ostendit.

The earth, then, is round, and is the immoveable centre of things. Certain sophists, indeed, with Pythagoras as their master, had taught that the earth moves about its own axis. But the absurdity of such a doctrine is evident to the simplest mind. What were the speèd of birds or of the winds compared with the speed at which the earth would

---

[1] "Singulari Dei providentia effectum est, ut terra aliqua sui parte aquis extaret, ad tuendam vitam animantium."—Burgersdicius, *Sacrobosco*, p. 9 (edit. 1647).

have to move to meet the conditions of the case?
Think, also, of the noise made by a boy's rattle
when whirled round his head, of the noise of a sling,
of the air issuing from a pair of bellows ; and conclude what must have been the din of the earth,
with all its mountains, forests, and cities, whirling
round itself, as these sophists taught.   Moreover,
if a bird took the shortest flight into the air, where
would its nest be by the time it descended ?

Nec se
Auderet Zephyro solus committere turtur,
Ne procul ablatos terra fugiente Hymenaeos,
Et viduum longo luctu defleret amorem.

Suppose two armies engaged in battle, the missiles
of the one would reach their aim, but what would
happen to the missiles of the other?   And then
how could the sea keep its limits?   Must it not
rush madly over the earth's surface, and sweep
before it all the works of man ?   On the insignifi-
cance of the earth in the scheme of things, as contrasted with the foolish pretensions of men, no
modern could descant more energetically than
Buchanan, as the following lines, which conclude
the first book, will show :—

O pudor ! o stolidi praeceps vesania voti !
Quantula pars rerum est, in qua se gloria jactat,
Ira fremit, metus exanimat, dolor urit, egestas
Cogit opes ; ferro, insidiis, flamma atque veneno
Cernitur, et trepido fervent humana tumultu.

In his second book, Buchanan expounds the
system of the Sphere by which Ptolemy sought to
explain the motions of the heavenly bodies.   Into
this exposition we need not follow him, as he strictly
follows the lines laid down for him by Sacrobosco.
One passage, however, may be quoted, as showing

what Buchanan thought of Copernicus and his
theory.   He has been speaking of the motions of
the heavenly bodies in their respective spheres.
" Although reason," he exclaims, " has clearly
shown all this to be true, yet blind ignorance,
forsooth, immersed in its own darkness, does not
cease to rail aloud, and audaciously to condemn the
heavens to rest, and to transform the sluggish earth
into a swiftly moving body."

In the third book, where he gives an account of
the various artificial contrivances by which men had
sought to simplify the study of the heavens, two
passages deserve special notice—a description of the
Milky Way, and a few lines of reference to the discovery of America.   The latter passage is introduced
as a final and conclusive proof that the sun and stars
circle round the earth.   " Although," he says, " the
god-like mind of Posidonius had clinched this truth
with sound argument, yet the force of reason and
the weight of his authority carried conviction to but
few, till the fleet of Spain, in search of a path to
shores abounding in glittering gems, and to the
Indian dusky from the nearer sun, revealed the
secrets of the earth, brought forth what had long
been hid in night, and beheld populous lands, where
the sun holds his course through mid-heaven, and
strikes the underlying earth with upright ray,
piercing the soil of rich Taprobane [Ceylon], and
the Brazilian plains—abodes of all delight, where
for every sense Nature pours forth her store : there
the trees, elsewhere barren, of their own accord bear
golden fruits, earth smiles in ever-rich hues, ambrosial
odours exhale from grateful flowers, and the soothing
breeze is quick with the songs of birds."   The above

passage gives an idea of the manner in which Buchanan relieves the technicalities of his subject.

Of the fourth book Buchanan wrote only about a hundred lines, though he had doubtless the intention of making it of the same length as the preceding three. The fifth book, which is also unfinished, treats of the eclipses of the sun and moon, with especial reference to the impostures of astrology. What Buchanan thought of judicial astrology, as it was called, does not appear from this poem. In all probability he was of the same opinion as his friend Élie Vinet, who, in the preface to his edition of Sacrobosco, remarks that " if one will but apply his judgment to the question, he will understand that the department of astronomy known as divination is as much a part of science as the predictions of doctors, that are rightly recognised as making part of medicine ".[1] Such is the poem on which Buchanan confidently trusted that his fame must rest secure against all the assaults of time.

While Buchanan was with de Brissac he wrote a few short poems, which deserve notice not only for their intrinsic merit, but also as having the most direct bearing on his life and opinions. One of these is his really fine ode addressed to Henry II. on the capture of Calais by the Duke of Guise in 1558. This ode is one more proof of how completely Buchanan identified himself with the fortunes of the French people. He glories in the humiliation of England, and in the future security of France from her invasion. Of Mary of England he speaks in the

---

[1] " Si quis adhibebit judicium, intelliget alteram partem artis, divinatricem, perinde esse partem physices, sicut medicorum predictiones pars quaedam physices esse existimantur."—Élie Vinet, *Sacrobosco* (1540).

following energetic fashion : "The queen, who knew
not how to endure peace, now mourns the treaties
she held at nought, now dreads the imminent
wrath of God, the scourge of the avenging fury.
The common leech of subjects and enemies, thirsting
equally for the blood of both, she hates and fears
subjects and enemies alike. By day the dread of
war is ever before her ; and a blood-guilty conscience
and ghastly spectres disturb her rest by night.
Thus doth offended justice exact expiation ; thus
doth Nemesis bear down stiff-necked pride ; and
thus to the mild and just doth mild and just heaven
lend its aid."

Another poem belonging to this period is among
the best known of Buchanan's productions. This is
his Epithalamium on the marriage of the Dauphin
Francis with Mary of Scotland in 1558. We may
readily believe that this marriage had his most
ardent approval. The idea of an English in preference to a French alliance, which by this period
had come to commend itself to many of the leading
men in Scotland,[1] had certainly not as yet presented
itself to the mind of Buchanan. England was still
for him the " auld enemy", and the only safe policy
for Scotland a more and more intimate union with
France. In this alliance, however, Buchanan stoutly
maintained that France was quite as much a gainer
as Scotland, and that the understanding between
the two countries must be as between two perfectly
equal Powers.

Buchanan's poem has the stamp of genuine
enthusiasm from the first line to the last. Even of

[1] Cf. Major, *De Gest. Scot.*, Lib. i. cap. 7 : " Dicere ausim Anglum
Scotumque Regibus male suis consulere, si inter eos non semper matri-
monia contrahant, quatenus de utroque regno unum Britanniae regnum
faciant."

poor Francis himself he has things to say which
seem odd if perversely construed.   But the grave
de l'Hôpital, who produced a poem on the same
occasion, leaves Buchanan far behind on this theme.
Having given the bridegroom full credit for all
his virtues and for the greatness of his fortunes,
Buchanan reminds him that he has by no means the
worst of the bargain.   In his bride he has every
grace of mind and person that he could desire.   In
the matter of birth she is the representative of the
most ancient line of sovereigns in the world—

> Haec una centum de stirpe nepotes
> Sceptriferos numerare potest, haec regia sola est,
> Quae bis dena suis includat secula fastis. [1]

As for dowry, does she not bring a country rich
in all the fruits of the earth, abounding in copper
and lead, whose mountains glitter with gold and
are compact with iron, whose rivers bear down all
manner of precious metals to the sea?   It is, of
course, only the vulgar who look to such things,
and who make light of everything but riches.   But
his bride will bring him something more precious
than gold.   And here follows his famous panegyric
of the Scottish nation :—

> Illa pharetratis est propria gloria Scotis, [2]
> Cingere venatu saltus, superare natando
> Flumina, ferre famem, contemnere frigora et aestus ;
> Nec fossa et muris patriam, sed Marte, tueri,

---

[1] As is well known, the Scots not only believed this themselves, but
actually succeeded in persuading other nations to believe it.

[2] In illustration of this line, Irving (*Memoirs of Buchanan*, p. 120)
quotes this sentence:—"Nostra autem aetate [Scotorum] complures cum
Carolo Francorum rege Italiam invaserunt, qui sub ejus signis militarent :
sunt enim in dirigendis maxime sagittis viri acres atque egregii."—
Crinitus, *De Honesta Disciplina*.   At home the Scots had a strong contempt for the bow as a weapon.

Et spreta incolumem vita defendere famam ;
Polliciti servare fidem, sanctumque vereri
Numen amicitiae, mores, non munus amare.
Artibus his, totum fremerent cum bella per orbem,
Nullaque non leges tellus mutaret avitas
Externo subjecta jugo, gens una vetustis
Sedibus antiqua sub libertate resedit.
Substitit hic Gothi furor, hic gravis impetus haesit
Saxonis, hic Cimber superato Saxone, et acri
Perdomito Neuster Cimbro. Si volvere priscos
Non piget annales, hic et victoria fixit
Praecipitem Romana gradum : quem non gravis Auster
Reppulit, incultis non squalens Parthia campis,
Non aestu Meroe, non frigore Rhenus et Albis
Tardavit, Latium remorata est Scotia cursum.

> " The glory of the quivered Scots
>   Is the bold breast and hardy frame
>   That fear, nor want, nor toil can tame ;
>   Whose joy is in their native woods
>   To chase and strike the various game,
>   And fearless breast their mountain floods ;
>   Whose good right hands their soil can keep,
>   Nor need high walls nor fosses deep ;
>   Who count all gone, if honour's gone ;
>   Whose faith can ne'er be bought nor sold ;
>   Who deem a friend heaven's dearest boon ;
>   Who barter not their soul for gold.
>   So was it, when of old each land,
>   A prey to every spoiler's hand,
>   Its ancient laws and rulers lost,
>   The Scot alone could freedom boast !
>   The Goth, the Saxon, and the Dane
>   Poured on the Scot their powers in vain ;
>   And the proud Norman met a foe
>   Who gave him equal blow for blow.
>   And I might tell, were not twice-told
>   The tale, how Rome, whose might controlled
>   The world beside, was taught to know
>   That bounds there were she might not pass,
>   Though never yet had been the foe,
>   Or man, or nature's direst force,
>   That e'er had stayed her onward course."

Having thus glorified the valour of the Scots
and their aptitude for war, he reminds the Dauphin

that their record is no less glorious in the arts of
peace. When the rest of the world was given up
to endless war, it was among the Scots that letters
found a home. When Charlemagne opened his
schools, it was to the Scots he appealed for his
doctors.[1] It was in the time of Charlemagne, also,
that the alliance between France and Scotland
was first begun—an alliance which no power had
yet availed to break up.[2] Many a time had France
had occasion to be grateful for the friendship of
Scotland. English, Batavians, Spaniards, all had
reason to know what France owed to the prowess
of the Scots. And the poet concludes with the
following prayer :—" Grant me, ye Fates, this length
of days, that I may behold united in soul, subject
to the sway of the brothers of one race, France and
Scotland, knit already through so many ages by
mutual service, by leagues, and solemn compact—
that I may behold as one people joined in concord,
enduring as the lights of heaven, those whom the
sea keeps apart by its waves, earth and sky by far-
stretching space." When we remember what the
next quarter of the century was to bring forth for
Scotland and France alike, we must find all the
irony and pathos of life in this prayer of Buchanan.
Before many years, he was led to think that the
alliance of France would be for Scotland the most
disastrous event that could befall her. And, as it
happened, at the very moment he wrote these lines

---

[1] As is well known, the Scots made unjust capital out of the confusion between Scotland and Ireland. Mr. Hill Burton has some interesting remarks on the subject in his *Scot Abroad*, vol. ii. Boece tells us that
Paris University began to flourish " by the industry of two Scotsmen ".

[2] This alliance with Charlemagne made part of the mythical history
of Scotland, as accepted in Buchanan's day.

it had come to pass in the inevitable process of things that the respective paths of France and Scotland were henceforth to be wide as the poles apart.

It is interesting to compare this poem of Buchanan with that of de l'Hôpital, afterwards Chancellor of France, which was produced on the same occasion. L'Hôpital's verses are bald and awkward compared with Buchanan's, and the spirit in which they were written is much more suggestive of the statesman than the poet. We learn from him what, indeed, we know from other sources, that the Scottish marriage was regarded by many in France as seriously compromising the dignity of the French Crown—

> Namque maligne
> Quidam homines etiam haec vulgo connubia rodunt.

On grounds of policy, however, de l'Hôpital strongly approves of the alliance. Mary, he reminds those who opposed the match, brings a kingdom as her dowry—a kingdom petty indeed compared with France, yet one which at many a lamentable crisis had brought saving aid to France. So populous a country is Scotland that she is able at once to send an invading army into England and an auxiliary army into France. If France should reject this union, England may accept it; and what would be the fate of France if she had to contend with Scotland and England both? Moreover, it would be highly impolitic to give such mortal offence to the Scottish Queen. Married to some other prince, she would make it the aim of her life to repay the insult with interest. Everything considered, therefore, l'Hôpital is of opinion that the

Scottish alliance is the wisest policy for France ; and
he concludes his poem in a fashion which contrasts
oddly with the enthusiastic prayer of Buchanan.
" By me, his bard," he says, " Apollo predicts these
happy results (that will flow from this union).   My
posterity, as I trust, will say—if, indeed, my strains
but live so long—' Long since our ancestor sang
that these things would be, when the majority of
men said they would never come to pass '."

In less than three years Buchanan saw the ruin
of all the hopes that had been founded on the alliance
he had celebrated with such enthusiasm.   Francis
died in December 1560, on the eve of the religious
wars that were to devastate France for the
remainder of the century.   On this occasion, also,
Buchanan wrote a poem ; and perhaps, among all
his productions, there is not one where he mounts
to a higher strain of impressive dignity.   The poem
is entitled *A Lamentation on the State of Affairs
on the Death of King Francis II.*   It is curious to
note that the poem does not contain a single reference to the bereavement of Mary.   The loss of its
king to the French nation at one of the most fateful
moments of its history, its humiliations abroad, its
dissensions at home—these are the themes on which
he now speaks in tones that remove the poem quite
out of the category of mere conventional effusions.
In the light of what befell France in the years
immediately succeeding the death of the young
King, the following personification of Discord has a
terrible significance.   It is to be remembered that
in less than two years after these lines were
written the Huguenot Wars began.   " Discord,
steeped to the lips in foulest venom, meditates

crimes more monstrous than all the rest. From their silent seats she summons to upper air her infernal sisters, and plants in men's minds the seeds of rage and hate. The thoughts of the chiefs of the people she turns to selfish aims, nor permits them to lay to heart the common weal." The last line of this poem, though it is a touch in perfect keeping with the age, has a somewhat grotesque effect on the modern reader. Having besought Heaven to avert further evils from France, the poet concludes with the request that Heaven may be pleased to let loose these same evils on the Turks!

Though we have no reason to suppose that it belongs to this period, we give a place here to another poem of Buchanan's, which affords the most conclusive proof, if any were needed, that poetry was indeed his natural language. This is his poem entitled *Calendae Maiae*. Of its poetic value we have fortunately the opinion of Wordsworth himself. The subject of the poem, it may be said, is one on which Wordsworth speaks with all his authority. " I think (he says, writing to the nephew who became his biographer) Buchanan's *Calendae Maiae* equal in sentiment, if not in elegance, to anything in Horace; but your brother Charles, to whom I repeated it the other day, pointed out a false quantity in it. Happily this had escaped me."[1]

---

[1] *Life of Wordsworth*, by Christopher Wordsworth, vol. ii. p. 466. The following note is attached to the above passage : " If I remember right, it is the line

'Ludisque dĭcatae, jocisque',

a strange blunder, for .Buchanan must have read Horace's ' Quid dedicatum poscit Apollinem ' a hundred times." False quantities are not uncommon with the best scholars of Buchanan's century. Mr. Christie notes that Saumaise points out false quantities in Milton's Latin poetry. Even in Gray Mr. Christie finds similar lapses. — *Life of Etienne Dolet*, p. 479.

M

Some readers may think that Wordsworth's praise might well have been more emphatic, and that Buchanan's ode, by its true poetic quality, is worthy of Horace when he transcends himself.

CALENDAE MAIAE.

Salvete sacris deliciis sacrae
Maiae Calendae, laetitiae, et mero,
  Ludisque dicatae, jocisque,
    Et teneris Charitum choreis.
Salve voluptas, et nitidum decus
Anni recurrens perpetua vice,
  Et flos renascentis juventae
    In senium properantis aevi.
Cum blanda veris temperies novo
Illuxit orbi, primaque secula
  Fulsere flaventi metallo
    Sponte sua sine lege justa :
Talis per omnes continuus tenor
Annos tepenti rura Favonio
  Mulcebat, et nullis feraces
    Seminibus recreabat agros.
Talis beatis incubat insulis
Felicis aurae perpetuus tepor,
  Et nesciis campis senectae
    Difficilis, querulique morbi.
Talis silentum per tacitum nemus
Levi susurrat murmure spiritus,
  Lethenque juxta obliviosam
    Funereas agitat cupressos.
Forsan supremis cum Deus ignibu
Piabit orbem, laetaque secula
  Mundo reducet, talis aura
    Aethereos animos fovebit.
Salve fugacis gloria seculi,
Salve secunda digna dies nota,
  Salve vetustae vitae imago,
    Et specimen venientis aevi.

THE FIRST OF MAY.

Hail! sweetest day,
Day of all pure delight ;
Whose gracious hours invite

To mirth and song and dance,
And wine, and love's soft glance.
Welcome ! with all thy bright hours bring
Of quickened life and beauty's dower—
The certain heritage of spring.
In thee each year doth hoary time
Renew the glories of his prime !

When, still rejoicing in her birth,
Spring brightened all the new-made earth,
And in that happy golden age
Men knew no lawless passion's rage,
Thy train of joys embraced the year ;
Soft breezes wooed the untilled field
Its blessings all unforced to yield.

Even in such mildest atmosphere
For ever bask those happy isles,
Those blessed plains, that never know
Life's slow decay, or poisoned flow.

Thus 'mid the still abodes of death
Should steal the soft air's softest breath,
And gently stir the solemn wood
That glooms o'er Lethe's dreamless flood.

And, haply, when made pure of stain
By cleansing fire, the earth renewed
Shall know her ancient joys again,
Even such mild air shall o'er her brood !

Thou crown of the world's failing age,
Of life's sad book one happy page,
Hail ! sweetest day—memorial bright
Of early innocent delight.
And sure pledge of the coming day
When it shall be eternal May.

THE first notice we have of Buchanan after his return to his native country is in a letter of Randolph, the English resident at the Scottish Court, to Cecil, the minister of Elizabeth. The letter is dated Edinburgh, 30th January 1561-2: "Ther is with the quene one called Mr. George Bowhanan, a Scottishe man, verie well lerned, that was the schollemaster unto Monsr. de Brisack's sone, very godlye and honest." On the 7th of April, also, Randolph wrote from St. Andrews: "The queen readeth daily after her dinner, instructed by a learned man Mr. George Bowhannan, somewhat of Lyvie." Randolph came to be better acquainted with Buchanan, and to esteem the acquaintance a privilege;[1] and it is him we have, in all likelihood, to thank for the Latin sketch of Buchanan's life which has formed the basis of all his biographies. In the following year we find another notice, which indicates that Buchanan had other employment besides reading with Mary. In the Register of the Privy Council there is an entry, under date 6th February 1562-3, to the effect that Buchanan, along with another, had been appointed

---

[1] Randolph had been a pupil of Buchanan in Paris.

"to interpreit the writtis producit in proces writtin in Spainis langage furth of the same in Franche, Latyne, or Inglis, that the Quenis grace and Counsale mycht thaireftir understand the samyn".

From all that we have·seen of Buchanan up to this point it may readily be believed that his feeling towards Mary must have been very different from that of Knox, who saw in her simply the victim of the most terrible of all delusions, and the most formidable of all obstacles in the way of national salvation. Buchanan had joined the Church of Knox on his return to Scotland; but his whole manner of life till then, his varied experience of men and things, the free play of thought and feeling that came to him from his humanistic training, would enable him easily to bridge the difference of religious faith, and fully to appreciate the grace and quickness of mind that distinguished Mary above most women of her time. On the other hand, Mary must have found in Buchanan what she could hardly have found in any other of her subjects. A peculiar bond between them must have been their common love and common memories of France. "Mary," says Sir James Melville, "was somewhat sad when solitary; and was glad of the company of such as had travelled to other kingdoms." It would appear, moreover, that Buchanan was not altogether wanting in the qualifications that make men acceptable at Courts. There is a certain discrepancy in the portraits of him that have come down to us; but from descriptions of him by different observers we can form a sufficiently distinct notion of how he looked and bore himself. In all his portraits he appears with strongly marked

features, the forehead of the same dome-like shape
as Scott's, and the mouth and chin indicative of
strength and individuality. His usual expression
was grave even to severity. He had a slight stoop
as he walked, and his general appearance was
homely and rustic.[1] In his latter years, at least,
he appears to have been careless in the matter of
dress, as the following curious reference to him
shows : " The dowblet ye caust mak to Duncane is
now vp at the slot of his breist. Ye wald say
that he wearis his belt as men sayis Mr. George
Buchanan did weare his, the dowblet is growen so
schort."[2]   But while his outward man was thus so
uncourtier-like, his manners and style of speech
were those of one familiar with the most polished
society.   Ronsard, on such a question the best of
judges, was in the habit of saying that Buchanan,
Turnèbe, Muret, and Gouvéa had nothing of the
pedant about them but the cap and gown.[3] And
Sir James Melville, who had himself seen more of
the world than most Scotsmen of his time, says that
Buchanan was " pleasant in conversation, rehearsing
at all occasion moralities short and instructive,
whereof he had abundance, inventing where he
wanted ".[4] According to the witness quoted below,
also, he had " the air and speech of a finished man

---

[1] "Erat austero supercilio, et toto corporis habitu imo moribus hic
noster subagrestis ; sed stylo et sermone perurbanus, quum saepissime,
vel in seriis, multo cum sale jocaretur.   Denique vir quem mirari
facilius quam digne praedicare possis."—David Buchanan, *De Scriptori-
bus Scotis Illustribus.*   (Quoted by Irving, *Memoirs of Buchanan*,
p. 314.)

[2] From a letter written in 1619 by Mr. W. Bowie, tutor to the sons
of Glenfalloch. (Given in Cosmo Innes's *Sketches of Early Scotch
History*, Appendix, pp. 521, 522.)

[3] De Thou, *Histoire Universelle*, vol. viii. p. 665.

[4] Melville, *Memoirs*, p. 250 (ed. Edin. 1735).

of the world, being in the habit of lighting up even his most serious conversation by humorous sallies ". With such a man, though he had now passed his fiftieth year, we may be sure that Mary, keen-witted as she was and delighting in originality of character, would not confine her intercourse to the letter of Livy. Both, as we know, in their own manner, were noted for a certain hardiness of speech ; and we may fancy that there would be many a trial of wits between the old scholar and his brilliant pupil. With the possible exception of her secretary, Mait- land, there was no man in Scotland whose conversa- tion could have been more piquant and refreshing to Mary.

The reading of Livy must have been but inter- mittent, since during the four years before her marriage with Darnley, Mary visited almost every corner of her dominions. As St. Andrews, however, came to be Buchanan's chief residence, he would be frequently brought into contact with the Court, Mary much preferring that town to Edinburgh. That he was on excellent terms, both with the Queen and the ladies who attended on her, is proved by various epigrams, whose tone implies at once the privilege of age and easy intercourse. To Mary Fleming and Mary Beaton he has addressed eight such epigrams, all written in a spirit of mock gallantry, which proves that in spite of his failing health and his new theological bent he still retained something of the old leaven of humanism. To Mary herself he addressed one of the best known and most admired of all his shorter poems—the charm- ing epigram in which he dedicates to her his para- phrase of the Psalms. The second edition of this

paraphrase, as has already been said, was published
by Henri Estienne at Paris in 1566 ;[1] and it was
doubtless mainly with the intention of superintend-
ing its publication that Buchanan about that date
paid a short visit to France.[2] Although the poem
referred to has been many times quoted, it cannot
but have a place in every biography of Buchanan :—

> Nympha, Caledoniae quae nunc feliciter orae
>   Missa per innumeros sceptra tueris avos ;
> Quae sortem antevenis meritis, virtutibus annos,
>   Sexum animis, morum nobilitate genus,
> Accipe (sed facilis) cultu donata Latino
>   Carmina, fatidici nobile regis opus.
> Illa quidem Cirrha procul et Permesside lympha
>   Pene sub Arctoi sidere nata poli :
> Non tamen ausus eram male natum exponere foetum,
>   Ne mihi displiceant quae placuere tibi.
> Nam quod ab ingenio domini sperare nequibant,
>   Debebunt genio forsitan illa tuo.

> "O daughter of a hundred kings
>   That holdest 'neath thy happy sway
> This ancient realm of Caledon ;
>   Whose worth outstrips thy destiny;
> Whose mind thy sex ; whose grace thy peers ;
> Whose virtues leave behind thy years—
> Behold in Roman garb I bring
> The work of Israel's prophet-King.
> Rude is my song as born afar
> From the Muse-haunted founts of Greece,
> Under the frigid Northern star ;
> And but that aught that pleases thee
> Must ne'er displeasing seem to me,
> It had not looked on eyes save mine ;
> Yet such a virtue flows from thine,
> Perchance my sorry child may own
> Some graces that are thine alone !"

---

[1] It should be said that the date of the first edition, also from the
press of Stephens, is not known. This edition bears no date.

[2] That Buchanan visited France at this time is proved by a letter of
Daniel Rogers, given in Ruddiman's general introduction to Buchanan's
Works ; by *Epist.* i. in Ruddiman's edition ; and, lastly, by a letter of
Randolph to the Earl of Leicester, January 29th, 1567.

During the first years after his return to Scotland, Buchanan seems to have held no fixed appointment, though from his close connection with the Court, and the frequent demands the Queen made on his poetical powers, we may regard him as in some measure fulfilling the function of a poet-laureate.   On three several occasions he wrote short Latin masques for the Court—on the return of Mary from France, on her marriage with Darnley, and on the baptism of her son James.[1]   On behalf of Mary herself he also wrote complimentary verses to Elizabeth, which in the light of the subsequent relations of all three now read strangely enough. Thus Mary, sending Elizabeth a heart cut in a diamond, accompanies her present with these lines expressly written by Buchanan :—

> Quod te jampridem fruitur, videt, ac amat absens,
>   Haec pignus cordis gemma, et imago mei est.
> Non est candidior, non est haec purior illo,
>   Quamvis dura magis, non mage firma tamen.

> " The pledge and image of a heart
>   Whose constant joy and pride thou art—
>   This gem is not more fair, more pure,
>   Nor, though more hard, will more endure."

As is well known, such a position in connection with Courts was common enough with scholars during the sixteenth century.   In the enthusiasm for the new studies, it came to be the fashion with princes and other great persons to have attached to them some scholar or scholars, who should make part of the adornment of their Court.   The mere presence of the scholar and his occasional services on State occasions of business or pleasure were supposed to deserve both honour and remuneration.

---

[1] For the manner in which these masques were represented see Joseph Robertson's *Inventories of Queen Mary.*

As scholars were not over-abundant in Scotland, and Buchanan was in simple truth the most celebrated then living in the British Islands, we may believe that Mary, who was not without a genuine interest in literature, was perfectly aware that a subject of Buchanan's distinction lent a certain lustre to her Court.

For Buchanan's general services we learn from two entries in the Treasurer's Accounts for 1562 that he received an annual pension of 250 pounds Scots.[1] As throwing light on the relative value of this amount, it may be mentioned that a few weeks before his murder Rizzio received from Mary and Darnley 200 pounds " for the reparatiounis of his chalmer",[2] and that the authors of the Book of Discipline fixed 200 pounds as the annual salaries of the principals of colleges. From the cases of Hector Boece and the poet Dunbar we gather that it was customary to grant such conditional pensions, pending the promotion of the recipient to some benefice.[3] It would seem that this pension of 250 pounds did not suffice to meet even the modest wants of a celibate scholar. It is certain, at least, that, during all his years in Scotland, Buchanan was constantly in straits for money. Both before and after the dethronement of Mary we have sundry begging epigrams which sufficiently indicate the state of his purse; and the condition of his affairs at his death is one of the commonplaces of literary history. What this chronic state of neediness may imply it is difficult to say. In

---

[1] " Item to Maister George Buchquhannane for his pensioun of the said [Whitsunday] terme [1562]   .   .   .   .   jᶜ xxv li."

[2] Robertson, *Inventories of Queen Mary*, p. xci.

[3] Laing, *Introduction* to Dunbar's Poems, p. 30.

the case of Erasmus, we have the same constant appeals (though in much less dignified fashion than Buchanan's) for pecuniary assistance ; but Erasmus was a person of far more luxurious habits than Buchanan could ever have been. It may be, however, that Buchanan had all the proverbial incapacity of poets for domestic accounts ; and we have it on the authority of Joseph Scaliger that he was a despiser of riches.[1] At all events, he came to hold appointments whose emoluments should have been amply sufficient to meet the wants of a scholar who, like Buchanan, was "something of a Stoick philosopher". Yet it is to be remembered that in this chaotic period of Scottish history the promise to pay by no means implied its fulfilment. In the scramble for wealth that followed the ruin of the old Church, and accompanied the incessant changes in the management of public affairs, the strongest and most unscrupulous laid hands on all the prizes, and diverted the public funds from their proper channels. Of this we have a signal example in the case of one particular gift of Mary to Buchanan, and it may be taken as an illustration of the precarious nature of the incomes of those peaceful persons who depended on grants from the State.

Among the rich spoils of the old Church was the famous Abbey of Crossraguel in Ayrshire, which for forty years before the Reformation had enjoyed the immediate protection of the Earls of Cassillis.[2]

---

[1] In his epitaph on Buchanan, already quoted, he says :—
   " Contemptis opibus, spretis popularibus auris,
        Ventosaeque fugax ambitionis, obis."
[2] For what follows regarding Buchanan's relations to Crossraguel, I am indebted to the *Charters of the Abbey of Crossraguel*, printed for the Ayrshire and Galloway Archæological Association, Edin. 1886. It

Its valuation, as rendered in accordance with a decree of the Privy Council in 1561, was £409, 13s. 4d. per annum.   On the 9th October 1564, Mary conferred on Buchanan, under a gift of Privy Seal, a pension of 500 pounds Scots from the lands of this Abbey, together with the whole temporality of the Abbey as well as the monastic buildings.   It was added in the terms of the gift, " gif the samyn sall not be fundin sufficient and eneuch for zeirlie payment of the said sum of fyve hundred poundis, in that case her majesty assynis to him [Buchanan] sa mekle as he sall lack of the said temporalitie of the readiest teyndis and fruitis of the spiritualitie of the said Abbaye, viz., of the Kirkis of Govane and Kirkoswald belangand thairto".   It thus seemed that, by the generosity of Mary, Buchanan's interests were thenceforth safe.   As the sequel shows, however, the gift proved one of doubtful felicity. Before the month was out in which the gift was granted, we find an order of the Privy Council bearing that Mr. George Buchanan had complained to them that the Earl of Cassillis (the son of Buchanan's former pupil) had entered within the Abbey of Crossraguel since the decease of Abbot Quentin, and would not deliver it to Mr. George Buchanan ; therefore the Lords of Council ordain letters charging the Earl of Cassillis to deliver the same to the said Mr. George within six days, under pain of horning.   The following year, 19th July 1565, the Abbacy was gifted by Mary to Allan Stewart, laird of Cardonald, and in February 1566-7 the Earl of

may be said that till the publication of these charters Buchanan's exact debt to Mary, as " pensionary " of Crossraguel, had never been accurately stated.   It is to be remembered that Buchanan's other pension ceased on the gift of Crossraguel.

Cassillis obtained a lease of the same Abbacy from Mary and Darnley, free from all rent. Thus, counting the Abbot who had succeeded Quintin Kennedy, there were no fewer than four persons interested in the Abbacy. Accordingly, though Buchanan styled himself " Pensionarius de Crossraguel ", the pension was by no means always forthcoming. In April 1568 he disposed of it to Allan Stewart for the yearly payment of 500 pounds ; and in the following January he assigned it to Cassillis, complaining that it had been " restand owand " to him for several years past. By this assignation the Earl agreed to pay to Buchanan the sum of 980 marks. On the way in which Cassillis kept his bargain we have a significant commentary in a letter addressed to him by the Earl of Mar so late as the 5th July 1572. In this letter Mar begs him to " remember Maister George Buchannan, and to bring with you sumquhat for his satisfaction of his pension ". Finally, in 1573, Buchanan sold his pension to the laird of Bargany for the annual sum of 400 pounds. Whether Bargany met his claim more satisfactorily than Cassillis is not recorded.

As illustrating the easy terms on which Buchanan must have stood with Mary, and as showing at the same time the impecuniosity of which we have spoken, the following two epigrams may be taken as examples. The lines are supposed to be accompanied by copies of verses :—

AD MARIAM SCOTIAE REGINAM.

Do quod adest : opto quod abest tibi : dona darentur
   Aurea, sors animo si foret aequa meo.
Hoc leve si credis, paribus me ulciscere donis :
   Et quod abest, opta tu mihi : da quod adest.

" I give you what I have,
    I wish you what you lack ;
And weightier were my gift
    Were fortune at my back.

Perchance you think I jest ?
    A like jest then I crave :
Wish for me what I lack,
    And give me what you have."

AD EANDEM.

Invida ne veterem tollant oblivia morem,
    Haec tibi pro xenio carmina pauca damus
Sunt mala; sed si vis, poterunt divina videri;
    Nam nunc quod magno venditur ære bonum est.

" A good old custom should not cease ;
    Receive these songs, then, as of old.
Poor stuff ?   But good or bad is now
    Just what things fetch in weight of gold."

While Buchanan was on this excellent footing
with Mary, he nevertheless distinctly showed on
what side his sympathies lay on the questions at
issue between her and the Protestant party.   From
1563 he sat for four successive years as a member of
the General Assembly of the Reformed Church.   In
1563 he was one of the Commissioners appointed
to revise the Book of Discipline.   In 1564, along
with Knox and others, he made one of the Com-
mitee " to confer about the causes appertaining to
the 'jurisdiction of the Kirk, and to report their
judgment to the next convention".   In 1565, he
and five others " were ordained to convene and sit
from six till eight in the morning, to decide questions propounded or to be propounded, and to report
their decision to the Assembly " ; and in 1566 he
made one of a similar commission.   It is well
known that Mary's special aversion was the General
Assembly, at which her government was discussed
with a frankness that must have contrasted pain-

fully with the subservience of French parliaments. That Buchanan, therefore, could thus take such a prominent part in these assemblies, and yet remain in friendly understanding with Mary, is conclusive proof that he stood on an entirely different footing in the country from Knox and the ministers of the Congregation. They were reformers, and nothing else. Buchanan approved of the same cause ; but he had other interests, and the memory of a life behind him which made genial intercourse possible with those who differed most widely from himself on the deepest questions.

That Buchanan was also on intimate relations with Mary's brother, the Earl of Moray, is proved by several circumstances. To him, also, he addresses begging epigrams in the same tone of mingled respect and familiarity with which he addresses Mary. In all probability it is to some period before 1567 that these epigrams are to be referred.

AD JACOBUM MORAVIAE COMITEM.

Si magis est, ut Christus ait, donare beatum,
    Quam de munifica dona referre manu :
Aspice quam foveam tibi : sis ut dando beatus,
    Non renuo fieri, te tribuente, miser.

> " It is more blest, saith Holy Writ,
>   To give than to receive ;
> How great, then, is your debt to me,
>   Who take whate'er you give ! "

AD EUNDEM.

Sera, Jacobe, quidem sunt, parvaque munera nostra :
    Hac in re vitium si quod inesse putas,
Ne sectare meam, sed contra corrige culpam,
    Et cito, sed larga munera redde manu.

> " Niggard and laggard came my gift, you say,
>   Then must I deem your duty clear indeed ;
> By good example this my fault amend :
>   Let thy gift come with bounty and with speed."

To Moray, also, he dedicated his *Franciscanus* in its completed form, and in terms which prove that he shared with the Protestant leaders their admiration of him. Having described the origin of the satire, and the persecution to which it had subjected him, he proceeds : " At length, after twenty-four[1] years of exile, when, by the consent of the Scottish nobility, the tyranny of the friars had been suppressed, I began to retouch my Satire, undertaken at the command of the King, and interrupted by the vicissitudes of public affairs, and the untowardness of my own. As soon as my circumstances permitted me to complete it, I determined to give it to the world under your name in preference to that of any one else, as the one man who above all others has done most to clear the country of these monsters—a work you performed with such vigour that you have made simple reality of those fables which the Greeks, the most ingenious and instructed of peoples, relate of Hercules in the wildest flights of their fancy. Moreover, by your notable virtue, you have so effectually restored simple primitive religion, that, now the seeming impossibility has been accomplished, our delight is not less than our admiration. Let me add that it seemed to me but just that the debt I left unpaid to your father, I should, though somewhat late in the day, make good to the son who walks so heedfully in that father's steps ; and this I trust I have now done in such wise that the years will seem to you to have brought a goodly interest." In 1566, Moray acknowledged Buchanan's attentions by appointing him to a post for which his training

---

[1] This statement is chronologically not quite accurate.

peculiarly fitted him. As Commendator of the Priory of St. Andrews, Moray had the right of nominating to the principalship of the College of St. Leonard; and a vacancy occurring in that year, he appointed Buchanan.[1] Of Buchanan's relations with St. Andrews University an account will be given in another place.

Till the murder of Darnley in 1567 Buchanan continued on the same friendly footing with Mary and the Protestant party alike. That he did not take the same view of the Darnley marriage as Moray and Knox is conclusively proved by the poems he wrote in its celebration, as well as by some lines he has addressed to Darnley himself. The objection of Moray and Knox to the marriage was that it threatened the newly established religion. Buchanan would certainly have considered it a national misfortune had the old religion been restored; yet it cannot be said of him, as of Knox, that he lived and moved in the questions that divided the two Churches. Moreover, there was a reason, which must have had a weight of its own in determining the view he took of Mary's second marriage. Darnley was the son of the head of the clan of Lennox, and in his exaltation to the throne Buchanan would see the glorification of the clan to which he himself belonged. Buchanan would have been no good Scotsman had he not been susceptible to such feelings, and Buchanan was a Scotsman to the core. Of the Court poem he wrote on the occasion it would be easy to make too much. Such poems of the Latinists of the sixteenth century are as purely official as the dresses and decora-

[1] *Sibbaldi Comment. in Vitam Buchanani*, p. 65.

N

tions made to order by the Court tradesmen.[1]   In
the poem, however, which he addressed to Darnley
himself, it may be supposed that he gave expression to his desires if not to his convictions.   It
was written in January 1566 or 1567; if in the
latter year, the prayer with which it concludes
received a terrible commentary a month later in
the tragedy of the Kirk of Field.   All men,
says Buchanan, pour forth their own prayers at
the beginning of a new year.   The farmer implores
a good harvest, the soldier active service, the mer-
chant peace.   Some pray for riches, some for power,
some for glory.   For his [Buchanan's] part, he has
but one boon to ask of Heaven—that Darnley may
be preserved.   "With thy safety," he concludes,
"all happiness must follow to thy kingdom."[2]   The
prayer is a singular one, as we now estimate
Darnley; but in his History also Buchanan has no
hard words to say of him, though he nowhere seeks
to credit him with virtues he did not possess.

Such being Buchanan's attitude towards the
marriage of Mary and Darnley, and his general
relations with the Court, it must be considered
as a singular testimony to his estimation in the
country that Knox, then at the height of his
antagonism to Mary, could in 1566 write the following sentence: "That notable man, Mr. George
Bucquhanane, remains to this day in the year of
God 1566 years, to the glory of God, to the great

---

[1] This fact cannot be too strongly insisted on with reference to the
Latin poets of the sixteenth century.   Even Mr. Joseph Robertson (*Inventories of Queen Mary*, xxxvi) takes Buchanan's lines on Darnley quite
seriously.

[2]   . . . quoniam te sospite nobis
        Succedent regno prospera cuncta tuo.

honour of the nation, and to the comfort of them that delyt in letters and virtue."[1]   As Knox could not have been ignorant of Buchanan's close connection with the Court since his return to Scotland, the sentence just quoted clearly proves that Buchanan's position in the country was peculiar to himself—that a liberty of thought and action was allowed him which the extreme representatives of either party in the State would have allowed to no other.   The most detestable of all things in the eyes of Knox was a lukewarm professor.   We may be sure, therefore, that had there been the faintest suggestion of trimming on the part of Buchanan the above sentence would never have been written.

The last occasion on which we find Buchanan in friendly relations with Mary was on the baptism of James VI. in December 1566.   As poet-laureate of the Court, he wrote the masque played at the supper that followed the celebration of the ceremony.   This is a singularly jejune performance, consisting only of some sixty lines, made up of the speeches of bands of satyrs, nereids, naiads, fauns, and oreads.   In succession they approach the young king and his mother, and offer their homage in the strain of high-flown flattery then used towards princes. As the piece, however, would afford ample scope for all manner of fantastic dresses, it doubtless very well served the purpose for which it was produced.[2]

---

[1] Knox, *History of the Reformation.*

[2] Mr. Joseph Robertson (*Inventories of Queen Mary*, lxxxvi) gives the following account of the performance of this masque of Buchanan : "The masque for the grand banquet at the Prince's baptism at Stirling in December 1566, was arranged, it would seem, by Buchanan, who supplied the Latin verses, and by Bastien Pagez, a French valet of the Queen's chamber, who devised the machinery. When the dishes were to be brought in, they were placed upon a table so constructed, that it

It may be deemed significant that the father of
the young prince is not once mentioned by any of
the speakers.   The omission may, of course, mean
nothing more than that Darnley did not take rank
with the mother and son; yet though Buchanan,
as principal of St. Leonard's, was not a resident at
Court, he must have heard of the strained relations
between Mary and her husband.   Buchanan afterwards learned and related in his History that
Darnley was actually in Stirling Castle at the time,
and yet was not present at the ceremony of his
son's baptism.

But the most noteworthy of all Buchanan's productions addressed to Mary before the tragedy of
the Kirk of Field is the poem he wrote on the birth
of James VI. in 1566.   Nominally addressed to the
infant prince, it is clearly for Mary's eyes it is
meant; and if we are to judge fairly of Buchanan's
subsequent feelings towards her, this poem must

seemed to move through the great hall of its own accord, accompanied
by musicians in female attire, singing songs, and playing upon instruments.   A procession of Rural Gods marched before, each groupe as it
passed the dais reciting a few lines of Latin.   The Satyrs, the Naiads,
and the Oreads, addressed the Prince; the Nereids and the Fauns
turned their speech to the Queen:

> ' Virtute, ingenio, Regina, et munere formae
>   Felicibus felicior majoribus,
> Conjugii fructu sed felicissima, cujus,
>   Legati honorant exteri cunabula:
> Rustica quem donis reverentur Numina, silvis
>   Satyri relictis, Najadesque fontibus.'

The Satyrs, as we learn from an eye-witness, not content with playing
the part assigned to them, chose to wag their long tails, in the hope, no
doubt, of creating a laugh among their companions in the hall.   But the
retainers of the English ambassador fancying that it was done in their
derision (there must have been Kentishmen among them), were so
incensed that the Queen and the ambassador had difficulty in appeasing
their wrath.   The masque, thus interrupted, was followed by a discharge of fireworks from a mimic fortress, the possession of which was
contested by motley bands of Moors, Highlanders, Centaurs, Lanz-
knechts, and Fiends.''

be read in connection with the terrible *Detectio*.
From this poem it distinctly appears that Buchanan
made no secret from Mary of his opinions as to
the true relations in which the prince stands to
his people. It is as distinctly implied here as
in the *Baptistes* and the *De Jure Regni* that kings
exist by the will and for the good of the people;
and in the concluding lines he hints neither more
nor less directly than in the *De Jure Regni* that the
death of tyrants is well-pleasing in the sight of God
—an opinion, indeed, which Buchanan shared with
Erasmus and many of the most eminent humanists.
In certain of its passages, also, it is impossible not
to see that a delicate animadversion is implied both
on Mary's private conduct and her private policy.
In short, Buchanan's subsequent attitude towards
Mary is distinctly implied in this poem; and the
tragic events of the next few months were alone
needed to convert a delicate rebuke into the fierce
denunciation of the *Detectio*.

The opening lines of the poem admirably show
what hopes Buchanan, with all patriotic Scotsmen,
based on the birth of James. For all such it was
the most auspicious event that could have happened
to Scotland, as they saw in it the surest promise
of that peaceful and honourable union with England
which every year showed to be more absolutely
necessary. "Grow and be strong, long-wished-for
boy, happy pledge for thy country's weal, to whom
ancient bards have promised the peaceful glories of
the golden age. And thou, happy Britain, joyfully
lift up thy head, thou so often stricken by foreign
foes, so often on ruin's brink from the swords of thy
own children; bind thy hair with olive, and repair

thy ruined homes, for the stars now promise thee
eternal peace.   Now Saxon oppresseth not Scot, nor
Scot Saxon, nor stain their swords with the blood of
their kindred, nor make the cities of the other their
prey.   They whose delight was mutual war now
join right hands ·in peace.   And ye, happy parents
of this happy child, train him from his tenderest
years to virtue and justice.   Let piety be his companion from the cradle, moulding his thoughts and
growing with his years ! "   As the ship answers the
helm, the poet proceeds, so the people direct their
steps by the example of their prince.   Prisons, and
harsh laws, the threats of death, fill a people with
terror ; but true virtue in their king and reverence
for authority are of more avail to win them to good.
What the sword cannot compel, love will gladly yield.
The people vie with their prince in mutual service,
love when they see they are loved, and obey as their
lord him whom they may freely obey.   If the prince
but relax the reins, of their own accord the people
draw them tight, and the yoke they reject when
thrust on them, if left to themselves they demand.
On the other hand, the true king and father of his
people imposes no laws which he himself is not
willing to obey.   In food, and dress, and lodging he
sets the example of moderation.   In love, also, he
is chastity itself.   Who would wear silk, if the
prince were content with wool ?   Who would find
fault with the marriage-law if the ruler were the
first to submit to it ?   Who would be intemperate,
if the king were not ?   But the concluding lines
of the poem must be given in Buchanan's own
words, as they may be regarded as a brief summary
of the teaching of the *De Jure Regni* :—

Scilicet humano generi natura benigni
Nil dedit, aut tribuet moderato Principe majus,
In quo vera Dei vivensque elucet imago.
Hanc seu Rex vitiis contaminet ipse pudendis,
Sive alius ferro violet vel fraude, severas
Sacrilego Deus ipse petet de sanguine poenas,
Contemtumque sui simulacri haud linquet inultum.
Sic Nero crudelis, sic Flavius ultimus, et qui
Imperio Siculas urbes tenuere cruento,
Effigiem foedare Dei exitialibus ausi
Flagitiis, ipsa periere a stirpe recisi.
Sic qui se justi macularunt sanguine Servi,
Et qui legitimos ferro flammaque petivit
Rectores patriae Catilina nefarius, acti
In furias misero vix tandem funere vitam
Invisam posuere, ignominiaque perenni
Foedavere suam ventura in secula gentem.

" In good sooth, nature hath never given and never will give a greater boon to man than a prince who is moderate in all things, in whom shines the true and living image of God. Whether the King himself defile this image by his own vice, or another violate it by force or fraud, God Himself will exact stern punishment for the sacrilege, nor will leave unavenged the slighted exemplar of himself. So was it that Nero, and Domitian, and the Dionysii, who dared by their misdeeds to pollute God's own likeness, were cut off root and branch. So the slayers of Servius Tullius, and the impious Catiline, who pursued the lawful rulers of his country with fire and sword, goaded to madness, died a wretched death, and to all time brought dishonour on their race."

CHAPTER XIV.

WE have seen that in December 1566 Buchanan wrote the Court masque for the festivities that followed the baptism of James VI. This, as has been said, was the last occasion on which we find Buchanan on friendly terms with Mary. However we may regard the events of the next few months, they at least made impossible any compromise between the two parties in the State; and they brought to direct issue which of the two, Catholic or Protestant, was to fashion the destinies of Scotland. These events may be told in one sentence. On the 9th of February 1567 Darnley was murdered in the Kirk of Field; on the 15th of May Mary married Bothwell; in June she was imprisoned in Lochleven; and in May of the next year she was a fugitive in England. By the part which Buchanan took in this revolution he has been made the object of the most vehement denunciation by all the champions of Mary from his own day to the present. As it was through him more than any other that the charges against Mary were made known to Europe, it has been the invariable custom of all who have believed in her innocence to make abuse of Buchanan an essential part of their case.

---

[1] *Detectio Mariae Reginae Scotorum.*

They represent him as a time-server, who, so long as Mary had it in her power to do him any favour, wrote beautiful poems in her honour, and danced attendance on her Court. When the hour of her misfortune came he deserted her for the side of her enemies, and wrote a malignant libel which did more to ruin her reputation in the eyes of Europe than all the efforts of her other enemies together. For writers of this class Buchanan is, in truth, only worthy of notice as the author of the *Detectio*, and the sycophant and afterwards the reviler of Mary. It is curious that in his Life written or inspired by himself he has not considered it worth while to mention that he wrote the *Detectio*, or that he accompanied the Commissioners who put the case against Mary before Elizabeth. His silence is certainly not due to any regret or shame for the part he played; for in his History he has stated with added emphasis every charge brought against her in the *Detectio*, and thus confidently left it to posterity to judge of his good faith and the truth of his indictment. As his good name, however, has seriously suffered at the hands of successive generations of special pleaders, whose sole concern has been to vindicate Mary at all costs, it is necessary to speak at greater length of this episode than it really deserves. And it may be said in passing that the writers who have thus denounced Buchanan have shown an ignorance of the facts of his life, of the scope and significance of his work, of his relations with certain of the finest spirits of the time,[1]

---

[1] These relations will be further illustrated in the chapter on Buchanan's Correspondence.

only to be justified by their praiseworthy desire to say all that can be said for the most interesting and most unhappy of women.[1]

The true relations of Buchanan to Mary have already been stated; but the charges brought against him of being first her pensioner and flatterer, and afterwards her libeller, have been so pertinaciously repeated that it is as well they should again be put before the reader.[2] The only so-called pension which Buchanan received from Mary was that from the Abbey of Crossraguel, and it has been seen that it brought to him as much worry and vexation as profit.[3] If Mary had seriously exerted herself, it is possible that the pension might have proved a more substantial boon. Moreover, it can hardly be denied that one of the most brilliant scholars in Europe, and beyond a doubt one of the great men of the age, in acting as classical tutor to Mary, and doing other services for which he was better fitted than any one else in her kingdom, had a distinct claim on her liberality which makes it preposterous to speak of him as her mere pensioner. The truth is, also, that whatever may have been Mary's generosity, Buchanan was in actual straits while she was in power.

Buchanan has been styled a flatterer and a time-server because in certain poems he has spoken of Mary in terms which flagrantly contradict what

[1] Thus Mr. Hosack actually confounds the *Detectio* with the *Actio.* Moreover, if one thing be more certain than another, it is that the *Actio* was not written by Buchanan.—Hosack, *Mary Stewart* (1888), p. 15. Cf. p. 213 (below).

[2] "An accomplished Latin scholar, Buchanan was without doubt the most venal and unscrupulous of men."—Hosack, p. 17. Other writers of the type of Mr. Hosack speak in the same strain.

[3] As Dr. Dickson has pointed out to me, the pension of 250 pounds would cease when that from Crossraguel Abbey was conferred. Cf. p. 186 (above).

he afterwards said of her in her misfortune. It has already been more than once remarked that it would be absurd to take as genuine expressions of opinion the panegyrics of the Latin poets of the Renaissance. We have seen how the University of Paris regarded its self-imposed function of addressing princes in terms of ill-deserved eulogy. Lord Bacon, himself an adept in the art, has told us what such panegyric meant in his day. "Some praises," he says, "come of good wishes, and respects, which is a form due in civility to kings and great persons. *Laudando præcipere*; when by telling men what they are, they represent to them what they should be."[1] It is assuredly in the light of these remarks of Bacon that we must understand Buchanan when he praises Mary, and de l'Hôpital when he praises Catharine de Medici and the Cardinal Lorraine.

But by his entire line of action previous to the dethronement of Mary, Buchanan left her in no manner of doubt as to the side he took in her contests with the reforming party. He took his place year after year in the General Assembly, and thus identified himself with a body which sought to traverse her policy at every step. He published his *Franciscanus*, one of the bitterest satires of the age on the religion which she professed, and dedicated it with a laudatory preface to her brother the Earl of Moray, whom at no time she regarded with much affection. And, finally, he won the unqualified approval of the most determined of all her opponents, Knox, the very last man in the world who would approve any time-serving compromise

[1] *Essays* : Of Praise.

with Papistry. It is difficult, therefore, to see what
more Buchanan could have done to show that whatever his relations to Mary, he retained all through
perfect mental independence and freedom of action.
It is indeed only utter ignorance of the facts of his
life, and the necessities of a precarious argument,
that could present Buchanan as the venal and
supple-kneed courtier. Whatever may have been
his faults or weaknesses, greed of money or place,
or cringing subservience to authority, were certainly
not amongst them. Again and again throughout
his life, in Scotland, in France, and in Portugal, he
injured his prospects and risked his safety by the
uncompromising frankness of his speech. As far as
his attitude towards the policy and religion of Mary
was concerned, it was that of antagonism from
the date of his return to Scotland till the date of
his death. That he was on good terms with Mary
till the murder of Darnley is to the credit of both,
since both understood that on the most important
questions that touch man's welfare each deliberately
sought to undo the work of the other.

From the murder of Darnley Buchanan's friendly
feeling for Mary was changed to indignation and
contempt, and thenceforward he took his place
among the most formidable of her enemies. It is
his share in the proceedings taken against her by
the insurgent party under Moray that has brought
down on him the obloquy of her champions from
that day to this. Yet when all he said and did is
temperately considered, nothing can be clearer than
that, holding the political and religious views he did,
he could hardly have acted otherwise as a patriot
and man of honour. In justifying the conduct of

Buchanan it will not be necessary to defame Mary. Whether she was guilty or not, Buchanan's good faith in either case must be perfectly manifest to every one but a partisan.

After Mary's marriage with Bothwell, it is unquestionable that the general conviction, not only in Scotland, but in England and Europe, was that she had her own share in the murder of her late husband. Her own ambassador in France gave her plainly enough to understand what men thought of her in that country; but a more interesting testimony than that of her ambassador Beaton is found in a Latin poem by one who stands as the highest type of civic virtue in the sixteenth century, the great Chancellor de l'Hôpital. L'Hôpital, it will be remembered, was one of the multitude of poets who, along with Buchanan, celebrated the youthful charm of Mary on her marriage with the Dauphin Francis. "The murder of Darnley," says Ste. Beuve,[1]

---

[1] Ste. Beuve, *Causeries*, 11 août 1851. This poem of De l'Hôpital was not to be found in any edition of his works at my disposal. I am indebted for a copy of it to M. Manget of the Lycée, Versailles, who found it in an edition of l'Hôpital published at Amsterdam in 1732. The poem is entitled *In Mortem Regis Scotiae*. I give the lines that specially refer to Mary. The poet has been speaking of the various inhuman crimes committed during his century, and he proceeds :—

"En aliud ! Juveni modo quae regina marito
Nupserat, et sobolem formosam mater alebat,
Illum ipsum vesana novis oppressit inermem
Artibus. At medium jam nox confecerat orbem,
Versa repente domus, subjecto fulgure et igni
Quo misere casu ambusti regalibus omnes
Qui tectis suberant, attritaque membra jacentum,
Exanimum Regis, nudum et sine vulnere corpus
Ad primum lapidem (flammae vis tanta) repertum est.
O diros hominum mores ! O tempora ! Quid non
Laesus amor spretis naturae legibus audet ?
Talia cum reges prospectant, posse tueri
Praesidiis hominum sperent se tempore nullo.
Non vis, non humana potest prudentia casus
Diffugere innumeros quibus est obnoxia vita.
Ergo communes cum sint hoc tempore casus,

"echoed beyond the seas; l'Hôpital, that representative of the human conscience during a fright-
ful age, heard in his country-house of the crime
(*égarement*) of her whose first marriage and early
grace he had celebrated; he gave solemn expression
to his indignation in a new piece of Latin verse, in
which he recounts the horrors of that fatal night,
and does not shrink from naming the wife and
young mother as the murderer of the father of the
child still at her breast." When such was the
general impression in Catholic France, we may judge
how Mary must have been regarded in Scotland,
and, above all, among those of her subjects who had
all along held that, alike by her religion and entire
manner of life, she was fast in the bonds of iniquity.
Among men of this type there can be no doubt
whatever that there was absolute certainty that
Mary was guilty of her husband's murder. But
these were the men with whom Buchanan was in
daily contact. Everything considered, therefore, it
would be manifestly unjust to question Buchanan's
good faith if he shared the conviction of those
whom, with all their excesses, we are bound to consider the saving element in the country.

But we have no reason to suppose that Buchanan
was convinced of Mary's guilt before a discovery
was made which of necessity must have put all his
doubts to rest. On the 20th of June, four months
after Darnley's murder, the famous Casket Letters
came into the hands of the Earl of Morton. The
recent discovery of the deposition made by Morton

Quumque premat reges eadem fortuna superbos,
Stulta sui fuerit vel inanis cura tuendi,
Adversante Deo, rumpit qui stamina vitae
Arbitrioque suo longos producit in annos."

before the English Commissioners appointed by
Elizabeth to sit on Mary's case has shed the fullest
light on the history of these letters.[1] On the day
following the seizure of the casket, the letters and
poems it contained were carefully scrutinised in the
presence of the Earls of Morton, Mar, Glencairn,
Lords Home, Semple, Sanquhar, the Master of
Grahame, Maitland of Lethington, and the Laird of
Tullibardine. Among these witnesses several were
Catholics, and others were known to be the staunch
friends of Mary; and it is they to whom Morton
refers in his deposition as evidence for the genuineness of the letters. Of this discovery, and the conclusive attestation to its genuineness, Buchanan,
from his close connection with the leading men in
the country, must have heard almost immediately.
Under these circumstances, can we wonder that
Buchanan should have been convinced of the
Queen's guilt, proved as it was by the testimony of
her best friends?

The month following the seizure of the casket
letters, the General Assembly met in Edinburgh,
and Buchanan for the first time acted in the
capacity of Moderator. The doings of the Queen
formed the great theme of discussion, and so stern
was the feeling against her, that but for the inter-
ference of Throgmorton, the English ambassador, it
seemed likely that the Assembly would recommend
sentence of death as the only sufficient punishment of

---

[1] For the details of this discovery see Henderson's *The Casket Letters
and Mary Queen of Scots* (Adam and Charles Black, 1890). Morton's
deposition disposes of the strongest argument against the genuineness of
the letters, viz., that Morton may have forged or tampered with them
between the date of the casket's falling into his hands and his delivery
of it to Moray—an interval of fifteen months. As the controversy now
stands, the probabilities are greatly in favour of the genuineness of the
letters ; and Maitland comes worst out of the whole case.

her crimes.[1]   After violent debate, it was at length
resolved that she should be called upon to demit the
crown in favour of her son.   As the leaders of the
Church acted at this time in the closest union
with the Protestant lords, in all likelihood these
proceedings of the Assembly are in part to be
explained by their privacy to the secret of the
casket letters.

In October 1568 Moray proceeded to York to
lay before the Commissioners of Elizabeth the
indictment against Mary. He took with him the
Earl of Morton, the Bishop of Orkney, Lord Lind-
say, and the Commendator of Dunfermline, as the
Commissioners for Scotland ; and added, as assistants
to these, Maitland, James Makgill, and Buchanan.
It must certainly be regarded as a tribute to the
character and high reputation of Buchanan that he,
a simple scholar, was chosen to make one of a body
charged with such weighty responsibilities.

Of the tedious and tortuous proceedings of the
Commissioners, first at York and afterwards at
Westminster, it is unnecessary here to give any
detailed account. The only question with which
we are concerned is, whether Buchanan, as a man
of honour, was in his place as an aider in these proceedings against his Queen. The charges which
Moray and his colleagues brought against Mary
were contained in the casket letters, and in a
document known as the Book of Articles, in which
the case against her was set down in a formal
indictment.   Until the recent discovery of the
original Book of Articles, it was generally supposed
that this document was the famous *Detectio,* written

---

[1] Tytler, *History of Scotland,* vol. iii. chap. viii.

by Buchanan himself.[1] As the veritable Book of Articles was written in Scots, and in legal form, it is unlikely that Buchanan had any hand in drawing it up. But whoever drew it up, the men responsible for its contents were Moray, Morton, and Lethington.[2] It is on their evidence that the indictment is based, and on their oath that it is authenticated. Of the charges enumerated in the Book of Articles, Buchanan could have known nothing from personal experience. His position, therefore, was this. Like all men of his way of thinking in politics and religion, he was disposed by the general course of events to believe that Mary was guilty; but when this presumption was supported by direct evidence sworn to by her friends and foes alike, it was no longer possible for him to resist the conviction of the Queen's guilt. This being the case, it is clear that, as a Protestant and a lover of his country, he was bound to do all in his power to prevent her return to the throne. He must have thought, and was certainly justified in thinking, that to restore to her throne a woman capable of the crimes laid to her charge, would be an outrage on society which no possible consideration of loyalty could justify. Personal feeling, also, must have intensified his indignation against her as a public enemy. There is no reason to believe that Buchanan had much affection for Darnley, yet as the

---

[1] This document was found among the Hopetoun Manuscripts, and published by Hosack in his *Mary Queen of Scots and her Accusers*. There seems no reason to doubt that it is the original Book of Articles laid before the English Commissioners. It may be said that Camden clearly distinguishes between Buchanan's *Detectio* and the Book of Articles.— *History of Elizabeth* (London, 1675), pp. 116, 117.

[2] Anderson's *Collections*: "The Copie of a Letter written by one in London to his Friend, concerning the Credit of the late published Detection of the Doynges of the Ladie Mary of Scotland," vol. ii. pp. 261-267.

O

head of his own clan, the fact that he had been the victim could not but have its own share in whetting the rhetoric of the *Detectio*. Moreover, the very youth and beauty of Mary (she was only twenty-five at the murder of her husband), to which Buchanan as a poet must have been more susceptible than most men, must, in the light in which he now regarded her, have added a certain loathing to his wrath, which need hardly excite our wonder. Such, then, is the simple account of Buchanan's attitude towards Mary after the murder of Darnley. It will be seen that he is equally justified whether she be regarded as innocent or guilty. If she were innocent, the odium must lie at the door of the "practical politicians"—a race of men, it must be admitted, who, in all ages, have had a conscience and a moral law peculiar to themselves.

It has been said that the Book of Articles was distinct from the *Detectio*, and that it, and not the *Detectio*, contained the original list of charges brought against Mary and laid before the English Commissioners. Whether the *Detectio*, in the form in which we have it, was also laid before them, it is difficult to determine. If we may believe an anonymous writer, who seems to speak from special information, in all probability it was.[1] "The book itself" (meaning the *Detectio*), says the writer, "was written by hym, not as of hymself nor in his own name, but according to the instructions to him given by common conference of the Lordes of the Privie Counsel of Scotland, by hym onely for hys learning penned, but by them the Mater ministred, the book ouerseen and allowed, and exhibited by them as Mater

---

[1] Anderson's *Collections*, vol. ii. p. 261.

that they have offered and do continue in offering
to stand to and justifie before our Soveraigne Lady,
or her Highnesses Commissioners in that behalf
apointed." The same writer says that a copy of
the *Detectio* was found in " one of the Duke of
Norfolk's men's houses " after that nobleman's arrest.
As Norfolk was arrested in October 1569, the
Detectio must at least have been in circulation long
before its publication. The form in which it is cast
would also lead us to believe that it was expressly
written to be submitted to the Commissioners, as
in the opening sentence the writer formally
addresses Elizabeth as if in her presence.[1]

The matter of the *Detectio*, we have seen, is
almost exclusively drawn from the Book of Articles;
but in Buchanan's production, it is presented with
a literary force and skill, and penetrated with a
passion, that transform it into a deadly indictment.
To the reader of the present day its tone must
hardly appear such as becomes an arraignment of a
sovereign, however great her crimes. But it would
be utterly uncritical to judge this performance by
present canons of taste and good feeling. The
Detectio, like all Buchanan's literary work, must be
judged by the standard it is necessary to apply to
all the productions of humanism. We have seen
how, in the case of his poetry—of his erotic verses,
his translation of the Psalms, his didactic poem of
the *Sphere*—his choice of subject and manner of
treatment were determined by the conditions of his
age. The *Detectio*, also, to be properly understood,
and to receive its due place in our final estimate of
Buchanan, must be read in the light of the amazing

[1] Yet in the *Detectio* Moray is spoken of as dead.

controversial literature of the humanists. A writer, who speaks with the highest authority on the learned literature of the sixteenth century, thus marks the traditions of humanism in its mode of conducting controversy: " It is impossible to defend, and difficult to excuse, the scurrility with which Dolet speaks of the greatest scholar and the foremost man of letters of his age (Erasmus). All that can be said in extenuation is, that scurrility of this kind was a common practice of the literary men of the day in writing of their opponents, that we find it in men distinguished for their ability, learning, and virtue, and that, violent as the language of Dolet appears, it is far less violent, far less scurrilous, and far less unseemly, than that which Julius Cæsar Scaliger used of the same great man, or that which Luther applied to Henry VIII. and his other opponents, whilst it is absolutely moderate in comparison with the language of Filelfo, of Poggio, and of Valla."[1] It is in view of these controversial methods of the humanists that we have also to judge one greater than Buchanan. Milton himself, in his controversial writings, has exhibited these ill-manners of the humanists in far greater degree, and certainly with far less provocation, than Buchanan in any invectives he has left us.[2]

It is quite in the spirit of humanism, therefore, that Buchanan wrote his *Detectio*. The matter was not his own; but, called on by Moray and his associates to present it in literary form, he did so in the most approved fashion of his contemporaries.

[1] Christie, *Life of Etienne Dolet*, p. 201.
[2] Those who would judge Milton and Buchanan aright in this matter should read the controversial pamphlets of Melanchthon and Sir Thomas More, two of the most finely-touched spirits the world has known.

The subject was one, indeed, after the humanist's own heart, commanding, as it did, the interest of Europe, and offering the most splendid scope for all the turns of Ciceronian rhetoric. Buchanan wrote it, therefore, in the full consciousness that his reputation as a scholar was in question. How he succeeded, the obloquy of three centuries on the part of Mary's advocates is the most significant commentary. It was published in London in 1571, accompanied by Latin translations of three of the casket letters, and a pamphlet entitled *Actio contra Mariam Scotorum Reginam*.[1] By some writers this pamphlet has also been attributed to Buchanan. But no one acquainted with his writings could for a moment imagine it to be his. It goes over exactly the same ground as the *Detectio*, in the most rambling fashion, and in a spirit compared with which Buchanan's philippic is strikingly judicial. Moreover, its feeble rhetoric and inconsequent logic have not the remotest suggestion of the masculine grasp and nervous energy of Buchanan.[2] Immediately afterwards appeared a translation of the *Detectio* into Scots, executed by an Englishman with imperfect knowledge of the dialect ; and in 1572 a Scots version was published at St. Andrews. This last translation has been ascribed, perhaps erroneously, to Buchanan himself. In certain passages the translator has missed the meaning of the original Latin, which could hardly

---

[1] Mr. Henderson (*The Casket Letters*, p. 46) has given an accurate account of the first edition of the *Detectio* and the various subsequent translations.

[2] Malcolm Laing, *History of Scotland*, vol. iii. pp. 247 *et seq.*, conclusively showed by external evidence that the *Actio* could not have been written by Buchanan. He shows that in all probability it was written by Dr. Thomas Wilson.

have happened had Buchanan himself been the translator.[1] In February 1573 a French translation appeared, ostensibly published at Edinburgh, but in reality at Rochelle by the Huguenots. Ultimately, Buchanan embodied the *Detectio* almost entire in his History, and thus pledged his faith to posterity for the truth of its statements. That he should have done so, in the full knowledge that these statements were mere libellous falsehoods, is so utterly inconsistent with the whole strain of his life and character, that to maintain it can be only the desperate shift of the blindest partisanship.[2]

The full title of the *Detectio* will sufficiently explain its character and scope. It is as follows : "De Maria Scotorum Regina, totaque ejus contra Regem conjuratione, foedo cum Bothuelio adulterio, nefaria in maritum crudelitate et rabie, horrendo insuper et deterrimo ejusdem parricidio, plena, et tragica plane Historia." As Malcolm Laing pointed out, this most unclassical title could hardly have been the work of Buchanan. The title of the Scots translation is as follows : "Ane Detectioun of the Duinges of Marie, Quene of Scottes, touchand the murder of hir husband, and hir conspiracie, adulterie, and pretensed mariage with the Erle Bothwell ; and ane Defence of the trew Lordis, mainteineris of the Kingis gracis, actioun and authoritie." It is, of course, impossible to present a summary of the *Detectio*, as it consists simply of a

---

[1] Ruddiman pointed this out, and was of opinion that Buchanan was not the translator. At the same time, the style of the translation appears to be exactly that of Buchanan's *Admonition* and *Chamaeleon*.

[2] On the supposition that the casket letters were forged, a forger had to be found, and at one time Buchanan, among others, was suggested. But apart from the absurdity of such a suggestion, as the controversy now stands, it is irrelevant.

long series of accusations whose only connection is
chronological.   We give the opening paragraph of
the Scots translation :—

"Quhairas of Thingis judiciallie determinit within ony Dominioun, to have Accompt demandit be
Strangeris, is to sic as be not subject to forane
Jurisdictioun, baith strange, and also for the
Strangenes displesant, to us above all uther it aucht
to be maist grevous, quha are drevin to yis Streicht of
Necessitie, yat, quhais Faultis we desyre to cover,
thair Lyves we ar enforcit to accuse, unles we will
our selfis be accomptit the maist wickit Persones
that live : Bot a greit Part of this Greif is relevit
be our Equitie, (maist excellent Quene) quha tak it
na les displesandly to se your Kinniswoman, than
we to se our Quene, thus in Speiche of all Men, to
be dishonorabillie reportit, quha alswa ar for zour
Part na les desyrous to understand the Treuth, than
we for ouris to avoide Sclander.   Thairfor we will
knit up the Mater als breifly as possibilly may be,
and declair it with sic Schortnes, as we may rather
seeme to have lychtly ryn ower the chief Pointis,
than to have largely expressit thame, beginning at
the Quenis first Inconstancie ; for as in making of
hir Mariage, hir Lichtnes was verray heidlang and
rasche, sa suddanely followit outher inwart Repent-
aunce, or at leist outward Takinis of Change in
hir Affectioun without ony causes Appering.   For
quhair befoir Tyme the King was not only Neglectit,
bot also not honorabillie usit, at length began oppin
Haitrent to brek out againis him, specially in that
Wynter quhen he went to Pebles, with small
Trayne, evin to meane for the Degre of ane private
Man ; not being sent thether a Hawking, bot as com-

mandit away into a Corner, far from Counsell and
Knawledge of publict affairis.   Nouther is it neces-
sarie to put in Wryting thay Thingis, quhilk as thay
wer than as a Spectacle notit of all Mennis Eyis, sa
now, as a fresch Image thay remane imprentit in all
Mennis Hartis.   And thocht this wer the Beginning of all the Evilis that followit, zit at the first
the Practises were secreit, sa as not only the com-
moun Pepill, bot alswa sic as wer richt familiar
and present at the doing of mony Materis, culd
not understand throuchly quhat Thing the Quene
than chiefly intendit."

While the Commissioners were in London,
Buchanan seems to have enjoyed the best society
the city could then offer.   With the family of Cecil,
Elizabeth's great minister, he was on the most intimate footing.   To the wife of Cecil he addressed
four short poems, which give us a curious glimpse
into the society of the time.   While he addresses
her in a strain that implies intercourse on the
friendliest terms, he does not hesitate to suggest
that a poet is a privileged person, who confers a
benefit in accepting a solid reward for his verses.
Lady Cecil perfectly understands the suggestion,
and not only meets the request with liberality, but
accompanies her present with a Latin poem, which
Buchanan, as a matter of course, declares to be
infinitely more precious to him than her gold.   To
Queen Elizabeth herself he also addressed two
poems—one an ode, in which he tells her that her
chief claim to honour is to have restored true religion and rid the country of idle monks ; the other
an epigram in which he concludes with the prayer
that she may ever remain simply as she is, since he

can wish her no gift she does not already enjoy.
But his most pleasant intercourse in London must,
we should think, have been with his friend Roger
Ascham, who held the same post with Elizabeth—
that of classical tutor—as he himself had lately
held with Mary. This was the last year of Ascham's life, and when they parted he presented
Buchanan with a copy of Virgil, accompanying it
with an inscription, which marks the affection and
admiration with which he had come to regard him :
"Rogerus Aschamus Georgio Bucchanano, Anglus
Scoto, Amicus amico, hunc poetam omnis veteris
memoriae optimum, Poetae hujus nostrae aetatis
optimo, amoris ergo, dono dat." Buchanan acknow-
ledges the gift in some graceful lines, which prove
that the esteem was mutual, and that he had lost
nothing of the happy skill in epigram which was
the envy of his contemporaries.[1]

Moray and his colleagues returned to Scotland
in the beginning of 1569, and Buchanan probably
accompanied them.[2] As they were the direct sequel
of the proceedings against Mary, this seems the
most suitable place to give some account of two
political pamphlets written by Buchanan in support
of the King's party. These are the *Admonitioun to
the trew Lordis*[3] and the *Chamaeleon*, both in the
Scots dialect. Both of these pamphlets had their
origin in the critical state of affairs that followed

[1] *Epig.* i. 39.
[2] At least he was in St. Andrews in April 1569.—Sibbald, *Commentarius in Vitam Georgii Buchanani*, p. 66.
[3] The full title is "Ane Admonitioun direct to the trew Lordis
maintenaris of Justice and Obedience to the Kingis Grace". In the
diary of Bishop Lesley there is the following reference to this tract,
under date 9th October 1571: "Attulit et libellum quendam famosum
compositum per Georg. Bocha. precipue contra Hamiltonios et Ducem
Norfolcie."—*Bannatyne Miscellany*, vol. iii. p. 155.

the assassination of the Regent Moray, and they prove that Buchanan was no mere theoretical politician, but one who was in practical contact with the affairs of the day, and who put his strength into what he believed to be the righteous cause. Both pamphlets are as far as possible from the idle declamation of the arm-chair politician. They show keen political insight into the situation, and put the case of the King's party with telling effect. It is proof of the shrewd sense that made the foundation of his character, that in a practical cause he avoided the rhetoric of literary politicians like Milton, and spoke in a manner that could make itself felt by plain men. In his pithy phrase and firm grasp of facts he suggests Swift and Defoe rather than Milton and Burke, though behind Buchanan's words there is a moral intensity of which Swift at least was unconscious.

In the *Admonitioun* Buchanan's main contention is that in the safety of the young King lies the only hope for liberty and religion in Scotland; and the object of the pamphlet is to place before James's supporters the national ruin that must follow the defeat of their cause. The great enemies they have to fear are the Hamiltons, whose triumph would only bring disaster to King and country alike. To make this statement good he sketches at length the history of that family through the last half-century, and proves that its action all along had known but one motive—the acquisition of the Crown for the head of their house. By religion and politics alike Buchanan was opposed to the aims of the house of Hamilton; and his feelings were whetted by the long-standing feud between them and the house of

Lennox. The Hamiltons had but lately murdered
the statesman whom Buchanan had admired most,
the Regent Moray ; they had taken an active part
in the murder of Darnley ; it was through them
that Darnley's father had been so long exiled from
Scotland ; and it was one of their house who had
brutally slain the grandfather of Darnley after he
had surrendered himself a prisoner of war. Such
being his relations with the house of Hamilton, it
was not to be expected that Buchanan's account of
their family history would be perfectly impartial.
Yet, in the main, all he has said against them is
fully borne out by the facts of their history as we
now know it. The party of Mary and the party of
Moray both stood on principles which high-minded
men could adopt in the honest conviction that in
enforcing them they were working for the best
interests of their country. But the Hamiltons
played fast and loose with either party according as
it served themselves, and steadily sacrificed the
interests of the country in the interests of their
own house. The only justification of their self-
seeking policy is that it was perhaps more than
human nature in that age could endure to have a
crown dangling at the ends of their fingers, yet
ever eluding their grasp.

The other pamphlet, the *Chamaeleon*, is directed
against Maitland of Lethington, whose policy since
the fall of Mary had been steadily, though stealthily,
directed against the party to which Buchanan belonged. In Buchanan's view of the best interests
of the country, Maitland's conduct was utterly
inexplicable, except on the supposition of sheer
factiousness or shameless love of intrigue. It was

through him more than any one else that Mary's party
still made head in Scotland, and thus prevented a
firm government from being set up, which, working
in union with England, should present a common
front against the great Catholic powers of Europe.
In this belief, and under the conviction that Maitland
was privy to the scheme for the assassination of
Moray, he wrote the *Chamaeleon*, and drew a portrait
of Lethington with just that amount of truth and
caricature which would make him at once odious
and ridiculous in the eyes of his countrymen.
Lethington's career certainly lends itself easily
enough to such treatment. At one time or other
of his public life he had worked in concert with all
the leading persons in the country, and his contemporaries are hardly to be blamed if they failed to
discover in his tortuous policy the unwavering purpose of the true patriot and great statesman. In the
seething elements of civil strife, fanatical zeal, and
hereditary feuds that make Scottish history of this
period, Lethington strikes us as one of the oddest
apparitions of that strange time. By his seductive
charm, his ironical wit, his lack of moral intuitions, his
insensibility to all enthusiasms, his utter irrelevance
to a time of revolution, he is perhaps as close an
approximation to a Talleyrand as Scotland could
produce.[1] The news had reached him, it appears,
that such a pamphlet by Buchanan was forthcoming, and the house of Lekprevik, the printer, was
searched by his order. Lekprevik, having had
warning of the visit, made his escape with "such

---

[1] The well-known *douceur séduisante* of Talleyrand seems to have
been equally remarkable in Maitland. Louis XI. had this quality in
equally high degree. The family likeness between all three is very
evident.

things as he feared should have hurt him ".[1] The publication of the *Chamaeleon* was thus stopped, and it was not printed till 1710. In his History of Scotland, Buchanan had again occasion to deal with the character and career of Maitland. He speaks approvingly of his early promise and striking talents, but still reprobates what he considers his unprincipled desertion to the enemy. The *Chamaeleon* is, in truth, but the humorous presentment of Buchanan's definitive judgment on Lethington's character and entire career.[2] The opening paragraph of Buchanan's tract will give the reader some idea of its general character and drift :—

" Thair is a certane kynd of beist callit Chamaeleon, engenderit in sic countreis as the sone hes mair strenth in than in this yle of Brettane, the quhilk, albeit it be small of corporance, noghttheless it is of ane strange nature, the quhilk makis it to be na less celebrat and spoken of than sum beastis of greittar quantitie. The proprieties is marvalous, for quhat thing ever it be applicat to, it semis to be of the samyn cullour, and imitatis all hewis, excepte onelie the quhyte and reid ; and for this caus anciene writtaris commonlie comparis it to ane flatterare, quhilk imitatis all the haill maneris of quhome he fenzeis him self to be friend to, except quhyte, quhilk is taken to be the symboll and tokin gevin

[1] Bannatyne's *Memorials*, p. 110. It has been asserted that Bannatyne is not a sufficient authority for this story. But it is in itself intrinsically probable ; and the fact remains that the pamphlet was not published till 1710. There must therefore have been some reason for its non-appearance.

[2] It has been inadvertently affirmed that in his History Buchanan presents Maitland in a very different light from that in which he presents him in the *Chamaeleon*. Any one who reads the nineteenth book of Buchanan's History, however, will see that this is far from being the case. The gravest accusations brought against Maitland in the *Chamaeleon* are also to be found in the History.

commonlie in devise of colouris to signifie sempil-
nes and loyaltie, and reid signifying manliness and
heroyicall courage.   This applicatioun being so usit,
zit peradventure money that hes nowther sene the
said beist, nor na perfyte portraict of it, wald beleif
sick thing not to be trew.   I will thairfore set furth
schortlie the descriptioun of sick an monsture not
lang ago engendrit in Scotland, in the cuntre of .
Lowthiane, not far from Hadingtoun, to that effect
that the forme knawin, the most pestiferous nature
of the said monsture may be moir easelie evitit : for
this monsture being under coverture of a manis
figure, may easeliar endommage and wers be escha-
pit than gif it wer moir deforme and strange of face,
behaviour, schap, and membris.   Praying the reidar
to apardoun the febilnes of my waike spreit and
engyne, gif it can not expreme perfytelie ane strange
creature, maid by nature, other willing to schaw hir
greit strenth, or be sum accident turnit be force
frome the common trade and course."

But these two pamphlets of Buchanan have
perhaps a stronger interest from a literary and
philological than a historical point of view.   The
vernacular style in which they are written is unique
in Scottish prose literature.   Buchanan, it is to be
remembered, spoke and wrote a foreign language
for more than thirty years of his life, and studied
it with such intensity that it became to him as
natural a vehicle of expression as his mother tongue.
When he came to write in Scots in his old age,
therefore, it is not surprising that he actually
thought in Latin what he wrote in Scots.   His
two pamphlets leave exactly the impression of
close translations from the Latin.   But while the

syntactical structure of his sentences is thus so distinctively Latin, no Scottish prose of the period is clearer or more effective. In none of the contemporary Scottish writers do we find any conception of the true nature of a sentence.[1] So long as they keep to short periods they contrive to convey their meaning with tolerable success, though wholly without rhythm or neatness of expression. When they embark on a long period, they hobble through it with a disregard for logical relations that fills a modern reader with despair. In the case of Knox, it is the sheer triumph of moral and intellectual force that gives his History its distinctive flavour. Even in England, as is well known, it was not till long after this date that the compass of the sentence was clearly apprehended. In speaking of the development of English prose, Coleridge has some remarks which find interesting illustration in the Scots style of Buchanan. " If you take Sophocles, Catullus, Lucretius, the better parts of Cicero, and so on," he says, " you may, with just two or three exceptions arising out of the different idioms as to cases, translate page after page into good mother English, word by word, without altering the order."[2] A few sentences from the opening of his *Admonition* will illustrate the truth of Coleridge's remarks. Individual words are given in modern English that the rhythm of the sentences may be more readily felt :—

".It may seem to your lordships that I, meddling with high matters of governing of commonwealths, do pass mine estate, being of so mean quality, and

[1] In *The Complaynt of Scotland* we have something of the conscious art of Buchanan.
[2] *Table Talk*, vol. ii. p. 56 (Murray, 1835).

forget my duty, giving counsel to the wisest of this realm. Not the less, seeing the misery so great appearing, and the calamity so near approaching, I thought it less fault to incur the crime of surmounting my private estate than the blame of neglecting the public danger. Therefore I chose rather to underlie the opinion of presumption in speaking than of treason in silence, and specially of such things, as even seem presently to redound to the perpetual shame of your lordships, destruction of this royal estate, and ruin of the whole commonwealth of Scotland. On this consideration I have taken in hand at this time to advertise your honours of such things as I thought to appertain both to your lordships in special, and in general to the whole community of this realm, in punishment of traitors, pacification of troubles among yourselves, and continuation of peace with our neighbours."

Nothing could be clearer than the syntax of this passage, yet, as we read, we are inevitably reminded of the grandiose periods of Roman oratory. In his familiar letters Buchanan has the same syntactical structure, but with a lighter movement and quicker turns. Unfortunately only two of these letters have been preserved. We give one of them in the original Scots. It will be seen that we have good reason to regret that more such have not come down to us. Its companion, also addressed to Randolph, is, however, the racier and more characteristic of the two.[1]

"To Maister Randolf Squiar, Maister of Postes to the Quenes Grace of Ingland. Maister, I haif resavit diverse letters from you, and yit I

---

[1] See also Appendix C.

have ansourit to nain of thayme: of the quhylke albeit I haif mony excusis, as age, forgetfulness, besiness, and disease, yit I wyl use nane as now, except my sweirness and your gentilnes: and geif ye thynk nane of theise sufficient, content you with ane confession of the falt w^{t}out fear of punition to follow on my onkindness. As for the present I am occupyit in writying of our historie, being assurit to content few, and to displease mony tharthrow. As to the end of it, yf ye gett it not or thys winter be passit, lippin not for it, nor nane other writyngs from me. The rest of my occupation is wyth the gout, quhilk holdis me besy both day and ny^t. And quhair ye say ye haif not lang to lyif, I traist to God to go before you, albeit I be on fut, and ye ryd the *post*; praying you also not to *dispost* my hoste at Newyerk, Jone of Kelsterne. Thys I pray you, partly for his awyne sake, quhame I tho^t ane gud fellow, and partly at request of syk as I dar no^t refuse. And thus I tak my leif shortly at you now, and my lang leif quhen God pleasis, committing you to the protection of the almy^{t}ty. At Sterling xxv. day of August, 1577.—Yours to command w^t service, G. BUCHANAN."

CHAPTER XV.

IN all schemes for the advancement of education in Scotland, it was to be expected that Buchanan would be consulted as the highest authority in the country. His European reputation as a scholar, and his wide experience as a practical teacher, marked him out as the one man fitted to place Scotland abreast of other countries in all the new studies and all the new methods. We have abundant evidence that he took the keenest interest in all matters connected with education, and that he not only had a leading share in the many schemes proposed for the improvement of the universities, but that more than once he was the prompter of substantial boons in their favour. At the same time, the protracted unsettlement of public affairs rendered all but abortive the best endeavours of himself and the reformers associated with him. Lack of funds, divided aims, religious dissensions, civil discord, made impossible that system of national education so nobly set forth in the Book of Discipline. As it is, therefore, Buchanan is not to be ranked with such educationists as his friend Jean Sturm, whose school at Strasburg was his so durable monument. Even had Buchanan had the administrative genius of

226

Sturm, which is very doubtful, it could never have been in his power, as things then went, to establish in Scotland such a school for secondary education as Sturm was able to set up in Strasburg. It is probable, therefore, that Buchanan's most effective service to education in Scotland was mainly through the inspiration of his own great name as a scholar, and his life-long devotion to learning. That his example had the most direct and potent influence on the studious youth of Scotland is amply proved by testimonies from Andrew Melville to Melvin of Aberdeen. His poems, also, especially his version of the Psalms—systematically used in schools in the teaching of Latin—themselves establish for him a solid claim on the gratitude of his countrymen.

In 1566, we have seen, Moray appointed Buchanan principal of the College of St. Leonard at St. Andrews. The College of St. Leonard had originally been the Hospital of St. Leonard, founded for the accommodation of pilgrims who came to see the wonders wrought by the bones of St. Andrew. In 1512 the Hospital had been converted into a College by Prior Hepburn, supported by Alexander Stewart, Archbishop of St. Andrews, natural son of James IV., best known as the pupil of Erasmus, and by that scholar's charming account of his character and accomplishments. This conversion had been made with the express desire "to preserve the tempest-tost bark of St. Peter, and to uphold the declining state of the Church".[1] Almost from the beginning, however, the pious desire of the founders was doomed to be thwarted. Its second principal, Gavin Logie

---

[1] Lyon, *History of St. Andrews*, vol. ii. p. 243.

(1523-37), was one of the earliest Scotsmen to be affected by the teaching of Luther; and from the date of his rule "to have drunk of St. Leonard's Well" became the current euphemism for heretical proclivities. According to the original foundation, there was to be provision for a principal, four chaplains (two of whom were to be regents), and twenty poor scholars.[1] The internal arrangements were as nearly as possible those of a convent—in diet, religious duties, and regulation of hours. The students were in turn to do all the menial work of the house, a cook and his boy being the only servants. Before bursars were admitted, they had to be tested in grammar (that is, Latin grammar), and in their knowledge of the Gregorian Chant. The subjects taught were those prescribed by all the medieval universities for the degree of Master of Arts— grammar, logic, physics, philosophy, metaphysics, and ethics. During the first years of its existence, the "College of Poor Clerks", as its founders termed it, was cramped by the poverty of its endowments; but a succession of energetic teachers and managers won it a reputation which brought students in large numbers from the ranks of the nobility and clergy. By the charter of Cardinal Beaton (1544), confirming the foundation of St. Leonard's, the Prior of St. Andrews was to have the right of naming the Principal; and his choice was to be made from the Canons of the Priory. The duties of the Principal were those of the head of a religious house. He was to superintend the domestic economy of the College, to lead all the religious exercises, and, on Wednesdays and Fridays, he was to "instruct the

---

[1] Lyon, *History of St. Andrews*, vol. ii. p. 243.

presbyters, regents, and all others who chose to attend, in sacred and speculative theology".[1]

Such were the internal arrangements of St. Leonard's on its original foundation. As the period of the Reformation approached, however, these arrangements must have been largely modified, both in form and spirit, and all the more that its principals and regents were in such marked sympathy with the new opinions. With all the other Scottish Colleges, St. Leonard's suffered greatly from the troubles that preceded the establishment of the reformed religion. In 1557, ten students in all attended St. Mary's, ten St. Leonard's, and eleven St. Salvator's. In 1560, the numbers were respectively seven, four, and seventeen; and in 1563, fifteen, twelve, and twelve.[2] At St. Andrews, the reformers had little difficulty in making the University their own. St. Leonard's, as was to be expected, of its own accord accepted the new conditions; and even the staff of St. Mary's College, founded as late as 1553-4 by Archbishop Hamilton, for the express purpose of checking the progress of heresy, all but unanimously declared for the enemy. The provost and most of the regents of St. Salvator's were more faithful to the intentions of the founders, and preferred to quit their posts rather than teach on the terms dictated to them. It would appear, however, that this purging was not so thorough as we might have expected. One of the duties imposed on the Commissioners appointed by Parliament in 1579 to inquire into the state of the University was " to

[1] Lyon, *History of St. Andrews*, vol. ii. p. 249. These duties were doubtless all performed by Buchanan, though not in the sense intended by the founders.

[2] *Ibid.* vol. ii. p. 179.

reform sic things as soundit to superstitioun, ydolatrie, and papistrie ".

The Reformers being now masters of the situation in St. Andrews, the progress of the new studies throughout Europe demanded of them something more than the mere suppression of discredited religious forms and doctrines. If the University was to hold its own with other seats of learning, the entire scheme of studies would have to be recast and adjusted to the new standards of the intellectual revolution. At the Reformation, the studies and methods pursued in all the three Colleges were wholly those of Medievalism. Canon law, that monstrous birth of the Middle Ages, the logic and metaphysic of the schoolmen, made the staple of the curriculum. Latin had a distinct place assigned to it; but it was Latin as known and handled by men like Major, the most eminent of the representative professors at St. Andrews before the Reformation. On the very eve of the Reformation, as we learn from the case of Andrew Melville,[1] Greek was still unknown in St. Mary's, the most fully equipped of the three colleges. While the curriculum was thus so completely antiquated, the overlapping functions of the three colleges stood in the way of the effective and economical organisation of the University. There was no organic connection between the colleges, and the various subjects of study were promiscuously taught in each. This was, of course, the case with all the colleges of the medieval universities; but at St. Andrews, where the number of colleges was so few, and funds were not over-abundant, a distinct function for each, and an

---

[1] James Melville's *Diary*, p. 39 (ed. 1842).

organic connection between all, was imperatively needed to meet the wants of the time.

It would be unjust to the successive authorities at St. Andrews to cast undue blame on them because so late as the middle of the sixteenth century the number of students was so limited and the programme of studies so antiquated. The keen religious dissensions, the poverty of the endowments, and the irresistible attractions of the great foreign universities for such a wandering nation as the Scots, sufficiently account for the meagre attendance without injurious inferences as to the energy and capacity of its teachers. As for any charge of obscurantism, St. Andrews was, in truth, in the same case with all the ancient universities of Europe. In following Buchanan's own career we have seen the general attitude of Paris to all the lights of the Renaissance. When Francis, inspired by Budé, founded the Collége Royal in 1530 for the study of Latin, Greek, and Hebrew, it was in the teeth of the whole University ; and past the middle of the century Greek and Hebrew were generally regarded at Paris as fit only for heretics. The canon law, also, and the medieval Aristotle, continued to make the most essential part of its university training long after their futility had been exposed by the labours of the humanists.[1]   At Oxford, in the opening years of the sixteenth century, Colet's novel methods of Biblical interpretation, though strictly within the lines of orthodoxy, were disapproved by the leading authorities,[2] and it was amid a storm of opposition that the study of Greek gradually made way in that

---

[1] Crevier, *Histoire de l'Université de Paris*, v. *passim*.
[2] Seebohm, *Oxford Reformers*.

university. In Cambridge, under the auspices of Bishop Fisher, Greek found readier acceptance, though Erasmus in 1511 had little encouragement as its teacher;[1] and it was not till 1535 that Medievalism had distinctly the worst of it at the English universities.[2] When we remember, also, that at Wittemberg, the cradle of the Reformation, Melanchthon, who died in 1560, had to struggle to the last for a liberal scheme of studies, it will be understood that St. Andrews, and with it the other Scottish Universities, were not, in fact, so very far behind their neighbours. It is worth while adding that, by the middle of the sixteenth century, the time had fully come when, in the interests of her intellectual not less than her political and religious development, Scotland should throw in her lot with England rather than with France. While the University of Paris was still in opposition to Renaissance and Reformation alike, Oxford and Cambridge had definitely accepted the new order. By contact with England, therefore, rather than with France, could she be a partaker in the best results of the revival of letters and religion.

In the deadly earnest which characterised all their action, the Scottish Reformers set about the work of reconstruction in the universities. The scheme they proposed, as set forth in the Book of Discipline (1560),[3] proved abortive for the time in

[1] J. B. Mullinger, *The University of Cambridge*, pp. 493, 496.
[2] *Ibid.* p. 631.
[3] The following paragraphs from "The Buke of Discipline" show how comprehensive were the aims of its authors :—"Of necessitie thairfore we judge it, that everie severall Churche have a Scholmaister appointed, suche a one as is able at least to teache Grammer and the Latine toung, yf the Toun be of any reputatioun. Yf it be Vpaland, whaire the people convene to doctrine bot once in the weeke, then must eathir the Reidar or the Minister thair appointed, take cayre over the children and youth

every case, but their ideals had a most direct influence on the subsequent form of Scottish university
education. With regard to St. Andrews, which was
to be the most fully equipped of all the universities,
they laid it down that each of the three colleges
should have a distinct sphere of its own—that one
should provide a course in philosophy, the second a
course in law, and the third a course in divinity.
But it was in the choice of subjects that the university was to provide, and the term allotted to
each, that we see the spirit in which the reform was
conceived, and the degree to which the reformers
had profited by the revival of letters.

In one circumstance they completely broke with
the tradition of the medieval universities, and
therefore with the tradition of St. Andrews itself.
By the arrangement they proposed, Latin grammar
and Latin literature were to have no place in the
curriculum of university studies. As is well known,
the medieval university was at once an elementary
school, a secondary school, and a university as well.
The slender provision for elementary and secondary
education in the various countries necessitated this
extended sphere of the university. It was one of

of the parische, to instruct them in thair first rudimentis, and especiallie
in the Catechisme, as we have it now translaited in the Booke of our
Common Ordour, callit the Ordour of Geneva. And farther, we think
it expedient, that in everie notable toun, and especiallie in the toun of
the Superintendent, be erected a Colledge, in whiche the Artis, at
least Logick and Rethorick, togidder with the Tongues, be read be
sufficient Maisteris, for whome honest stipendis must be appointed ; as
also provisioun for those that be poore, and be nocht able by them selfis,
nor by thair freindis, to be sustened at letteris, especialle suche as come
frome Landwart.

"Last, The great Schollis callit Universiteis, shall be replenischit with
those that be apt to learnyng ; for this must be cairfullie provideit, that
no fader, of what estait or conditioun that ever he be, use his children at
his awin fantasie, especiallie in thair youth-heade ; but all must be compelled to bring up thair children in learnyng and virtue."

the largest benefits of the revival of learning that it created and did much to supply the want of secondary education.[1]   The great secondary school at Bordeaux, with which we have seen Buchanan connected—that at Carpentras, over which another Scotsman, Florence Wilson, for a time presided—the famous school at Strasburg, remodelled by Sturm in 1537—are examples of the efforts made by humanists at once to relieve the universities, and to bring a sound education within the reach of those whom circumstances prevented from attending them.[2]   It was therefore in the spirit of the most advanced educationists that those who drafted the Book of Discipline cancelled what had hitherto formed the elementary portion of the Arts course at the university.   Had their project for establishing secondary schools throughout the country been carried into effect, it is easy to see that the whole system of education would thus have been placed on a broader basis, and the result been the immensely quickened intellectual life of the nation.   It was doubtless to Geneva and Strasburg that Knox and his associates mainly owed their far-sighted views on national education.   Calvin's academy at Geneva was not founded till 1559;[3] but on a subject so near to the hearts of them both, we may be sure that Knox and Calvin must often have held serious discussion. Sturm was as notable a figure in the religious as in the scholastic world; and Knox and his coadjutors could not but have heard of the radical reforms he

---

[1] Cf. Schmidt, *Vie de Sturm*, p. 222.

[2] Cf. Gaufrès, *Claude Baduel et la Réforme des Études au xvie Siècle* (Paris, 1880).

[3] Calvin's academy was based on the plan of Sturm's school at Strasburg.

had so successfully carried out at the Strasburg Gymnasium.

In the time of study prescribed for the various degrees we likewise see the changed attitude as regards the claims of life and duty that had been wrought by the revolution of the sixteenth century. By the arrangements of the medieval university, the degree of doctor of divinity could not be taken before the age of thirty-five; by the arrangement of the Book of Discipline a degree in divinity could be taken by the age of twenty-four. The term required for the doctorate in law was similarly shortened. The object in thus curtailing the curriculum was clearly at once to prevent stagnation in the university itself, and to let society have the benefit of that superabundant energy which made the more mature section of the students the torment of the university authorities.[1]

The reforms proposed in the Book of Discipline were thus far in the spirit of the most eminent educationists of the time. Nevertheless, though these reforms owed much to the labours of the humanists, the spirit of humanism is conspicuously absent in all the plans for the reconstruction of the Scottish universities. According to these reforms, all knowledge of the Latin and Greek classics was to be gained at the secondary schools, that is to say, by the age of sixteen or seventeen, when the student was supposed to be ripe for the university. After a three years' curriculum in dialectic, mathematics, and natural philosophy, he was expected to

[1] As is well known, it was the more mature students who gave by far the most trouble to the authorities of the medieval universities. Cf. Mullinger, *The University of Cambridge*, p. 131.

make choice of divinity, law, or medicine as the
profession he should eventually adopt. The peculiar
studies of the humanist were thus made the work
of boys; and the universities being closed against
them, no sphere was left for scholars who should
devote their lives to the disinterested study of
antiquity. The truth is that humanism, in the
proper sense of the word, never found a home
in Scotland, as it did more or less in the other
countries of Europe. The true humanist of the
fifteenth and sixteenth centuries was one who was
not only consumed by zeal for classical learning,
but who consciously or unconsciously exalted the
classical over the Christian tradition, and who regarded life with a kind of good-natured irony,
which made him shrink alike from asceticism and
rigour of creed. Of the last two notes of humanism, Scotland, whether for good or ill, learned
nothing from the Revival of Letters. Had the
Renaissance touched her before the Reformation
it might have been otherwise. But as it was, the
Renaissance came to her through the Reformation,
and theology dominated her schools from the moment of her new birth. In England, on the other
hand, the Italian Renaissance and the German
Reformation had an equal share in building up the
national life; and the Elizabethan drama was made
possible not less than Puritanism and the English
Church. A Scotsman like Andrew Melville might
hold his own against any foreign scholar in the
matter of classical attainments; but the light in
which he viewed these attainments was peculiar to
him as a Scotsman. Drummond of Hawthornden
is the only Scotsman of eminence in whom it is

possible to find the humanist even in his milder form ; and Drummond all through his life felt himself an alien in a strange land. In the so-called Moderatism of the eighteenth century we have for the first time after the Reformation the somewhat shabby manifestation of the less worthy side of humanism.

The proposals of the Book of Discipline were not carried into effect ; and during the next few years the University of St. Andrews fell into a state of the most wretched inefficiency. By an Act of Parliament, 1563, commissioners were appointed to investigate matters in that University, on the ground that there was "waisting of the patrimony of sum of the fundatiounis maid in the Collegeis of the City of Sanctandros and uthers placis within this Realme for the intertenement of the youth, and that few sciences and speciallie thay that ar maist necessaire, that is to say the toungis and humanitie, are in ane part not teicheit within the said Citie to the greit detriment of the haill liegis of this Realme". The most notable among the commissioners were Moray, Maitland, and Buchanan. They were to report the result of their inquiry the following year. This they failed to do ; and the only memorial of the Commission is a scheme for the reconstruction of the three colleges, which has been attributed to Buchanan himself.[1] This scheme differs greatly from that of the Book of Discipline, and is, perhaps, to be regarded as a compromise necessitated by the state of the time. Buchanan's plan, however, resembles that of the Book of Discipline in assigning

---

[1] This scheme is printed by Irving (*Memoirs of Buchanan*, Appendix III.) from a manuscript in the Advocates' Library, Edinburgh.

a separate function to each college.   One of the
colleges was to be merely a secondary school, where
the "tongues and humanity" should be learned by
way of preparation for the studies of the other two.
As the scheme for a system of secondary schools had
fallen through, it is evident that such a college was
a simple necessity.   In this college there were to be
at least six successive classes, in which Latin and
Greek were to be taught—Greek only in the three
highest classes.   In certain of the rules for its
administration there are points which afford a presumption that this scheme is rightly attributed to
Buchanan.   The rule for the Saturday disputations,
for example, is exactly that of the college at Bordeaux.   So also is the rule that the pedagogue or
regent in charge of the bursars in their private
rooms was not to "ding his disciples," nor to give
distinct lessons of his own.

The second college was to supply a three years'
course of philosophy and medicine, and was to be
conducted by the Principal, aided by four regents,
and a "reader" in medicine.   The third was to be
set apart for divinity and law—its entire staff to
consist of a principal, who was also to act as reader
in divinity, and a reader in law.   If this draft of a
university scheme appear ludicrously inadequate, it
would be unjust to make it a reproach against
Buchanan.   Things had not gone so prosperously
with the reformers as they had anticipated ; and
they had been taught by somewhat bitter experience that to draw up constitutions was one thing,
to embody them another.   The plan of Buchanan,
therefore, is to be considered, not by any means as
expressing his ideal of what a university should be,

but merely what in the circumstances seemed to him possible.

But not even the modest scheme of Buchanan could be carried into effect; and things at St. Andrews grew gradually worse, in spite of the ardent wishes of the reformers. " Eftir the first zeall of the Reformation," says James Melville, who speaks with personal knowledge of the University, " regents and schollars carit na thing for divinitie . . . ; and for langages, arts, and philosophy they haid na thing for all, bot a few buiks of Aristotle, quhilk they lernit pertinatiouslie to battle and flyt upon, without right understanding or use thairof." To remedy this state of things the Parliament once more appointed commissioners (1579) to report on the University of St. Andrews. The powers given to the commissioners show how complete the disorganisation had become. They were to visit and consider the foundations, to remove all superstition and Papistry, to displace all unqualified persons, and to plant qualified persons in their places; to redress the forms of teaching by more or fewer professors, to join or divide the faculties, to annex every faculty to such college as should be found most proper, and generally to establish such order as should most tend to the good of the commonwealth. As the result of their inquiry, the commissioners drew up a scheme for reforming, or rather reconstructing, the University. This scheme used to be known as Buchanan's, he being the most distinguished scholar among the commissioners. It is now generally spoken of as being mainly the work of Andrew Melville. Buchanan and Melville would doubtless be listened to with respect by their fellow-

commissioners ; but as all were men of weight and
experience, it may be regarded as the joint production of the whole body.[1]   It certainly has little of
that sobriety of judgment which so pre-eminently
distinguished the plan of the Book of Discipline.
By this new scheme St. Salvator's and St. Leonard's
were both to be Arts colleges, the former being
additionally equipped with regents in law and
medicine.   St. Mary's was to be exclusively a college of theology.   The course of study prescribed
for this particular College bears the stamp of Melville's discursive mental habit, and ardent though
somewhat impracticable temper.   Buchanan, with
his delicate exactness of mind, could hardly have
suggested an impossible course of study, which
could only have produced a race of sciolists.   In
the College there were to be five professors, and the
course was to be four years.   The first professor
was to teach Hebrew, Chaldee, and Syriac the first
year ; the second was to apply these languages to
the critical explanation of the Pentateuch and historical books ; the third to apply them to the
prophetical books ; the fourth was to compare the
Greek Testament with the Syriac version, and the
fifth to lecture on systematic divinity.   According
to James Melville, this theological school was pri-
marily intended as an " anti-seminary " to the
Jesuit seminaries ;[2] yet in the list of studies
Church History is not even mentioned.   This plan
received the ratification of Parliament ; but, as

---

[1] M'Crie (*Life of Andrew Melville*, vol. i. p. 246) says that " we
have direct evidence that Melville had the principal hand in drawing
up " this scheme.   The proofs which he gives hardly justify such a
broad statement.

[2] James Melville's *Diary*, p. 76 (ed. 1842).

might indeed have been expected from its one-
sided and impracticable character, did as little for
the University as its predecessors.   When Buchanan entered St. Andrews, therefore, not one of these
many schemes had been carried into effect.

Buchanan was Principal of St. Leonard's from
1566 till 1570.   Of the details of his life there, or
of the manner in which he discharged his duties,
nothing has come down to us.   The few facts that
have been gleaned from the University records may
be briefly related.[1]   For the three successive
years after his appointment he was one of the
electors, assessors, and deputies of the rector ; and
in each case his name is entered with the addition,
" Poetarum nostrae memoriae facile princeps ".[2]
From November 1566 to November 1567 he was
one of the auditors of the quæstor's accounts.   He
was never either rector or dean of the faculty of
Arts.   "It is remarkable," says the writer from
whom these details are quoted, "that no students
are enrolled as belonging to St. Leonard's College
in 1566 and 1567, though the numbers both in
St. Mary's and St. Salvator's are considerable.   In
1568 more students entered St. Leonard's than
even St. Mary's, which had generally been the most
numerously attended of all the colleges ; and in
1569 the numbers enrolled for the first time in St.
Leonard's were 24, while those at St. Mary's were
only 11, and those at St. Salvator's only 8."   It is

---

[1] This information was communicated by Dr. Lee to Irving (*Memoirs of Buchanan*, Appendix IV.).

[2] Florent Chrestien, in his translation of Buchanan's *Jephthes*, speaks of Buchanan as "*prince des poètes de nostre siècle*".   Henri Estienne, also, as we have seen, in his edition of Buchanan's *Psalms*, speaks of him as "*poetarum nostri saeculi facile princeps*".

natural to suppose that the great name of Buchanan may have had something to do with this pro-
sperity of St. Leonard's at the expense of its rivals.

There is a tradition to the effect that Buchanan
was in the habit of preaching during his stay in St.
Andrews.[1] The origin of this tradition may have
been the divinity lectures, which by the original
foundation of St. Leonard's he was bound, as Principal, to deliver every Wednesday and Friday. It
may also have originated in appearances Buchanan
may have made at the weekly exercise of "prophesy-
ing", which by the Book of Discipline was to be held
in every town " where schools and repaire of learned
men are ". Besides the ministers of religion, the
learned men of the neighbourhood were expected to
take part in this " exercise ", and as one of these
" learned men ", Buchanan may have distinguished
himself in this new part.

While Buchanan was thus so closely connected
with the University of St. Andrews, he seems
always to have been keenly interested in that of
Glasgow, and never to have lost an opportunity of
doing it substantial good. In a document of the
latter University, of February 1578, it is stated, in
the name of Andrew Melville, principal of the College, that a certain boon is conferred on one John
Buchanan for the " singular favour that ane honourable man George Buchanan teachar of our Sovereign
Lord in gude lettres hes borne and shawen at all
times to our College ".[2] As Mary's grants to Glasgow were conferred before Buchanan's breach with
her, it is probable that he should have some credit

---

[1] M'Crie, *Life of Knox*, Note A, Period Sixth.
[2] *Munimenta Alme Universitatis Glasguensis*, vol. i. p. 123.

in prompting her generosity. In the new foundation of the College of Glasgow made by the town in 1572, by which Queen Mary's foundation was overthrown, Buchanan undoubtedly took an active part. It has been suggested, in fact, that the Latin of the deed may be the work of Buchanan. The opening sentences have certainly all the freedom and impetuosity of movement that give his Latin style its distinctive character. In the desire the writer expresses also that Glasgow College may turn out as many scholars as the Trojan horse turned out heroes, we are reminded of the common saying regarding Buchanan's old College of Ste. Barbe. What is known as the *Erectio Regia* was, likewise, in all probability, largely due to Buchanan's influence with Morton. His name is attached to the deed as "our dear Privy Councillor, George Buchanan, Pensioner of Crossraguel, and Keeper of the Privy Seal".[1] A valuable gift of Latin and Greek books gave further proof of Buchanan's good-will towards the College of Glasgow.[2]

A humbler example of Buchanan's eager interest in education also deserves to be mentioned. In Scotland, as in other countries, the multiplicity of Latin Grammars that followed the growth of the new studies became a serious drawback to the efficient teaching of the language.[3] Accordingly, a committee of four scholars, with Buchanan as president, was appointed to consider the difficulty. They decided that three of their number should compile a Grammar which should supersede those in use.

---

[1] *Munimenta Alme Universitatis*, vol. i. p. 103.
[2] *Ibid.* vol. iii. p. 407.
[3] Cf. Schmidt, *Vie de Sturm*, chap. iii. part ii.

Prosody was the part of the task assigned to Buchanan. All three accomplished their tasks, but the Grammar, though the joint production of three of the most eminent scholars in Scotland at the time, failed to serve the purpose for which it was intended.

It was said in connection with Buchanan's regenting in Ste. Barbe that the labours of the practical teacher were probably little to his mind. However this may be, he seems to have possessed in rare degree the faculty of interesting and attracting youth. "Buchanan," says one, who as a young man had been personally acquainted with him, —"Buchanan was of such flexibility of mind that with boys he became a boy ; he had alike the faculty and the will to adapt himself to every time of life, yet always in such a way as never to forfeit the respect due to himself."[1] To the very end, when broken in body and harassed in mind, he never lost that most delightful trait of old age, the surest proof of a genial and simply sincere character—a sympathetic interest in the young. Of this trait in his character we have almost pathetic evidence in his relations with two young men, who seem to have won his special affection. One of these, Jerome Groslot, was the son of a man from whom Buchanan had received much kindness during his sojourn in France ; and the last letter written by Buchanan that has come down to us was addressed to Beza on his behalf. This letter deserves to be

---

[1] "Erat enim vir ille ea ingenii dexteritate, ut cum pueris repuerascere, et ad omnes omnium aetatum usus modeste et sapienter sese accommodare et posset et vellet."—Julius, *Ecphrasis Paraphraseos G. Buchanani in Psalmos Davidis*, epist. nunc. Lond. 1620, 8vo. (Quoted by Irving, p. 239.)

given in full, as it brings before us a side of his character which the *Detectio* and such lines as his epigram on Major are apt to make us forget. It is dated Edinburgh, 15th July 1581, that is to say, a year and two months before his death.

"Distracted though I am by manifold engagements, and so poor in health that I have hardly leisure for the ordinary duties of life, yet the departure of Jerome Groslot has deprived me of every excuse for not taking up my pen. During my stay in France, his father, a man of some eminence in the State, overwhelmed me with kindness, and his son while in this country has honoured me as a second parent. Had I ignored the kind offices of the one, or the pleasant intercourse of the other, or your own unvarying good feeling towards me, I should have justly incurred the gravest charge of ingratitude. Let me say, however, that those who best know the present state of my affairs would readily have cleared me even from this charge. This is, indeed, my best apology, that I am in simple truth but the shadow of my former self. I have not even the hope of forming new friendships, or of keeping up the old. I speak thus the more freely, as you will have the opportunity of learning from Groslot how things really stand with me. Him I fancy I need not recommend to you. His character and acquirements will speak for themselves. Still, I have obeyed custom, and have supplied him with the accompanying testimonial. As to myself, since I am no longer equal to the interchange of friendly offices, I shall indulge in silence." The following is the testimonial :—"Jerome Groslot, a youth of Orleans, the bearer of this letter, though born in a distinguished city, and of distinguished parents, is yet much more notable by his misfortunes. In the political confusions of his native country, and the universal infatuation of its citizens, he lost his father and his inheritance, and narrowly escaped with life. Unable to live in safety at home, he chose Scotland as his place of abode till the violence of civil strife should somewhat abate. In the present comparative lull, his private affairs calling for his return, he has resolved to travel by way of England, in order that, like Ulysses of old, he may, as far as a passing visitor may, become acquainted with the various manners and cities of men—certainly not the least important part of civil wisdom. This journey, as I am justified in hoping from the manner in which he profited by his previous one, he will not make without large benefit to himself. While in Scotland he lived not as a foreigner, but as our fellow-citizen. To learning he has devoted himself with the aim that it should not be merely a solace in his misfortunes, but a means of livelihood for himself and those dependent on him. In a case like this, it is not for me to persuade or exhort you to show kindness to a youth so full of promise. This the whole tenor of your life and the bond of a common faith demands, nay, constrains, you to show, if you are to be worthy of yourself."

The other youth (whom Buchanan seems to have regarded with still warmer feelings than Groslot) was Alexander Cockburn, who died in 1564 at the age of twenty-eight. Cockburn was a pupil of Knox, who mentions him more than once in his History. The dates of his birth and death are wrongly given by Dempster. The right dates are

supplied by the mural brass at Ormiston.[1] Buchanan
has given expression to his keen regret on the
death of Cockburn in two poems, which justify us
in believing that his early death was a loss to the
literature of his country. The best of the two
poems may be given here :[2]—

> Omnia quae longa indulget mortalibus aetas,
>   Haec tibi, Alexander, prima juventa dedit.
> Cum genere et forma generoso stemmate digna,
>   Ingenium velox, ingenuumque animum.
> Excoluit virtus animum, ingeniumque Camoenae
>   Successu, studio, consilioque pari.
> His ducibus primum peragrata Britannia, deinde
>   Gallia ad armiferos qua patet Helvetios.
> Doctus ibi linguas, quas Roma, Sion, et Athenae,
>   Quas cum Germano Gallia docta sonat.
> Te licet in prima rapuerunt fata juventa,
>   Non immaturo funere raptus obis.
> Omnibus officiis vitae qui functus obivit,
>   Non fas est vitae de brevitate queri.[3]

Another young Scot, whose meteoric career has
left a faint trail even to the present day, the
Admirable Crichton, made it a boast to the great
printer Aldus Manutius that he had been a pupil
of Buchanan. The boast is a tribute to the fame
of Buchanan ; but, like many other assertions of
Crichton, it is probably untrue. Crichton was
first enrolled as a student at the College of St.
Salvator's in 1570, at the age of ten. But Buchanan,
as we have seen, had no connection with St. Salvator's, and it was in 1570 (probably in the beginning

---

[1] See *Proceedings of the Society of Antiquaries of Scotland*, vol. iv.
[2] *Epig.* ii. 26.
[3] These lines were engraved on a mural brass in the aisle of the old
church at Ormiston Hall. The brass still exists, and, according to David
Laing, is of the same date as that in St. Giles', Edinburgh, to the memory
of the Regent Moray, the inscription on which was also written by
Buchanan.

of the year) that he gave up the principalship of St. Leonard's to become tutor to King James.

Of Buchanan's relations with the most notable of all his pupils, King James himself, a special account must be given in a separate chapter.

CHAPTER XVI.

FOR about a year after his return to Scotland
Buchanan still continued to act as Principal of
St. Leonard's. Of that year the most important
event was the assassination of the Regent Moray,
in whom Buchanan lost one of his best friends, and
whose death, as affairs then stood, he deemed the
heaviest calamity that could have befallen Scotland. "Buchanan," says Randolph in a letter to
Cecil, "hath not rejoiced since the Regent's death." [1]
We have seen from the poems Buchanan addressed
to Moray on what terms he stood with him. From
his History we also gather that he was occasionally
a guest at the Regent's house. [2] When all allowance
is made for the partiality of friendship, and identity
of conviction on the deepest subjects, the estimate
Buchanan has given of Moray is probably nearer
the truth than any other that has come down to us.
What he says amounts to a panegyric; yet there is
a careful precision in his words which gives the impression that he is tracing a portrait, not drawing
on mere partial fancy. It is certainly the Moray

[1] Calendar of State Papers (Scotland). In this letter Randolph
encloses Buchanan's epigram on the death of Moray.
[2] Rer. Scot. Hist. lib. xix. p. 385.

of Buchanan who became the tradition of the Scottish people.

The death of Moray was a heavy blow to the King's party; but its leaders were resolved that Mary should never again sit on the throne. Lennox was appointed Moray's successor, and every step was taken to give credit to James's government. At a meeting of the Privy Council in March 1570, it was resolved that provision should be made for the education of the King, then only four years of age. As the most eminent Scotsman in the scholastic world, Buchanan was naturally thought of for this responsibility. He was accordingly directed to leave St. Leonard's, and thenceforward to devote himself to the young King.[1]

It has abundantly appeared that all through life Buchanan had a noble interest in the cause of education. It was to be expected, therefore, that he would enter on his new duties with the fullest sense of the responsibility that would lie upon him both to his pupil and the country. He was now sixty-four years of age, and his infirmities made him even older than his years. He was not, therefore, in all respects specially fitted for the task imposed upon him. Yet as the larger half of his literary work, and, as he himself considered, the more important half, was produced after this date, it is clear that the energy of his mind was in no degree abated.

---

[1] Privy Council Records. The Act begins thus : "The Lords of Secret Council and others of the nobility and estates, being convened for taking order in the affairs of the Commonwealth, among other matters being careful of the King's Majesty's preservation and good education, and considering how necessary the attendance of Mr. George Buchanan, Master of St. Leonard's College within the University of St. Andrews, upon his Highness shall be, and it behoves the said Mr. George to withdraw himself from his charge of the said College," etc.

It is difficult to determine the exact share Buchanan himself took in James's education. In the dedication of his History to the King he expressly states that he had been prevented by incurable ill-health from discharging that part in James's education which had been assigned to him, and mentions as one of his motives in writing his History that it would in some degree make amends for the unavoidable neglect. After 1578, when James began to be made use of by the enemies of Morton, his studies must have been somewhat interrupted. By that date, also, Buchanan was in his seventy-second year, and his chronic ill-health had almost overpowered him. From James's fourth to his twelfth year, however, we are justified in thinking that Buchanan not only exercised a general super-intendence over his education, but in certain branches himself gave his pupil instruction.

In the school-room in Stirling Castle several youths of noble family received their education along with the young King. Among these were the young Earl of Mar, Sir William Murray of Abercairney (a nephew of the Countess of Mar), Walter Stewart, afterwards Lord Blantyre and Lord High Treasurer, and Lord Invertyle.[1] The family of Mar were the hereditary guardians of the King, and on the death of the Regent Mar in 1572 the care of James's person was intrusted to his widow and his brother, Sir Alexander Erskine. David and Adam Erskine, Commendators of Dryburgh and Cambuskenneth, were appointed to superintend the King's training in bodily exercises and accomplishments. In the care of his studies Buchanan had

---

[1] M'Crie, *Life of Andrew Melville*, vol. i. p. 105.

for assistant Peter, afterwards Sir Peter, Young,
of whom he speaks with cordiality and respect.[1]
Among Young's papers there is a sketch of a day's
work at a particular period of James's education.[2]
After morning prayers he read Greek—the New
Testament, Isocrates, and Plutarch ; after breakfast
Cicero and Livy or modern history.   The afternoon
was devoted to composition, and, when time permitted, to arithmetic or cosmography, or logic and
rhetoric.   It has been suggested that James's
Essayes of a Prentise in the Divine Art of Poesie,
published in 1585, three years after Buchanan's
death, may have been themes written by him for
his teachers.[3] The twelve " sonnets " that make up
these *essayes* are certainly near the level of a school-
boy's performance, and they have all the marks of a
theme written to order.   But even if it were so, it
would be a mistake to conclude that Buchanan had
any disposition to give the vernacular an important
place in his pupils' studies.   Like his friend Sturm,
Buchanan confidently believed that Latin must one
day be the universal language of Europe, and that
it was only a question of time when the common
people of each country should abandon their respective mother tongues.   This, with the majority of
the humanists, they regarded as the necessary and
legitimate result of the revival of letters.   Sturm's
end in education was what he called *pietas literata*
—true religion combined with thorough knowledge
of the Greek and Latin classics ; and for him the
mark of the highest culture was the command in

---

[1] *Epist.* vi. and vii.
[2] Irving, *Memoirs of Buchanan*, p. 160.
[3] M'Crie, *Life of Andrew Melville*, vol. i. p. 102.

speech and writing of pure and elegant Latinity.[1]
There can be no doubt whatever that Sturm's ideal
was also the ideal of Buchanan. Though he was a
master of the Scottish dialect, and had Knox's
example before him, he yet deliberately chose to
write the History of his native country in the
language which he knew would give him all Europe
for his readers.[2] With such training, and under such
masters, James, with his natural cleverness, could
hardly fail to make rapid progress in learning.
What the result was everybody knows. He became
"the only English prince who has carried to the
throne knowledge derived from reading or any considerable amount of literature".[3] Late historians
have formed a somewhat higher opinion of James's
character and capacity than what had become the
traditional one;[4] yet after the most generous construction the fact remains that his mind was essentially of that type which knowledge neither broadens
nor enriches.

While Buchanan impressed on James "that a

[1] "Quid enim utilius in hac vita quam pura mens et pura oratio,
quid jucundius quam elegans vita et elegans oratio?"—Charles Schmidt,
Jean Sturm : Sa Vie et ses ouvrages, p. 247.

[2] The following passage from Buchanan's History (p. 4) is interesting
as directly bearing on this subject:—"Quod ad me attinet, malim
ignorare veterem Scotorum et anilem priscorum Britannorum balbuticm
quam dediscere quodcunque hoc est sermonis Latini, quod magno cum
labore puer didici. Neque aliud est, cur minus moleste feram priscam
Scotorum linguam paullatim intermori, quam quod libenter sentiam
barbaros illos sonos paullatim evanescere, et in illorum locum Latinarum
vocum amœnitatem succedere. Quod si in hac transmigratione in
alienam linguam, necesse est alteros alteris concedere, nos a rusticitate
et barbaria ad cultum et humanitatem transeamus : et quod nascendi
infelicitate nobis evenit, voluntate et judicio exuamus: aut, si quid
opera et industria possimus, id omne eo conferamus, ut linguam Græcam
et Latinam, quas orbis pars melior tanquam publicas recepit, pro viribus
expoliamus, et si quis ex contagio barbari sermonis adhaesit situs et
squalor, quoad fieri possit, extergeamus."

[3] Mark Pattison, *Life of Casaubon*, p. 296.

[4] Mr. Gardiner, for example. *History of England*, vol. i. p. 48 (1883).

king ought to be the most learned clerk in his dominions", he was far from thinking that mere learning was a sufficient qualification for a good ruler. In a poem addressed to his friend Sir Thomas Randolph, the English resident in Scotland, he has told us in few words what to his mind a good prince should be : " You often urge me to paint for you what manner of king I should wish, were God to grant one according to my prayer. Here, then, is the portrait you want. In chief, I would have him a lover of true piety, deeming himself the veritable image of highest God. He must love peace, yet be ever ready for war. To the vanquished he must be merciful ; and when he lays down his arms he must lay aside his hate. I should wish him to be neither a niggard nor a spendthrift, for each, I must think, works equal harm to his people. He must believe that as king he exists for his subjects and not for himself, and that he is, in truth, the common father of the State. When expediency demands that he shall punish with a stern hand, let it appear that he has no pleasure in his own severity. He will ever be lenient if it is consistent with the welfare of his people. His life must be the pattern for every citizen, his countenance the terror of evil-doers, the delight of those that do well. His mind he must cultivate with sedulous care, his body as reason demands. Good sense and good taste must keep in check luxurious excess." [1]

Buchanan certainly lost no opportunity of im-

---

[1] *Epigram.* ii. 27. With these lines of Buchanan it is interesting to compare the epigram in which James dedicates his *Basilikon Doron* to his son Henry.

pressing on James this ideal of his future duties. The three works in which he has set forth his conception of the true relation that should hold between king and subject, he dedicated to him in plain-speaking prefaces, which in after years James regarded as little short of blasphemous. The dedication of the *Baptistes* has already been noted. In the dedication of his History he says that he was largely influenced in undertaking it by the desire that it might tend to the profit of his Majesty. We shall afterwards see from what point of view Buchanan regarded the constitutional history of Scotland. At present, it is sufficient to say that it ran counter at every point to what was eventually James's own. That Buchanan should have dedicated to James his *De Jure Regni*, a tract which every crowned head in Europe was bound to regard as the most monstrous compound of treason and impiety, cannot but provoke a smile in the light of what his pupil was afterwards to become. What James came to think of these well-meant efforts to make him a man and a king, his manner of speaking of Buchanan and his works very plainly showed. Yet it is clear that Buchanan must have made an impression on him which he never forgot. Of a certain personage, James, when come to manhood, was wont to say "that he ever trembled at his approach, it minded him so of his pedagogue".[1] He had a certain pride also in the great name of his master. At the close of a scholastic disputation at Stirling, a certain English doctor who was present expressed his admiration at the King's mastery of Latin. "All the world, "he replied, "knows that my master,

---

[1] Osborne, *Advice to a Son*, p. 19.

George Buchanan, was a great master in that
faculty.   I follow his pronunciation both of the
Latin and the Greek, and am sorry that my people
of England do not the like; for certainly their
pronunciation utterly spoils the grace of these two
learned languages.   But you see all the university
and learned men of Scotland express the true and
native pronunciation of both." [1]

Of Buchanan's bearing towards his pupil compared with that of his assistant Young, we have an
interesting account in the Memoirs of Sir James
Melville.   Melville had been a courtier and diplo-
matist all his life, and was at the opposite pole from
Buchanan in character and opinions.   His words
regarding Buchanan, therefore, must be taken with
due reserves.   In his account of Buchanan's independent attitude towards his royal pupil, however,
we have seen that he is borne out by James's own
subsequent testimony.   "My Lady Mar," Melville
writes, "was wise and sharp, and held the King in
great awe; and so did Mr. George Buchanan.   Mr.
Peter Young was more gentle, and was loath to
offend the King at any time, carrying himself
warily, as a man who had a mind to his own
weal by keeping of his Majesty's favour; [2] but
Mr. George was a Stoick philosopher who looked
not far before him.   A man of notable endowments
for his learning and knowledge of Latin poesie, much
honoured in other countries, pleasant in conversa-

---

[1] Craufurd, *History of the University of Edinburgh*, p. 86 (Edin. 1808).
Ben Jonson informed Drummond of Hawthornden that he had told
King James "that his master Mr. George Buchanan had corrupted his
ear when young, and learnt him to sing verses when he should have read
them".
[2] As the Acts of the Parliament of Scotland show, Young reaped
the benefits of his complaisance.

tion, rehearsing on all occasions moralities short and instructive, whereof he had abundance, inventing where he wanted." The remainder of the passage may be given, though it is not quite relevant : " He was also religious, but was easily abused, and so facile that he was led by every company that he haunted, which made him factious in his old days, for he spoke and wrote as those who were about him informed him ; for he was become careless, following in many things the vulgar opinion ; for he was naturally popular, and extremely revengeful against any man who had offended him, which was his greatest fault." With reference to his general bearing towards James, we have already seen that Buchanan had a natural faculty for engaging the affection and admiration of youth. If therefore he showed himself somewhat of a hard taskmaster to James, we may conclude that his bearing was influenced by what he saw in his pupil's character and by the general attitude of those who attended on him. As for Melville's concluding words, they must also be set over-against the testimonies of those who understood Buchanan better than himself.

Two curious glimpses into the school-room at Stirling are given us by two very different observers —the one by Killigrew, Elizabeth's resident in Scotland, the other by James Melville, nephew of the famous Andrew. Killigrew, it appears, had paid a special visit to Stirling to see the young King. James, he says, showed that he had greatly profited by the instructions of his masters, made " pretty speeches ", and " translated a chapter of the Bible from Latin into French, and from French

R

into English extempore ".   His preceptors Buchanan
and Peter Young, he adds, made the King dance
before him, which he did " with a very good grace".[1]
James Melville's visit was made in company with
his uncle, who wished to consult Buchanan regarding the reforms he was contemplating in the College
of Glasgow.   They found him engaged on his History
of Scotland.   Regarding James, Melville is even
more enthusiastic than Killigrew.   Speaking of the
King's performances before him he says that "it
was the sweetest sight in Europe that day for
strange and extraordinary gifts of ingine, judgment,
memory, and language ".   " I heard him discourse,"
he adds, "walking up and down in the auld Lady
Marr's hand, of knawledge and ignorance to my great
marvell and astonishment."[2]   Melville's wonder was
doubtless none the less great that the youthful
performer was a king.   Still, after every abatement,
there can be little doubt that James was something
of a youthful prodigy both in attainments and
quickness of mind.

Two anecdotes of Buchanan's method of dealing
with his pupil are related, which, though characteristic enough, do not rest on very satisfactory authority.   We give them here for what they are worth.
The young Earl of Mar had a sparrow which his
royal playmate greatly coveted, and one day, in a
struggle between them for its possession, the sparrow
met its end.[3]   The affair was reported to Buchanan,
who, lending James a box on the ear, told him that
" he was himself a true bird of the bloody nest to

[1] Calendar of State Papers (Scotland).
[2] Melville's Diary.
[3] As bearing on the truth of the story it should be said that Mar
was eight years older than James.

which he belonged ". On another occasion Buchanan
was even more emphatic. A theme had just been set
for James on the conspiracy at Lauder Bridge, where
the Earl of Angus acquired the *sobriquet* of Bell-
the-Cat. After dinner young Mar and the King
were so noisy as to disturb Buchanan at his studies.
He requested them to be quiet, but the noise went
on as before. Buchanan then told them that if they
did not attend to his words, he would use a more
forcible reminder. " But who will bell the cat ? "
asked the young prince. His master at once applied
such condign punishment that James's cries brought
the Countess of Mar to the spot. The Countess
demanded of Buchanan how he dared to lay his
hands on the Lord's anointed. Buchanan's reply,
though quite in the taste of the time, will not bear
a modern rendering.[1]

On the authority of Buchanan's nephew another
story is told which has a certain air of probability.
Buchanan, it seems, had discovered in James an
undue facility in complying with every request
that might be made of him—a trait, it may be
said, which signally showed itself in the favouritism
of his later years. Buchanan took the following
method of correcting this weakness. One day, presenting two papers to James, he requested his signature. After a careless question, James did as he was
desired. One of the papers conferred on Buchanan
the sovereignty of the kingdom for fourteen days.
He at once assumed the part of king, much to the
astonishment of James, who began to think his

[1] Mackenzie, *Lives of Scots Writers*, vol. iii. p. 180. Mackenzie is
always to be taken with large reservations. He says, however, that he
had the above two anecdotes from the Earl of Cromarty, whose grandfather, Lord Invertyle, was Buchanan's pupil along with James.

master had lost his wits. On asking an explanation, he was informed that it was with his own
consent that Buchanan was now king. James was
more amazed than ever, but Buchanan, presenting
the document with his own signature affixed, read
him a lecture on the folly of his conduct.

Was it the fault of Buchanan that James grew
into the man and king he did? Of all scholars
Buchanan strikes us as the least of a pedant. His
age was pre-eminently the age of pedantry; but in
Buchanan, the man is never for a moment lost in
the scholar. In spite of what we must regard as
his essentially artificial training, his fiery Celtic
nature proclaims itself in every page he wrote, in
every opinion he advocated. In religion and politics, also, he thought with the most advanced
section of the Protestant party. It is remarkable,
therefore, that in both points his pupil should have
grown into the very antithesis of himself—in his
learning a pedant, in his views of the prerogative of
kings an absolutist. It might be said, of course,
that Buchanan himself was too old and James too
young for the most fruitful relations of master and
pupil. Still, in the case of one of Buchanan's varied
experience, individuality of character, and natural
sympathy with the young, we might have expected
that he would have left some mark of himself even
on the narrow and perverse mind of James. The
case of Fénelon and the young Duke of Burgundy
naturally occurs to us in connection with Buchanan
and James. It will be remembered that Fénelon,
by sheer tact and sympathetic insight, transformed
the Duke from something very like a wild beast
into a prince with the highest consciousness of

duty and the humanest of tempers. Fénelon had undoubtedly the advantage of Buchanan in setting about his task when his own powers of body and mind were at their best. On the other hand, it might seem from what we read of the inhuman ferocity and vicious propensities of the Duke, that Fénelon had the more difficult subject to deal with. But Fénelon himself did not think so. " Lively and sensitive natures," he says, "are capable of going far astray ; passion and presumption drag them on ; but such natures have likewise great resources, and often make recovery when they seem to have gone furthest astray." In truth, no character is less easily moulded than such as we know James's to have been. He had by nature that pragmatical self-conceit which is as triple brass against the influence of other minds. Of spontaneity, of self-abandonment, of, in short, what we call essentially qualities of soul, James was utterly destitute ; and it is precisely in such qualities that the teacher finds the springs by which he directs, transforms, and elevates his pupil's nature.

Buchanan's position as tutor to the young King gave him a real political importance in the eyes of his contemporaries. During these years the struggle between the Protestant and the Catholic powers of Europe was passing through its sternest crisis ; and it was matter of momentous concern to both on which side James should eventually take his place. In a few years he would possibly be King of Great Britain and Ireland, and according as he made his choice it seemed that the balance would be turned. With Buchanan at the young King's ear, the Protestants naturally hoped that he

would imbibe notions on religion and politics very
different from those of his mother. From many of
the leading Protestants, therefore, Buchanan received letters emphasising the responsibility of his
position, and pointing out the vital importance of
James's future decision. A few of these letters
have been preserved, and they plainly show the
anxiety with which the situation was regarded.
Among them is one from Philip de Mornay,[1] the
devoted servant of Henry of Navarre. Henry had
intrusted Mornay with a letter to Buchanan, in
which he called upon him to do what lay in his
power to make the young King think well of him.
Mornay, however, had fallen into the hands of
pirates, and the letter was lost. He therefore
communicates to Buchanan what he knew to be the
purport of Henry's message. It is of the highest
importance, he says, that there should be an understanding between Henry and the Scottish king.
At that moment (he is writing in 1577) it seemed
as if "all the Christian kingdoms of the world were
going headlong to destruction, and that impiety
and tyranny must overrun the earth". Unless he
is deceived, however, Buchanan is educating a new
Constantine to save the world. It were in the
fitness of things, he adds, that the same region
which produced the world's first deliverer should
also produce the second. From another Huguenot,
Lemaçon de la Fonteine, there are two letters in
French, urging Buchanan to do all in his power to
bring about a marriage between James and the
sister of Henry of Navarre. Scholars also, Beza
among the rest, send him their latest books as pro-

[1] Duplessis-Mornay.

pitiatory offerings to the young King. With Beza
Buchanan had begun a friendship in France many
years before—probably in Paris after Buchanan had
left Bordeaux. Both had evidently the highest
esteem for each other; but what is interesting to
note is that Beza, since Calvin's death the most
distinguished Protestant divine in Europe, writes
to Buchanan as an acknowledged superior, and distinctly recognises him as of a genius higher than
his own.

Along with Peter Young, Buchanan was twice
(in 1572 and 1578) confirmed by decree of the
Privy Council in his office as "maister" to the
King.[1] The fall of Morton in 1578, which put a
temporary end to the Regency, practically emanci-
pated James from his tutors. Till his own death
in 1582, however, Buchanan still nominally held
his post. In his Testament-dative he is described
as "preceptour to ye Kingis majestye the tyme of
his deceis"; but his charge over James must practically have ceased two or three years earlier.

Besides his post as tutor to James, Buchanan
during his last years held other appointments,
which must have given him at least a certain social
status in his day. The election of Lennox as
Moray's successor in the regency was, of course,
favourable to Buchanan's fortunes. During Lennox's brief rule he was first made Director of
Chancery, and afterwards Keeper of the Privy Seal,
an office which he held till 1578. As Keeper of
the Privy Seal he was entitled to a seat in Parliament, a privilege of which he seems to have availed
himself. As member he served on one Commission

[1] Privy Council Records.

which, had it effected its object, would have kept
green the memory of himself and his fellow-commissioners. The object of the Commission was " to
mak ane body of the civile and municipale lawis,
devidit in heidis conforme to the fassone of the law
Romane, and the heidis as thai ar reddy to be
brocht to the Parliament to be confirmit ".[1] It is
needless to say that the Commission proved an
abortive one. While he was thus both " maister "
to the King and Keeper of the Privy Seal, Buchanan would seem to have been no easier in money
matters than formerly. The following epigram to
Lennox both suggests this, and shows the familiar
terms on which he stood with that nobleman :—

AD MATTHAEUM LEVINIAE COMITEM, SCOTIAE PROREGEM.

Cum mihi quod donem nil sit, tibi resque supersit,
  Accipe, cui dones officiosus opes.
Non ego sum nimius voti : ex tanto aeris acervo
  Sufficient animo millia pauca meo.
Denique da quidvis, podagram modo deprecor unam :
  Munus erit medicis aptius illa suis (tuis ?).[2]

" Since I am poor and you are rich,
    What happy chance is thine !
  My modest wishes, too, you know—
    One nugget from your mine !
  Only, whatever be your gift,
    Let it not be your gout :
  That, a meet present for your leech,
    I 'd rather go without."

Lennox was succeeded by the Earl of Mar in
September 1571. Of Mar Buchanan speaks with
the highest respect, and in this good opinion he is
supported by men of all parties in the State. Mar
was Governor of Stirling Castle, and hereditary
guardian of the King, so that Buchanan in his

[1] *Acts of the Parliaments of Scotland*, vol. iii. p. 40.
[2] *Epig.* iii. 19.

duties as tutor to James must have seen much of him. The new Regent died after little more than a year's tenure of office. In a short poem, Buchanan commemorated his virtues, and in a strain which is not that of mere conventional panegyric. The truth of the last two lines is borne out by other testimony besides Buchanan's. "This," he says, "is peculiar to himself, that in the course of a long life, envy and hatred have no charge with which to reproach him." [1]

Mar was followed in the regency by the Earl of Morton, a man of far more masterful character, but unscrupulous even for that age in his dealings with his enemies. To Morton Buchanan was not so favourably disposed as to the three previous Regents. With the religious party to which he belonged, he disapproved of Morton's attitude towards the Church. But his chief ground of opposition was the Regent's persistent attempts to gain possession of the King. It was, indeed, mainly by the advice of Buchanan, and Alexander Erskine, the Governor of Stirling Castle, that James was induced to support the party opposed to Morton, which brought about his temporary abdication in March 1578.[2] A council of twelve was then formed for the direction of the King, Buchanan being one of its extraordinary members. The council was of short duration, as by April of the same year Morton was again in power. During Morton's second regency Buchanan still continued in the Privy

---

[1] *Miscell.* xxv. Knox was of a different opinion.—*History*, vol. ii. p. 128.

[2] So at least says Sir James Melville : " Be whais [Buchanan's] advyse and counsaill his majeste was easely movit to depoise the Regent out of his office."

Council, though in 1578 he had resigned the Seal
to his nephew, Thomas Buchanan.   Of the two
Councils which met in Morton's second regency,
Buchanan occasionally attended the first, but at the
second he seems never to have appeared.   In the
first Council, Buchanan, assisted by Peter Young,
acted as *interim* secretary during the absence of the
Commendator of Dunfermline on an embassy to
England.[1]

During this period of Scottish history the agents
of Elizabeth were especially busy in Scotland, her
policy being to make sure of a strong party in that
country which she could always have at her disposal.   With this in view her agents kept Cecil
informed as to the persons upon whose support she
could count, or whose support it was politic to gain.
In July 1578 two lists were transmitted to Cecil,
one containing the names of *Biencontents*, the other
those of *Malcontents*.   In the latter, Buchanan's
name appears with the explanatory addition that he
is a Malcontent "in respect of the Erle Morton's
cominge againe into the king's favour".[2]   The following year Cecil had three other lists sent to him, the
first, " of persons who were commended by the Earl
of Morton, when he was Regent, as most meet to
be entertained"; the second, " of persons who were
also fit to have entertainment, though they were not
recommended by, the Regent"; and the third, " of
persons who were not commended by the Regent, yet
by others thought meet to be entertained ".   In the
last list appear the names of " Mr. George Buchanan,
a singular man", and of Peter Young, " another tutor

---

[1] Privy Council Records.
[2] Chalmers, *Life of Ruddiman*, p. 340.

to the King, specially well affected, and ready to persuade the King to be in favour of her majestye ".[1] In still another list are to be found " the names of such as are to be entertained in Scotland by pensions out of England ". In this list there are twenty-four names in all, the names of the Regent Morton and six earls coming first. Opposite Morton's name is placed the sum of £500 ; against those of the earls, in some cases £200, and in others £100. Opposite Buchanan's name is placed £100, and opposite that of Peter Young £30.[2] The list has a certain interest, as showing Buchanan's relative political importance in the eyes of the astute agents of Elizabeth. Whether the pensions were actually paid, or whether the intended beneficiaries even knew of these purposes in their favour, we have no means of knowing. But even had Buchanan accepted such a pension, it would be absurd to consider it any serious blot on his scutcheon. The habit of receiving pecuniary assistance from England had, in fact, during the sixteenth century become an accepted condition of public life in Scotland.

From these notices it will be seen that Buchanan was not among the leading political figures of his time. This is indeed conclusively shown by the place he occupies in the later Histories of Scotland. While the names of Knox and Andrew Melville are written large in all these Histories, that of Buchanan but rarely occurs, and then only as that of a mere public servant. At no time of his life, as we believe, were the instincts of Buchanan those of the practical politician; but even had he possessed these instincts,

[1] Chalmers, *Life of Ruddiman*, p. 342.
[2] *Ibid.* p. 343.

the advanced age at which he returned to Scotland,
as well as his chronic ill-health, must have debarred
him from taking a prominent part in public affairs.
In the religious strifes of his last years, the struggle
between Presbytery and Episcopacy, he seems to
have taken no part.   But the same reasons which
debarred him from politics sufficiently account for
his not taking his stand either with or against
Andrew Melville.[1]

[1] That his sympathies were with Melville, however, there can be no
doubt ; though he would certainly have disapproved of much that
Melville said and did.   In his History he has the following passage
regarding bishops : " Creditur idem Palladius primus Episcopos in Scotia
creasse.   Nam ad id usque tempus, Ecclesiae absque Episcopis per
monachos regebantur, minore quidem cum fastu et externa pompa, sed
majore simplicitate et sanctimonia."—*Rer. Scot. Hist.* lib. v. p. 79.

CHAPTER XVII.

By his dialogue *De Jure Regni apud Scotos* (Concerning the Rights of the Crown in Scotland) Buchanan holds a distinct place in the development of political thought in Britain. The dialogue is far indeed from being a material contribution to the subject it professes to discuss, yet its history conclusively proves that till the Revolution of 1688 its influence was seriously dreaded by the successive Governments of the country. In 1584, five years after its publication, and two years after Buchanan's death, this dialogue and his History of Scotland were condemned by Act of Parliament, and every person possessing copies commanded to produce them within forty days, that they might be purged of the " offensive and extraordinary matters " they contained.[1] In 1664 the Privy Council of Scotland issued a proclamation prohibiting all subjects from translating and circulating copies of a manuscript translation of the dialogue, and in 1688 this order was repeated.[2] In 1683, also, the University of

[1] *Acts of the Parliaments of Scotland,* vol. iii. p. 296.
[2] Wodrow, *Hist. of the Sufferings of the Church of Scotland,* vol. i. p. 218. Edin. 1721-2, two vols. fol.

Oxford publicly burned the political works of Buchanan, Milton, Languet, and other writers of their way of thinking.[1] These public censures sufficiently prove the importance of Buchanan's tract in the clash of political strife during the century that followed his death. During that century his reputation seems to have increased rather than diminished. His word, therefore, as that of the most illustrious of British scholars, could not be slighted even by the most distinguished supporters of the royal prerogative. Moreover, the dialogue itself, though of little value as a political treatise, yet by the elegance and force of its Latin style was well fitted to win readers in an age when Latin was still the language of learned discussion.

Immediately on its publication it was assailed by writers of the opposite school from Buchanan; and we may say that till the Revolution of 1688 the attacks on Buchanan's motives and opinions grew rather more than less bitter. In his own country the controversy was carried on into the following century with even increased asperity, his opponents seriously maintaining that it was impossible he could have been an honest man and have advocated the political opinions he did.[2] These opinions, they said, were, in the first place, new to Scotland; secondly, they were false; and lastly, they were brought forward simply to justify the unconstitutional proceedings against Mary. With

[1] Irving, *Memoirs of Buchanan*, p. 261 note.
[2] Ruddiman, in his later years, and after the failure of the '45, was unsparing in his denunciation of the man whose works he had edited. Chalmers, also, in his *Life of Ruddiman* (1794), leaves the humanists themselves behind in the scurrility of his abuse. But, like Ruddiman (though out of due time), he was likewise a rabid Jacobite.

the knowledge we now possess of the development of political ideas in Europe we see that such controversies are entirely beside the mark. By his natural affinities, and by every condition of his life and training, it was impossible that Buchanan in the sixteenth century could have adopted other political theories than he did.

Buchanan's main positions in the *De Jure Regni* are, that kings exist by the will and for the good of the people, that they may be brought to account for misgovernment, and that under certain circumstances tyrannicide is justifiable. But before giving a more detailed account of the dialogue, it is necessary that we should mark the conditions out of which it sprang. Humanism had undoubtedly its own influence in this as in every other of Buchanan's productions; but other currents meet in the *De Jure Regni*, which distinctly stamp it as a typical product of the time.

Among the ideas the humanists had gained from the study of antiquity was that of the paramount importance of liberty to the true growth and happiness of men. The passages they admired above all others in the Greek and Latin writers were those which proclaim the dignity of free citizenship and denounce the evils of tyranny. Their favourite heroes were such characters as Brutus and Timoleon, whom they extolled as personages a country should rejoice to have produced. Much of the rhetoric of the humanists on this subject was doubtless the mere echo of the writers they admired, yet the political conditions of their own day gave the reality of striking contrast to the tradition of the ancient republics. It was in large measure the suggestion of this contrast that inspired the biting sarcasms of Erasmus at the expense of contemporary princes.

But, independently of humanism, medieval Europe bequeathed its own legacy of opinion as to the claims of the people and the prerogatives of princes. From the rise of the various Christian powers in Western Europe this subject engaged the best minds of each successive generation. The opinion which all along had the approval of the Church was that all power comes from God, and that as the Pope was God's vicegerent, supremacy over kings of necessity pertains to the Church, which alone had the power to loosen the bonds of allegiance. This twofold conception of the sanctity of kings and their responsibility to God alone— that is, to the Church as God's representative—is expressed with great clearness as early as the sixth century in an address by Gregory of Tours to King Chilperic. "O king," he says, "if any one of us should desire to stray from the path of justice, thou canst correct us; but if thou shouldst go astray, who will arraign thee? We address ourselves to thee, it is true; but thou hearkenest only if thou wilt. Against thy will who will condemn thee, unless it be He who is justice itself?" This was the view approved by the Church, and received by men so little subservient to authority as Gregory; but an unbroken line of thinkers did not hesitate to assert that the people is the source of all kingly power, and that princes exist solely by the will and for the good of their subjects. It is the essence of the Christian doctrine that it gives the individual a dignity and importance he never had under

Paganism. That a whole people, therefore, should submit to one arbitrary will, implied the forfeiture of all that raises man above the beasts. A few quotations will show how strongly these views were held by many of the most distinguished teachers of the Middle Ages.[1]

"Kings are called kings," says Isidore of Seville in the sixth century, "because they do well. They retain the name so long as they act rightly; when they act amiss, they lose it."[2] In the eighth century a certain bishop of Verona declared "that all men are naturally equal, and that men ought not to recognise inequality, which has often the result of placing the best under the dominion of the worst". In the middle of the tenth century free notions regarding the divine origin of kings seem not to have been uncommon. "I know some persons among our contemporaries," says a writer of that century, "who believe that royalty has its origin, not from God, but from men ignorant of God, accustomed to live by plunder, treasons, and murders—covered, in short, with every kind of crime, who at the beginning of the world had, by the inspiration of the devil, the blind ambition and the unspeakable temerity to lord it over other men who were their equals." In the twelfth century John of Salisbury speaks in words that might pass for Buchanan's : "When he is the true image of God, the king should be loved, honoured, obeyed ; when he is the image of all that is evil, he should in most

---

[1] For the quotations in the following paragraph I am indebted to a singularly interesting paper (*La Royauté française et le Droit populaire d'après les Écrivains du Moyen Age*) in M. Jourdain's *Excursions historiques et philosophiques à travers le Moyen Age.*

[2] "Reges a recte agendo vocati sunt, ideoque recte faciendo, regis nomen tenetur, peccando amittitur."

cases be put to death." [1]   In the thirteenth century
Thomas Aquinas taught that the end of government
is the good of the community, that governments are
not instituted for the personal satisfaction of those
who are at their head, but for public utility, that
kings are the shepherds of their people, and that a
good shepherd thinks before everything of the good
of his flock. Duns Scotus, however, goes much
further than this, and boldly represents the people
as the sole source of political power. In a treatise
written about the year 1324 by Marsilius of Padua,
the rights of the people are emphasised with a bold-
ness and clearness that might have satisfied Knox
and Buchanan themselves. One sentence will show
the length to which this writer, who at one time
was rector of the University of Paris, was prepared
to go. " Est enim multitudo dominus major." " Of
people and prince, the former is the superior power."
One quotation more may be given, and it is the
most remarkable of all. Gerson, Chancellor of the
University of Paris, from whom the quotation is
taken, was one of the most notable figures in the
intellectual world of his day; and from him, perhaps, more than any other, John Major learned
the political opinions which have gained for him the
name of " the first Scottish radical ".[2]   " If kings,"
says Gerson, " fail in their duty towards their subjects, if they conduct themselves unjustly, above all
if they persist in their misgovernment—this is
exactly a case for applying the law of justice, that
it is permissible to repel force by force. Has not

---

[1] " Imago deitatis princeps amandus, venerandus est et colendus ;
tyrannus, pravitatis imago, plerumque etiam occidendus."
[2] The phrase is Professor Masson's.

Seneca said that there can be no more acceptable sacrifice to God than a tyrant ? " Neither Buchanan nor Milton went beyond this.[1]

These citations conclusively prove that it was not left to the humanists to make known the principles on which free States are based. Before the sixteenth century it is clear that educated men were perfectly familiar with doctrines that afterwards came to be identified with the Huguenots of France and the Puritans of England. How widespread these doctrines were, is signally proved by the speech, so often quoted, of Philippe Pot before the French States-General in 1484 : " As history relates, and as I have heard from my fathers, it was the people who first created kings by their suffrage, specially preferring men who surpassed others in virtue and capacity. Each people chose a king for his usefulness."

But these bold notions as to the inherent right of a people to govern itself, of necessity remained simple theory till the sixteenth century. So long as the Western nations owned universal allegiance to the Pope, the fundamental principles on which society rests could never be the subject of practical discussion. For the mass of the people the king and his prerogative made as much a part of the system of nature as the sun and the moon. The fiery spirits who led the great Protestant schism were made to feel that this habit of mind, produced by centuries of unquestioning submission to authority, could not be transformed in a day.[2] But it was the sixteenth

---

[1] It will be remembered that Milton translates Seneca's verse and thus stamps it with his approval.

[2] In the present age the following sentences from Buchanan's *De Jure Regni* strike us somewhat oddly : " Reliqua est imperita multitudo,

century that converted these theoretical discussions
into burning questions of conduct and policy.   This
fact may, of course, be broadly set down as the
result of the generally awakened intelligence of
Europe ; yet a few special causes stand out as so
powerfully operative that they deserve particular
mention.

During the latter part of the fifteenth century
there had been a rapid movement towards absolute
power on the part of all the great princes of Europe.
In the sixteenth century this tendency still continued, and an actual rivalry arose between the
rulers of the various countries as to which could
most completely override the will of his people.[1]
The Prince of Machiavelli reduced to a system the
means by which a ruler might attain the end at
which all were aiming.   Such men as Erasmus and
More, inspired alike by the Christian and the classical
tradition, had, before the publication of *The Prince*,
given the most forcible expression to their views of
the duties of kings to their subjects.   But the
appearance of *The Prince* still further excited the
alarm and indignation of thinking men throughout
Europe.   The fame of Machiavelli's book is proved by
the numberless references to it in the writings of the
century.   But the most significant tribute to the
widespread alarm it produced is the fact that Bodin
wrote his great work *De Republicâ* expressly to
counteract its teaching.[2]   It may be taken also as a

quae omnia nova miratur, plurima reprehendit, neque quicquam rectum
putat, nisi quod ipsa aut facit, aut fieri videt.   Quantum enim a consuetudine majorum receditur, tantum a justo et aequo recedi putat."
    [1] During his visit to Francis I. in 1539, Charles V. expressed his
admiration and envy at the French king's control over his people.
    [2] "Peu d'écrivains ont exercé une action plus directe [than Machia-
velli], plus profonde sur les hommes et sur les événements.   C'est à le
combattre que nous verrons s'appliquer Bodin."—Baudrillart, *J. Bodin
et son Temps* (Paris, 1853), p. 17.

curious proof how wide and deep the evil repute of
Machiavelli had gone, that his name, corrupted into
Mitchell Wylie, was in Scotland applied to Maitland
of Lethington.[1]

But it was the great Protestant revolt from
Rome that brought to direct issue the question of
the mutual relations of king and people. From
the very beginning of that revolt it was felt on
both sides that the old relations could no longer
hold if Luther should succeed. It was therefore
the policy of the supporters of Rome to hold out
the constant threat that Lutheranism meant not
only defection from the Church but universal
anarchy. The excesses of Anabaptism and the
Peasants' War gave them as strong a case as they
could have wished ; and in France especially, during
the first half of the sixteenth century, the dread of
a social cataclysm undoubtedly did much to arrest
the movement towards reform.

On the other hand, the reformers themselves had
equally soon to recognise the new position in which, as
subjects, their defection from Rome had placed them.
In a country where, being in a minority, their religious views should not be tolerated; or where, being
in a majority, the ruler should interfere with the duty
they owed to God—what in either of these cases was
the line of conduct they ought to pursue ? The
leaders of the Protestant party fully realised the
gravity of their position. The charge of extreme
counsels has been so constantly brought against them,
that the following testimony of de l'Hôpital to

---

[1] The name *Mitchell Wylie* appears in the *Memorials* of Knox's
servant, Richard Bannatyne. *Wylie*, of course, is *wily*. There is
frequent reference to Machiavelli in the Scots vernacular literature of
the time.

their moderation will surprise many. "Among all those," says this very highest authority, "who have gone over to Protestantism, there is not one who wishes to unsettle the supremacy of the king; for this is manifestly against the principles of their religion."[1] That this could be said of the Huguenots after the civil war, and after St. Bartholomew, is certainly a singular tribute to their great legislator Calvin.

In Germany, the political question was not thrust on the Reformers in the direct and critical form it took in France and Scotland. Luther had to face the orgies of Anabaptism and the revolt of the peasants as the result of his breach with Rome; but neither of these cases necessitated a full and precise definition of the relations of ruler and subject. As Ranke has said: "In Germany the Protestant churches were founded under the protection, the immediate influence, of the reigning authorities, and their form was naturally determined by that circumstance."

In France, however, the new opinions had to create for themselves a set of conditions for which no provision had hitherto been made in any Christian State. And it is to be remembered that those who held these opinions claimed not only sufferance, but the liberty of propagandism. How to provide this liberty and yet not seriously endanger the central authority of the State was the delicate question which Calvin had to solve in his *Institutes of the Christian Religion*. That he did not solve it is simply to say that a people cannot be fitted with a ready-made constitution, but must grow into it

[1] Baudrillart, *J. Bodin et son Temps*, p. 67.

by a natural process of adaptation. It was not till after three centuries that the question which engaged Calvin settled itself by the unconscious growth of educated opinion. Calvin taught that under no circumstances—always excepting where his religious faith was concerned—was the individual citizen justified in resisting his prince. The advisers of the prince, however, and any representative body in the State, Calvin did not forbid from withstanding the tyrannical exercise of authority.[1] It is evident that this position completely covers the entire policy of the Protestant party in Scotland in their proceedings against Mary. As the religious struggle grew fiercer, and at the same time more equal, the followers of Calvin were forced into bolder statements of the rights of the people against tyrants ; yet in the most extreme statements of their views they never forgot that obedience to the State is incumbent on every man professing to be a follower of Christ.

Calvin's *Institutes* appeared in 1535 ; but as the century went on, the great question of the true limits of the allegiance of the subject became more and more pressing, and more and more difficult of satisfactory definition. In France, the horrible treatment of Bordeaux by the Constable Montmorency for its refusal to pay the *gabelle*, gave a formidable impulse to free opinions regarding the

[1] " Neque enim, si ultio Domini est effrenatae dominationis correctio, ideo protinus demandatam nobis arbitremur : quibus nullum aliud quam parendi et patiendi datum est mandatum. De privatis hominibus semper loquor. Nam si qui nunc sint populares magistratus ad moderandam regum libidinem constituti, adeo illos ferocienti regum licentiae pro officio intercedere non veto."—*Institutio Christianae Religionis,* lib. iv. chap. xx.

" At vero in ea, quam praefectorum imperiis deberi constituimus, obedientia, id semper excipiendum est, imo in primis observandum, ne ab ejus obedientia nos deducat, cujus voluntati regum omnium vota subesse," etc.—*Ibid.*

rights of the Crown.[1] In the year of the revolt of
Bordeaux, 1548, "in face of the scaffolds erected in
the public places of the towns of Aquitaine," the
celebrated *Contr' Un* of la Boëtie, the friend of
Montaigne, was written, in which it was maintained,
in a torrent of youthful eloquence, that for the many
to be the slaves of the one was a disgrace to the
dignity of human nature. This pamphlet was not
published till many years after ; but the fact that
it was written before the civil war and St. Bartholomew is but one proof among many that the
boldest opinions regarding the rights of the people
were in the air long before these events.

The sketch of opinion that has just been given
applies in the first place to France ; but the political and intellectual bond between France and Scotland was for centuries so close that we need not
wonder to find in the one the ideas and aspirations
of the other. Before Buchanan, the two writers of
note who dealt with the rights of the Crown in
Scotland were Major and Boece. As Major's History was published in 1521, and that of Boece in
1527, neither was influenced by the great political
and religious impulses of the sixteenth century.
As has already been said, Major remained through
life a schoolman pure and simple. His intellectual
interests as well as his medieval Latin put this
beyond question. But he was a schoolman in the
line of those independent thinkers whose political
views have been cited above. We have seen how
he was regarded in Paris as one of the champions
of the privileges of the University against the
Pope. His opinions regarding the true source of

[1] Martin, *Histoire de France*, vol. viii. livre iv.

authority in a nation are equally bold and hetero-
dox. Everything, indeed, that Buchanan himself
has said regarding the Royal prerogative in Scotland, Major said before him with the quaint blunt-
ness and directness that mark his style. That his
political opinions were really abiding convictions is
proved by the fact that he expresses himself with
the same decision in his History and in his purely
scholastic writings. In his History we have such
sentiments as these : " As it was the people who
first made kings, so the people can dethrone them
when they misuse their privileges." [1] Elsewhere he
is still bolder, in the statement of his views as to
the measure that should be dealt to bad kings.
" As it is for the benefit of the whole body," he
says, " that an unhealthy member is removed, so is
it for the welfare of a State that a tyrant should be
cut off." [2] This is as explicit a statement on the
subject as anything we find in Knox or Buchanan.

Though a contemporary of Major, Boece belonged to the Renaissance rather than to Scholasticism. His Latin style and his whole manner of
conducting his narrative is so distinct from that of
Major, that the difference implies not only an
essentially distinct type of mind, but essentially
distinct intellectual ideals. Yet Boece's political

---

[1] The following sentences will illustrate Major's Latin style as well
as his political opinions : "Populus liber primo regi dat robur, cujus
potestas a toto populo dependet ; quia aliud jus Fergusius primus rex
Scotiae non habuit : et ita est ubilibet et ab orbe condito erat commu-
niter. Si dicas mihi ab Henrico Septimo Henricus Octavus jus habet,
ad primum Anglorum regem ascendam, quaerendo a quo ille jus regni
habuit ? et ita ubivis gentium procedam."—*De Gestis Scotorum*, lib. iv.
cap. xvii.

[2] " Cum licentia totius corporis veri tollitur hoc membrum ; etiam
facultate totius corporis mystici, tu, tamque minister comitatis, potes
hunc tyrannum occidere, dum est licite condempnatus."—Quoted by
M'Crie, *Life of Knox*, vol. i. (Note D).

philosophy is identical with that of Major, though his ideas of liberty were drawn, not from the school-men, but from the classical writers, whom he had evidently studied in the true spirit of the humanists. He does not present his political teaching in the dogged, logical form of Major : his notions regard-ing popular rights are wrought into his narrative and quietly taken for granted. Thus, when he relates how Theseus, one of the legendary kings, was dethroned and exiled for misgovernment, he makes no comment on this exercise of popular authority, but seems to think that his readers will take it as a matter of course. Yet there is so little uncertainty about his opinions, that Bishop Nicol-son could say that "Boece's principles in polity were no better than those of Buchanan".[1]

From what has been said, it abundantly appears that the political doctrines laid down by Knox in his famous interview with Mary had, in truth, the support of many of the ablest doctors of her own Church, and that so far from being new or peculiar to Scotland, they had their advocates in all the kingdoms of Europe from the very beginning of the Middle Ages. Though they have been quoted so often, the sentences may once more be given in which Knox lays down his doctrine of the people's right of resistance to bad rulers. "Do you main-tain," asked Mary, "that subjects having power may resist their princes ?" "Most assuredly," said Knox, "if princes exceed their bounds ; God hath nowhere commanded higher reverence to be given to kings by their subjects than to parents by their children : and yet, if a father or mother be struck

---

[1] *Scottish Historical Library*, p. 37 (London, 1736).

with madness, and attempt to slay his children, they may lawfully bind and disarm him till the frenzy be overpast. It is even so, Madame, with princes that would murder the children of God, who may be their subjects. Their blind zeal is nothing but a mad frenzy, and therefore to take the sword from them, to bind their hands, and to cast them into prison, till they be brought to a more sober mind, is no disobedience against princes, but just obedience, because it agreeth with the word of God." [1]

The events of the few years that followed this interview were the practical commentary on this teaching of Knox. In accordance with that teaching, a large number of Mary's subjects thwarted her government by all the means in their power, and in 1567 dethroned her on the plea that she had forfeited the allegiance of her people. It was to meet the animadversions on these doings of his countrymen that Buchanan wrote his *De Jure Regni*. So far, and so far only, the dialogue is to be regarded as the product of immediate temporary circumstance. As far as its political theories are concerned, these were an inheritance that lay at his hand.

The dialogue was published in 1579 ; but it had been written several years before. Writing to a correspondent in 1579, he says that he sends him the *De Jure Regni*, written in turbulent times, but now given to the world after a moderate period, when the tumult was subsiding, and men's ears had grown accustomed to opinions of the kind it contained.[2] In his dedication to King James, he also

---

[1] Knox, *History of the Reformation,* vol. ii. p. 282 (Laing's Edition). The above modern rendering is that given by Tytler, *History of Scotland,* vol. iii. chap. vi. p. 154 (Edin. 1873).

[2] *Epist.* xxiv.

says that it was written when Scottish affairs were in a state of unsettlement, and that his object was to put before his readers the origin and limits of the Royal prerogative in Scotland. The book, he continues, had served a good purpose at the time, by silencing the clamour of those who had protested against the existing arrangement in the State ; but as affairs had become more settled, " he had dedicated his arms to public concord ". In looking through his papers he had lately come upon his dialogue, and it occurred to him that its publication might be of real service to James himself, in showing him in true colours what a king of Scotland should aim at being.

The book must therefore have been written shortly after the return of the Commissioners from London, possibly even before the assassination of Moray in 1570. Its leading motive is identical with that of Milton in his *Defence of the People of England*—the justification of his countrymen in the eyes of Europe. Dryden, indeed, goes so far as to accuse Milton of having stolen his *Defence* from Buchanan.[1] But though the motive and teaching of both is the same, and though Milton had certainly read Buchanan's dialogue, this charge is irrelevant. It is interesting to note, however, how keenly both resent foreign criticism on their countrymen, as at once insolent and ungenerous. With Buchanan this is the first and last word of his treatise.

The book is in the form of an imaginary dialogue between Buchanan and Thomas Maitland, a younger brother of Secretary Maitland. Young Maitland

---

[1] Preface to *The Medal*.

is represented as having recently returned from France; and, by way of introduction, Buchanan asks him how late events in Scotland are being talked of on the Continent. He is told that men speak very freely of the seditious character of the Scots, as shown in the murder of Darnley, and in the proceedings against Mary. But, objects Buchanan, if they are so indignant at the murder of Darnley, why are they so full of pity for Mary? If Mary was guilty of Darnley's murder, she certainly deserved punishment. Those who will not admit this must belong to one of three classes—those who pander to the desires of princes, because they hope to profit by their misdeeds; those who, for their own selfish ends, approve peace at any price; or, lastly, the ignorant multitude, who are unwilling to quit the beaten track, because they think every novelty a crime.

The argument of the dialogue now begins; but Buchanan first asks that it may be allowed him as a provisional postulate that king and tyrant are contradictories. This being granted, he proceeds to consider the origins of all society. Primitive men had no fixed homes, no settled laws; how did they come in time to have both? Utility, which some have suggested, is not a satisfactory explanation, since if individual men always considered their own interest, it would lead rather to the dissolution than the building up of society. The true explanation is that in man there is a natural instinct which leads him to associate with his fellows.[1] Utility is rather

---

[1] Buchanan's contemporary, Bodin, like many subsequent thinkers, thought that violence created society. "Nos ipsa ratio," he says, "deducit imperia scilicet ac respublicas vi primum coaluisse."—*De Republicâ*, lib. i. cap. vi. p. 40 (Ed. 1591).

the handmaid than the mother of justice and equity.
Now, as in our bodies there are conflicting principles, which induce disease, so it is with society.
What the physician, therefore, is to the body, the
king is to society. The various names by which he
is known, father, shepherd, and the like, prove that
the king exists not for himself but for his people.
The aim of physician and king is the same—to preserve health, and to restore it when lost. In the
State as in the body there is a certain *tempera-
mentum.* For the State this is justice. Maitland objects that temperance is the apter virtue.
Buchanan replies that the term is immaterial.

But how can kings *justly* arise ? The answer is,
When they are chosen by the people, and continued
in their office by its will. But as no vote of the
people can make a man an artist or a physician, so
it may be said that the people cannot make a king.
But in the case of the artist a collection of precepts
guide him in the exercise of his art. In the case of
the king these precepts make what we call *law.*
Prudence is the art which the king has to practise ;
but as kings are not all gifted with prudence, the
law is added as something outside by which he must
be guided.

Maitland here objects that Buchanan would
unduly limit the power of kings, which is, indeed,
exactly what might have been expected from his
extravagant praise of the ancient republics and of
Venice. Buchanan replies that it is immaterial to
him what form of government a people may choose
so long as it is legitimate. King, doge, consul, all
are alike to him. Kings exist only for the administration of justice. Because they failed in this

the law was added. *Rex, lex loquens; lex, rex mutus.*

As the people are the authors of kings, so they are and ought to be the authors of the law. They must also be its interpreters, since otherwise they could have no assurance that their interests would be safe. Such limitations of their powers is no dishonour to kings, for it still leaves them the function of the true physician—that of relieving the State from all the evils to which it is incident. While it is forbidden them to override the law, the glorious task is assigned them of preserving and administrating it in its integrity—and could a god desire a more exalted one?

Buchanan then proceeds to distinguish between kings and tyrants. He finds the distinction to be that the latter seize and hold the power against the will of the people, and make their own will the law.[1] Here Maitland urges that as in Scotland kings are hereditary and not elective, the people must needs be content with whatever ruler chance may bring them. Buchanan's answer is that the Scottish people have always retained and exercised the right

---

[1] We have seen that the questions—What constitutes a tyrant, and under what circumstances is a people justified in calling him to account? —intensely agitated men's minds about the period the *De Jure Regni* was written. After St. Bartholomew numberless writings discussing these questions made their appearance. Bodin, a supporter of authority, differs considerably from Buchanan in the answer he gives to the above questions. This is his definition of a tyranny : " Tyrannis est in qua unus homo, divinis ac naturae legibus sublatis, rebus alienis ut suis, et liberis hominibus quasi mancipiis ad libidinem abutitur."—Lib. ii. cap. iv. p. 261. In the case of such rulers Bodin justifies tyrannicide. In the case of a lawful king, he will not allow his subjects under any circumstances to sit in judgment on him. He thinks, however, that they are at liberty to call in a neighbouring prince to dethrone him. This position of Bodin almost justifies the views of such men as Buchanan. As is well known, the Catholics of the League taught the same doctrine regarding tyrannicide as the Huguenots.

of calling bad kings to account, and of punishing violence offered to good ones.   The murderers of James I. were treated with every severity ; the death of James III. was allowed to go unpunished. The coronation oath by which the Scottish kings swear to preserve the laws of the country clearly proves the limited nature of their authority.   John Baliol was rejected by the Scottish nobility because he acknowledged the suzerainty of Edward I.

The treatment of tyrants is next discussed. Paul, Maitland suggests, taught obedience to the higher powers under all circumstances ; and Caligula and Nero then reigned.   The answer is that Paul speaks not of kings, but of the principle of authority. That this must have been his meaning is proved by the fact that if he had meant unconditional obedience to every kind of ruler, his words would equally apply to all grades of office.   Judges, therefore, and other subordinate officials, could not be punished for their misdemeanours.   Moreover, it is the express command of Scripture that every criminal should be punished, and nowhere is any immunity from punishment granted to tyrants.   Though Scripture may contain no instance of a king punished by his subjects, this would by no means imply that it disapproves such punishment.   Besides, in the case of the Jewish kings, God himself was their founder : to Him, therefore, it was fitting they should directly render account.   If we take other countries, all precedent favours the right of the people to punish bad kings.   Twelve or more bad kings of Scotland might be named who were imprisoned, exiled, or put to death by their subjects.   The case of James III. puts this right of the Scottish people beyond question.

In the Assembly of Estates it was enacted that James had justly suffered death, a clause being added that no one should be injured who had been concerned in the conspiracy against him. But, says Maitland, the very law by which the Estates justified themselves is more likely to be called in question by foreign nations than the deed itself. In that case, Buchanan replies, every law may be called in question. It is the king who receives authority from the law, and not *vice versâ.* But as it is the people who made the law, they must surely possess the power of dealing with the king who breaks it. Nor is it derogatory to a king to be tried by his own subjects, since the law by which he is tried is in reality but his own voice. A king, if guilty of any crime, should be judged by the same law as the private citizen. If he refuse to submit to a trial, force should then be applied, since he has broken his compact with his people, and has become a tyrant. Nay, since he is now a public enemy, individuals as well as the people collectively do well to slay him. Here Buchanan professes simply to answer the question how far the rights of the people against tyrants extend. The interests of the people must determine when the punishment of a tyrant is advisable.[2] The dialogue then closes with an indignant protest against the impertinent criticism passed on Scottish affairs by foreign nations. The Scots little deserve the charge of being seditious, since no nation has been more faithful to its kings, and has more steadily sacri-

---

[1] As is well known, the lawyers of the seventeenth century sought to efface this precedent by mutilating the record in which it is set forth.

[2] These are his words : " Praeterea ego in hoc genere quid fieri jure possit aut debeat explico, non ad rem suscipiendum exhortor."

T

ficed the interests of the few to the interests of the many. It is the best proof of this, says Buchanan, that there is no older monarchy in Europe than that of the Scots.

From this analysis it will be seen that Buchanan's tract is no contribution to political science like the *Republic* of Bodin, or even the *Francogallia* of his other contemporary Hotman. Buchanan makes no attempt, like Bodin, by the application of philosophical thinking to the facts of history, to educe a form of government which should abide the test of practice and best serve the wellbeing of a people. Neither does he, like Hotman, endeavour to base his theory of the government of the Scots on a solid array of facts that will stand the simplest historic test.[1] But to expect philosophic thinking or scientific research in Buchanan is to expect what was alien alike to his own habit of mind and the genius of his century. The dialogue is to be regarded simply as a party pamphlet; and as such its success was triumphant. Three editions of it appeared in three successive years. On the Continent its publication was expected with eager interest by the most distinguished scholars. "I have received your *De Jure Regni*," writes one of his correspondents, the very year of its publication, "which you sent me by the letter-carrier of our friend Sturm. The gift would have been a most welcome one had the importunities of certain friends permitted me to take advantage

---

[1] Hotman's object in his *Francogallia* is much the same as that of Buchanan—to prove that originally France had the right of electing its kings, and of sitting in judgment on its bad ones. Hotman's treatise, however, though also that of a strong partisan, has a much higher historic value than Buchanan's *De Jure Regni*.

of it. But the very moment of its arrival, Dr. Wilson borrowed it from me. He lent it to the chancellor, the chancellor to the treasurer, who has not yet returned it, so that to this day it has never been in my hands. Your book has the approval of all men of judgment and experience, and all who have eyes to see the present political situation. The parasites of princes, and such as think that laws are made to be altered at their pleasure, will have nothing of it. Almost everybody admires the genius which at your advanced age can so skilfully catch the manner of the Platonic dialogue. . . . Sturm, Hotman, and others are all eagerness to have a sight of it." [1]

As we have seen, it continued to be widely read during the next century, and to be regarded as a highly dangerous document by all the upholders of the divine right of kings.[2] Its small bulk, and the singular clearness and simplicity of its arguments, gave it the advantage over Milton's rambling and incoherent *Defence of the People of England* and the tediously pedantic *Lex Rex* of Samuel Rutherfurd. It might have been supposed that the interest of Buchanan's dialogue would have ceased with the English Revolution of 1688. Yet no fewer than three editions of it in separate form were published during the eighteenth century. It is also worthy

---

[1] *Epist.* xxvi.

[2] Hannay (*North Brit. Rev.* vol. xlvi.) quotes the following squib produced during the English Civil Wars of the seventeenth century. The Jesuit is Mariana, who in his *De Rege et Regis Institutione* taught similar doctrines to that of Buchanan :—

> " A Scot and Jesuit, hand in hand,
>   First taught the world to say
> That subjects ought to have command,
>   And monarchs to obey."

of note that in the year of the French Revolution, 1789, an English translation was published in London;[1] and that in the year of the secession of the Free Church of Scotland, 1843, another translation appeared, bound up with the *Lex Rex* of Samuel Rutherfurd.[2]

However slight, therefore, may be the scientific value of Buchanan's tract, it is evident that it has a very distinct place in the development of political thought. The doctrines he taught, which by many in his own day, and in the century that followed, were regarded as subversive of all government, were in every point carried into practice at the great English Revolution. As for his ideas regarding tyrannicide, the realisation of his views of the mutual relation of king and people rendered unnecessary even their theoretic discussion. In accounting for the democratic tendencies of modern Scotland, Buchanan has to be considered as well as Knox and Andrew Melville.

[1] Irving, *Memoirs of Buchanan.* p. 247.
[2] Robert Ogle, and Oliver and Boyd, Edinburgh, 1843.

CHAPTER XVIII.

BUCHANAN's most ambitious literary work was his
last. This was his History of Scotland in twenty
books, that all but fills the thicker folio in Ruddiman's edition of his works.[1] To write history in
Buchanan's day was something very different from
writing it in ours. The limited number of authorities he had to consult, the easy standard of accuracy he had to satisfy, made his task a far lighter
one than a similar undertaking would be at the
present day. Yet, produced as it was in advanced
age, in broken health, and apparently in other untoward circumstances, Buchanan's History must be
regarded as a signal proof of the native vigour of
his mind, and of his ardent and indomitable temper.

When he actually began his task we cannot
exactly determine. In his dedicatory letter to
James, he tells how the idea of his undertaking
first came to him. Shortly after his final return to
Scotland, when engaged in preparing a complete
edition of his poems, his friends had unanimously
besought him to produce a work "more worthy of
his advanced years and of the expectations his

[1] *Rerum Scoticarum Historia.*

countrymen had formed of him ". Such a work, they urged, would be a history of his native country, than which none could bring him more applause or assure him a more enduring reputation. He was the more easily persuaded to the undertaking, " since our island of Britain is the most famous in the world, and its history embraces events in every respect worthy of narration ". Moreover, in the long lapse of ages, hardly a single writer had dared to undertake the task, or had proved himself equal to its execution. In telling the story of James's ancestors, also, he would in some measure atone for his inability, through confirmed ill-health, to perform the daily duties imposed on him of fostering James's talents. Such, by his own account, was the origin of the most arduous of all his labours.

In a letter dated 1576, one of his correspondents says that " three years ago Buchanan had given him hopes of seeing a book which he had written on the origin of the British peoples ".[1] But it is not till 1577 that we hear from himself that he is actually at work on his task. In a letter dated from Stirling in that year he tells Randolph that his History is his main occupation. " As for the present," he says, " I am occupiit in writyng of our historie, being assurit to content few, and to displease many thairthrow. As to the end of it, yf ye gett it not or thys winter be passit, lippin not for it,[2] nor nane other writyngs from me. The rest of my occupation is wyth the gout, quhilk haldis me besy both day and nyt."[3] Writing also to another correspondent in 1579, he speaks of his various literary occupa-

---

[1] *Epist.* xiv.
[2] Do not reckon on receiving it.   [3] Letter already quoted.

tions, and specially mentions his History. " To my other labours," he proceeds, " I must add that of my History, a task irksome enough at the best period of life ; but, with death immediately before my eyes, and the disgrace of leaving undone what I have once undertaken, both tedious and ungrateful, since I am neither permitted to desist, nor have any pleasure in going on." [1] By 1579 his correspondents had heard that his work was nearing completion, and begin to express their desire for its appearance. In that year Randolph writes to him as follows :— " This putteth me in Mynd of many things more great prayse worthie donne by you, especially the *Historie of our whole Isle*, wherein I may justly complayne of you, my good Maister, that I shall not have so much as a sight therof, before myne Eyes be cleane shutt up, that nowe are become for Age very dymme. What maketh yow to doubt to let it come foorthe, a Spectacle unto the World, no lesse famous then *Apelles* Table was, and as voyde of comptrollement as his Worke was, howe curiouse soever the Souter would seme to be ? I pray yow deferre no more Tyme; at the least let us knowe what yow mynd to doe with it, and employ my Labor, and charge me so farre as yow please, that shortly we may enjoy our longe desyrid Hope in a Matter of so great Weight. Wherin yow will I am ever at your Command." [2] Randolph's words lead us to believe that, when he wrote, the work was already finished, but for some reason or other was held back from publication. That this was the case is proved by a letter of Bowes to Cecil dated from Stirling the previous year [3]:—" Buchanan hath ended

---

[1] *Epist.* xxvii.   [2] *Epist.* xxii.
[3] Murdin, *Collection of State Papers*, p. 316 (Lond. 1759, fol.).

his story wryttin to the death of the Erle of Murray. He proposeth to command it to print shortly : but *one thing of late hath been withdrawen from him,* which he trusteth to recover, or else to supply of new with soever travell.   He accepteth your lordship's commendations with great comfort, and returneth to your lordship his humble duty and thanks."   As another book continues his History after the assassination of Moray, the delay may have been due to the lack of certain materials to complete his task.

It need not excite our wonder that Buchanan, who was " easily the greatest poet of his age ", should also have undertaken to write history. Division of intellectual labour was hardly understood by the humanists ; nor had they realised that special faculties and special- types of mind are demanded for special studies.   It was the belief of Buchanan's friends that as he wrote the best verses of his time, the probability was that he would also write the best History.   We have just seen in his letter to James what motives had prompted him to his work.   Yet the fact that he wrote his History in Latin and not in Scots, of which he was really a master, proves that to the very last Buchanan belonged to Europe rather than to Scotland.   It was certainly open to him, as to Knox and Bishop Lesley,[1] to have written his last and most important book in the language in which all his countrymen could have understood him.   But the instincts of the humanist were still too strong for him, and the ambition to speak to learned Europe overbore the more patriotic motive to speak in their own language to the limited circle of his own countrymen.   At the

---

[1] Lesley afterwards published a version of his History in Latin.

same time it may be urged for Buchanan that he, like his friend Sturm, confidently believed that sooner or later Latin was bound to supersede all the vernacular languages of Europe. By writing in Scots, therefore, he may have thought that he would but help to delay this desirable end, and would, moreover, doom the great work of his life to speedy oblivion.

Of the spirit and temper in which Buchanan carried through his work we have a glimpse in certain casual references in his letters to Randolph. In that already quoted we have seen that he believed that his History " would content few and displease many ". In another letter to Randolph he is more explicit : " As to my occupation at this present time, I am besy w^t our story of Scotland to purge it of sum Inglis lyis and Scottis vanite, as to maister knoks his historie is in hys freindis handis, and thai ar in consultation to mitigat sum part the acerbite of certaine wordis and sum taintis quhair in he has followit to much sum of your inglis writaris as M. hal *et suppilatorem eius.*" It has of late years been shown that it is precisely the " English lies and Scottish vanity " of which Buchanan speaks that have been the main causes of the extraordinary distortion of Scottish history from the beginning.[1] In the conscious endeavour not to be misled by either of these motives, Buchanan's attitude was, therefore, distinctly critical. That he kept the two stumbling-blocks of his predecessors in view, many parts of his History very forcibly remind us. But to expect from Buchanan a critical handling of early Scottish history in the

[1] See Mr. Skene's Introduction to Fordun's History.

spirit of the nineteenth century, would, of course, be ridiculous. With the best intentions in the world, indeed, Buchanan was as incapable of a purely objective treatment of men and things as his countryman Carlyle himself. On the other hand, everything we know of him goes to show that Carlyle was not more incapable than Buchanan of deliberate misrepresentation of facts, or compromising deference to opinion. Intensity of conviction and the vagaries of a powerful nature may often mislead him as to facts and principles, but his errors are those of an independent thinker, who believed in the sacredness and infinite importance of truth. When Buchanan said that his History would "content few and displease many", he gives us the key at once to his History and to his entire work and character. But even had Buchanan been a man of the purest scientific temper, the time was yet far off when early Scottish history could possibly be placed on a historical basis. It would be absurd, therefore, to blame him for not divining results which have been reached only during the last quarter of a century.[1]

Buchanan had no such philosophic conception of the task he undertook as that which had been lately announced by Bodin in his *Historical Method*. According to Bodin, "the task of the historian is above all the study of political conditions, and the explanation of human revolutions".[2] In that part of his work which he knew best, the history of his

---

[1] Buchanan's latest translator, Aikman (Glasgow, 1827), thinks that he is meeting a *desideratum* in supplying a new translation of Buchanan's History. He says in his preface that Buchanan's list of the first forty kings was "at best doubtful", and he is inclined to accept Buchanan in spite of Father Innes, Pinkerton, and Chalmers.

[2] Baudrillart, *Bodin et son Temps*, p. 152.

own time, Buchanan had an excellent opportunity of putting in practice this maxim of Bodin. But, as we shall see, though this section of his History has an undoubted value of its own, Buchanan shows no real insight into the drift and scope of the great movements that passed under his very eyes. While he has thus no philosophical conception of his subject, he has at the same time little of the practical sense of de Comines and Machiavelli, which came of their actual experience of affairs. In his mode of presenting facts, and the character of the reflections he passes upon them, he is simply the theorist to whom forms of government and their various functions are subjects of keen feeling and conventional speculation, and not actualities that are constantly being modified by the friction of human experience. His History is a brilliant and powerful narrative of the lives of the successive Scottish monarchs, of their wars, their battles, their quarrels with their subjects, their understandings and misunderstandings with foreign powers. Of the growth of the Scottish nation, the significance of special periods in its development, the gradual fusion of the races that compose it—of these things we learn little from Buchanan. His conception of history was, in short, the conventional one of the humanists, who in history, as in everything else, were content to imitate to the best of their ability the examples they most admired among the ancients.

In his first book, Buchanan, following the example of Boece and other predecessors, gives a geographical description of the country whose history he is about to write. This was, of course, from no such philosophical conception as that in which

Bodin anticipated Montesquieu—the influence of climate on man.[1] Yet this chapter is in some respects the most valuable of Buchanan's whole work. The most interesting part of his description he could give from direct personal observation, as at one time or other he had visited most corners of the Lowlands of Scotland. It gives an additional value to this report that his extensive travels on the Continent supplied him with contemporary standards by which he could measure the relative advantages of Scotland. More than half of his description is devoted to the islands of Scotland—"a part of British history," he says, "which is involved in the gravest errors". In this part of his description, however, he professes not to speak from personal knowledge, but on the authority of one "Donald Monro, a pious man and careful observer, who has himself traversed all these islands, and examined them with his own eyes". The following is Buchanan's description of the islanders themselves, which may have a certain interest in these days of Crofter Commissions :—

"In food, dress, and all their domestic arrangements they practise a primitive economy. They live by hunting and fishing. In cooking their fish they use the stomachs or skins of the beasts they kill. During their hunting expeditions, they sometimes squeeze out the blood and eat the flesh raw. Their drink is the broth of boiled flesh. At their feasts they also drink with avidity the whey of milk after it has been preserved for some years. This beverage they call *Bland*.[2] The majority quench their thirst with water. They make bread

---

[1] Baudrillart, *Bodin et son Temps*, p. 150.
[2] This beverage is still in general use in Shetland.

of oats and barley (the only crops produced in that region). This bread is not unpleasant, as they make it with the skill that comes of daily practice. A little of this in the morning satisfies them for a day's hunting or other labour. They delight in gay-coloured garments, especially striped. They are especially fond of purple and blue colours. Their ancestors wore plaids of various colours, the colours being different in different districts (as is, indeed, still generally the case). Most of them now wear clothes of a dark brown colour, very like heather, so that when lying amongst the heather no brilliant colour may betray them. Their clothes hang loosely about them, yet they brave every in- clemency of the weather, and sometimes sleep under the snow. At home, also, they lie on the ground, placing under them fern or heath with roots down- ward in such wise that they have a couch as soft as down, and far more wholesome. The heath, with its natural dryness, absorbs all the superfluous moisture of the body, and restores its vigour to such a degree that he who lies down at night wearied and faint rises in the morning sprightly and active. As for mattresses and bed-clothes, they not merely disregard them, but profess the most eager desire for hardiness and simplicity. If occasion or neces- sity ever call them into another country, they toss the mattress and bed-clothes on the ground, and compose themselves to sleep in the clothes they have on—and this they do from their anxiety lest that barbarous self-indulgence (as they call it) should corrupt their native and inbred hardiness. In war they cover their bodies with an iron helmet and a coat of mail constructed of iron rings, which gener- ally reaches almost to the heel. Their weapons are bows and arrows—the latter generally pointed with barbs, with prongs protruding on both sides, so that unless the wound be laid open they cannot be extracted. Some fight with broadswords and axes. In place of the trumpet they use the bagpipe (*tibia utriculari*). They take great delight in music, though their instruments are peculiar to themselves. Some of these instruments have brazen strings, others gut ones. These they strike with quills, or their nails, which they wear very long. Their one ambition is to bedeck their instruments with a great show of silver and jewels. The poorer class substitute crystal ornaments for jewels. They also sing songs not inartistically composed, whose themes are generally the praises of heroes. Their bards have almost no other theme. They speak in somewhat modified form the ancient language of the Gauls."

In his second book, Buchanan addresses himself to a problem which in his day, as in ours, exercised all patriotic antiquaries—the origin of the various races that found their way into Britain. By his contemporaries Buchanan's treatment of the question was considered both learned and critical. He is aware of the difficulty of the investigation. " In my endeavours," he begins, " to recall the events of British history of more than a thousand years ago, many difficulties present themselves, but this in chief, that in these very regions where the knowledge of our origin ought to be found, for a long period no learning existed, and, when late in the day it did arrive, it perished almost in its birth." Both "English lies" and " Scottish vanity" come in here for the most vigorous animadversion. Of Albion and the fifty daughters of Diocletian, and Brutus, and the rest of the legendary English history, Buchanan speaks as sarcastically as Milton himself. But the Scottish legend of Gathelus, the successor of Moses in Egypt, who with his wife Scota founded the nation of the Scots, is treated with equally little ceremony.[1] Like Milton, he takes the trouble to tell this mythical history, but with the apology to the reader that he does so " because certain people stand by it as pertinaciously as if it had been a Palladium dropped from Heaven ".

Coming to what he considers historical times, he affirms that three peoples anciently possessed the whole island—Britons, Picts, and Scots. The Britons came from Gaul, though not from that part of it known as Brittany. The Scots came from Spain through Ireland into Scotland. To distinguish the Scots of Ireland from those of Scotland, the former were called Irish Scots, the latter Albyn Scots. In time, however, the name *Scots* was dropped, and these additions came to be their only distinction. The name *Picts* he does not think to have been the original name of that people ; but either a name given by the Romans, or a Latin word adopted by that people themselves. From their habit of marking their skins with iron, and adorning them with the figures of various animals, he conjectures whence the Picts must originally have come. The Getini, a people of Thrace, had also this habit, and, as Tacitus has said, also spoke Gaelic. The inference, therefore, must be that the Picts are kindred to the Getini, and, therefore, came from their country—either, that is to say, from the shores of the Baltic, or from the banks of the Danube.

---

[1] Major is equally sceptical.—*De Gestis Scotorum*, lib. i. cap. ix.

Buchanan is especially wroth with the theories of
Humphrey Lloyd, a Welsh antiquary, who had
lately published a tract on the antiquities of Britain.
Lloyd had maintained that the Caledonians were
Britons and not Picts, and that the Scots and Picts
are not found in Britain before the reign of Honorius
in 420 A.D.   On this subject, as Bishop Nicolson
remarks, " Buchanan is so intemperately hot, that
he appears to an unprejudiced English reader to
have more Welsh blood in him than he's aware of;
proving unadvisedly what he will not allow his
antagonist to have done, that the ancient Britons
and Scots are of one family and kindred."[1] It
further excites his wrath that Lloyd should have
made " a scurrilous attack on Hector Boece, a
man not only distinguished beyond his time, but
remarkable for his high-toned feeling and kind
consideration of others ".

His third book Buchanan devotes to extracts
from ancient authors, who support the opinions he
has just advanced.   The reasons he gives for making
these quotations throw a curious light on the
heated controversies then current on subjects which
of all others might be supposed to permit of " dry
light ".   But such questions, we must remember,
had, before the Union of the Crowns, a certain
political importance which in a measure justified this
liveliness of feeling.   " Although," he thus begins
his third book, " I have sufficiently proved in the
two preceding books how not only fabulous, but
monstrous, are the matters which historians have
handed down regarding our ancestors, and have
shown, by the most convincing argument, that the

[1] Bishop Nicolson, *Scottish Historical Library*.

Britons originally sprang from Gaul; nevertheless, because I have here to deal rather with men who doggedly shut their eyes to self-evident truth, than with men who have heedlessly stumbled into error, I have thought it worth while to try if, from writers of the highest authority among the learned, I might not put some check on the presumption of idle meddlers, and supply weapons to good men and lovers of truth, wherewith to restrain their licence of statement."

In his fourth book, Buchanan thinks he is on firm ground, and, with Fordun and Boece as his principal guides, confidently embarks on that extraordinary history of the legendary kings, whose portraits adorn the walls of Holyrood.[1]   Here and there he applies the pruning-knife to Boece's astonishing narrative, but his story is virtually the same as that of Boece. Beginning with Fergus, the first king of the Scots (330 B.C.), he describes the reigns of sixty-eight monarchs before Kenneth Macalpine, with a circumstantiality of detail admirably fitted to carry the profoundest conviction to the innocent reader. The most trivial acts of these kings, the exact dates of their births and deaths, the names of their wives and children and various relations, are all given with a confidence and precision which, now that we know that the whole is absolute fiction, remind us of the tales of Swift and Defoe. Buchanan is charier than Boece in putting elaborate speeches in the mouths of his kings, but he also does not hesitate to produce them on occasion. He shows his scepticism most in largely rejecting the " sundry

[1] Major is much more cautious on the subject of these legendary kings than Boece and Buchanan.

U

merveilles"[1] with which Boece continually seasons
his narrative.   Yet Buchanan also has his own
marvels to relate, though of a kind more adapted to
the taste of his more sceptical generation.   In his
history of these legendary kings, Buchanan, like
Boece, is careful to unfold his own theories of the
Scottish constitution.   Thus of King Finnan, his
tenth king, he gravely tells us " that in order that
he might remove tyranny root and branch, he made
a decree that kings should pass no law of importance without the authority of the public council".
Tyrannical kings are invariably deposed by the
people, though the royal authority is always
regarded with reverence.   Durst, for example, the
king who followed Finnan, proved an insufferable
tyrant, and his people were forced to take up arms
against him.   But " though all orders detested him,
yet, for the reverence due to the royal name and
the memory of his ancestors, he was buried in the
place of his fathers ".

In the part of his work dealing with the period
of Roman occupation, Buchanan, as we should
expect, is more critical than his predecessor Boece.
Thus Boece boldly claims as a king of the Scots the
famous British hero Caractacus, who, in the reign
of Claudius, made such a gallant stand against the
Romans.   Buchanan also gives a Caradoc as a king
of the Scots in the time of Claudius, but he pru-
dently confines his exploits to Scotland.   One of
Boece's doughtiest heroes is King Galdus, whom
he unhesitatingly identifies with the Galgacus of
Tacitus, and on whose exploits he enlarges in his
best manner.   Buchanan is more cautious.   " There

---

[1] The phrase is Bellenden's, the translator of Boece.

are some," he says, "who think that this Galdus is the Galgacus of Tacitus"; and he proceeds to remark that, in his opinion, Galdus was the first Scottish king who bore arms against the Romans, thus disposing of Boece's other champion Caradoc.

As we should expect, Buchanan's opinions on the early religious history of Scotland differ widely from those of Major and Boece. His account of the Culdees is curious, and seems to mark a tradition (now more cautiously accepted) that they differed essentially from the later Roman Church in Scotland. In the reign of Fincormac, his thirty-fifth king, he tells us that, the country being freed from the attacks of the Romans, the Scots seriously turned their attention to the state of religion. As it happened, at this particular moment the persecution of Diocletian drove many pious men to take refuge in Scotland. After lives of solitude, these men left behind them such a name for sanctity, that the cells in which they lived were converted into churches. Hence arose the custom of the ancient Scots of calling their churches cells. "These monks," he proceeds, "were called Culdees, and their name and discipline remained till a later race of monks, divided into many sects, expelled them. These monks were as inferior to their predecessors in learning and piety as they were superior to them in wealth and ceremonial, and in all other rites which catch the eye and delude the mind." In the same way, Buchanan has nothing but praise for Columba, and only reprobation for St. Augustine. His account of the latter shows how completely he had identified himself with the views of Knox and the other Scottish reformers. "In the reign of

Aidan (his forty-ninth king), there came to Britain, sent thither by Pope Gregory, a certain monk named Augustine, who, by his own self-seeking, wrought great confusion in the old religion by teaching a new one; since it was not so much Christian doctrine he taught as the ritual of Rome. For the Britons of former times, having learned Christianity from the disciples of John the Evangelist, were instructed by monks, whom that age had hitherto esteemed both learned and pious. But this monk, by making the See of Rome supreme in Britain, by giving himself out as the one archbishop of the whole country, and introducing a dispute neither necessary nor profitable concerning the time for celebrating Easter, brought much confusion into the churches; and by his new ceremonial and fictitious miracles so crushed the ancient discipline, already tending towards superstition, that hardly a trace of sincere piety was left."

When he reaches the strictly historical period of his subject, it is the "English lies" rather than the "Scottish vanity" that come in for Buchanan's censure. Though he does not, like Fordun and Boece, boldly claim the foundation of Paris University for two Scotsmen, yet, in his account of the union of the Picts and Scots, he is as credulous as his predecessors. Through the prowess of Kenneth Macalpin, king of the Scots, he maintains that "the rebellious and perfidious Picts" were brought under the subjection of the Scots, and ever afterwards remained an inferior people. The English historians had been in the habit of asserting that in the reign of Constantine III. (that is, Buchanan's Constantine III.) Athelstane was sole king of Britain, and that all other kings in the island were his feudatories. This calls forth one of those scathing passages, which show that, in spite of his old age and his gout, Buchanan had lost little of the fiery spirit of his youth. "Those who maintain this," he says, "quote approvingly many wretched English scribes, and to corroborate their story add Marianus Scotus, a writer of high reputation. On this matter, however, I have thought it right to warn the reader, that in the edition of Marianus published in Germany there is no mention whatever of this circumstance. If they have another Marianus different from the one the rest of the world knows, interpolated and touched up by themselves, I wish they would produce it. Moreover, these men (being for the most part quite devoid of letters) do not sufficiently understand their own writers, nor perceive that Bede, William of Malmesbury, and Geoffrey of Monmouth, generally speak of that country as Britain over which the Britons ruled, namely, that which is within the wall of Hadrian, or, when its boundary extended further, within the wall of Severus." [1]

It is in Buchanan's treatment of such important reigns as those of Malcolm Canmore, David I., and Alexander III., that we miss that philosophical conception of history which we find in Bodin and Machiavelli. Buchanan is as lavish as the chroniclers who preceded him in his praises of Malcolm. Yet from his different religious standpoint, Malcolm's ecclesiastical policy, prompted by his wife Margaret,

---

[1] Buchanan is here in accordance with the latest antiquaries in distinguishing the wall of Hadrian between the Tyne and the Solway from that of Severus between the Forth and the Clyde. Until recent years, antiquaries, misled by Bede, have associated the name of Severus with the wall connecting the Tyne and the Solway. Buchanan draws special attention to the fact that Bede was in error.

could hardly have had his unqualified approval.
But the national tradition was too strong for him,
and he has no words of blame for Malcolm's nursing
of the religion which as a reformer he was bound to
detest.   Indeed, it may be said in passing, that it
seems to have been a point with the early Scottish
historians, and with Buchanan among the rest, to
say the best they could of their kings.   Of the
immense importance of the English immigration
into Scotland during David I.'s reign Buchanan
makes no more than either Boece or Major.   He
notes the fact that the English speech then began
to predominate in the country; but he evidently
thought that the new-comers hardly brought a
blessing.   " Malcolm," he says, " made all but fruit-
less attempts to check the luxury, which, already
prevailing through the presence of multitudes of
English, and the intercourse with other countries,
now, through the entertainment of many exiles of
English race over the whole country, began to be a
serious evil."   Of Donald Bane, the usurper who
followed Malcolm, Buchanan says, " that all good
men, who revered the memory of Malcolm and Margaret, detested him".   It is curious that Buchanan
should thus unconsciously have reprobated in Donald
the dying struggle of that Celtic race whose glories
he was so fond of celebrating.   In his account of
David I., Buchanan faithfully follows Fordun and
Boece, even to assigning him a brilliant victory over
the English at Northallerton.   He also follows the
national tradition in exalting the virtues of David;
but with Boece and Major he is disposed to question
his wisdom in so lavishly enriching the Church at
the expense of the Crown.   In this reference he

makes kindlier mention of Major than in his autobiography, and seems pleased to have the weight of
his authority on his side. "John Major," he says,
"who had a great name in theology when I was a
boy, though he highly eulogises all the other acts of
this king, yet censures him (and would that his
censure had been less true) for this prodigality
towards the monasteries." It is from David's reign,
Buchanan thinks, that true learning and true
religion in the Church mainly date their decline.
With reference to William the Lion's acknowledgment of the feudal superiority of England, Buchanan
makes larger admissions than his predecessors. It
is evident, however, that he does so sorely against
his will. After making the admission he goes on to
remark, "But some say that the meeting between
William and Henry had not for its object the question of superiority, but the payment of certain
tributes, and the surrender of certain fortresses till
such time as these tributes should be paid." And
he proceeds to say that, in view of the treaty afterwards renewed by William and Richard, this opinion
seems to him nearer the truth.

In the period of the Wars of Independence
Buchanan found materials which bring out his
strongest points as a historian. Modern research
has here, as elsewhere, discredited much that he tells
us. We can now only smile at what he calls the
"ingenuous reply" made to Edward i. by Bruce,
the rival of John Baliol—"that he was not so
desirous of reigning as to curtail the inherited
liberties of his country". But his narrative of the
gallant struggle of his countrymen against England
is told with a force and picturesqueness which prove

that he put his full strength into this part of his work. Buchanan had undoubtedly something of Scott's eye for local details, and in his descriptions of battles he never fails to present a careful map of the field. He had also Scott's own relish for battle and adventure. Of Wallace and Bruce he writes with all the fervour of a Scotsman, convinced that their memory is his country's best possession. "Such was the end of a man," he says of Wallace, " by far the most distinguished of the age in which he lived; for greatness of soul in undertaking tasks of danger, and for courage and counsel in the conduct of affairs, easily comparable to the most famous leaders of antiquity; second to none in affection for his country; who, alone a freeman among slaves, could neither be induced by rewards, nor constrained by fear, to abandon the public cause which he had once undertaken to defend; whose death seemed the more deserving of commiseration, that while he was still unconquered by the enemy, he was betrayed by those who should have been the last in the world to have proved false." His portrait of Bruce is one of the classical passages of his History. It will be seen how entirely he has in this portrait caught the manner of the ancients :[1]—

"To put as shortly as possible what I have to say, Robert Bruce was certainly a man in every respect of the very highest distinction, and one to whom, even from heroic times, we shall find few equals in all manner of virtue. As he was of the first courage in war, so in peace his justice and moderation were supreme ; and although unexpected

---

[1] " Few modern histories are more redolent of an antique air than Buchanan's History."—Hallam, *Lit. Mid. Ages*, vol. i. p. 257. (1842.)

success, and (after fortune had sated, or rather wearied, herself with his misfortunes) an unbroken series of victories gave a noble lustre to his life, yet in his adversity he seems to me more worthy of admiration. For what was the strength of that mind which was not to be overwhelmed, nay, not even to be shaken, by the united attack of such an army of ills? What that constancy which was not to be moved by a wife in captivity, four brothers (all men of the most sterling courage) cruelly put to death, friends vexed at one and the same time by every species of calamity, those who were able to escape with life exiles and beggared, himself not only spoiled of his own ample patrimonial domain, but of his kingdom, by a prince the most powerful of those times and the most prompt in counsel and action? Beset at one time by all these evils, and reduced to the extremest need, he never doubted that the kingdom should one day be his, and never said or did aught unbecoming a king. He neither, like the younger Cato nor like Marcus Brutus, laid violent hands on himself, nor did he, like Marius, driven to madness by his calamities, give the loose to his hatred against his enemies. For when he had regained his ancient condition, he lived in such wise with those who had made his life so hard, that he seemed to remember not so much that he had once been their enemy, as that he was now their king. At the approach of his end, even when a most painful disease made more grievous his failing age, he was still so true to himself that he put on a stable foundation the existing state of his kingdom, and made careful provision for the tranquillity of his descendants; so that for most excellent reasons did

all men at his death grieve as for one who had not
been only a just king, but their affectionate parent."

As our object is not so much to appraise
Buchanan's History as to mark his own character
and opinion in his work, we give other two quotations which have a distinct biographical interest.
In his account of Robert III. he makes a short
digression to relate the exploits of the Earl of
Buchan in France. He seldom makes such digressions, and when he does so, he usually thinks it
necessary to make an apology to his readers. The
apology on this occasion is that " the detractions of
certain English writers have forced him into it".
" These writers," he proceeds, " enviously seek to
throw contempt on achievements which they dare
not deny. Even if history were silent, the magni-
ficence of kings, the decrees of states, and the noble
monuments at Orleans and Tours, put them beyond
question. What then is the ground of the cavil-
ling ? They tell us, forsooth, that the Scots are too
poor to maintain such bodies of troops abroad. If
they deem poverty a fault, it is the fault of the
land and not of the people. Nor should I have
taken it as a reproach had these writers not shown
that they meant it as such. I will only make this
reply—that these same poor, and (as they will have
it) needy Scots, have gained many a notable victory
over the wealthy English. If they do not take my
word for it, let them take that of their own historians. If they do not believe what their own
writers have written, let them not ask us to do so."
But, he curtly adds, let us return to the affairs of
the Scots.

The other passage also refers to what Buchanan

considered "English lies" regarding Scottish history.
On this occasion his wrath is especially directed
against " Hall and his plagiarist Grafton " [1] for
charging James I. with base ingratitude to the
English king in marrying his daughter to the
Dauphin, afterwards Louis XI. of France. These
writers had maintained that in educating James,
and afterwards supplying him with a wife, Henry IV.
had put the Scottish king under a lifelong debt of
gratitude. In view of the real circumstances of the
case, Buchanan naturally thought these statements
somewhat barefaced, and gives us a specimen of his
most pungent style. He closes his digression as
follows : " But leaving these half-instructed men,
who forget all moderation and modesty in their
writings, to count favours received as benefits conferred, what must we think of the lying effrontery,
the unbridled slanders, which they permit themselves in speaking of the daughter of the same
king (James I.) ? These writers tell us (for against
her character, insolent though they are, they did
not dare to imagine a charge) that this princess
was displeasing to her husband by reason of her
mal-odorous breath. But Monstrelet, a contemporary writer, relates that she was both virtuous
and beautiful ; and the author of the Pluscardine
Book, who accompanied the queen on her voyage,
and was present at her death, has left it on record,
that as long as she lived she was much beloved by
her father-in-law, mother-in-law, and husband ; as
indeed appears by her epitaph at Châlons on the
Marne (where she died), a poem ascribing to her

---

[1] It is worth noting that the Latin expression here is the same as
that in Buchanan's letter to Randolph quoted above.

every virtue, and which, translated into the Scots
tongue, is in the possession of most of our countrymen
at the present day. But leaving these slanderers of
another people's reputation, who are yet so careless
of their own that they pay as little heed to what
they say of others as to what others say of them,—
let us proceed to the subject in hand."

Buchanan's account of the reign of James III.,
through no fault of his own, is of less value than
his account of the other Jameses,[1] but it contains
the most famous passage in his whole History—the
speech he puts into the mouth of Bishop Kennedy.
This speech of Kennedy, and that of Morton in the
twentieth book, embody Buchanan's political creed,
and, taken together, they are simply another statement of the doctrines of the *De Jure Regni*. It
may be said that they also give us the measure of
the very limited circle of political ideas familiar to
Buchanan. As the oration of Kennedy fills rather
more than three folio pages it cannot be produced
here. The point to which the bishop addresses
himself is the expediency of appointing the queen-
mother as Regent during the minority of James III.
It is needless to say that Buchanan is of exactly
the same mind as Knox with regard to "the
regiment of women". In the bishop's speech he
had doubtless the nation's experiences of Mary in
his thoughts, but it would be a mistake to think
that these experiences determined his opinions. The
two arguments he ascribes to Kennedy—that female
rule is at once contrary to nature and to Scottish
tradition—were in fact what as a Scotsman and an

---

[1] The publication of the *Foedera Anglica* discredited both Buchanan's
and Lesley's account of this reign.—Tytler, *History of Scotland* (Notes
and Illustrations. Letter P, vol. ii.).

admirer of the ancients, he was bound to maintain. It deserves to be noted that Buchanan bestows the highest eulogy on Kennedy, in this case as in others showing that his religious convictions did not blind him, as they blinded Knox, to merit in those of another faith from his own. With an evident reference to Major, he says "that Kennedy caused a magnificent tomb to be erected to himself at St. Andrews, which the malignity of men grudged him, though as a private citizen he had deserved well of most, and, as a statesman, of all".[1]

From the reign of James IV., Buchanan's History assumes the special interest of a contemporary narrative. What he henceforth has to say is either from direct personal knowledge, or from the information of men who had such knowledge. It is to be remembered that in all the years which he spent in Scotland, he was at the very centre of the nation's life. As a youth he had studied at St. Andrews, in his second sojourn in Scotland he was in the closest contact with the Court itself, and in the last years of his life he was himself a public man who had his own share in the great events of his time. As one who had had daily intercourse with Mary, who was intimate with Moray, Lennox, Mar, Knox, and other leaders of the people, his narrative must needs have an importance which it would be a serious mistake to undervalue. In his account of his own century, Buchanan puts before us the construction of its main tendencies as they appeared to the party to which he belonged. Such a statement from a man

---

[1] Major speaks thus of Kennedy: "Duo in viro non laudo, scilicet commendam cum tali episcopatu tenuisse, licet exigua erat; nec sepulchri sumptuositatem approbo."—*De Gestis Scotorum*, lib. vi. cap. 19.

of Buchanan's powers of mind, with his wide experience of men and things, and intense interest in
the great movements of life, puts us in a far truer
relation to his century than any modern reconstruction we may base on piles of State documents. It
is the drawback of such documents, that in presenting us, it may be, with unquestionable facts, they
give us the mere death-mask, not the living features,
of the past.

In his account of the reign of James IV.
Buchanan thrice specially vouches for his facts on
the evidence of contemporaries. In each of the
three cases it will be seen that a special voucher
was certainly called for. The first is his description of " a new kind of monster born in Scotland",
which would appear to have been an anticipation of
the Siamese twins. The King, he tells us, took a
great interest in the creature, and had it taught
several languages, and also music, "in which it
made wonderful progress". "Concerning this
affair," Buchanan adds, " I speak with the greater
confidence, that many honest men are still alive
who saw these things." It is a quaint circumstance
that Buchanan, a man with all the culture of the
age in his head, should thus break his stately narrative of the nation's destinies to give a minute
description of this wretched abortion. But the
notable cases of Melanchthon and Bodin remind us
that this curiosity in the monstrosities of nature
was a weakness of the best spirits of the sixteenth
century. The above, it should be said, is only the
best example of many of the same type to be found
in Buchanan's History. More interesting is his
reference to Sir David Lyndsay as his authority for

the story of the apparition in Linlithgow Church
warning James IV. against his fatal expedition into
England. "Among those present," he says, "was
David Lyndsay of the Mount, a man of noted
honesty and veracity, devoted to learning, and
whose whole life showed how utterly incapable he
was of a lie." Buchanan's intercourse with Lyndsay must belong to the period when he was acting
as tutor to the natural son of James. This glimpse
of the actual contact of the two brightest geniuses
of their day in Scotland, with this quaint specimen
of their talk, is as if we caught the sudden glance
of an eye, or felt the living touch of a hand from
out the depths of the past. Speaking of the various
stories that went regarding the fate of James IV.,
he also says, "However it may have gone with
him, I have thought that I should not keep back
what I have heard more than once from Lawrence
Tallifer, a man of learning and virtue. He used to
tell (for as one of the King's pages he was a spectator
of the battle) that when the fortune of the day was
decided, he saw the King mount a horse, and cross
the Tweed." Buchanan was seven years old when
Flodden was lost, and his story of the battle and
its fateful consequences to Scotland has a peculiar
interest as the expression of the mingled grief and
shame and indignation which the memory of that
day awoke in every Scotsman. "Such was that
famous fight at Flodden," he says with a pathetic
pride that touches the heart of a Scotsman even to
the present day, "memorable among the few de-
feats sustained by the Scottish nation, not so much
by reason of the numbers slain (for in other battles
double the numbers were lost), as that by the

destruction of the King and his nobles, few remained to rule a populace fierce by nature, and
unrestrained by the dread of punishment."

From the battle of Flodden onwards, Buchanan's
History of necessity becomes more deeply tinged
with personal feeling. On the feuds of the houses
of Lennox and Hamilton it was impossible that a
man with Buchanan's character and connections
should speak with judicial impartiality. It was
during this period also that the struggle between
the old and the new religions began, and Buchanan
wrote of that struggle at a time when the bitter-
ness of the strife was still at its height. Moreover,
his long absence from Scotland made it necessary
that he should take much of his narrative from men
who would put their own construction on the facts
with which they supplied him. Of the secret dealings with the Courts of England and France, which
so powerfully affected the course of Scottish affairs,
Buchanan could only have had the most imperfect
knowledge. Thus, his account of the policy of such
nobles as the Earls of Lennox and Cassillis, whom
he did not know to have been so deeply pledged
to Henry VIII., could be given in all good faith,
being as he was in complete ignorance of the real
position in which these nobles stood.[1]

When all these deductions have been made,
however, the fact remains that Buchanan's History
of his own time is the honest attempt to produce a

---

[1] Considering the severe judgments passed by Pinkerton, Tytler,
and others on the prejudiced inaccuracy of this period of Buchanan's
History, it is remarkable that Professor Brewer, on the authority of the
State Papers of Henry VIII., is able to say that " Buchanan's information for this portion of his History was evidently derived from trustworthy sources ".—*Reign of Henry VIII.* vol. i. p. 557. The above
paragraph was written before I met with this statement of Brewer.

narrative such as he believed would be finally accepted as just and true. Partisan though he is, Buchanan's estimates of the chief personages of his time in Scotland display a studious attempt to be fair, even where his antipathies are strongest. Thus the character he has given of Arran, the head of the detested Hamiltons, is that accepted by historians of the most different ways of thinking. Nor could we wish anything fairer than his final judgment on the Queen-Regent, Mary of Lorraine. We have but to compare Buchanan's summing up of her character and policy with the expressions of Knox on the same subject, to see the wide difference in spirit and method between the two champions of the same faith. Of Cardinal Beaton Buchanan never speaks but with the utmost scorn and indignation. We have seen Beaton's deliberate attempts both in Scotland and elsewhere to have Buchanan disposed of as a heretic. Buchanan had therefore special reasons for entertaining no kindly feelings towards the great Cardinal. But, apart from personal feeling, Buchanan had certainly ample justification in denouncing Beaton as the most unscrupulous public man of his day in Scotland. A recent discovery has shown that Beaton was capable, to the full, of all that his worst enemies laid to his charge. Buchanan, as well as Knox, relates that on the death of James v. the Cardinal produced a forged will, in which James was made to appoint himself and three others as tutors or guardians to the infant Queen. By this arrangement the chief power in the country would have been placed in Beaton's hands. This story has been questioned by certain writers, though it was

x

confirmed by the positive testimony of the Regent Arran.[1] But the recent discovery of the forged instrument among the Hamilton papers now places Beaton's guilt beyond question.[2] It should be said that Buchanan's method all through his History is in the first place to present his own opinion with all the clearness and emphasis of which he is master. Where he was aware that wide difference of opinion existed regarding any person or event, some letter or speech is introduced which exhibits the arguments of the other side. These arguments certainly lose nothing of their force as he states them. It is evident, indeed, that it is a matter of conscience with him to put the case of his adversaries in the best light. The most notable example of this is the message that Mary is made to put into the mouth of her French envoy after her marriage with Bothwell. All that can be said for Mary is there put with a force and ingenuity which none of her modern advocates has surpassed.

It has already been said that from Buchanan's sketch of his own time we gain no adequate conception of the significance and scope of the great Protestant revolution in Scotland. Of this the best evidence is the strangely insignificant place his narrative assigns to Knox. For us, Knox is by far the most important figure of his time in Scotland. In Buchanan's History his name occurs only four times, the reference on each occasion being of the most casual kind. He is first mentioned as denouncing the impiety of his fellow-inmates in the castle of St. Andrews previous to its capture by the

---

[1] Tytler, *History of Scotland*, vol. iii. chap. i.
[2] Historical Manuscripts Commission. The Manuscripts of the Duke of Hamilton, K.T., pp. 205-220. The editor regards the forgery as incontestable.

French. We next hear of him in 1559 as addressing
his famous sermon to the inhabitants of Perth. He
is again referred to as delivering an "excellent
sermon"[1] at Stirling in the same year, which had
the effect "of uplifting the minds of many with the
sure hope of a speedy escape from present evils".
Lastly, at the coronation of James VI. he is again
represented as delivering "an excellent sermon".
On each occasion the reference made to him is contained in a single sentence. As has already been
pointed out, Knox in his History of the Reformation speaks of Buchanan in the most respectful and
admiring terms, and there is no reason to believe
that Buchanan of deliberate intention kept silence
regarding the great part played by Knox among his
contemporaries. The truth probably is that in
Buchanan's eyes Knox was not the commanding
figure he now appears to us. By their contemporaries, indeed, there can be no doubt that Buchanan,
with his European reputation, was considered much
the more distinguished man of the two. It is more
probable than not that for Buchanan, with his
humanistic instincts and his scholar's training, there
was much in Knox that repelled rather than
attracted him. That a popular preacher and (as
he must have regarded him) a somewhat ignorant
theologian should be reckoned a great historic
figure, would probably have appeared to Buchanan
as something of an absurdity.[2]

---

[1] *Concio luculenta* is the phrase.

[2] Buchanan's History ends before the death of Knox. In his edition
of Knox's History Mr. David Laing points out that the reformer in all
probability obtained from Buchanan his account of the death of
Francis II. Mr. Laing was also of opinion that the Scots translation of
the Latin verses in the same passage was supplied to Knox by
Buchanan. The Scots version would certainly do no discredit to
Buchanan.—Laing's *Knox*, vol. ii. pp. 134-136.

In the twentieth and last book of Buchanan's History the most notable and characteristic passage is the speech of Morton before Elizabeth's Council, in which he justifies the proceedings of James's supporters against Mary. As the speech is mainly a reproduction of the arguments of the *De Jure Regni*, it is unnecessary to repeat them here. In Buchanan's narrative Morton is represented as restating this defence before the Convention of Estates on his return to Scotland. Since Buchanan, as Keeper of the Privy Seal, sat as a member of the Convention, it is possible that he may have been present when Morton gave the account of his mission. We know, indeed, from the comparison of other reports given by Buchanan that in the case of contemporaries these long speeches are really based on what was actually said. The speech of Morton may therefore be regarded as the manifesto of the King's party, and as possessing a real historic value, in placing the policy of the Protestant party in the best light of which it was capable.

Buchanan's History closes with the death of the Regent Lennox and the appointment of his successor Mar. As in November 1579 his work still engaged him, the pen would seem literally to have fallen from his hand. Had he been able to continue his narrative over the Regency of Morton, it is probable that he would not have spared that nobleman, of whose policy he so strongly disapproved.[1] His work was published at Edinburgh in 1582, the very

---

[1] Buchanan disapproved of Morton's policy, but it appears that he had also reasons for personal dislike of the Regent. Certain of his merciless critics, therefore, suggested that he closed his History where he did that Morton might not have a place in his work. But, as Irving has said, "the completion of his History and the termination of his life took place about the very same period".—*Memoirs of Buchanan*, p. 303.

year of his death. The next year another edition was published at Geneva, and the year following a third at Frankfort. Four editions in all appeared during the sixteenth century, nine in the seventeenth, and three in the eighteenth—the last in 1762. A translation into Scots was made by John Reid or Reed, who is described by Calderwood as "servitur and writer to Mr. George Buchanan". Many translations continued to be made both in England and Scotland during the seventeenth and eighteenth centuries. An English translation published in 1690 passed through no fewer than seven editions. As Buchanan anticipated, his work was received with indignation by a certain section of his countrymen. Even in the eighteenth century, writers of opposite political views from his own accused him of manipulating Scottish history to support his own theories, and to justify the party to which he belonged. As we know, historians of a later day than Buchanan's have been accused of similar motives without being stigmatised as miscreants. But in the heated political controversies of the last century, Buchanan's hereditary opponents did not stop short of this. It has already been told that Buchanan's History and *De Jure Regni* were condemned by Parliament in 1584. His pupil James, as was to be expected, regarded his master's work with horror, and lost no occasion of denouncing its untrustworthiness as a record of Scottish affairs. When he recommends his son Henry to read the history of his own country, he warns him that it must not be " those scandalous libels of Buchanan, which whoever may have in his hands, even in your days, let him feel the weight of

my laws". James is probably responsible for a
story told by Camden,[1] to the effect that as his
death approached Buchanan expressed his sorrow
for having maligned Mary. What truth is in this
story will be seen from the testimony, afterwards to
be quoted, of one who had certainly the best opportunity of knowing.[2]

By his contemporaries Buchanan's History was
regarded as a work of the first order. Even into
the eighteenth century it was seriously debated
whether Caesar, or Livy, or Sallust was to be considered his model. By almost universal consent he
was acknowledged to have equalled or even surpassed his masters. But the finest contemporary
tribute paid to Buchanan's work is that of de Thou,
whose opinion carries the greater weight that his
own History of his time was long the source at
which every practical statesman sought political
wisdom. "In his old age," he says, "Buchanan
undertook a History, which he wrote with such
purity, sagacity, and insight (although from that
inborn love of liberty, peculiar to his nation, somewhat severe on the pride of kings), that his work
seems the production, not of one trained in the dust
of the schools, but of one who has passed his life in
the conduct of affairs".[3] Archbishop Usher also said
"that no one had investigated his country's antiquities more thoroughly than Buchanan".[4] This
note of praise was maintained for fully a century and
a half after his death; and the following passage
from Dryden shows in what estimation Buchanan's
History was held a century after its publication :—

[1] *Annales,* vol. i. p. 130 (Hearne's ed.)   [2] See next chapter.
[3] *Hist. sui Temporis,* vol. iv. p. 99.
[4] *Epist. de Brit. Eccles. Primordiis,* c. 16.

"Buchanan, for the purity of his Latin, and for his learning, and for all other endowments belonging to an historian, might be placed among the greatest, if he had not leaned too much to prejudice, and too manifestly declared himself a party of a cause, rather than an historian of it. Excepting only that (which I desire not to urge too far in so great a man, but only to give caution to his readers concerning it), our isle may justly boast in him a writer comparable to any of the moderns, and excelled by few of the ancients."[1] Such being the fame of Buchanan and his work, it is not wonderful that the history of Scotland became a subject of interest to educated Europe. What Scott did for his country in the nineteenth century, Buchanan did as effectively in the seventeenth and eighteenth. In the present century Buchanan's classical Latin stands him in little stead, and his work is now estimated on its bare merits as a national record. As such, it has met with but scant approval even from writers most kindly disposed to him. "Buchanan's History," says Hill Burton, "stands among those remarkable instances where the author's estimate of his own works is inverted by public opinion. His Psalms, and all the poetry for which his name is illustrious, he spoke of as fugitive trifles when weighed with that effort which is of little more use and value than as a bulky exercise in the composition of classical Latin."[2] For all popular purposes Buchanan's History is for ever superseded; but to speak of it "as of no more use

---

[1] Dryden, *Life of Plutarch.* (*Works,* vol. xvii. p. 58, Scott's edit., Edin. 1821.)

[2] *History of Scotland,* vol. v. p. 479, ed. 1870. Burton expresses a somewhat different opinion elsewhere (*ibid.* vol. iii. p. 101 note, ed. 1872).

and value than as a bulky exercise in the composition of Latin " is a somewhat unguarded expression.
A work which could call forth such judgments as
those of men like de Thou and Dryden must always
remain something more than what Burton calls it.
Moreover, as has already been more than once
stated, Buchanan's narrative can never be neglected
by any one who wishes to place himself in contact
with the mind and heart of Scotland during the
sixteenth century.

But granting Burton's judgment to be correct,
it still remains the fact that few histories have
maintained a permanence of interest to be compared with Buchanan's. If we put the classical
histories aside, which owe their perennial interest to
many other reasons besides their intrinsic literary
value, it is astonishingly few of which it can be said
that they have been read with interest by educated
Europe for nearly two centuries. Yet this was the
fortune of Buchanan's History of Scotland—the
materials of which, be it remarked, possessed in
themselves no superiority of interest or importance.
We shall best judge of the significance of this
statement, if we remember what place is now held
by the famous Histories of Buchanan's countrymen,
Hume and Robertson. These Histories were regarded by contemporaries as in the highest order
of their kind. Yet the single century that has
elapsed since their appearance has effaced them as
completely as the Latin History of Buchanan.
Nay, for the purpose of the specialist, Buchanan's
History must at the present day be deemed of
higher value than the Histories of Robertson and
Hume.

CHAPTER XIX.

CORRESPONDENCE.

It has already been said that Buchanan counted among his correspondents men of the first rank in letters and affairs. Without some acquaintance with his correspondence, therefore, we can hardly form an adequate estimate of the place he held in the minds of his contemporaries. In the case of Buchanan, also, his correspondence is specially needed for a fair judgment of his character. His set literary performances are either purely impersonal, such as his poem on the Sphere, or merely conventional, such as a large number of his minor poems, or, lastly, controversial, as the *De Jure Regni.* In comparatively little of his work, prose or verse, does he speak without some disturbing motive that partially obscures him behind mere temporary circumstance. In his letters we see him in his relation with friends or sympathisers; and both from his own and those of his correspondents we receive an impression which in many respects exhibits him in an entirely new light. If we may judge from the few that have come down to us, Buchanan's letters differ from the typical letters of the humanists in not being mere exercises in imitation of Cicero or Pliny. In all of them he has something to say, and he says it shortly and pointedly, with none of that flourish of phrase which the humanists were apt to affect. Those of his letters which we possess were all written after his final return to Scotland, and this may partly account for the fact that they contain none of those sallies we naturally look for in the correspondence of a man like Buchanan. "Calm of mind, all passion spent," is their prevailing note. Yet, at the same time, they leave us with the clearest impression of an essentially elevated and benignant nature. Only such a nature could have preserved in the most advanced age and broken health the genial interest which Buchanan never failed to show in his young fellow-countrymen. It will be seen that often his sole motive in taking up his pen was either to encourage them in the pursuit of learning and virtue, or to commend them to the interest of his friends abroad.

In Ruddiman's edition of Buchanan's Correspondence, there are forty-one letters in all, of which only fourteen are Buchanan's own. From his own words we gather that he must have written many more. As they were in Latin, however, we have not perhaps the same reason to regret their loss. What we must regret is, that only two in Scots have been preserved.[1] In selecting for translation the letters that follow, we shall be guided solely by their biographical value.

The following letter to Pierre Daniel, a French scholar of some repute, and one of Buchanan's

---

[1] Only one of these is given in Ruddiman. See his General Introduction to his edition of Buchanan's *Works.*

most respected friends, is dated Edinburgh, 1566.
" What with ill-health and my duties at Court, I
have hardly been able to steal a moment either for
my friends or myself. Hence my rare letters to my
friends, as also the fact that my poems are still un-
collected. As far as I myself am concerned, I made
no great efforts to preserve them. The truth is,
that their subjects are mostly so trifling, that now,
in my old age, I am half ashamed and half chagrined
at ever having written them. At the importunities
of friends (Pierre Mondoré in special), however, to
whom I neither can nor should refuse what they ask,
I have at odd times brought together some of my
poems, and arranged them under different heads.
At present I send you one book of Elegies, one of
Silvae, and one of Hendecasyllabics. Pray be good
enough to show them at your leisure to Mondoré or
de Mesmes, and other learned friends, and do nothing
without their advice. I hope some day soon to send
you a book of Iambics, one of Epigrams, and another
of Odes, and perhaps some other pieces of the same
kind. These also I should like you to submit to
our friends, as I have made up my mind to be
guided by their judgment rather than my own. I
have corrected many *errata* in my Psalter, and have
also made certain changes in my text. When you
treat with Estienne, therefore, you will tell him not
to issue a new edition without consulting me. I
have not had leisure to complete my second book of
the *Sphere*, so that I have not as yet made a copy
of the first."

This letter was addressed to Daniel in Orleans,
where, it would appear, there was a colony of
Scotsmen. In the letter addressed to Buchanan

from Orleans, following the one just quoted, the
writer says that he is on intimate terms with
"Gordon, Cunningham, Guthrie, and other Scottish
youths devotedly attached to Buchanan". On
the strength of his acquaintance with Buchanan's
friends, he asks him for any emendation of the text
of Caesar that may have occurred to him. Failing
Caesar, his correspondent will be glad to have suggestions regarding the text of any Latin author.
In return for this favour, he undertakes to keep
Buchanan informed on matters of general interest,
although, he adds, this is somewhat unnecessary, as
"many correspondents are continually in communication with you". Buchanan's astronomical poem, he
also tells him, is eagerly expected by everybody.

Buchanan's next letter is addressed to Daniel
Rogers, an ardent Protestant, and a person of some
standing at the English Court, as is proved by his
frequent embassies to the Continent. He seems to
have been one of Buchanan's closest friends, and
Buchanan exchanged more letters with him than
with any other of his correspondents. The following
letter refers to the proposed marriage between
Elizabeth and the Duke of Anjou, and it shows the
keen interest Buchanan took in the political life of
the day. It is dated Leith, 1571. "I received
your letter three months after it was written—for
which very many thanks. As occasion serves you, I
wish you would keep me informed of the state of
affairs in France. Although the new match is now
given out almost for a certainty, I cannot think
that it will really take place. Such ill results must
follow this marriage, that France and England
both could hardly survive it. It would so compro-

mise the interests of religion, and raise such a strife
in the neighbouring countries that we have not seen
in our time the confusion that must follow in
Europe. I am astonished that prudent men on both
sides do not see this. If I had only a few hours'
talk with you, I think I could easily show you what
pernicious results will follow from this marriage.
For, not to mention other reasons, if Anjou, when a
simple duke, could not endure his brother to be
greater than himself, how will he feel disposed to
him, when by this marriage he will have such
resources behind him? Then, though England
bases some hope on the result of a war, in the first
place the result would be uncertain, and, in the
second, such a war would so strain the resources of
both kingdoms that, whichever should have the best
of it, the victory would also mean the ruin of the
victor. Again, if Aegisthus should once cast eyes
on Clytemnestra,[1] he is simply blind who does not
see that this would threaten the ruin of the
English queen. As regards our affairs in Scotland,
if any of your countrymen do not see that it is
your queen's interest more than ours, that the
honester party here should hold the power, him also
I hold equally purblind. If any one see this and
yet conceal his opinion, he is even more a traitor to
his own country than an enemy of ours. Our affairs
are now in such a state that the very show of
assistance on your part would be enough to put
down our common enemies. If this opportunity
should be lost, I fear there will be no occasion for our
appealing to you again. I was delighted to hear what
you had to say regarding the state of religion and

---

[1] The reference is, of course, to Mary and the Duke of Norfolk.

letters.   When you write to me, direct your letters
to the Countess of Lennox, the relative of your
queen, and wife of our Regent, at the English Court.
In this way they will reach me most directly."

The following letter is dated Stirling, and,
from internal evidence, must be referred to the year
1571.   It is addressed to a countryman of his own,
Henry Scrimgeour, who was settled in Geneva as
a professor of Civil Law.   The letter will explain
itself.   "You have more than once heard from me
during the last two years how eager Lennox, our
late Regent, was to make your acquaintance, and
what generous offers he enjoined me to make you.   It
was his intention not only to assign you some public
office, and to treat you liberally, but also, as far as
his leisure from public business would permit, to
refresh himself with the pleasure of your society.
Lennox died lately, but his successor, the Earl of
Mar, is even more urgent, and for the same reason
as his predecessor.   He also promises to make you
a partaker in all his good fortune.   But even if
these promises should not be fulfilled, it would
hardly become a man of your virtue and learning
and knowledge of affairs to refuse his offer, were it
only for the sake of your country, to whose interests
you cannot be wanting without actual criminality.
Nor do I consider it necessary here to remind you,
versed as you are in all Christian and Pagan wisdom,
what your country, your friends, and your kindred
have a right to demand of you.   Much less need I
recall to you the examples of those who, in the hour
of their country's trial, gladly gave their lives in its
interest.   This only I will add to what I have
already said in my former letters.   If anything in

the past (as I have never doubted) could in some measure delay your decision, every excuse of that kind is now removed. Our prospects are now somewhat brighter, and we have at our head a man who is not only better known to you than his predecessor, but in whom you can place even more implicit confidence. Does not the same reason also urge you to this step as that which moved the illustrious Epaminondas, who deliberately chose to remain childless in order that when the need should arise, he might more freely give his life for his country? But if you are one of those who set greater store by lucrative ease than honourable employment, still, neither the high reputation you have gained by so many years of foreign travel, nor the distinction of your family, nor the just solicitations of your country, can allow you to yield to such poor-spirited suggestions, unless you wish to forfeit at one stroke all the honour of your past life. . . . Of my zealous affection towards you I shall say nothing at present, nor of Peter Young, whose attentions to me are such that I have come to think him as much my own kinsman as yours. Pray salute Beza and Henri Estienne in my name. Our friend Knox is still in life, but he is fast hastening to its term." In spite of Buchanan's urgency, Scrimgeour did not respond to his appeal, alleging old age and the troubles in Scotland as his sufficient excuse. To Buchanan, he states these excuses in a long Latin letter; to the Regent Mar himself, in Scots.

The following letter of Beza to Buchanan will show the relations that existed between them. It is dated Geneva, 1572. " I was unwilling to let slip the present opportunity of writing to you,

partly that you may know with what fidelity I hold
you in remembrance and with what reverence I
ever regard you, and partly that I might congratu-
late yourself, or, to speak more truly, every one of
your countrymen, on the circumstance which you
mentioned to our friend Scrimgeour—that to you
has been assigned the charge of the King, who even
already, while yet a child, has given such proofs of
piety and every excellence as to raise the highest
hopes for the future wellbeing of himself and
your whole nation. Heaven grant that the same
event may not happen in your case which in former
times befell your neighbour England![1] But rather
let this be your lot, that Scotland, having obtained
a king adorned with every gift of mind and person,
may at length, after her protracted wars and re-
verses, enjoy the benefit of sacred peace. As for our
own affairs, Scrimgeour, as I hope, will give you full
information. I am immensely delighted with your
version of the Psalms. But though they are such
as could have come from you alone, I yet wish
(what would be a very easy matter for you) that
you would perfect those which are already good, or,
as I should rather say, improve that which is
already perfect."

The following letter shows the kindly interest
Buchanan took in the younger generation of his
fellow-countrymen, and how he made his great
reputation abroad serve their interests. It is
addressed to Monsieur de Sigongues, Chevalier de
l'Ordre, et Capitane et Gouverneur de la Ville et
Chasteau de Dieppe. This Sigongues, it may be
said, was at one time an agent of the French

---

[1] The reference is, of course, to Edward VI.

Government in Scotland. We give the letter in the original French, as the only specimen we possess of Buchanan's acquaintance with that language. From other sources we know that he spoke French fluently. "Monsieur, ce que j'ay tant differé de vous escrire a esté pour l'occasion des troubles qui ont universellement regné, tant en ces quartiers, qu'en la *France*, au grand prejudice des deux roy- almes. Et comme par la grace de Dieu nous avons en la fin quelque relasche de nos maux, il me semble (je le dis avec regret) que les vostres ne font que recommencer. Mais pour laisser ce propos, la pre- sente sera pour me recommander humblement a vostre bonne grace, ensemble ce present Porteur *Thomas Fairlie*, qui est fort de mes amys, et autant amy qu'aymé de tous les miens. Le bien et plaisir que vous luy ferez, je l'estimeray fait a moy mesme, comme je fais celuy qu'avez par le passé fait a tous ceux que je vous ay recommandé, qui se louent grandement de vostre faveur, pour laquelle je vous demeure tres obligé ; vous asseurant, Monsieur, que si je puys quelque chose pour vous par deca, ou pour les vostres, que vous me pouvez livrement com- mander, comme celui qui sera tousjours prest a vous obeyer et fair service. A Sterlin, ce dousieme de Janvier, 1573, Celui qui est de tout vostre,

"GEORGE BUCHANAN."

One of the most distinguished of Buchanan's correspondents was the Danish astronomer, Tycho Brahé; but the following letter of Buchanan's is the only memorial of their intercourse that has been preserved. In 1590, when King James visited Tycho in his castle of Uranienburg, he saw the

Y

portrait of Buchanan in the library. Sir Peter
Young, Buchanan's assistant in the education of
James, had presented it in one of his embassies to
the Court of Denmark.[1]   Buchanan's letter is dated
Stirling, 1576 : " Another year has already passed,
most learned Tycho, since William Lumsdale, on his
return from Denmark, brought me your book, *De
Nova Stella*.   For many reasons your gift was most
grateful to me, but above all because it came from
you, a man, that is to say, illustrious by descent
and genius, and equally remarkable for his accomplishments, who has raised from its low estate, and
transported from the sordid hands of the vulgar to
its true home, the palace, that part of philosophy,
which in the words of your favourite Manilius,

> ' Regales animos primum dignata movere,
> Proxima tangentes rerum fastigia coelo.'

Great as is your gift, your kindness and courtesy
have still more increased its value.   From the
height where rank and learning alike place you, not
only have you cast favourable eyes on my humble
self (*penitus penitusque jacentes*), but by your own
example you encourage me also *Nube vehi, vali-
disque humeris insistere Atlantis,* and by the monuments of your own industry refute that false
though generally received opinion, that under our
cold northern sky men's minds are doomed by
nature to lethargy.   Since every northern people is
thus so deeply in your debt, and I myself most of
all, you will not, I trust, think me guilty of rudeness because I have not acknowledged your gift till
now.   All who know me are well aware how far
any such rudeness is from my character and con-

---

[1] Irving, *Memoirs of Buchanan,* p. 200.

stant habit. My friends also know how, during
the last two years, my life has been a constant
battle with the most serious illnesses, and that I
have had hardly an hour at my disposal for correspondence. I have, therefore, been forced not only
to give up my lighter tasks, but also to leave half
finished my five books on the *Sphere*, and finally to
abandon the hope of producing a poem worthy to
preserve my name with posterity. Yourself I con-
gratulate on a rank due to your ancestors, on
your genius, the gift of nature, and your learning
acquired while still in the prime of life by your own
labour and zeal. Though myself reduced to the
helpless torpor of age, I shall gladly applaud you
who are still in the course ; and any services
besides, which you may ask of me, I shall be grati-
fied to perform to the extent of my ability. I
have requested William Lumsdale, the bearer of
this letter, carefully to inform me of the state of
your affairs. I would also request that with your
usual courtesy and kindly zeal you would help him
to recover, if possible, a small sum of money which
is due to him."

In the letter which follows we again see
Buchanan in the character which his age and reputation entitled him so gracefully to assume—that
of general mentor to the thoughtful young Scotsmen of the time. Neither the date nor the person
addressed is known. " I received your letter some
days since. I received it with much pleasure for
many reasons, but specially because you were the
writer, and because it gave no mean proof of your
capacity, as well as a sure hope that in no long time
your country will reap the happiest fruits from the

same soil.   Moreover, by the same letter it seems
to me that you have, as it were, bound yourself by
a pledge to future usefulness.   When such a
foundation is laid, it can be only your own sloth if
the rest of the building do not correspond.   Surely
it is not likely that you alone, to the extent of your
other good qualities and gifts of person and fortune,
will be found wanting when nature has supplied all
the rest.   I wish you, therefore, not only to lay
seriously to heart what you owe to yourself, your
friends, and your kinsmen, but meanwhile to remember that I also, who hold you bound by such
a pledge, will never cease to remind you of your
duty, as knowing that good things do not usually
become bad by their being called such.   But if you
should disappoint our hopes, although many will
grieve along with me, yet my sorrow will be so
much greater than that of everybody else, because
I feel myself bound to you for so many more
reasons.   But if, as all desire, you shall achieve
what is worthy of yourself, you will at once give a
common pleasure to myself and others, and do what
is worthy of your descent, and thus renew the
ancient lustre of your family, whose glory it is
incumbent on you to serve.   I would have you
especially to remember that in this same race for
glory you have a competitor (the King himself, I
mean), your equal in genius, but younger than yourself in years, and in his tender age even more
engrossed by the attentions of flatterers than yourself, who in your quiet retreat, free from all solici-
tude, ought to give yourself up to study both out of
respect for yourself and from the inspiring example
of others.   I add no more, lest I should seem to

imply doubt of your character and talents." Nothing could show more forcibly than this letter the eager interest Buchanan took in the generation rising around him. A significant reference to this trait in his character occurs in another letter, in which one of his correspondents refers to George Keith (son of the Earl Marischal), a young man in whom Buchanan seems also to have taken an interest, as being well aware that "Buchanan was always ready to seek the friendship of good men, and that no one could be more faithful in the discharge of the duties of friendship ".[1]

We have seen Buchanan recommending the young Huguenot, Jerome Groslot, to Beza. In the following letter we have Beza similarly recommending another young man to Buchanan : "Not so long since, my Buchanan, I sought to renew our friendship by writing to you. You will now see what trust I place in your goodwill to me, when I actually take the liberty of recommending my friends to you.[2] The youth who bears this letter comes of a distinguished family, and is the son of a father held by us in the highest esteem. On his being sent on a mission to your king I deemed it my duty to make him acquainted with yourself, that by your counsel and authority he may be stimulated, young as he is, and in a foreign land, to persevere in that course of piety and virtue on which he has already entered. Although I have no doubt that as a true lover of all good men you would of your own accord have done this kindness, yet I persuaded myself that on my recommendation of this young

[1] *Epist.* xviii.
[2] Buchanan's letter recommending Groslot was written after the above.

man you will do so even more gladly, and with
still greater eagerness to serve him. I earnestly
request that you will not deceive me in this my
hope. As for myself, I am as well as men of my
age usually are. I suffer not so much from my
labours, though of these I have undergone not a
few, as from chronic vexation of spirit, for which
there is too great justification. For how can I for-
bear to indulge my grief for the Churches in France,
so cruelly persecuted, spoiled, and oppressed? I
confess myself unable to bear with becoming
patience this heavy visitation, yet it is my hope
that God will in brief space ordain its end, and
so restore me to a happier frame of mind. Pray
God, therefore, for me, dearest brother, that I
may happily finish the course I have yet to run,
as I in turn pray Him that He may bless with increasing blessing the happiness of your old age."

The letter which follows is perhaps the highest
tribute ever paid to the character and career of
Buchanan, and it is the tribute of one who was
himself among the noblest spirits of his age—Hubert
Languet, the revered friend and mentor of Sir
Philip Sidney. To Languet himself, it will be
remembered, Sidney in the *Arcadia* expresses his
deepest debt :

> "The song I sang old Languet had me taught—
>   Languet, the shepherd best swift Ister knew
> For clerkly reed, and hating what is naught,
>   For faithful heart, clean hands, and mouth as true.
> With his sweet skill my skill-less youth he drew
>   To have a feeling taste of Him that sits
>   Beyond the heavens, far more beyond our wits."

Buchanan and Languet were in many respects
kindred spirits. They thought alike in religion and

politics,[1] they had both the same impetuous temper,
and they both showed the same vehemence in their
denunciation of what they deemed tyranny or irre-
ligion. From Languet's letter it will be seen that
he regarded Buchanan with much the same feelings
as Sidney regarded himself: "So well are you
known to the whole Christian world by your virtue
and the many monuments of your genius, that there
is hardly a lover of learning and sound instruction
who does not pay you the tribute of his ardent
reverence and admiration. I count it my great
happiness that in Paris some twenty years since it
was my good fortune not only to see you and to
enjoy the benefit of your learning and the delightful
charm of your conversation, but also to entertain
you as my guest along with others of the highest
distinction, Turnèbe, Dorat, and others. We then
heard much from you to our utmost profit and
delight. Of all this I now write to see whether I
can recall to you who I am. But be I who I may,
be certain that your virtues are my profoundest
admiration. For many years I lived with Philip
Melanchthon, and I then thought myself happy.
On his death, after many vicissitudes, I at length
came to this country as to a safe port, finding none
safer elsewhere, though here also for many years
the storms of civil war have been raging. Nevertheless, amid these storms the light of the Gospel is
shining, and the true way of salvation is preached
to us, and superstition driven out of the churches
to the great indignation of Spain, which is still

---

[1] Languet was supposed to be the author of the famous political
tract *Vindiciae contra Tyrannos*, which advocates much the same doctrine as Buchanan's *De Jure Regni*. The authorship of this tract is still
under discussion.

under its dominion.   It was by the command of the
Prince of Orange, the chiefest ornament of our age,
that I came here with himself.   By his courage and
genius he has till now so successfully coped with
the mighty resources of the Spanish king that he
has won for himself undying fame.   Under him as
their leader, these provinces, after their rupture from
the tyranny of Spain, have with happy auspices set
up other states and churches, and by their confede-
ration hitherto withstood the arms of the enemy.
The king of Spain, after vainly attempting for
many years to put the Prince down by force, has at
length had recourse to weapons which seem hardly
to become so great a king.   He has published a
document in which he denounces him as an outlaw,
and by the offer of rewards encourages his assassination.   As in that document there are many false
charges against the Prince, his friends urged him to
publish a manifesto (which I herewith send you) as
a reply to the calumnies of the Spaniards.   I have
spent this last winter in these marshes of the
Netherlands, which seem more fitted to be the
abodes of frogs and eels than of human beings.
This, however, is a very fine town.[1]   At a distance
of some three hours' journey is Leyden, where are
to be found Justus Lipsius, the poet Douza, and the
French jurisconsult Donellus, all of them men of
learning and reputation.   By going outside the
town we at once come in view of Rotterdam, the
sight of which recalls not only the great Erasmus,
the boast of his fellow-citizens, but yourself also,
since I can never cease wondering that such countries
and climates can give birth to men whose equals in

---

[1] Delft, in the Netherlands.

genius can nowhere be found among their contemporaries. Erasmus was invited to undertake the education of Ferdinand, the brother of the Emperor Charles, but refused the task. You I count both more fortunate and more noble in consenting to the request of your countrymen to imbue the youthful mind of your prince with precepts which, if his manhood follow them, will lead to the highest happiness of himself and his subjects. I am extremely eager to learn, if I am not too curious, when we may look for your History of Scotland. You will learn from Melville, a man of the highest character, how things are at present with myself."

The last letter but one[1] of Buchanan is addressed to his old friend and colleague, Élie Vinet. Their friendship, begun at Bordeaux, had been cemented by common dangers and misfortunes at Coimbra. The two friends, it appears, were in the habit of exchanging letters once a year through the wine-merchants who traded between Scotland and Bordeaux. It should be said that Vinet was now at the head of the Collége de Guyenne, in Bordeaux. " When our merchants from Bordeaux bring me tidings of you, it rejoices my heart, and my youth seems to return, for then I learn that a remnant still survives of our notable Portuguese expedition. Now in my seventy-fifth year, I sometimes recall through what cares and toils (passing every port where men are wont to find joy and refreshment) I have in my voyage of life at length struck on that rock beyond which, as it is most truly said in the ninetieth psalm, nothing

---

[1] At least of those that we possess.

remains but labour and sorrow. The memory of
friends, of whom you are almost the only survivor—
this is now my one consolation. You, though
I believe as advanced in years as myself, are still
able to give your fellow-citizens the benefit of your
labour and your wisdom. I have long bidden farewell
to literature; and my only thought now is, with as
little noise as possible, to leave a generation with
which I am no longer in sympathy—as one dead,
that is to say, to leave the haunts of the living.
Meanwhile I send you the last-born of my little
books. When you see its clear proofs of my dotage,
you will have no great desire to see its fellows. I
hear that a young Scotsman, by name Harry Wardlaw, and come of a good stock, is at present in Bordeaux prosecuting his studies with some success.
Although I know well your unfailing kindness and
courtesy, and though you are aware that foreigners
have a peculiar claim upon you, still I wish the
young man to understand what our ancient friendship avails with you." De Thou tells us that, when
he was in Bordeaux, Vinet showed him this very
letter of Buchanan. It was written, he says, " in a
trembling hand but in a magnanimous spirit", the
writer "complaining not so much of the irksomeness
of old age, as of the weariness of a life prolonged
beyond its due limits ". De Thou was especially
struck by one sentence in the letter, which he says
he always preserved in his memory: " Nunc id
unum satago, ut minimo cum strepitu, ex inaequa-
lium meorum, hoc est, mortuus e vivorum con-
tubernio demigrem."[1]

    To this letter of Buchanan Vinet replies as

    [1] De Thou, *Commentar. de Vita Sua*, lib. ii.

follows :—" Your letter, dated 16th March, reached me on the 3rd of June. Nothing could well give me greater pleasure than a letter from yourself, now so far down the vale of years, with seas between us, and so many a day since we met. And that mention of our Portuguese journey, and those times when we were far happier than now ! I have read it again and again, as likewise the book that accompanied it. If I may trust my own judgment and that of friends, many of whom are your own former scholars, it was no ' dotard ' that wrote it. I hear, however, that a countryman of your own, a councillor of Poitou, is of a different opinion. He has written a book, which I shall send you as soon as it is published in Poitou. Of the companion volumes, which you say I am desirous of seeing, I know nothing ; but George Buchanan's Tragedies, Psalms, Elegies, and Epigrams, are for sale here. Many persons here, myself not least, are looking for your *Sphere*, which we are told you composed some time since ; but perhaps it is not quite ready for publication. My own treatises of which you speak are merely elementary, and are intended for the use of my pupils. If you doubt this, the commentary on the *Somnium Scipionis*, which I send you with the letters of Gelida, will satisfy you. As regards Henry Wardlaw, whom you so warmly commend to me, since I made your acquaintance here, and came to know your character and attainments, I have for your sake loved and cherished all your countrymen, and done all in my power (limited as it is) to advance their interests. Our school is rarely without a Scotsman. At present we have two,

one a professor of philosophy, the other of
Greek and mathematics, both men of learning and
character, and acceptable to the students. Farewell! Look henceforward for many letters from me
as I have opportunity of sending them."

CHAPTER XX.

DURING the last years of his life Buchanan lived mainly in Edinburgh, in what part of the town no tradition has reached us.[1] At Sheriffhall, in the parish of Newton, near Dalkeith, however, a room is still shown where he is said to have written part of his History.[2] Fortunately, just one year before his death, he received a visit, which has been described for us with a minuteness and fidelity of detail that make it by far the most valuable contemporary notice of Buchanan we possess. In September 1581, the diarist James Melville, with his uncle, Andrew Melville, and Buchanan's own cousin, Thomas Buchanan, crossed from St. Andrews to Edinburgh with the express purpose of visiting the old scholar. Melville has devoted a page of his diary to an account of this visit,[3] which is not only a vivid page of biography, but has in it a strain that

---

[1] But see note to page 353.

[2] As being on the lands adjoining Dalkeith, the house in which Buchanan lived at Sheriffhall would belong to the Earl of Morton. During Morton's regency it was necessary that Buchanan, as Keeper of the Privy Seal, should be near him; and we actually have documents, dated from Dalkeith, with Buchanan's signature attached to them. The tradition is that it was in the tower of Sheriffhall House, known as the "Dove-cot", that Buchanan wrote his History. It may be added that the room where Buchanan lived in St. Andrews is also still shown.

[3] *Mr. James Melvill's Diary*, p. 86, 4to, Edin. 1829.

reminds us of Plutarch at his best. As Buchanan
is here presented to us, we can hardly help recalling
Sir James Melville's description of him as " a stoick
philosopher, who looked not far before him ".

"That September [1581], in tyme of vacans, my
uncle, Mr. Andro, Mr. Thomas Buchanan, and I,
heiring that Mr. George Buchanan was weak and
his Historie under the pres, past ower to Edin-
bruche annes errand, to visit him and sie the wark.
When we cam to his chalmer, we fand him sitting
in his chaire, teatching his young man that servit
him in his chalmer to spell a, b, ab; e, b, eb, etc.
Efter salutation, Mr. Andro sayes, ' I sie, sir, yie
are nocht ydle.'

"'Better this,' quoth he, ' nor stelling sheipe,
or sitting ydle, qhuilk is als ill.'

"Therefter he schew us the Epistle Dedicatorie
to the King; the quhilk, when Mr. Andro had read,
he tauld him that it was obscure in sum places, and
wanted certean words to perfyt the sentence.

"Sayes he, ' I may do na mair for thinking on
another mater.'

"' What is that?' sayes Mr. Andro.

"'To die!' quoth he; ' bot I leave that and
manie ma things for you to helpe.'

"We went from him to the printars wark hous,
whom we fand at the end of the 17 buik of his
Cornicle, at a place quhilk we thought verie hard
for the tyme, quhilk might be an occasion of steying
the haill wark, anent the buriall of Davie.[1] Therfor,
steying the printer from proceiding, we cam to Mr.

---

[1] David Rizzio. In his History Buchanan states, as one among other
proofs of Mary's guilty relations with Rizzio, that she caused his body to
be removed from the place in which it was first laid, and to be buried in
the tomb of James v.

George again, and fund him bedfast by[1] his custome,
and asking him, whow he did, 'Even going the way
of weilfare,' sayes he. Mr. Thomas, his cusing,
schawes him of the hardnes of that part of his
Storie, that the King wald be offendit with it, and
it might stey all the wark.

" ' Tell me, man,' sayes he, ' giff I have tauld the
treuthe ? '

" ' Yis,' sayes Mr. Thomas, ' sir, I think sa.'

" ' I will byd his fead, and all his Kins, then,'
quoth he: ' Pray, pray to God for me, and let him
direct all.'

" Sa, be the printing of his Cornicle was endit,
that maist lerned, wyse, and godlie man, endit this
his mortall lyff."

In August 1582, a month before Buchanan's
death, occurred the famous Raid of Ruthven. By
that date he must have been so feeble that he could
take but little interest in an event that threatened
Scotland with another revolution. According to
Camden, the conspirators tried to win him to their
side, but failed.[2] This is improbable. If Buchanan
was able to take any interest whatever in the affair,
all his past record leads us to conclude that his
sympathies would be against the favourites of the
King, and the policy they had been teaching him.

As in the case of every Protestant of eminence,
many foolish stories came to be circulated by Roman
Catholic writers regarding Buchanan's last days.[3]
It is needless to say that these stories rest on no
satisfactory evidence, and that they are stupidly
inconsistent with the character of the man they were

---

[1] *i.e.* contrary to.   [2] *Annales*, vol. ii. p. 386.

[3] Some of these stories are given in Bayle.

meant to discredit. We have seen from his correspondence that for years he had looked for death
even with longing, as one who had fully accomplished
his work, and to whom life could henceforth be but
"labour and sorrow". Two stories we may accept
as at once in keeping with his character, and as
resting on fair authority. According to Wodrow,
Buchanan was visited towards his end by a Pres-
byterian minister, John Davidson. Buchanan expressed to him his belief in salvation through the
sacrifice of Christ, but, in the course of the interview, ridiculed, in his usual caustic vein, the
absurdities of the Mass. The other story is thus
told by Mackenzie.[1] As will be seen, it is admirably
true to all we know of Buchanan :—

"When Buchanan was dying, he called for Mr.
Young, his servant,[2] and asked him how much
money he had of his, and finding that it was not
sufficient for defraying the charges of his burial, he
commanded him to distribute it among the poor.
Upon which Mr. Young asking who then would be
at the charges of burying him, he answered that he
was very indifferent about that, for if he was once
dead, if they would not bury him, they might let
him lie where he was, or throw his corpse where
they pleased; and that, accordingly, the City of
Edinburgh was obliged to bury him at their own
expenses." This story of Mackenzie is supported
by the fact that in Buchanan's will, it is stated
that his only "goods and gear" in the world is

---

[1] *Lives of Scots Writers*, vol. iii. p. 172. Mackenzie says that he
had this story also from the Earl of Cromarty, who had it from his
grandfather, Lord Invertyle.

[2] This "Mr. Young" is, of course, not to be confounded with Sir
Peter Young, Buchanan's assistant in the education of James.

the sum of a hundred pounds due to him from his Crossraguel pension.[1]

Buchanan died on the 28th of September 1582, and was buried on the following day, Saturday, his funeral being attended "by a great company of the faithful".[2] The grounds of the Greyfriars had lately been converted into a public burying-ground, and Buchanan was "the first person of celebrity" laid there.[3] From a minute in the Town Council Records of Edinburgh, 1701, it would appear that at some date a stone must have been placed over his grave. By that year, however, the stone had sunk out of sight, and the Council gave orders that it should be raised, and its inscription renewed.[4] At a later date, the stone seems again to have disappeared, as George Chalmers could find no trace of it.[5] Within recent years, however, it was re-discovered, and actually removed and appropriated to the memory of one of the grave-diggers.[6] A simple tablet marks the spot where Buchanan's grave is supposed to be,[7] and in another part of the church-

---

[1] See Appendix D.

[2] Calderwood. I am indebted to Mr. John Taylor Brown for the following interesting note : "The following note was extracted about sixty years ago from a memorandum-book kept by George Paton, the antiquary. 'George Buchanan took his last illness and died in Kennedy's Close, first court thereof on your left hand, first house in the turnpike above the tavern there ; and in Queen Ann's time this was told to his family and friends, who resided in that house, by Sir James Stewart of Goodtrees, Lord Advocate.' Kennedy's Close was the second close above the Tron Church, and is now absorbed into Hunter Square."

[3] David Laing, Introduction to *Epitaphs and Monumental Inscriptions in Greyfriars Churchyard* (Edin. 1867), p. xxii.

[4] It seems, however, that there was no inscription on the stone.— *Ibid.* p. xxiii.

[5] Chalmers, *Life of Ruddiman* (Lond. 1794), p. 270 note. Irving, *Memoirs of Buchanan* (p. 309 note), is very severe on Chalmers's unfortunate misreading of Adamson's Epigram, which is not, as he thought, a monumental inscription.

[6] *Epitaphs and Monumental Inscriptions in Greyfriars,* p. xxiv.

[7] *Ibid.* p. 18 : "A few years ago, a humble blacksmith erected at

Z

yard a monument has been erected, consisting of a large pedestal with a bust of life-size.[1]   Within the Old Greyfriars Church itself, a memorial window, with Buchanan's portrait and the arms of his family, has also within recent years been erected to his memory.[2]   It may be added that what on good authority is supposed to be Buchanan's skull is preserved in the Anatomical Museum of the University of Edinburgh.   Its general outline is exactly that of the best portraits, and by its dome-like shape and extreme tenuity, it has all the marks of a high cerebral development.[3]

From the preceding pages it will have sufficiently appeared what manner of man Buchanan was, and what the scope and general direction of his life.   The type of mind to which he belonged we can have no difficulty in determining.   He was no religious reformer like Knox, or Calvin, or even Colet, nor was he a born educationist like Jean Sturm.   He belonged to that class of men who feel strongly and generously, but who by the mobility of their feeling and their very keenness of insight are incapable of being enthusiasts or great practical reformers.[4]   During the last quarter of his life he

his own expense the small tablet which now marks the spot where Buchanan was buried." The grave (regarding which, however, there is some uncertainty) is near the eastern wall of the churchyard, to the right of the main entrance.

[1] This monument was erected by the late Mr. David Laing, at his own expense, in 1878. The bust was executed by Mr. D. W. Stevenson, after the Boissard portrait approved by Drummond and Laing.

[2] By the late James Buchanan, Esq., father of the present Member for Edinburgh.

[3] The skull was obtained from Greyfriars by John Adamson, Principal of the University of Edinburgh. After Adamson's death it became the property of the University.—Sibbald, *Commentarius in Vitam Georgii Buchanani*, p. 62 ; Irving, *Memoirs of Buchanan*, p. 310.

[4] Mark Pattison (*Essays*, i. 79, Clar. Press, 1889) says of Erasmus

was in full sympathy with the Protestant revolution, and he was profoundly convinced that in a complete breach with Rome lay the only hope for the future of Christian Europe. At the same time, he held these convictions in a fashion very different from Calvin and Knox. This, indeed, could hardly have been otherwise, seeing that, till past middle age, his mind had been far more deeply engaged by the ideals of humanism than those of religious reform. The free play of thought and feeling which this discipline naturally induced made it impossible for him to be dominated by a single idea like Knox, or to be a theological doctrinaire like Calvin. Buchanan spoke with sufficient vehemence of what he deemed the corruption and false teaching of Rome ; but we measure the difference between him and Knox, when we compare their respective treatment of that period of Scottish history in which they themselves lived and acted. For Knox the one all-absorbing series of events is the gradual schism from Rome and the establishment of an independent Church, based on a purer conception of the essentials of the Christian teaching. Buchanan's aim in his History was, of course, a more general one than that of Knox; yet, had he been equally absorbed in the great religious revolution, he could never have referred to it in the merely casual way he does.

The truth is, that Buchanan belonged essentially to that class which we now recognise as distinctively *men of letters.* He has always passed for

that "the humanist and reformer were pretty well mixed " in him. In Buchanan, of course, there was still more of the reformer, seeing that he actually identified himself with the Protestant revolution.

the most famous scholar whom Scotland has produced, but from the account that has here been given
of his work it must be clear that Buchanan was
no scholar like Budé, or Casaubon, or the younger
Scaliger.   Their life's effort was to add to our
knowledge of classical antiquity.   Buchanan was
regarded by his contemporaries as one of the most
learned men of his age;[1] but the direction of his
activity was far from being that of the scholar pure
and simple.   Buchanan is best described as a man
of letters of 'the sixteenth century, who used Latin
for the same purpose as a modern writer does his
mother tongue.   In his own fashion, Buchanan was
a general critic of men and things, like Erasmus himself, though he had neither the range of thought
nor the flexibility or openness of mind which make
Erasmus the supreme type of his class.   On the
other hand, Buchanan undoubtedly possessed what
Erasmus with all his gifts cannot claim—a distinctive vein of genius clearly perceptible under all his
foreign guise and artificial inspiration.

We have no detailed account of Buchanan's
relations with a single friend or enemy, such as
enable us to mark those delicate traits that distinguish men of the same type from each other.
Of his general aims and modes of thought, however,
of the total impression he made on those with
whom he came in contact, we have full material for
forming our judgment.   In view of the course the

---

[1] Turnèbe bears testimony to Buchanan's minute knowledge of Latin.
(Ruddiman, *Buchanani Opera*, vol. ii. p. 104).   In Greek, Buchanan,
like many of the best scholars of his century, was self-taught.   Those
of his contemporaries best entitled to have an opinion, speak of him as
equally learned in Greek and Latin.   Buchanan's writings certainly
give the impression of very wide knowledge in all the learning of the
time.

world has taken since his day, we are justified in saying that Buchanan was on the side with which the best interests of the future lay. In the reform of studies and religion alike, the part he took gives him a distinct place in the front rank of the representative men of his century. In his own country his great name and the inspiration of his example have been among the strongest influences in maintaining the tradition of the higher studies. For such studies Scotland has always had the most meagre provision ; yet in every generation since Buchanan's day there has never failed a line of students with the highest ideals in learning and national education, and it is undoubtedly to Buchanan, more than to any other, that this tradition is due.[1] He took no such direct part as Knox and Andrew Melville in the religious and political struggles of his time. The main direction of his influence, however, was identical with theirs, so that he has his own merit and responsibility for the types of thought and feeling which the world now recognises as distinctively Scottish. Though less obtrusive than that of Knox and Melville, Buchanan's influence on subsequent Scottish politics was perhaps more persuasive and permanently active. In his History of Scotland and his *De Jure Regni*, the political leaders of the Scottish people during the seventeenth century had what they deemed the classical statement of the principles of civil and religious liberty, and Buchanan's universal fame as a scholar gave a weight to his teaching beyond even

[1] Thus, Calderwood in the seventeenth century says, " No man did merit better of his nation for learning, nor thereby did bring it to more glory."—Vol. ii. p. 300.

that of Melville and Knox. It is, in truth, only in comparatively recent times that the work of these two has been realised in all its significance. In the seventeenth century their names carried no such fulness of suggestion as they now imply for us.

In Buchanan's literary work, what first strikes the modern reader is the variety of forms in which his genius expressed itself. He wrote prose and verse indifferently, and verse in all its traditional classical forms. This is not, of course, to be set down to any undue consciousness of universal talent on Buchanan's part. It was simply because the age had no notion of special talent and the necessity for its special direction. Many of his contemporaries who did not attain to the fame of Buchanan displayed their powers in the same dispersive fashion. Underlying all Buchanan's work, both prose and verse, there is the solid foundation of strong sense quickened by strong feeling, and this for Buchanan's age, with all its fatuous pedantries and affectations, is praise that can be estimated only after some acquaintance with his contemporary humanists. In his History of Scotland there is no suggestion of the great original thinker; but in the firm texture of its style, and the logical process of the narrative, we feel ourselves always in contact with a mind eminently sane, and a character bent on making itself felt on every page that he wrote. Verse, however, and not prose, was Buchanan's natural language. He tells us this himself, and there can be no doubt that he judged himself aright. The range of his poetical faculty is certainly remarkable. In *Franciscanus* we have humour as broad as that of *The Jolly Beggars*, and in his version of the Psalms there is a strain of spiritual feeling which not even its artificial form can wholly obscure. That he had a delicate play of fancy, both sportive and serious, many of his shorter pieces prove beyond a doubt; and it is impossible to read his ode on the First of May, and not recognise that on occasion he had also at command the special note of the poetic imagination.

We have no knowledge of Buchanan in any of those intimate domestic relations which alone enable us to form a true and comprehensive judgment of a man's character and habitual mood. From his correspondence, however, we gather that he inspired lasting attachment and reverence in men themselves of outstanding worth and accomplishments. In the everyday intercourse of life the charm of his manner and conversation is attested by friends and foes alike. It is the best proof of his strenuous individuality that his friends and foes speak of him with the same keenness of feeling. Those opposed to him on all the principles that underlie human life spoke of him in terms that refute themselves by their own excess. The faults of Buchanan, as has been said, were those of a powerful nature. In the pungency of his satire, and the vehemence of his denunciation, he seems when tried by modern standards to pass the limits of generous controversy. Yet it must not be forgotten that in this matter Buchanan can be fairly judged only by reference to the licence of speech that characterised his age, and especially the generation of humanists to which he belonged. The men of the sixteenth century staked life and fortune in the expression of their convictions; and in controversy carried on under such conditions, words were real battles and not mere broadsides of ink. Whatever his defects, Buchanan through his long and varied career was faithful to the ideal of honourable manhood. He had little care for those prizes in life by which most men set such store. His aims were all of the noblest, and it may be said that only with his life did he abandon them. Taking him all in all—having regard at once to the variety and scope of his work, to the striking individuality of his character, and to the fact that for nearly two centuries he stood before Europe as the one man of genius his country had produced— we seem justified in asserting that in the history of Scotland there is not a greater personality than Buchanan. Scotland has produced more original thinkers, men of perhaps higher literary genius, of greater practical power; but in no other Scotsman do we find conjoined with the same range and quality of gifts that uniqueness of personal character which, in its blended humour and austerity, recalls to us certain of the great figures of classical antiquity.

APPENDIX.

APPENDIX A.

(Page 180.)

To THE RIGHT WORSHIPFULL, MY VERY LOVINGE FREIND,
MAISTER PETER YONGE, SCHOLEMAISTER UNTO THE KINGES
MAJESTIE OF SCOTLAND.

After my verie hartie Commendacions. Beinge lately mouid
with the remembrance of my Maister, Mr. G. *Buchanan*, by the
Sight of a Booke of his, *De Jure Regni apud Scotos*, and callinge
to Mynde the notable Actes of his Lyfe, his Studie, his Trauayle,
his Danger, his Wisdome, his Learninge, and to be short, as
muche as could be wished in a Man; I thought the Kinge your
Maister more happie that had Buchanan to his Maister, then
Alexander the *Great*, that had *Aristotell* his Instructor. I thought
you very lukye that had his daily Company, ioynid in Office of
lyke Seruice, and thanckid God not a litle for my self, that euer
I was acquaintid with him. For one that hath so great
acquaintance as he hath with many learnid, and Compaignons of
his Lyfe, and that hath so wel deseruid of the Worlde, I maruaille
that no Man hath written of it: beinge a thinge so common
unto all famous Personnes, and most peculiar to the best learnid.
Heerin I might chieflie blame you, my good Freind Maister
Yonge, so neere unto him, so deere unto him, that nothinge can be
hid of that which you desyre to knowe. If you say that Tyme
yeat seruithe, and that he yeat liuethe whose Life I wishe to be
sett foorthe, surelie yeat I say unto you, that yf it be donne
after his Deathe, many Things may be omittid that were
worthie of famous Memorie, by him to be better knowen then
after his Deathe. The cause of the wrytinge against the *Grey
Friars* is knowen to many, but afterwardes howe they preuailed
against him, that he was fayne to leave his Contrey, howe he
escapid with great hazard of Lyfe at Godes Hand, the Thieues
on the Borders, the Plague in the North of England, what
Reliefe he found heere at a famous Knightes Handes, Sir *John*

Rainsforde, the onlie Man that maintaynid him against the Furie of the Papistes; none doth knowe so wel as him self, or can giue better Notes of his Life then him self can. As he liuith vertuouslie, so I doubt not but he will dye Christianly, and may be addid, when the former is perfectlie knowen. This is desired by many, specially looked for at your Handes, that can best doe, and are fittest to trauayle in so worthie a Worke. As I craue this at your Handes, so shall you command what is in my Power. And thus wishinge unto yow, my good Freind, hartely well, I take my leave. *London*, the 15th of *Marche*, 1579.

Your verie lovinge Frende

THO. RANDOLPHE.[1]

GEORGII BUCHANANI

VITA

AB IPSO SCRIPTA BIENNIO ANTE MORTEM.

Georgius Buchananus in Levinia Scotiae provincia natus est, ad Blanum amnem, anno salutis Christianae millesimo quingentesimo sexto, circa Kalendas Februarias, in villa rustica, familia magis vetusta quam opulenta. Patre in juventae robore ex dolore calculi exstincto, avoque adhuc vivo decoctore, familia ante tenuis pene ad extremam inopiam est redacta. Matris tamen Agnetis Heriotae diligentia liberi quinque mares et tres puellae ad maturam aetatem pervenerunt. Ex iis Georgium avunculus Jacobus Heriotus, cum in Scholis patriis spem de ingenio ejus concepisset, Lutetiam amandavit. Ibi cum studiis literarum, maxime carminibus scribendis, operam dedisset, partim naturae impulsu, partim necessitate (quod hoc unum studiorum genus adolescentiae proponebatur) intra biennium avunculo mortuo, et ipse gravi morbo correptus, ac undique inopia circumventus, redire ad suos est coactus.

Cum in patria valetudini curandae prope annum dedisset,

---

[1] In the concluding sentence of the following Latin sketch of his life, it is stated that Buchanan was in his seventy-second year when it was written. From this we should infer that it was written before Randolph's letter. But the phrase "septuagesimum quartum annum agens" should not, perhaps, be taken too literally. Ruddiman was of opinion that Randolph's letter was the occasion of Buchanan's writing his autobiography.

cum auxiliis Gallorum, qui tum in Scotiam appulerant, studio rei militaris cognoscendae in castra est profectus. Sed cum ea expeditione prope inutili, hieme asperrima per altissimas nives reduceretur exercitus, rursus in valetudinem adversam incidit, quae tota illa hieme lecto affixum tenuit. Primo vere ad Fanum Andreae missus est, ad Joannem Majorem audiendum, qui tum ibi dialecticen, aut verius sophisticen, in extrema senectute docebat. Hunc in Galliam aestate proxima sequutus, in flammam Lutheranae sectae, jam late se spargentem, incidit: ac biennium fere cum iniquitate fortunae colluctatus, tandem in Collegium Barbaranum accitus, prope triennium classi grammaticam discentium praefuit. Interea cum Gilbertus Cassilissae comes, adolescens nobilis, in ea vicinia diversaretur, atque ingenio et consuetudine ejus oblectaretur, eum quinquennium secum retinuit, atque in Scotiam una reduxit.

Inde cum in Galliam ad pristina studia redire cogitaret, a rege est retentus, ac Jacobo filio notho erudiendo praepositus. Interea pervenit ad Franciscanos elegidion per otium ab eo fusum, in quo se scribit per somnium a D. Francisco sollicitari, ut ejus ordini se adjungat. In eo cum unum aut alterum verbum liberius in eos emissum esset, tulerunt id homines mansuetudinem professi, aliquanto asperius, quam patres, tam vulgi opinione pios, ob leviculam culpam decere videbatur: et cum non satis justas irae suae immodicae causas invenirent, ad commune religionis crimen, quod omnibus quibus male propitii erant intentabant, decurrunt: et dum impotentiae suae indulgent, illum sponte sua sacerdotum licentiae infensum acrius incendunt, et Lutheranae caussae minus iniquum reddunt.

Interea rex e Gallia cum Magdalena uxore venit, nec sine metu sacrificulorum, qui timebant, ne puella regia, sub amitae reginae Navarrae disciplina educata, nonnihil in religione mutaret. Sed hic timor brevi secuto ejus decessu evanuit. Subsecutae sunt in aula suspiciones adversus quosdam e nobilitate qui contra regem conjurasse dicebantur. In ea caussa cum regi fuisset persuasum, non satis sincere versatos Franciscanos, rex Buchananum, forte tum in aula agentem, ad se advocat et ignarus [1] offensionis, quae ei cum Franciscanis esset, jubet adversus eos carmen scribere. Ille utrosque juxta metuens offendere, carmen quidem scripsit, et breve, et quod ambiguam

---

[1] As has been pointed out, we must here read *gnarus*.

interpretationem susciperet. Sed nec regi satisfecit, qui acre et aculeatum poscebat; et illis capitale visum est, quenquam ipsos nisi honorifice ausum attingere. Igitur acrius in eos jussus scribere, eam Silvam, quae nunc sub titulo *Franciscani* est edita, inchoatam regi tradidit. At brevi post per amicos ex aula certior factus se peti, et Cardinalem Betonium a rege pecunia vitam ejus mercari, elusis custodibus in Angliam contendit.

Sed ibi tum omnia adeo erant incerta, ut eodem die ac eodem igne utriusque factionis homines cremarentur, Henrico VIII. jam seniore suae magis securitati quam religionis puritati intento. Haec rerum Anglicarum incertitudo, et vetus cum Gallis consuetudo, et summa gentis humanitas, Buchananum ad se traxerunt. Ut Lutetiam venit, Cardinalem Betonium pessime erga se animatum ibi legatione fungi comperit. Itaque ejus irae se subtraxit, Burdegalam invitante Andrea Goveano profectus.

Ibi in scholis, quae tum sumptu publico erigebantur, triennium docuit : quo tempore scripsit quatuor tragoedias, quae postea per occasiones fuerunt evulgatae. Sed quae prima omnium fuerat conscripta (cui nomen est *Baptista*) ultima fuit edita ; ac deinde Medea Euripidis. Eas enim ut consuetudini scholae satisfaceret, quae per annos singulos singulas poscebat fabulas, conscripserat : ut earum actione juventutem ab allegoriis, quibus tum Gallia vehementer se oblectabat, ad imitationem veterum, qua posset, retraheret. Id cum ei prope ultra spem successisset, reliquas *Jephthen* et *Alcestin* paulo diligentius, tanquam lucem et hominum conspectum laturas, elaboravit. Sed nec id temporis omnino ei fuit expers sollicitudinis, inter cardinalis et Franciscanorum minas. Cardinalis etiam de eo comprehendendo ad archiepiscopum Burdegalensem literas misit : sed eas forte fortuna Buchanani amantissimis dederat. Sed hunc metum regis Scotorum mors, et pestis per Aquitaniam saevissime grassata sedavit.

Interea literae a rege Lusitaniae supervenerunt, quae Goveanum juberent, ut homines Graecis et Latinis literis eruditos secum adduceret, qui in scholis, quas ille tum magna cura et impensis moliebatur, literas humaniores et philosophiae Aristotelicae rudimenta interpretarentur. Ea de re conventus Buchananus facile est assensus. Nam cum totam jam Europam bellis domesticis et externis, aut jam flagrantem, aut mox conflagraturam videret, illum unum videbat angulum a tumultibus liberum futurum, et in eo coetu qui eam profectionem susceperant, non tam peregrinari, quam inter propinquos et familiares agere existimaretur. Erant enim plerique per multos annos summa benevolentia conjuncti, ut qui ex suis monumentis orbi claruerunt, Nicolaus Gruchius, Gulielmus Garentaeus, Jacobus Tevius, et Elias Vinetus. Itaque non solum se comitem libenter dedit, sed et Patricio fratri persuasit, ut se tam praeclaro coetui conjungeret. Et principio quidem res praeclare successit, donec in medio velut cursu Andreas Goveanus morte, ipse quidem non immatura, comitibus ejus acerba, praereptus est. Omnes enim inimici et aemuli in eos primum ex insidiis, deinde palam animo plane gladiatorio incurrerunt : et cum per homines reis inimicissimos questionem clam exercuissent, tres arripuerunt, quos, post longum carceris squalorem, in judicium productos, multis per eos dies conviciis exagitatos, rursus in custodiam abdiderunt. Accusatores autem ne adhuc quidem nominarunt.

In Buchananum certe acerbissime insultabant, ut qui peregrinus esset, et qui minime multos illic haberet qui incolumitate gauderent, aut dolori ingemiscerent, aut injuriam ulcisci conarentur. Objiciebatur ei carmen in Franciscanos scriptum, quod ipse, antequam e Galliis exisset, apud Lusitaniae regem excusandum curavit, nec accusatores quale esset sciebant; unum enim ejus exemplum regi Scotorum, qui scribendi auctor fuerat, erat datum. Crimini dabatur carnium esus in Quadragesima, a qua nemo in tota Hispania est qui abstineat; dicta quaedam oblique in monachos objecta, quae apud neminem nisi monachum criminosa videri poterant. Item gravissime acceptum, quod in quodam sermone familiari inter aliquot adolescentes Lusitanos, cum fuisset orta mentio de eucharistia, dixisset, sibi videri Augustinum in partem ab ecclesia Romana damnatam multo esse proniorem. Alii duo testes, Joannes Tolpinus [1] Normannus, et Joannes Ferrerius e Subalpina Liguria, (ut post aliquot annos comperit) pro testimonio dixerunt, se ex pluribus hominibus fide dignis audivisse, Buchananum de Romana religione perperam sentire. Ut ad rem redeam, cum quaestores prope sesquiannum et se et illum fatigassent, tandem ne frustra hominem non ignotum vexasse crederentur, eum in monasterium ad aliquot menses recludunt, ut exactius erudiretur a monachis, hominibus quidem alioqui nec inhumanis, nec malis, sed omnis religionis ignaris. Hoc maxime tempore psalmorum Davidicorum complures vario carminum genere in numeros redegit.

[1] Talpinus. Cf. p. 134 (above).

Tandem libertati redditus, cum a rege commeatum redeundi in Gallias peteret, ab eo rogatus ut illic maneret, pecuniola interim accepta in sumptum quotidianum, donec de conditione aliqua honesta prospiceretur. Sed cum procrastinationis, nec in certam spem, nec certum tempus, taederet, navem Cretensem in portu Olisipponensi nactus, in ea in Angliam navigavit. Nec hic tamen substitit quamvis honestis conditionibus invitaretur. Erant enim illic omnia adhúc turbida sub rege adolescente, proceribus discordibus, et populi adhuc animis tumescentibus ab recenti motu civili. Igitur in Galliam transmisit, iisdem fere diebus, quibus urbis Mediomatricum obsidio fuit soluta. Coactus est ibi per amicos ea de obsidione carmen scribere, idque eo magis invitus, quod non libenter in contentionem veniret cum aliis plerisque necessariis, et in primis cum Mellino Sangelasio, cujus carmen eruditum et elegans ea de re circumferebatur.

Inde evocatus in Italiam a Carolo Cossaeo Brixiacensi, qui tum secunda fama res in Ligustico et Gallico circa Padum agro gerebat, nunc in Italia, nunc in Gallia, cum filio ejus Timoleonte quinquennium haesit, usque ad annum millesimum quingentesimum sexagesimum. Quod tempus maxima ex parte dedit sacrarum literarum studio, ut de controversiis, quae tum majorem hominum partem exercebant, exactius dijudicare posset; quae tum domi conquiescere coeperant, Scotis a tyrannide Guisiana liberatis. Eo reversus nomen ecclesiae Scotorum dedit. E superiorum autem temporum scriptis quaedam velut e naufragio recollecta edidit. Caetera vero quae adhuc apud amicos peregrinantur, fortunae arbitrio committit. In praesentia septuagesimum quartum annum agens, apud Jacobum Sextum Scotorum regem, cui erudiendo erat praefectus, senectutis suae malis fractae portum exoptans agit.

Haec de se Buchananus, amicorum rogatu.
Obiit Edinburgi, paulo post horam quintam matutinam, die Veneris xxviii. Septembris, anno M.D.LXXXII.

George Chalmers, in his *Life of Ruddiman* (p. 68, note) dogmatically asserts that the above sketch was not written by Buchanan but by Peter Young. "The writer," he says, "whoever he were, talks of John Major as being *in extrema senectute* in 1524, when he was but fifty-five. He speaks of Henry VIII. as *jam seniore* in 1539, when he was but forty-eight. He

makes Buchanan meet Cardinal Beaton at Paris in 1539, a
twelvemonth after he had returned to Scotland." These
objections are groundless. As every one acquainted with the
sixteenth century knows, a man at fifty was then considered far
advanced in life. With regard to Beaton, the State Papers of
Henry VIII. (v. 154 and 156) distinctly state that he was in Paris
that year. In one point there is an inaccuracy in the sketch.
It leads us to infer that Buchanan went to St. Andrews the
spring following Albany's expedition, that is, the spring of
1523-4, whereas Buchanan's entry of matriculation in the University records is of the date 1524-5. There seems hardly
any reason, however, for questioning Buchanan's authorship of
the document. The general texture of the style is certainly
Buchanan's; and there are touches here and there (notably the
account of the Portuguese expedition) which, as we think, could
only have come from him. It may be questioned whether there
was any one in Scotland save Buchanan himself who could have
written Latin with such strength and incisiveness.

APPENDIX B.

(Page 76.)

THE following extracts, which I have had copied from the archives of the University of Paris,[1] are Buchanan's own record of his procuratorship. They are interesting not only as a part of Buchanan's own biography, but also as affording a curious glimpse into the university life of the time. It will be seen that Buchanan does not depart from the official dog-Latin of his predecessors. But even in these meagre official notes he shows his sarcastic humour.

M. ROBERTI WAUCHOP. [1529]

Quinto maii anni supradicti congregata fuit invictissima Germanorum natio apud divum Mathurinum super procuratoris electione et ad audiendum partes de discordia inter Magistrum Georgium Drappier et Magistrum Georgium Bochananē Scotum magistros et regentes prefate nationis, quorum uterque dicebat se procuratorem fuisse, nam Drappier allegabat turnum pertinere ad altos Alemanos et se fuisse functum procuratorio magistratu pro vice bassorum, precedente procuratorio, insuper quod erat continuatus ab omnibus altis septima Aprilis. Alter vero, scilicet Bochananē, allegabat se fuisse electum legitime ab omnibus Scotis et Anglis qui constituebant provinciam Britannorum juxta statutum M[agistri] Roberti Fergusson factum de duabus provinciis, et virtute ejusdem statuti dicebat vicem electionis pertinere ad prefatos. Insuper dixit Drappier conclusisse a pauciore numero et decanum nationis conclusisse recte pro eo et eum in possessionem posuisse, etc. . . .

---

[1] Bibliothèque de l'Université ; Archives : Registre 16, fol. 169v° 174.

SEQUITUR PROCURATURA GEORGII BUCHANAM
LEVINIANI SCOTI ANNO 1529.

Anno domini millesimo [quingentesimo] vicesimo nono die vero tertia mensis Junii convocata fuit fidelissima Germanorum natio apud ædem divi Mathurini duobus super articulis consultura. Primus concernebat novi procuratoris electionem, secundus communis erat supplicationibus et injuriis. Quod ad primum articulum spectat a decano provincie Scotorum nominatus est Georgius Buchananus Levinianus diœceseos Glasguensis e comitatu Leviniæ et omnium communi consensu procurator electus qui statim prestito jurejurando et inito magistratu gratias egit nationi pro tam propenso erga se animo et supplicuit ut natio ei favorem consilium et auxilium in omnibus prestaret.

GEORGIUS BUCHANANUS.

Eodem anno et mense die xix. convocata fuit universitas in templum divi Mathurini quinque super articulis consultura : primus concernebat processionem rectoris quam quominus fieret die] qua constituerat rector impediebat mandatum regium qui per dominum episcopum parisiensem mandaverat ut fieret omnium parechiarum generalis processio pro pace impetranda. Statutum est ut rectoris processio in diem lunæ differretur protestatione facta ne id in fraudem privilegiorum universitatis fieret. Secundus articulus communis erat supplicationibus et injuriis.

Eodem anno et mense die vero vigesima tertia congregata fuit [natio] Germanorum super electione intrantis apud ædem Cosme et Damiani super duobus articulis deliberatura. Quoad primum qui electionem intrantis concernebat, decanus provinciæ Scotorum exhibuit et presentavit virum egregie doctum Magistrum Robertum Fergushil qui prestito juramento et solitis ceremoniis peractis, omnium consensu admissus est. Secundus communis erat supplicationibus et injuriis.

Eodem mense pridie divi Joannis Baptiste convocata fuit Germanorum natio apud edem Cosme et Damiani deliberatura super duobus articulis. Primus qui electionem intrantis spectabat, secundus vero communis. Quoad primum decanus Scotorum cujus tum iuris erat presentavit egregie doctum et idoneum magistrum Robertum Fergushil, qui, prestito juramento, ab omnibus admissus est.

Eodem die paulo post facultas artium ad divum Julianum

congregata super electione rectoris. Ibi acta per magistrum Ludovicum Fabrum defunctum rectorem habita sunt rata et gratie acte ab intrantibus post rem divinam auditam, via spiritus sancti electus est rector vir doctissimus Hylarius Cortesius et ejus supplicationi ut dispensaretur de diebus legibilibus annuit facultas.

Nono die mensis Julii congregata fuit Germanorum natio apud divum Mathurinum super provisione nunciatus Lismorensis in Scotia per mortem vacantis. Electus est nuncius Joannes de Puys.

XXIII. die Julii apud Mathurinos Petrus Lamy factus est nuncius diœceseos Existerciensis per mortem Egidii Sumel. Item Petrus Belin nuncius Clusiensis per resignationem.

Eodem anno die [1] mensis Augusti collecta facultas fuit apud divum Julianum super appellatione domini Joannis Benedicti adversus Claudium Roillet primarium collegii Burgundiorum. Natio dedit deputatos magistros Robertum Vauchop et Joannem Douglas. GEORGIUS BUCHANANUS.

Pridie divi Barthomei congregata fuit universitas ad Mathurini super duobus articulis quorum primo Universitas promisit auxilium et favorem rectori. Secundo : multi supplicuerunt ut reciperentur in locum Pergamenarii mortui. Nostra natio elegit Antonium Monpignon. Reliquæ vero nationes et facultates elegerunt Petrum Petit. Tertio : supplicuit procurator Universitatis ut reficeretur sigillum Rectoris. Cui ab omnibus assensum. Quarto : supplicuit quidam preceptor collegii Coqueretici Petrus Tyllier nomine cujusdam preceptoris eiusdem collegii qui iniuste in carceres censoris criminum coniectus erat. Item, nomine cuiusdam pedagogi qui in carceribus officialis Parisiensis detinebatur per virum insigni crudelitate et avaritia primarium collegii Coqueretici ob panem unius assis ab eis comestum, et utriusque epistolas super ea re protulit. Natio ex consensu etiam totius facultatis prefecit virum gravissimum magistrum Martinum Doletium qui incarceratos repeteret. Primarium vero privavit privilegiis Universitatis quod contra statutum fecisset quod prohibet quempiam Universitati subiectum vocari in ius ante alium judicem priusquam vocetur ante rectorem, et tota facultas undem refractarium iudicavit iussitque reformatores adire collegium Coqueretici et pro magistratu agere et tumultus componere. GEORGIUS BUCHANANUS.

---

[1] The day is omitted in the original text.

CONTINUATIO MAGISTRI GEORGII BUCHANANI LEVINII.

Postridie divi Barthomei apostoli Germanorum natio congregata
fuit ad divi Mathurini in qua congregatione procurator omnium
consensu in proximum mensem continuatus est gratiasque
maximas nationi egit et suam operam sedulam et fidelem eidem
est pollicitus.　　　　　　　　　　GEORGIUS BUCHANANUS.

Congregata fuit facultas artium apud sanctum Julianum super
novem articulis deliberatura. Primus erat de danda nomen-
clatura regentum juratorum domino rectori cui in forma assensum. Secundus de salutandis procuratoribus nationum ad
convivia supplicationum rectoriarum veluti salutantur decani
facultatum, de quo articulo ita decretum est ut cum facultas
ostendat sese maxime liberalem in externos, indignum esse suos
negligi ; rursus dignum esse ut mutua benevolentia procuratores
cum rectore certent ideo invitandos esse procuratores ; rursus ut
procuratores post prandium cappati rectorem ad Mathurinos
usque comitentur. Tertius articulus super negocio pergamena-
riorum iuratorum qui nocent iuri rectoris. Decretum ut statuta
antiqua servarentur. Quartus ut scriba denuo publicitus repetat
conclusiones factas a domino rectore vel in facultate vel in
Universitate, cui conclusioni maxime assensum est.

Quintus ut qui recturi sunt proferant literas gradus in sua
natione ante quam admittantur propter nonnullos abusus.
Huic item assensum. Sextus super querimonia cuiusdam
regentis volentis repetere via juris supellectilem quam dicit
detineri ab avarissima harpya magistro Roberto Dugast primario
collegii Coqueretici ; quem idem regens vocavit in ius coram
eadem facultate. Dictus vero primarius solita pervicacia usus
non comparuit. Septimus super supplicatione Magistri Jacobi
Staphet volentis repetere quemdam quem asserit tum scolasticum
esse qui, uti ait idem Staphet, divertit alio ad capessendum
ingenii cultum. Quem scho[la]sticum qui se non suo arbitrio
id facere negabat, sed servire cuidam mercatori, et cum sepe
cubiculum petiisset in collegio Plessiaco non impetrasse. Ideo
voluntate mercatoris predicti se ad collegium Cenonense contulit,
asserens se tantum novem menses in collegio Plessiaco fuisse.
Itaque permissum est ut illic maneret.

Octavus ut nullus rector permittat sigillatori suo signare
litteras vectigales testimoniales citationes aut alia id genus,

[margin note:] Quod si invitati non fuerint non tenean[tur] venire ad processionem rectoris.

veluti fiunt multe obsignationes passim, uti dicitur, in fide parentum; idque se facturum, si opus, rector iuret quando elegetur. Cui articulo assensum cum etiam id iuret rector se servaturum privilegia. Nonus erat communis supplicationibus et iniuriis. G. B.

Kalendis septembribus fidelissima Germanorum natio necnon reliqua Universitas apud divum Mathurinum congregata fuit super duobus articulis consultura.

Primus, resignationem questure generalis; secundus, communis supplicationibus et iniuriis. Quod ad primum spectat articulum, natio admisit resignationem et iussit ut defunctus receptor pecuniarum acceptarum rationem redderet intra mensem et in locum eius substituit virum probum [1] primarium collegii Thesaurariorum voluitque ut in singulis annis sine ulla delatione computum redderet. Quoad secundum, supplicatum est ut nomen cuiusdam rectoris in album et catalogum aliorum rectorum inseretur. Cujusdam supplicationi assensit natio oravitque ut idem in aliis quibus fieret, cum negligentia quorumdam nomina rectorum et tempus magistratus non satis constet; ut que comperirentur in catalogum aliorum referrentur, subscripto anno et mense; et ita per rectorem conclusum est.

Eodem anno decima octava die mensis septembris facta est congregatio Universitatis apud divum Mathurinum super tribus articulis. Primus concernebat resignationem cuiusdam sacellaniæ. Secundus vero causam Roberti Dugast primarii collegii Coquereti, qui ter contumax fuerat; bis quia non comparuit cum citatus esset. Tertio vero cum comparuisset appellavit a rectore et ad quesita reddere recusavit. Tertius communis erat supplicationibus et iniurii[s]. Supplicatum est nomine cuiusdam magistri incarcerati ut pecunia ei pro victu impenderetur. Quod ad primum spectat articulum, natio censuit non admittendam esse resignationem nisi constaret illum cui fiebat resignatio gradum Parisii in aliqua facultate suscepisse; et cum compertum esset eum omnino juramento rectorio non adactum esse, nihilominus in favorem theologorum alie facultates eum admittebant ad sacellaniam ea lege ut intra quindecim dies iuraret; quod cum in fraudem commodorum Universitatis fieret, appellavit vir gravissimus procurator Universitatis magister Martinus Dolet; ob cuius appellationem consensu omnium res dilata fuit in proxima

---

[1] A word omitted in text.

comitia. Quod ad secundum spectat, egit pro se dictus Robertus Dugast cum multis gratiis adversus rectorem, cui modestissimus rector Hylarius Cortesius modestissime pariter et doctissime respondit et eius maledicta refellit. Supplicavit etiam Magister Philippus Roguet, qui dictum Dugast in ius vocaverat, ut sibi redderetur sua supellex iniuste detenta a dicto Dugast et obligatio quedam quam ei dederat qua pecuniam promiserat ei cum ad regendum admissus fuit. Cum tamen id contra statuta Universitatis esset, ad eam rem dati sunt deputati qui de dicta causa iudicarent et morem legendi in collegiis respicerent. Supplicationi incarcerati annuit natio. De summa vero que ei daretur, id ad deputatos remisit. Annuit item supplicationi Bede, videlicet ne dialectica Melancthonis prelegeretur pueris cursum inchoantibus.

Vigesimo die mensis eiusdem facta est congregatio venerande nationis Germanorum apud Mathurinos super tribus articulis. Primus erat de admissione Germanorum quos bassos vocant ad jura pristina nationis que pro tertia congregatione celebrata est. Secundus spectabat electionem novi rectoris. Tertius communis erat supplicationibus et iniuriis. Quod ad primum spectat, natio Germanos admisit revocando statutum de duabus provinciis secundum congregationem prius factam, nempe ut tres essent provincie quarum prima esset superiorum Germanorum, secunda Scotorum, tertia Germanorum inferiorum et Anglorum. Statutum tum tertio ut illud inviolabiliter observaretur, consentibus (*sic*) omnibus Germanis bassis qui aderant. Aderant autem quatuor magistri Cornelius Ceratinus et Hugo et Gerardus Morrhius et   quorum consensum suo decreto confirmavit reliqua natio. Quod ad secundum, dati sunt ex natione aliorum magister Titus   [1] ex natione Scotorum, magister David Henrisom ex natione Bassorum, magister Cornelius Hugo qui antiquo receptori in redditione rationum adessent. Qua reddita, pecunia recepta excessit expensam duodecim libris duodecim solidis parisiensibus et septem denariis turonensibus. Item electus est in Receptorem proximi anni Corneliis (*sic*) Ceratinus et magistro Roberto Vauchop defuncto receptori de dono gratuito supplicanti natio annuit.

Item magnas distributiones dari jussit. Item bedellis pro clavis suis quas massas vocant et regentibus pro scolis supplicantibus annuit et hec ita per me conclusa sunt.

GEORGIUS BUCHANANUS.

---

[1] A word omitted in text.

Eodem die apud rectorem conquestus est Magister Franciscus
Zampinus regens in collegio Lexoviensi quosdam a se discessisse
ad collegium Plessiacum quos repetebat iudicio.

Audita [querela] utriusque regentis et juvenum, procuratores
reformatores et deputati nationum censuerunt juvenes debere ad
prefatum preceptorem redire. Et ita per dominum rectorem
conclusum est magistro Joanne Arboreo apud quem juvenes
erudiebantur Universitatem appellante.

GEORGIUS BUCHANANUS.

———

NOTES.

Bacchalaureorum anni domini 1527 nomina . . .

Licentiatorum nomina . . .

Dominorum magistrorum de novo incipientium nomina . . .

Dñs Georgius Buchanam, dioc. Glasguensis, cuius bursa valet
4 sol. paris.

Isti duo post
continuationem
fuerunt recepti,
ut patet in
continuatione.

Dñs Joannes Redmaynus dioc. Eboracensis, cuius bursa valet
8 sol. paris.

Signé :

CL. POLLATIUS.[1]

Continuatio Magistri Claudii Pollatii, Helvetii Lausanici
diocesani in munere procuratorio 1527.[2]

Anno eodem, 1528.

Nomen unius incipientis.

Dominus Georgius Buchanam, dioc. Glasguensis, cuius bursa
valet 4 sol. paris. . . .[3]

[1] Fol. 141.   [2] Fol. 143 verso.   [3] Fol. 144 verso.

APPENDIX C.

(Page 224.)

[ORIG. BRIT. MUS., LANSDOWNE MSS., NUM. 15–24.]

LETTER FROM GEORGE BUCHANAN TO SIR THOMAS RANDOLPH.[1]

To his singular freynd M. Randolph, maister of postes to the
Queines g. of Ingland. In London.

I resauit twa pair of lettres of you sens my latter wryting to
you. wyth the fyrst I ressavit Marianus Scotus, of quhylk I
thank you greatly, and specialy that your ingles men ar fund
liars in thair cronicles allegying on hym sic thyngs as he never
said. I haif beyne vexit wyth seiknes al the tyme sens, and
geif I had decessit ye suld haif losit both thankis and recompens,
now I most neid thank you bot geif wear brekks vp of thys
foly laitly done on the border, than I wyl hald the recom-
pense as Inglis geir. bot gif peace followis and nother ye
die seik of mariage or of the twa symptomes following on
mariage quhylks ar jalozie [and] cuccaldry, and the gut cary not
me away, I most other find sum way to pay or ceis kyndnes or
ellis geifing vp kyndnes pay you w^t evil wordis, and geif thys fasson
of dealing pleasit me I haif reddy occasion to be angry wyth you
that haif wissit me to be ane kentys man, quylk in a maner is
ane centaur, half man, half beast. and yit for ane certaine consideration I wyl pas over that iniury, imputyng it erar to your
new foly than to ald wisdome, for geif ye had beine in your ryt
wyt ye being anis escapit the tempesteous stormes and naufrage
of mariage had never enterit agane in the samyng dangeris. for
I can not tak you for ane Stoik philosopher, having ane head
inexpugnable w^t the frenetyk tormētis of Jalozie, or ane cairless
[*margin*, skeptik] hart that taks cuccaldris as thyng indifferent.
In this caise I most neidis praefer the rude Scottis wyt of capi-

---

[1] This letter was first printed by Dr. M'Crie in the Appendix to his
Life of Andrew Melville.

taine Cocburne to your inglis solomonical sapience, quhylk
wery of ane wyfe deliuerit her to the queyne againe, but
you deliverit of ane wyfe castis your self in the samyn
nette, et *ferre potes dominam saluis tot restibus ullam.* and so
capitaine cocburne is in better case than you for his seiknes is
in the feitte and youris in the heid. I pray you geif I be out
of purpose thynk not that I suld be maryit. bot rather consider
your awyn dangerous estait of the quhylk the spoking has thus
troublit my braine and put me so far out of the way. As to my
occupation at this present tyme, I am besy w^t our story of
Scotland to purge it of sum Inglis lyis and Scottis vanite, as to
maister knoks his historie is in hys freindis handis, and thai ar in
cõsultation to mitigat sum part the acerbite of certaine wordis
and sum taintis quhair in he has followit to much sũ of your
inglis writaris as M. hal et *suppilatorem eius* Graftone &c. As to
M. beza I fear y^t eild quhylk has put me from verses making
sal deliure him sone a Scabie poetica, quhylk war ane great
pitye for he is ane of the most singular poetes that has beine
thys lang tyme. as to your great prasyng gevin to me in your
lre geif ye scorne not I thank you of luif and kyndnes towart
me bot I am sorie of your corrupt ingement. heir I wald say
mony iniuries to you war not yat my gut comandis me to cesse
and I wyl als spair mater to my nixt writings. Fairweall and
god keip you. at Sterling the Sext of august.

Be youris at al power

G. BUCHANAN.

APPENDIX D.

(Page 353.)

BUCHANAN'S TESTAMENT DATIVE.[1]

Maister
George Buchannane
Vigesimo Febr[ii]
1582

THE Testament Datiue, & Inuentar of ye gudis, geir, soumes of money, & dettis, perteining to vmquhile ane rycht venerabill man, Maister George Buchannane, preceptour to ye kingis majestie the tyme of his deceis, quha deceist vpoun ye xxix day of September,[2] the zeir of God j^mv^clxxxii zeris, faithfullie maid & gevin vp be Jonet Buchannane, relict of vmquhile Mr. Thomas Buchannane of Ibert, his bruyer sone, executrix dative, decernit to him be decreit of ye commissaris of Ed^r as ye same decreit of ye dait ye xix day of December, the zeir of God foirsaid, at lenth proportis.

In the first, ye said vmquhile Maister George Buchannane, perceptour to ye kingis majestie, had na uyer gudis nor geir (except ye dett vndirwrittin) pertening to him as is awin proper dett ye tyme of his deceis foirsaid : viz. Item, yair wes awand to ye said vmquhile Mr. George be Robert Gourlaw, custumar burges of Ed^r for ye defunctis pensioun of Corsraguell, restand of ye Whitsonday terme in anno j^mv^clxxxii zeris, the soume of ane hundreth pundis.

Summa of ye inuentar . . . j^c l.

No diuisioun.

Quhairof ye quot is gevin gratis.

[1] From the Records of the Commissary Court.
[2] It will be observed that the date of Buchanan's death given here differs from that of the note affixed to the Latin sketch of his life. With Irving, I have followed the latter date.

We, Maisteris Eduard Henrysoun, Alex^r Sym, & Johne Prestoun, commissaris of Ed^r specialie constitut for confirmatioun of testamentis, &c., vnderstanding yat efter dew summonding & lauchfull warning maid be forme of editt oppenlie, as efferis, of ye executouris intromettouris with ye gudis & geir of vmquhile Mr. George Buchannane, & of uyeris hafand entreis, to compeir judicialie befoir us at ane certane day bypast, to heir & sie executouris datiuis decernit to be gevin, admittit, & confermit be us in & to ye gudis & geir quhilk justlie pertenit to him ye tyme of his deceis, or ellis to schaw ane caus quhy, &c. we decernit yairintill as our decreit gevin yairupoun beris ; conforme to ye quhilk we in our soverane lordis name & autoritie makis, constitutis, ordanis, & confermes ye said Jonet Buchannane in executorie datiue to ye said Mr. George, with power to hir to intromet, vptak, follow & perseu, as law will, ye dett & soume of money abone specifeit, & yairwith outred dettis to creditouris, and generalie all & sindrie vyer thingis to do, exerce, & vse yat to ye office of executorie datiue is knawin to pertene ; prouiding yat ye said Jonet, executrix foirsaid, sall ansuer & render compt vpoun hir intromissioun quhan and quhair ye samin salbe requirit of hir, & yat ye said dett & soume salbe be furthcumand to all parteis haifand entres, as law will ; quhairvpoun scho hes fundin cautioun, as ane act maid yairvpoun beris.

INDEX.

Printed by T. and A. CONSTABLE, Printers to Her Majesty,
at the Edinburgh University Press.